DATE DUE

MAR 29 1994	
APR 29 1994	
FEB 1 3 1996	
NOV 9 1998	
FEB 2 3 2001	
MAR 1 0 2006	
JUN 2 7 2012	
WITHDRAWN	

GRASS KINGDOM

Tor books by Jory Sherman

Horne's Law
The Medicine Horn
Song of the Cheyenne
Winter of the Wolf

GRASS KINGDOM

JORY SHERMAN

A TOM DOHERTY ASSOCIATES BOOK
NEW YORK

GRASS KINGDOM

This book is printed on acid-free paper.

A Forge Book
Published by Tom Doherty Associates, Inc.
175 Fifth Avenue
New York, N.Y. 10010

Design by Lynn Newmark

Library of Congress Cataloging-in-Publication Data

Sherman, Jory.
    The grass kingdom / Jory Sherman.
        p.   cm.
    "A Tom Doherty Associates book."
    ISBN 0-312-85360-2
    1. Cattle trade—Texas—History—Fiction.   2. Ranch life—Texas—History—Fiction.   3. Family—Texas—History—Fiction.   4. Texas—History—Fiction.
    I. Title.
    PS3569.H43G73   1994
    813'.54—dc20   93-33507
                                                               CIP

First edition: January 1994

Printed in the United States of America

0 9 8 7 6 5 4 3 2 1

For Nat Sobel, a man of vision and intelligence

Cast of Characters

THE AGUILAR RANCH—ROCKING A BRAND

Ernesto "Ernie" Alfonso de Lopez y Aguilar—ranch owner

Elena Corazòn Mercado de Peña y Alicante—Ernie's wife

Hector Fernando Aguilar—Ernie's son

Alicia Luz Aguilar—Ernie's daughter

ROCKING A HANDS

Francisco "Paco" Velez—foreman

Randolph "Randy" Connors—segundo

Alberto Horcasitas—cook

Rafael Mendoza—line rider

Alfonso Serrano—wrangler

Silvino Marcos—handyman

Jesus Roxas—cowhand

THE KILLIAN RANCH—LAZY K BRAND

Benjamin Orly Killian—ranch owner

Edith Baron Killian—Matt Baron's first wife (deceased)

Frances Beverly Killian—Ben's wife, nee Butler

Jane Houston Killian—Ben's mother

Ralph Houston—Jane Killian's father (deceased)

Doris Houston—Jane Killian's mother (deceased)

George Killian—Ben's father (deceased)

Roy Killian—George's father (deceased)

Stephen Norris Killian—Ben's son

Constance "Connie" Paige Killian—Ben's daughter

April Jennifer Killian—Ben's daughter

Lucas Albert Killian—Ben and Edith's oldest son

LAZY K HANDS

Charlie Stone—foreman

Harvey Leeds—wrangler

Reed Packer—segundo

Jared Rutman—wrangler

Jack Bellaugh—line rider

Nancy Fellows—maid

Consuela Delgado—cook
Jefferson "Jeff" Rogers—stableman
Warren Finnerty—wrangler
Old Silvero—ranch hand
Lew Carmody—ranch hand
Lester Balcom—ranch hand
Lewis "Ike" Ikert—ranch hand
Shorty Coots—cowhand, powderman

INDIANS

Jack Bone—Lipan Apache
Ned Feather—Kickapoo
Jay Black Horse—Yaqui
Eddie "Eddie Blue" Blue Sky—Mescalero Apache
Virgil Coldwater—mixed breed, Yaqui, Apache

BARONSVILLE TOWNFOLK

James Harding—veterinarian
Henry Emberlin, M.D.—physician
Katherine "Kitty" Emberlin—Henry's wife
Faith Emberlin—Henry's daughter
Roy Blanchard—sheriff
Harlan Doakes—deputy sheriff
Raymond Naylor—deputy sheriff
Fred Beane—deputy sheriff
Porfirio Delgado—horticulturist
Jack Kearney—attorney-at-law
Dale Wilker—newspaper reporter (*Baronsville Bugle*)
Naomi "Nomi" Tyler—owns Naomi's Café
Burtrand "Burt" Tyler—Naomi's husband
David Tyler—Naomi's son
Theodore "Ted" Womack—mayor, banker
Delmer Mudd—pool-hall owner
Orville Treacher—Klansman
Giacomo Ingianni—Delmer's partner in pool hall
Jo-Beth Vermeil—telephone operator
Melba Orr—sheriff's dispatcher

Merle Chandler—owner Chandler's Feed Store
Bob Filbert—gas-station owner, Bob's Oil Company
Wilma Sisler—Mayor Womack's secretary
Eunice Baker—clerk, Baronsville Land & Title Co.
Grady Tippetts—owner Baronsville Mercantile
Susy Dillard—waitress
Nancy Hogan—telephone operator
Willie Powell—pharmacist
Bill Letterman—used-car dealer
Ken Loehon—owner Main Street Barber Shop
Lew Pettibone—grocer
Martin Longerbeam—rancher
Andy Erickson—store clerk
Betty Swain—clerk in courthouse
Richard S. Wheeler—physician
Georgeann Sinton—legal secretary
Lupe Carvaljo—owner Lupe's Cantina
Barbara Amos—secretary
Susie Loomis—court clerk

Houston Residents

Keith Sherwood—oilman
Samantha Deane—Ethan Baron's girlfriend
Jim Goff—advertising man, entertainer
William "Billy" Cameron—pilot
Frank Anthony—geologist, oil expert
Barr Sherwood—Keith's son
Leroy Deane—Senator

Others

Martin Longerbeam—rancher
Tamar Longerbeam—Martin's wife
Curtis Longerbeam—son of Martin and Tamar
W. Lee O'Daniel—governor of Texas
Bernard Bedford Huff—schoolmaster
Deane—Senator
James Ferguson

Jimmy Allred—governor
Larry Braden—geologist
Bob Kleberg—rancher
Liggett—ranch hand
Miriam Ferguson—politician
Governor Sterling
Judge Chowney
Morris Sheppard—senator
Coke Stevenson—governor

The history of every country begins
in the heart of a man or a woman.

—Willa Cather

East were the
Dead kings and the remembered sepulchres;
West was the grass.

—Archibald MacLeish

1

THE GENERAL SPIT out the tarantula.

He had dragged the lethargic arachnid from its hibernation place under an overturned chunk of two-by-four only moments before. Now, he eyed its shriveled hairy body on the ground as he chewed a severed leg, softened it with saliva.

He stood on the fence rail of the chicken coop, stretched his neck out and flapped his wings as he voiced his morning proclamation of territorial rights. His golden neck feathers with their ragged trim flowed over his chest and shoulders like military epaulets, giving him the look of a gaudy South American general. And that's just what the ranch hands called him: The General. The bird filled his lungs with air, puffing out his chest. He piped the morning stillness to a halt with his throaty cry of dominance over the still-sleeping hens draped like lifeless feather balls on their roosts inside the coop.

In the stables, Silvino Marcos, the handyman on the Rocking A ranch, muttered to himself.

"*El gallo cabrón se levanta,*" he said, as he tugged both ends of the big Mexican saddle atop the black gelding. "*Es un generál chingado sín ningun ejército.*"

Silvino adjusted the single cinch, whacked the gelding in the belly with his fist. The black sucked up its gut and Silvino pulled the cinch tight through the O-ring, made a neat symmetrical knot.

He raked the tangles out of the shiny dark mane with a currycomb, checked the martingale, the curb in the grazing bit. The gelding was six years old, the Sunday horse of *el patrón*, fourteen hands high, sleek as a satin sash, its hide glistening with a high sheen like sunshot anthracite.

The familiar whistle interrupted Silvino's rambling, directionless thoughts. He clucked to the gelding, grabbed up the trailing reins, headed for the open stable doors.

"Feliz Feliz! Feliz! *Ben pa' 'ca!* Come here, boy. Here, Feliz." The call was not loud, but subdued, as if *el patrón* did not want to be heard calling his dog by those still sleeping inside his massive, sprawling house atop the grass-crowned knoll.

Silvino emerged from the dark stable leading the saddled horse. There was a faint auroral glow in the eastern sky. It was early for *el patrón* to go riding, especially on this day, he thought, rubbing the backs of gnarled fingers over the stiff bristles spearing his leathered cheeks and chin. He had not even shaved with the straight razor yet and he dearly loved brushing the hot lather from the mug onto his face when he was fully awake. His body had risen like Lazarus' from his death pallet, but his eyes were still half asleep, the lids hooding them so that they looked like oily ball bearings in egg cups.

"Have you seen my dog? The setter?"

"*No he visto aquel perro este mañana, Patrón,*" said Silvino. "He is probably hunting the rabbits."

The rancher whistled again, but he did not call the dog's name. Instead, he took the reins, grabbed the saddle horn, swung up into the saddle, ignoring Silvino's querulous expression. Without a word, he ticked the horse's flanks with the silvery sunset rowel spurs. The horse bunched its muscles, pranced under the tug of reins that held him in check until the rider cleared the maze of fences and outbuildings scattered helter-skelter some two hundred yards from the shadowy house surrounded by live oaks and sycamores. A '29 Reo flatbed, its green paint fading, stood under the barn loft, a pair of hands working in concert to load the truck with twine-wrapped bales of alfalfa.

"*Pa' 'onde va', Patrón?*" asked Silvino, his stubby hands clasping the tortilla-layered ring of fat around his middle. "*Que temprano in la mañana. . . .*"

The rider did not reply or look back. Silvino removed his battered sombrero with the deep crease in the center of the high-domed crown. He blinked the owl-flaps of his eyes and decided he might sleep another hour with no one the wiser. The General crowed again. Silvino picked up a chunk of wood and sailed it like a boomerang toward the chicken coop. He heard it slap against a rail. The rooster teetered, then deserted the rail in an awkward lurch toward solid ground, his stubby wings riffling scarcely enough to soften the shock. He skidded on his fluffy rump and toppled over on his side.

Silvino laughed and for a moment his rheumy eyes flickered with a faint glowworm wink of light.

The rider faded into the morning mists and it was quiet.

Where does he go so early? thought Silvino. *Ah, what does it matter? Don Ernesto has his reasons. Perhaps he just wants to think some little thoughts by himself.*

The Rincon was a dark and somber place to meet a hated man on such a day. It was the corner where the three ranches met, where the boundaries knifed into the seventy-five-mile-long, five-mile-wide *brasada* like three sharp wedges of a *torta*. The stillness, as he rode the jittery black Arabian gelding, reeked of a coming storm. Clouds of redwinged blackbirds wheeled over the marsh edge of the *brasada,* their dark silhouettes framed like antic darts against the dull cream sky of morning. Ernesto Alfonso de Lopez y Aguilar, that was his formal baptismal name, Ernie Aguilar to his friends and hands, hated to sneak away from the hacienda this morning, but he dared not ignore the summons from a man he thought, had hoped, was dead.

Aguilar sat stiff-backed in the saddle, a short, slender man, muscular and lean under his flat-crowned black Spanish hat, his black hair just beginning to streak with needles of silver, cut short, the sideburns long and flaring over his sun-browned cheeks, his thin flannel shirt crisscrossed in a red and black pattern of thick lines. He wore faded Lee jeans, form-fitting as a glove, worn, comfortable Judson boots burnished to a rich mahogany luster. A wallet jutted out of his back pocket, his name carved into the leather. Like Silvino, he too had not shaved, and his chin bristled with the shadows of an emerging growth like magnetized iron filings clinging to his swarthy flesh. He passed one of his windmills, its blades whirling in a high-speed blur, the pump screeching as it plumbed for deep water to fill the trough of galvanized iron, its waterline rimmed with a thin green slime.

He wore the nickel-plated Smith & Wesson .38 in a braided leather holster on his flower-etched cowhide belt, a double-action pistol with custom maple grips, crosshatched to give him a good grip. His gloves were worn smooth, almost to a chamois thinness, the calfskin dyed black, soft and pliant.

The gelding, Gorguz, which meant "javelin" in Spanish, stepped briskly over ground speckled with thistles, pigweed, wild privet, cat-claw, tansy mustard, snakeweed and mesquite, its small hooves freshly shod, its regal neck arched gracefully as it moon-eyed the unfamiliar shapes of flora, listened with coned ears bristled for any startling sound.

Ernie held the reins loosely in his right hand, let his left arm hang straight. His rump fit the contours of the high cantle like an olive in a spoon. He seemed part of the horse, in exact harmony with its single-footed gait that was as smooth as sitting in a rocking chair, even over rough country.

To the north, the sky was sooted dark as the inside of a stovepipe; to the west, an uncertain gray mantled the horizon, neutral as a mourning dove's breast, the high cloud layer as yet untinged by the gild of the pallid morning sun trying to clear the eastern mists, break through the fog of the distant Los Olmos River and the gulf below Corpus Christi.

He rode through a desolate stretch of country, fenced and cross-fenced to the north, but open range here, broken only by the hideous hulks of rusted oil derricks, abandoned by wildcatters who leased the land, dreamed of fortunes in black gold. Behind the barbed wire the humped gray Brahmin cattle grazed on clumps of gamma grass, an experimental range newly opened. It looked like some Moorish land-scape in the shrouds of mist that drifted on the morning breeze, patches of wisp carried westward from the dank swamp of the *brasada,* ghostly shrouds that blurred the frozen hulks of the "Braymers," made them seem even more unreal to him. Later on, Ernie planned to run the biggest, sturdiest bull in with his most promising white-face cows when they came fresh, as Matt Baron was already doing on his Box B north and east of the Rocking A.

He rode past another section where he kept the last remnants of those beef cattle descended from animals brought to Mexico by Spaniards, beasts who went wild on the river plains and wilder still in the old *brasada.* He saw them now, relics of a past he never knew, but nobler, he thought, than the ungainly Brahmin cattle, with their long sweeping horns doubled up and soaring backwards for half their huge length, cattle with heavy, thin heads, long, graceful legs and narrow, powerful flanks. The longhorns lowed as he passed, their calico hides looking like patchwork quilts in the morning light, no two alike, haired in cream and red and brown, some with patches the color of liver or pale orange. Maybe someday, he thought, someone would once again find a use for such a hardy breed.

His grandfather had settled this land, obtained more than a million acres by Spanish Land Grant, fought for it after Santa Ana's defeat when Texas became a republic, held onto it when the carpetbaggers came down from the north after the War Between the States and demanded outrageous taxes. Ernie had listened to his old grandfather tell his stories and had hung breathlessly on every word. His father, Lafcadio, also told him many stories of those days when he was but a boy and Ernie's grandfather freighted goods from the Gulf to upriver crossings, or from the States into Mexico where bandits lurked on every trail.

Once, his grandfather had taken goods into Mexico, delivered his cargo, and returned with nearly four hundred thousand dollars in Mexican silver and fifty thousand pounds of copper, destined for France. He had fought off Mexican brigands in Mexico and Texas soldiers of fortune across the border, but earned over twenty thousand dollars for the trip.

Ernie remembered his grandfather, Granpapá Miguelito, as they called him, telling him of the freighting life so long ago, of how he had come to love Texas, the vast land so full of riches that a man could possess only in his heart, for this was the wealth of the blue sky and the starred night and the moondusted desert landscape. His grandfather's freighting company, whenever they could, held a dance after supper when they were on the trail. They would lay several wagon sheets on the ground inside the corral made by the surrounding wagons. On the tall wagon wheels they stuck lighted candles. If they were near a town, the mariachis would come out, bringing their stringed instruments to play. If not, the teamsters made music with what they had in their wagon trunks—a banjo, a violin, bones, spoons, washboards, tubs, deer antlers clacked together in rhythm to the makeshift bass and drum. The wagon sheets on the level hard ground made a fine dance floor for the dancers. They danced all night, sometimes, until the train corporal drove in the herd at daybreak to hitch it up to the wagons. Sometimes Miguelito would send riders to the ranches in the open country, invite the people to be his guests. And, after breakfast in camp, the best people Ernesto had ever met rode back through the wilderness to their isolated and solitary homes and the wagon train rumbled off on its destined route, rolling and pitching like a convoy of ships slowly making its way over the great flat lands through which the Rio Grande ran. As they journeyed, his grandfather said, his eyes full of dream dust and tears, they would see other freighters or cattle drovers in the distance and wave their hats, but they did not call out because the wagon train or the cattle on drive were too far away for their voices to carry to their ears.

Now, Ernesto rode toward the forbidding place and remembered that, too, from when he was a boy bucking the brush with his father, listening to him at noon camp tell of the fearsome *brasada* when it covered a wide band of territory from the Nueces to the Rio Grande. His father had brought him to this fringe and taken him into it, so that he could see how it had been before Lafcadio and his father, Miguelito, had cleared the brush and made huge bonfires that blazed into the night and burned for days on end. Men of dreams and muscle, they had worked for years to harness the wilderness, bring it under their dominion, not for themselves, but for their children and their children's children. For Ernesto and his heirs and for all the generations to come.

The *brasada* was a ghostly sight when it had been dusted gray by the blistering winds that whipped sands up from the gulf beaches and carried them inland to this great barrier thicket, gaunt as a boneyard when beaten by torrential downpours that hissed as they struck the hot ground or when raked mercilessly by freezing white blizzards that swept down from the north with a whistling keen of wind. In its interlocking thickets that encircled small clearings, there grew curly mesquite grass where once cattle grazed by the thousands and could scarcely be seen by mounted horsemen who invaded the brush in search of a herd to drive to market.

In summer heat, the green cicadas clamored in noisy insect voices that deafened the ears and the stiff-haired javelinas rooted among the thorns. Blue-scaled quail darted shyly among the wiry shadows of the mesquite bushes and rattlesnakes threaded their way to the water-holes, silently hunted wild turkey or muskrat.

This was, Aguilar knew, a place of hard secrets. Once laced by streams and rivers, it had grown thick and impenetrable until his grandfather had begun to clear the land for growing grass. Later, his father had taken up the axe and the machete and cleared still more.

"A man could die of thirst in there," his papá had told him, "if he does not know where to find the streams, the hidden rivers."

The rivers and creeks ran in random trenches walled with yellow, pink or slate-blue limestone and could not be seen until one stood on their banks.

Ernesto was glad that he would not be going into the *brasada* this day. Even now, with thousands of acres cleared, the brush seemed interminable. Once, Ernesto, hunting a mossy-horned bull and some calves during spring roundup, had sat his horse atop a mound in the depths of the *brasada* and felt a terrible loneliness smother him as he looked into the distance for something familiar and certain, a mountain or a clump of tall trees to break the monotony.

Instead, the land bristled as it rose up and stretched toward the white sky in gentle rolls and shimmered in the heat that blended the ashen hue of the ground with the olive greens of brush until the horizon seemed to be veiled with a cheesecloth scrim of dusty lilac.

Aguilar rode Gorguz to the edge of the *brasada,* reined the horse in at the point of the wedge that ended the cleared land of his property. The bright spring sun had cleared the horizon. Frogs croaked from somewhere inside the slough; a meadowlark trilled chromatically in the fringe, then went silent. Moments later, a covey of scaled quail flushed out of the swamp, spooked Ernesto's horse. He tightened down on the bit, backed the horse down until it was once more under control.

Then he saw Bone.

The man stepped soundlessly out of the tangled brush, the burly mesquite, dressed in grimy duck trousers, patched at the left knee, a loose-fitting shirt dotted with red and blue flowers. He wore boot moccasins and a red bandanna tied around his skull. His straight black hair hung shoulder-length. He wore a long-bladed knife in a beaded sheath on his wide brass-studded belt. He was dark-skinned, with high sharp cheekbones, Oriental eyes slitted and deep-sunk. His thin lips parted mirthlessly.

"Don Ernesto," said the Indian. "Long time no see, eh man?"

"You got some *juevos* coming here, Bone."

"Ay, sonofabitch, eh? You don't look like you want to see me. By the Jesus, you should. Better Jack Bone than the sheriff, huh? Where in hell you think I been, Ernie?"

"I thought you were dead."

"Dead my Apache ass. I was in prison, goddamnit. Goddamned

prison. They locked my Injun ass up, by the Jesus, and I didn't even do nothing."

"You blame me? I knew nothing about it, Bone."

"Hey, I wrote you a letter, man. I asked you for a little money. You don't send me a goddamned penny."

"I got no letter from you, Bone." Aguilar's voice was flat and toneless, yet underneath there was a quaver that he hoped the Indian could not detect.

"Hell, man, I sent you a whole bunch of letters. You got 'em. Damned if you didn't get 'em."

Ernesto looked at the man and all the bitter memories returned. Bone was half Yaqui, half Apache, or so they said. A misfit. Once he had worked for the Rocking A, as had his father, but Bone was lazy and a drunkard. When he got drunk, he got mean. He fought, he bit, he kicked, he used a knife or a club or a barstool. He wrecked things and he swore loud and long, ranted against the white race and the brown in three mutilated languages.

"You 'member that little white girl?" asked Bone, a cagey edge to his tone. "I hear her goddamned brother is looking for the bastard who killed her ass."

Ernesto's jawline hardened. His stomach knotted, the muscles in his diaphragm tautened like strands of piano wire.

"Bone, you better not talk about that. It's hard times. You need some money? I can give you twenty dollars." Ernie reached in his back pocket, pulled out a worn leather wallet. He pried it open, fingered a bill inside.

Bone's mouth rose in a curl on one side. He snorted with a vented fury.

"I want some goddamned land, Ernie. You got plenty. I want some land and some beef cattle for me and my people."

"What people?" Aguilar slammed his wallet shut, shoved it back in his pocket.

"I got people," Bone said warily. "In there." He cocked a thumb back toward the *brasada*. "I come back to my people's land. You stole it from us."

"No!" Aguilar exploded. "Get off my land. Go away and don't ever come back here."

Ernesto rammed his spurs into the gelding's flanks, rode up on Bone. He lashed at the Indian with the trailing ends of the reins, slashed at his face with the whipping leather. Bone stumbled backwards, throwing his arms up to escape the fury of Aguilar's onslaught. His eyes squinted to porcine slits and crackled in their nut-brown depths with animal fury.

Then, Bone turned and ran into the *brasada*. Ernesto heard the brush crackle.

"You are going to be very sorry, man. I want my goddamned land. I ain't jokin', sonofabitch."

"You go to hell, Bone."

It was quiet for a moment. Aguilar heard a yelp, a thrashing noise. Then, Bone reappeared, holding his bloody knife and grasping something, a bundle, in his hands. He thrust the bundle at Aguilar. The rancher grabbed it, his face stricken with a look of surprise.

"No, you go to hell, Ernie," screeched Bone, and then he disappeared into the tangled jungle of mesquite.

Aguilar hefted the bundle in his hands. Puzzled, he stripped the rags away from the enclosed object. The sun caught the reddish hair, made it shine like fire. He stared down at the once beautiful head of his Irish setter, Feliz. The red silken strands of its fur glistened with an auburn glow and there was blood rusting the strands of hair where the neck had been severed from the body. The setter's eyes stared fixedly up at Ernie, frosted to a hideous glaze that glittered in the sunlight as if the dog were still sentient. Its mouth was open, slack, the tongue lolling over the teeth as if it was thirsty.

He dropped the head to the ground as if he had suddenly burned his hands.

Ernie cringed, and then crumpled in the saddle as tears welled up in his eyes, stung like salt on a raw wound. He could no longer look at Feliz's once majestic head lying there in the dirt with the flies already starting to swarm over the fresh blood and the purpling glass of the eyes.

A moment later, he unsnapped the strap on his holster, drew his pistol. He fired into the *brasada,* pulling the trigger until the cylinder was empty.

2

MATT OPENED HIS eyes, tried to see the dawn through the mist, the warm smothering shroud of darkness. That first chunk of morning was all murked up, but the clock in his mind and the hard ground under his bedroll told him it was time to get up. His jake leg was horning in on his sleep, wooden from the nightchill, stiff as a twenty-year-old slab of oak, painful as a big toe swollen rosy-red with the gout. He rubbed the brittle granules of sleep from his eyes, peered across the clearing to a spot where his foreman, Casebolt, ought to be.

"I'm already up," said Tom, his cockleburred voice floating to Matt Baron's ears from another direction.

Matt heard the creak of saddle leather, the faint ring of Tom's jinglebobs. That man had to hear music when he rode. It was damned annoying this early of a morning when things ought to be quiet so a man could think. There was a lot to think about. He saw the orange glow winking from Tom's cigarette.

"You can't see to saddle," said Matt, moving his bad leg just to see if it still had blood in it.

"I'm just gettin' it ready. I want Blister to suffer some, knowin' it's comin'." The disembodied glow from Tom's cigarette floated in a sudden arc, scrawled a hieroglyph on the darkness like a child's Christmas sparkler. Then, the light disappeared for a moment as if it had been swallowed up in the night's black maw.

Blister was Tom Casebolt's cowpony, a bullet-headed, Roman-nosed, fire-snorting mustang when first saddled up, but a good working horse once it had ironed out its orneriness with a few jumps and kicks under leather. Tom, Matt knew, dreaded putting a saddle on the horse, but liked riding it better than any he had ever forked. It was an ugly horse, too, a gimlet-eyed blue roan whose sire must have been a pinto because it had liver-splotches on its hide, as well as the roan flecks, and its left eye was blanched white as a boiled egg, its right eye a mustard color that Tom called "shit-brindle brown." The term was meaningful to anyone who had ever twisted a calf's tail to get him in the chute and been surprised and humiliated by the anal stream of wet crap that oozed all over his hand and wrist.

Casebolt, Matt Baron's foreman on the Box B, was ten or twelve years younger than Matt, but they were as close as brothers. Closer, maybe, because Matt didn't have any brothers, only an older sister, spinster Louise Alice Baron, who had her own house on the Box B. His only other sister, Edith, had married Ben Killian, died young, leaving behind a son who drifted like a tumbleweed from one town to another, spending some of his time in jails, working when he felt like it. Luke Killian was what folks called a black sheep, and the only visible memory of Matt's dead sister.

Somewhere, off in the distance, a nightjar bleated and Matt realized that a similar sound had awakened him. He listened to the monotonous cry, a querulous plaint that he had always translated into human speech as a plea to "whip poor Will's widow." The bird sounded far away, but he knew that it could be very close. He had seen only one whippoorwill in his life, back when he was a boy of fifteen or so, a sick or wounded one he had found lying on the ground one morning when a milk cow was calving. He had brought it inside, tried to feed it flies and bits of fresh ground beef. But it had died the next day. He had looked for them on many a summer morn in the trees outside his bedroom window, but had never seen more than a shadow on the glass pane.

"Be in for some weather, maybe," said Matt as he shook free of the blankets and stood, sniffing the dewy tang of night, almost tasting the cistern metal dampness on his tongue. "Sky was red as a barn yesterday mornin'."

"And flyin' mares' tails yesterday evenin'," said Tom.

The weather was always uppermost in a cowman's mind, the easiest and most natural thing to talk about, especially when things were going bad, like now. Two days before, Tom had discovered a small bunch of Box B cattle missing. The tracks showed they had been driven off their spring pasture by a half dozen men on horseback. The line rider, Jamey Dobbs, was gone, too, and from the looks of it, Casebolt figured he hadn't gone of his own accord. He had found Jamey's wire tools by a hole in the fence, scattered like the cats had gotten into a box of tacks. He found one of Jamey's boots lying among the cattle tracks, crumpled up like a squeezed-out tube of pink-eye salve.

Matt's horse, Esquire, snorted. The big rangy Tennessee Walking Horse paced at the end of his manila tether. The sorrel gelding stood sixteen and a half hands high, with four white stockings, flax mane and tail, a small white blaze on its forehead. The horse was six years old, the usual high sheen of its curry-combed hide fading after two days of trail dust and range sweat. This section of the Box B, La Golondrina, covered more than five hundred thousand acres and was the smallest of the Baron ranchos. A man could ride for days and never get out of it.

"Esky knows we're in for a change," said Matt, not wanting to talk about Jamey. Jamey was like a son to him. That boy wouldn't steal a single head of Box B stock, much less a couple of dozen. And Dutch Zee. Jamey put a lot of stock in Matt's prize bull. Matt knew Dobbs wouldn't drive a fifteen-hundred-pound animal thirty miles over rough ground.

"Smells wet, all right," said Tom. "God knows we need it. Seldom seen such a case of the drys."

Matt thought of Ben Killian over at the Lazy K. Ben had been hit by the drought worst of all. Last week Killian hands had been burning dead cattle. You could smell the kerosene and the roasting flesh from miles away. A kind of sweetish smell that made a man sick to his stomach. The buzzards so thick they looked like horseflies swirling over carrion.

A hesitant light, like cream pouring out of a pitcher, spread through a dark rent in the eastern horizon. The whippoorwill went silent abruptly, as if an iron door had been slammed in its face. Matt stepped away from the sour puddle of his sweat-soaked bedroll. They had left the main ranch two days ago, figuring the cattle had been rustled the afternoon before that. The dusty tracks verified the time frame. Tom told Matt he thought Jamey might have discovered that hole in the fence, might have started to fix it when the rustlers jumped him. Matt agreed that this was likely what had happened.

Blister whickered. Matt saw Casebolt now. The foreman held a fist under the cowpony's rubbery nose. His hand-rolled cigarette hung like a limp icicle from his lips.

"You've spoilt that measle-hide so bad now he'll probably want to set at Gracie's table when we get back," said Matt. Grace Baron was Matt's wife.

Tom grinned, opened his hand. The smoke clung like plaster to his lower lip. Blister nibbled at the tiny cone of sugar in Casebolt's palm.

"Hell, when he was a colt this was the onliest way I could throw a rope on him."

"I don't know who's more fool, you or Blister."

Matt flexed the jake leg, walked over to the grain bag. The spreading light cut edges to his features, honed him out of the last frieze of darkness. He was a tall, lean man in his early fifties, with steeldust threaded through his meager sideburns. A few strands of gray laced his small, thick moustache, traces of ash sprinkled on a handful of coaldust. His hazel eyes flickered with green tidepools and tiny wedges of gold and amber that shifted colors with the light and the climate of his temper. He had broken the leg in a long fall from a high horse on open range. He had set the bone himself with a chunk of mesquite and a bandanna. That had been ten, twelve years ago when it didn't matter a whole hell of a lot to a man still in his prime.

Matt dipped his hand into the cowhide and heavy denier grain bag, scooped up cracked corn and oats. He carried it like water to Esquire.

Casebolt laughed harshly.

"Well, no use in Esquire gettin' jealous," said Matt.

"No use a-tall," said Tom, his lips curled back in a smile. Matt caught it.

"You grin like a cat lickin' the butter churn," said Baron.

"You want a sugar-tit for that hoss, Matt?"

"This horse runs on grain, not cane sugar."

The two men bantered with one another as if to avoid talking about the missing cattle, the prize bull and Jamey. That was all they had been talking about for two days of riding across the vast spaces of the Baron ranch holdings, but only when they were on horseback. It didn't seem right to talk about it when they were on the ground, not moving anywhere in particular. But each knew he couldn't avoid it much longer. Stealing cattle was serious business. In another time, they would have been justified in hanging the culprits from the nearest cottonwood tree. No questions asked.

"You going to feed your face, Matt?"

"I'll gnaw me a biscuit when I've paid out some sweat. Let's get some yonder under us first."

"Yeah, I figure they had to bed those cattle down last night. They still got the best part of a day on us."

"Yeah, maybe."

Matt knew what Tom was talking about. They had found the beds from the night before some fifteen miles back. Tracks all roiled, cracked ground crumbled and smoothed by the heavy bodies of beef cattle fattened on winter hay and spring grass.

Baron thought about those cattle now, wondered who was thief enough to take them like that. Twenty-five head, he figured, twenty-six counting Dutch Zee, his prize Hereford shorthorn bull.

"I'll grain Esquire and saddle up," said Matt. "It's already light enough to squirrel hunt."

"I reckon I can face it," said Tom, patting Blister on the withers. Blister curled back his lips and laid his ears back like a cat ready to claw hair. Tom backed away, out of reach of the cowpony's sharp teeth. "You bite me, Blister, and I geld you all over again."

Matt chuckled. He poured some grain into a feed bag, set it close to Esquire. The horse arched its neck and began to nibble inside the bag. Matt walked over to his bedroll, hunkered down. He shook it out, folded it, rolled it tight, tied it with a pair of leather thongs.

"I'll fetch 'em some water, if they's any," said Tom, walking over to the pathetic trickle they called Spring Creek. The cottonwoods were lit up now, but mist hung along the creek and in patches over the greening plain. He picked up a canvas bag that had been parafinned to hold water. Matt's saddle straddled an oak log. Matt picked up his hat, which he had impaled on the saddle horn the night before. It was a broad-brimmed Stetson, splotched with sweat stains, made of 4X beaver felt. It had held its stiffness over the years, drained water like a duck's tail, kept the sun off his face most of a bright day.

Matt sat down on the log, watched as Tom stooped over the creek, whacking the sullen branch water into the canvas bag. He dug into his saddlebags, fished out his pipe and a battered can of Prince Albert. He shook tobacco into the briar bowl, tamped it down with his thumb. Wedging the pipestem between his teeth, he took a small box of wooden matches from his shirt pocket. He took one stick out, raked it along the sandpaper side. The sulfurous head exploded into flame with a hiss of escaping gas. Matt touched the flame to the tobacco, drew air through the pipe. The tobacco caught and he shook out the match. He mashed the charred head between his thumb and forefinger until it grew cold. He had seen fires start from "dead" matches. A grassfire, Matt knew, was a fearsome sight.

Tom lugged the waterbag back from the creek. It seemed to Matt that it was just barely half-full. Tom didn't strain at all, and no water sloshed out. Tom's bowed legs made him walk with a rolling gait, like that of a sailor when first stepping on dry land. Casebolt watered Blister first, then carried the bag over to Esquire, set it down. He walked over to the log, stood there as he reached for the paper medallion dangling from the Bull Durham sack in his left shirt pocket. He rolled a smoke one-handed, cracked a match into flame with his thumbnail.

That was one thing about Tom, Matt reflected. He didn't waste much movement. Casebolt stood a hair over five-foot-nine in his stockinged feet, seemed to be made of heavy-gauge wire and iron instead of bone and gristle. He was as tough as a boot, Matt knew, with so many scars on him you could play tic-tac-toe most anywhere on his skin if you had a piece of charcoal to make a mark. Casebolt's eyes were a dusky blue like the Texas sky early of a foggy spring morning. He had a sharp crag of a nose, bent hard at the bridge and scarred where a drunken fool had laid a pool cue across it one Saturday night in Laredo back in twenty-two. Tom was lean as a whip, not an ounce of fat on his bones to slow him down. He had the high cheekbones of his Cherokee mother, the dark sandy hair of his Missouri-born father. His face was richly tanned even to the crevices of the crow's feet at the edges of his eyes.

"Likely we'll be shakin' out the chaps before this Sunday ride is over," said Tom, drawing the smoke from his cigarette deep into his lungs.

"That's another burr under my saddleblanket," said Matt, his visage partly veiled by streamers of blue pipe smoke. "I thought sure they'd head for the border."

"Ain't much south 'ceptin' that goddamned brush," said Tom, exhaling less smoke than he had sucked in.

"Mighty peculiar, Tom," said Matt. "Who do we know who's got balls enough to ride onto my ranch and steal beeves?"

"I been to a couple of county fairs, once roped me a goat and saw a damned punkin'-rollin' contest in Sweetwater, but I ain't seen anybody steal over two head of cattle in fifteen er twenny years."

"Pretty serious when they kidnap a good hand to boot," said Matt, wincing with the enormity of it.

"Yeah. I keep seein' Jamey's tools a-lyin' there by that damned hole in the fence."

"Let's get to it, Tom." Matt stood up, tamped the pipe bowl on the heel of his boot. He crushed the dottle underfoot, put the pipe and can of Prince Albert back in his saddlebags. He shook out the wool saddle blanket, carried it and his saddle over to Esquire. The horse stood hipshot as Matt threw on the blanket, fitted the single-cinch saddle to it. He heard Blister fighting with Tom, but did not look over at them. Sometimes it was downright embarrassing to see that horse act like a colt with a case of the frights. The damned horse was old enough to know better.

Matt mounted Esquire, slipped on a pair of calfskin gloves. He checked the .30-.30 Winchester '94 in its boot, pulled on it slightly to make sure it would draw free. He looked up then, saw Casebolt pull himself into the saddle. Blister got a hump in his back, bucked as soon as Casebolt settled his weight against the cantle. Tom snubbed hard on the reins, pulling Blister's nose back against his chest, straightened his legs in the stirrups.

"Hang on, Tom," said Matt.

Blister snorted and began to dance stiff-legged in a little circle. He arched his back, hopped several times, then kicked out his hind legs. He fishtailed twice more, but Matt saw no daylight between Casebolt's butt and the saddle. Tom grinned wide as he brought the cowpony under control, turned the hurricane deck into a rocking chair.

"Smooth," said Tom.

"If you and Blister are through squaredancin', let's do some serious trackin'," said Matt, looking at the north sky with a wary glance. The sky was slightly overcast, with dark cotton batting rolled against the distant horizon like rugs against the weather crack in a door. To the east, the sun was burning feebly through the gulf fog. He could already feel its searing, moisture-heavy, tropical heat.

The trail was easy to follow. The rustlers were keeping the cattle bunched, driving them at a pretty fair clip. Tom found the bedding ground of the previous night. The tracks drifted southwest, toward brush country. Tom and Matt stopped just after noon, shook out their chaps, put them on. "They know where they're goin', Tom?"

"I reckon they do. They could hide 'em for forty years in that brush."

"It thins some just before you get to the dry lake."

"Yeah. More of it beyond."

They rode into the mesquite a half hour later. The tracking was harder and they had to guide the horses slow so they wouldn't get cut up. The cattle had stomped down some of the brush and left sharpened spears that could pierce a horse's hide or break a rib. There were old prairie dog holes to guard against, homes for snakes and muskrats now, perfect traps for a horse to break an ankle in if they went too fast.

The brush thickened. Blackbirds flushed from the stretch of slough they crossed. The swamp, probably fed by an underground spring, stood in a low place that held the water dank and stagnant through the driest weather because the brush was so thick. Thorns slashed at their leather chaps, scored the horses' legs, making them skittery.

Casebolt swore under his breath when he rode up to a stand of mesquite so thick it was like an adobe wall. It took him ten minutes to find the track, and they had to dismount to go through a narrow tunnel in the brush that someone had widened with a machete.

They knew damned well where they were going, all right, thought Matt. A man didn't take the hard way unless he had a reason. On the other side of the tunnel, Tom had to push away a pile of cut brush the thieves had stacked up after they passed through. His face was greased with sweat, grimed with dirt. They rode on, single file, until the trail broke out of the brush, into the open.

They crossed the Laguna Salado, two miles of cracked dry earth, heading almost due east. In the distance, a coyote slunk out of a gully, its gray coat washed pale by the sun. It disappeared as soon as they noticed it, as if the earth itself had swallowed it up. Then, the trail cut southeast, back toward the angling course of the *brasada*, a strip of brush that ran for seventy-five miles or so, was some ten miles wide in places. The two men halted two hundred yards short of a plain that was cut by shallow arroyos, bleak little draws slashed by ancient rivers, centuries of hard rains and flash floods. They nibbled on dry biscuits and swallowed water from their canteens. A pair of barn swallows, way off course, streaked by overhead, little specks against the desolate bleakness of the terrain. The horses were sleek with sweat; flies nipped at their flanks, striping them with erratic streaks of dark blood. For several moments the only sound came from the whick of the horses' tails. Matt looked at the swath of cattle and unshod pony tracks leading into the broken country, a desert landscape dotted with *cholla* and *nopal*, little clumps of prickly pear bristling with spines and pastel flowers. The land there looked like the naked back of a man flayed with a pirate's cat-o'-nine.

"Somebody's a-comin'," said Tom, looking off to the north.

"Goddamnit," said Matt. "That's Lou."

"Oh, Christ."

"Just steady down, Tom. Don't make it no worse."

Tom rolled his lips together in a fleshy clamp.

Lou rode a plump cowpony, a spayed mare they all called Butterball although her name was Buttercup. Butterball was agile in brush and could take the slack out of a rope quicker than any horse on the Box B. Lou could take the slack and the starch out of any hand just as quick.

"Thought you might need another pair of hands," said Lou, fixing Matt with a skewering look as tough and final as a hayhook sunk in a bale of alfalfa. "I see you both have your thumbs up your butts."

"Havin' a smoke, Lou," said Matt.

"Any sign of Jamey or Dutch?"

"Nary," said Tom.

Lou dismounted, tied Butterball to a sassafras bush. She shook out her heavy denim skirt, tucked her blouse inside her skirt a little tighter and fished a packet of cheroots from her pocket. She put the small cigar in her mouth, leaned down and pulled a pack of matches from Matt's shirt. She struck one on the side of the box, touched the tip of the cheroot to the flame and drew in air. The flame caught and she inhaled deeply. Matt winced to see his sister draw the acrid smoke into her throat.

"You must have leather lungs," said Matt, as Lou handed him back the box of wooden matches.

Lou blew a smoke ring and sat down on a rock, her legs wide, denim skirt pulled up to the top of her boots.

"How'd you know where to find us?" asked Casebolt. "We come forty mile since yesterday."

"I could track a flea acrost an anthill," said Lou. "Half the time, neither you nor Matt could find your ass with both hands."

"Where'd you let out?" asked Matt. He knew she had hauled her horse some eighty or ninety miles from the main ranch at La Loma de Sombra just to get close to this place. She was right about her tracking ability. She could see and taste dust long before anyone else could. He often wondered if his sister wasn't part Indian.

"Over to Hundred Mile Ditch. I figured you and Tom would be somewhere within five or ten miles of the creek."

"Pretty damned good figuring," said Tom, his tone a compost of "grudge and admire," as he would have put it.

Lou walked around, studying the tracks the men were following. She shaded her eyes from the sun and scanned the horizon above the plain, beyond the trees.

"Those sonsofbitches are making a beeline for the *brasada*," she said. "Be like looking for a single cuckleburr in a brier thicket."

"Let's get to it," said Matt.

Lou smudged the tip of her cheroot against the rock where she had been sitting a few moments before. She saved the stub, tucking it behind her ear like a pencil.

Tom, Matt and Lou steamed in the mid-afternoon heat. The sun boiled their shirts, plastered them to their torsos. Sweat coursed down their grime-streaked faces. Tom smeared a bandanna across his eyebrows, swept it down to his dripping chin. He stuffed the kerchief into his hip pocket, where it drooped like a sodden flag.

Lou rode ahead of them, her back straight as a rod.

Casebolt built a smoke. Matt didn't break out his pipe. The last thing he wanted was heat. He stood up in the stirrups, as Lou pointed a finger straight up over her head, twisted to look at the north sky. Tom looked too, and then they looked at each other in amazement.

"Snuck up on us, I reckon," said Tom.

"Christ! That sky makes black look pert' near gray."

"Be a frog strangler, all right."

"And not very damned far off," said Matt.

They caught up with Lou.

"We'll have to break out our slickers, sure as shit's brown," she said.

As they stared at the dark, ominous sky, thunder rumbled in the distance, rumbled hard and long, like someone rolling heavy casks across the floor of an empty upstairs room.

"We better look for some high ground pretty quick," said Tom.

Matt nodded. They all knew how quick a flash flood could spring up in this country. You didn't hear much when one came. It sounded like a far-off train rolling on iron track and then a wall of water came out of nowhere and swept away everything in its path. Each had seen cattle and men try to outrun a flasher, only to be caught out in the open, swept under and taken away, never to be found.

"That's no one-day norther," said Matt as he touched soft blunt rowels to Esquire's flanks.

Lou rapped Butterball on the butt with a gloved hand. The horse responded as if it had been spurred, loped after Esquire.

Tom passed Lou and Matt, riding at an easy lope, Blister as docile as a forty-year-old country mule, grinning at the fresh breeze generated by his speed. Esquire broke into a lope without any urging from Matt. He brought the horse back down to a rolling trot that was easier on his seat.

Ahead, Tom pulled up abruptly, hauling Blister to a jolting stop at the head of a shallow gully. Blister backed away as if shying from a rattlesnake.

"Matt," called Tom, "it don't look too damned good."

"What you got?"

"It's Jamey, Matt. Jesus."

Lou Baron's lips tightened to a thin crack. Her dark eyes seemed to smolder and brighten, throw shadowy light on her sharp, aquiline nose. People said that if she wore makeup she'd be a beautiful woman. As it was, they said she was "handsome." Were it not for her long hair, she could pass for a man if she wore pants, she was that skinny. But every inch of lean was tough and supple as oiled rawhide. Her breasts had never filled with milk, were pert and firm. They were so small, it seemed only as if she had a pair of kerchiefs stuffed in her shirt pockets.

Matt rode up, followed the line of Tom's pointing arm. He winced, felt the stinging bile rise up in his throat.

Lou came up alongside, saw where they were both looking.

Jamey Dobbs lay at the bottom of the gully, staring sightlessly up at the burning sun. His throat was slashed, grinning at them hideously as his head lolled to the side at a sickening angle, obviously just barely attached to his spine.

"Goddamn," breathed Matt. A muscle tightened in his jaw and his eyes narrowed to shadowy slits.

He swung out of the saddle, barely conscious that his hands were clenched to fists and that Tom was throwing up all over Blister's mane.

3

FRANCES KILLIAN SNAPPED the tortoiseshell barrette shut, looked in the mirror to see if it was a symmetrical match to the other one in her auburn-tinted hair. It was too symmetrical, she thought, pouting; made her look like a mannequin. She unsnapped it, shook that side of her hair out so that it flowed gracefully serpentine along the side of her face. She patted the curl that arched over her forehead, smiled with pleasure when she saw it spring back to shape, intricate and quiet as a seashell.

Ben liked to see her hair all combed when she woke him in the mornings. She used little makeup; a faint tinge of rouge to give a pastel color to her cheeks, the slightest smear of red to give her lips definition. He didn't like to see her in her robe or with her hair mussed up, so she arose long before he did, to bathe leisurely before she dressed and made the coffee. She was a comely woman, still slender as a girl, with square shoulders, soft brown eyes, dimples in her cheeks, petite breasts that held their shape under the simple gingham and cotton dresses she wore in spring and summer. This morning, she had let Ben sleep later than usual because she had seen how tired he was the night before, felt his chained anger surge through her when they made love after the children were asleep. He had not read before he fell asleep as he usually did.

She turned from the mirror, got up from the bench quietly, looked over at Ben asleep on the big brass bed, his rugged face peaceful against the pillow. A robin chirped outside the open, but curtained, window. She had not pulled the sash down for the past several nights. It had been unseasonably warm all during February. The window was edged with a pulsing pale light and she could smell the fresh-turned soil of the garden drifting through the open frame, the fragrance of the wisteria that clung to the trellis, the tang of mint thick as clover under the cistern.

She blew out the lamp, watched the tendril of smoke rise from the glass chimney. The bedroom ticked with silence, bathed now with a soothing gray light. She walked to the open door, glanced down the hall to the room occupied by Ben's mother, Jane. There was no light streaming through the small space under the door. Only the sewing room separated their bedroom from Jane's. The children had two bedrooms downstairs, but there was a guest room at the other end of the hall, separated from the walls of her and Ben's bedroom by a large linen closet and a cedar-lined, walk-in closet. She knew that Mother Jane had probably stayed up late, reading. She sighed and picked her way down the stairs to the first floor, through the quiet, comfortable frame house, with five bedrooms, a parlor, office, living room, to the spacious kitchen. Ben had added on to the house over the years until it sprawled over half an acre of ground. He had built playhouses for the children, a small stable for the goats that had pulled little carts the children rode in when they were small. The coffee had boiled while she was fixing her hair and she set out two cups and saucers. She poured some in her own cup, tasted it. Ben liked his coffee strong enough to float a fourpenny nail in it, but she had to add water from the tap to hers. She ground the beans fresh once a week, kept the grounds in a tightly sealed tin. Ben always drank two cups before he took his morning whiskey, and he liked her to sit with him so they could talk quietly before he began his day.

She opened the tap, let a tablespoon of water cascade into her cup, carried the coffeepot, cups, saucers, sugar bowl, into the bedroom atop a tin RC Cola tray she had gotten from Mr. Tippetts, who owned the grocery in Baronsville. Grady had gotten a gross of them when he began handling RC Cola and he gave them out to his biggest customers. Grace Baron, Frances knew, would never serve anything on such a gaudy and cheap tray. In fact, she had seen the Baron family's tray over there one day, on the edge of the porch. The Baron kids were making mudpies in it, baking them in the sun while they splashed in a stock trough by the side fence.

She set the tray down on a table, opened the curtains at the big window that faced the east. She pulled up the shade, looked through the glassless frame down at the garden. Consuela Delgado was already out there, breaking up the clumps with a hoe. She looked like a chubby harlequin with her dark hair swathed in a red and yellow shawl, her multicolored dress hiding her tiny sandaled feet.

"You can fix breakfast now, Consuela," said Frances. "Jeff can tend to the garden."

"*Señora, tengo una cosa a decirle.*"

"*Luego.*"

"*Si, Señora.*"

Frances wondered what Consuela had to say. Whatever it was, it could wait, she was sure.

Consuela never entered the kitchen until she knew Frances was finished making coffee. The Delgado woman then made breakfast for herself and for the Killian children, Stephen, Constance and April, then got the kids off to school while Frances worked on the ranch accounts, made up supply lists, checked expenditures and profits at the big rolltop desk in the study. Frances's mother-in-law, Jane Houston Killian, would double-check her figures once a week. Ben called it "toting up the tally," no matter what it was she did. Frances smiled. There was considerably more to her task than summing numbers and Ben knew full well how complicated her job was, what with the taxes and the leases Humble Oil held on better than three hundred thousand acres. The oil company would begin drilling the first well next year, in 1933.

At eight o'clock, Consuela would fix toast with salt rising bread and slice an orange, boil strong coffee for Ben's mother, Jane, who lived in a separate upstairs wing of the house. Jane was seventy-five years old, spry as a bantam pullet. She stayed up all night listening to shortwave radio and reading Zane Grey and B. M. Bower. She was related to Sam Houston, somehow. Some said her mother was Sam's illegitimate daughter by an Osage Indian woman he had consorted with in Arkansas when he was hiding out from Texas politics. The people in Baronsville said she had Comanche blood, but Jane insisted it was Osage.

Consuela nodded, whacked another clod with the blade of the hoe and waded through the furrows like a duck waddling down a bumpy road. Consuela's dress looked more like a quilt than a garment. She must have used ten different flour sacks to make it, but somehow the colors complemented one another, the yellows, greens, reds, browns and oranges all blended together in a sensible pattern.

Jeff Rogers, the stableman, had plowed the garden the day before, better than half an acre that would give up fresh vegetables not only to the Killian family but to Consuela's and Nancy's, as well. Frances made the children plant seeds, onion sets, and tend to some of the simpler crops: radishes, peas, carrots and lettuce. But she and Consuela planned the garden, worked it at odd moments during the day. Jeff sometimes helped, but he hated stooping over to pull weeds. He would hoe and rake some, but was always sullen when he had to work with the women. She and Consuela and Nancy Fellows, the maid, enjoyed canning outdoors when they had harvested the last of the beans and squashes, and waited only for the pumpkins to ripen in early fall.

Frances watched as Consuela leaned the hoe up against the garden trellis, walked over to the pump to wash the dirt from her hands. Then, Frances turned from the window, walked over to the bed. She shook Ben gently, delighting in the muscular strength of his shoulder as she cupped it in her palm.

"Ben," she said softly. "Coffee's ready. Sun's up."

Ben cracked open a watery blue eye, looked up at her like a Cyclopean giant. She stepped back, assumed a flapper pose, one leg cocked forward so her dress draped its shapely form, one hand on her hip. She smiled and batted her eyelashes like Betty Boop.

"Hoo boy," he gruffed, his voice gravelly with nightphlegm, "you're still the prettiest woman I ever laid eyes on. Pretty as a speckled pup."

"Oh, Ben, you silly flirt," she teased, flattered as always by his thoughtfulness.

He rose up from the bedclothes like a mountain birthing, his massive shoulders freckled and bare as stone, fixed her with both eyes, eyes a powerful cobalt blue. He ran fingers through his thick, kinky hair, tawny now with only faint traces of the Irish red he was born with, forty-four years before. Frances was eight years younger than he and he constantly wondered how he had been so fortunate to have married her. She was soft and well-mannered; he was a man with the bark still on, crude as a Kansas yahoo by her standards.

"You flirt pretty fair yourself, Fran," he said. He looked through the open window, squinted his eyes to tiny fists. "Ye gods, you slept me late." That was as close as Ben got to swearing around Frances.

On the range, with the men, he used every Anglo-Saxon invective known to man, and some he'd coined himself.

"You were plumb tuckered last night, Ben," she chided in her soft southern drawl, gliding away to the table. She poured the coffee from the blackened cast-iron pot so that he could smell the earthy aroma. Steam vapors wisped up in lazy spirals from the two cups like meadow mist in summer. She sat down and spooned coarse granules of sugar into her watered-down coffee. Ben liked his black as Indian pepper and neither cared for cream.

Ben swam out of the bedclothes, pulled on a clean chambray shirt Frances had set out for him on the brass knob adorning one bed-leg. The ornate knob looked like a miniature Turkish steeple. He wore only the bottoms of thin, hip-hugging pajamas that looked like anemic winter underwear. Frances had sewed them using his winter longjohns for a pattern. She made a top for him, too, but he never wore it. He said the hair on his chest and back kept him warm enough.

Ben clambered over to the table barefooted, his shirt front open, the hair on his chest tangled and curly, like an explosion of fine copper wire. He was still red-haired between his legs, too, and Frances blushed every time she thought of it.

"How's 'at coffee?" he asked.

"Taste it."

"You put branch water in yours?"

"You know I did." Her voice was languid and sweet as summer wisteria when she spoke. It made him think of honey on his tongue, the singing of a choir.

He engaged the chair. Ben didn't just sit in a chair, he possessed it, made it conform to his bulk as if it were a horse to be broken to the saddle. Any chair he sat in always seemed to be too small for him. Frances had always marveled at the way he took command of something so ordinary. He sat in the chair like a lord, like a king, and when he laid his forearms on the table, he possessed that too. She felt a strange tingle when he leaned forward and looked at her over coffee. It was a thrilling, intimate moment, one she looked forward to every morning.

Ben grasped the handle of his cup, brought it to his lips. His index finger was missing the tip, burned off at the first joint by a rope. She tried not to look at the stub, as always, but it took an effort of will not to touch it, to kiss it as she once kissed honeysuckle when she was a girl. She wanted to. She secretly fumed that she was not brave enough to do it. She had touched it once; had tapped its blind blunt tip with her index finger, wanting to caress it, kiss it, make it whole. Ben had snatched his hand away from her, glowered with all the darkness and bulging rage of a smoke-black thunderhead, and she realized that she had stepped away from her place. But the stubby finger fascinated her, mesmerized her, and she found herself constantly thinking about it when he made love to her or when she was close to him, and the finger shouting at her to grasp it and feel the smooth mutilation of the scar, magically restore the missing joint. Ben would misunderstand her intentions if she touched it now, and she felt a poignant sadness wash through her, a deprivation that left her feeling empty and strangely unrequited.

Ben blew away the steamy cobwebs rising from his cup with sensuously pursed lips. Frances watched him in solemn adoration. He closed his eyes as he drank the first swallow, and she hooded her own eyes, fearful of looking too boldly at the nub of his mutilated finger.

"Mmmm. Tastes better'n corn, near 'bouts."

"Aw, Ben, you know nothing tastes better to you than corn."

"First off it does. You make a mighty fine cup, Sugar."

She basked in the glow of his praise, brushed the loose locks away from her face as he looked at her across the table. They sipped their coffee quietly for a few moments, listening to the birds sing. A meadowlark piped a rippling strand of chromatic lyric and the thrushes in the orchard whistled back and forth in short, mellifluous phrases.

"Where will you be going today?" she asked.

"I'm going to drive the truck over to Bandera Creek, meet up with Charlie and Reed. We'll saddle up and ride the creek, see why it's dried up so bad. Might be the spring's blocked with brush or a dead critter. You tell Ma where I'll be and not to worry."

"You'll be gone all day."

"And then some. May have to batch it with the boys tonight. You tote up the tally, hear?"

Frances laughed.

Bandera Creek was almost a separate ranch, crossed a hundred seventy-five thousand acres, ran a good hundred and twenty miles, into Rocking A land. It was fifty or sixty miles from the main house over rough roads. Charlie Stone was Ben's foreman; Reed Packer, his segundo. Most of the drought-stricken cattle had died on that range over the past week. She knew Ben was sick about it. It wasn't as bad

as the drought they had experienced in 1916 that lasted through
1918. The average rainfall then had been less than eight inches on
some of the ranges. This year they had lost two dozen head. They had
drifted onto another range from Bandera. Ben had come in last
night, too tired to talk about it, but she saw his smoke-blackened face
and knew that he'd been burning dead cattle to keep from spreading
disease through his herds.

She hadn't told him about Luke last night, nor would she mention their oldest son now. Lucas was something of a problem, a sore
point with Ben. She had gotten a letter from him yesterday, post-
marked San Angelo. Luke was in jail, needed bail money. He hadn't
said much in his letter, but she could read between the lines. And, she
knew Luke. He had probably gotten into a fight over a woman, or
perhaps had been arrested for trying to sell something he didn't
outright own legally. Luke wasn't dishonest, he was just not very
careful about making the right friends. He had always gotten into one
scrape or another. This latest one sounded serious. He had asked for
a hundred and fifty dollars. Not from his father, but from her. He said
he'd pay her back as soon as he got out of San Angelo, that his arrest
was all a big mistake.

"You must have sent Charlie and Reed over last night," she said,
shaking Luke out of her mind. She didn't know if she could scrape up
a hundred and fifty dollars to send to him. She could, but it would
mean depriving the household of certain staples for a few weeks. She
didn't dare ask Mother Jane.

"How'd you know?"

"Your mother, Ben. She sits in her room and knows everything
that goes on in the world. How does she do it?"

"Ma's always been bright," he said. "More'n bright. I reckon she
has her ways of findin' out what she wants to know."

"Then you did send the boys over?"

"Yesterday afternoon. Just a hunch. Harvey Leeds was tendin' the
Bandera herd. He came up on us where we were noonin', said the
cattle were bawling real pitiful, leaving the dry country through a
fence they tromped down."

"My, my," she said. "We might have to haul water down there.
You want me to have Jared and Jeff load some stock tanks onto the
flatbed? They could fill them at the field pump and drive to Bandera
this afternoon."

"Not yet. There ought to be water in that creek, Frances." His tone made her tummy twitch. Ben's anger seldom flared up, but ran deep like an underground river. It could come bursting out at any time and break things. She knew well enough to leave the subject alone until he had figured things out for himself.

"Two weeks ago, we brought in twenty-five thousand head. We may have to take them over to the Arenas Range, now. Have to get some of the hands to burn pear and we may have to bring in cottonseed cake. The stock could get by on the sacahiste grass and prickly pear if we burn the thorns off. I'll make up my mind tonight, or in the morning. Probably tomorrow morning. I don't think well on high heat."

The Arenas comprised more than six hundred thousand acres. Part of the land was planted in prickly pear, for insurance against drought. All of the ranches kept prickly pear growing along the fence rows. With the spines burned off, the meat provided sustenance for cattle. By adding two pounds of cottonseed cake to a cow's diet of cactus, the animal might even fatten.

"I'll look for you tomorrow, then," she said. "Shall I have Consuela pack you a basket?" She reached over, touched the back of his good hand, rubbed it as she would polish piano wood.

"No. I'll get me some beans over to Bandera," he said, slipping back to his Texas drawl. Ben could, she knew, speak like an orator when he wanted to. That came from reading so many books, a side of him that few of his hands knew about. His mother had instilled a love of books in him. She had always read to him aloud when he was a boy. They still exchanged books and talked about them. That was a side of him Frances could never reach. She was far too busy to have time to read. She let Ben and his mother have those private moments together, when they talked books and old times, without rancor.

She finished her coffee. Ben drank another cup. She left him while he dressed, carried the tray back downstairs to the kitchen. Consuela had the table set for the children, raisin bread and butter set out, milk glasses at each place setting. The cookstove was warm now. She saw the flame through the slits in the firebox, heard the faint roaring wind inside, the tick of metal turning from cool to hot. Consuela was probably waking up the children for school. Nancy had not yet arrived, for her apron was still hanging on a nail inside the pantry.

"*Señora?*"

Frances, startled, brought a hand to her throat, turned suddenly. She hadn't heard Consuela come into the kitchen.

"Consuela. You—you scared me half out of my wits."

"Con permiso, Señora. Aquel cheriff dice que va a San Angelo hoy para—"

"Will you please speak English, Consuela. What in the name of heaven are you talking about?"

"Cheriff Blanchard. He say to tell you he goin' to San Angelo to pick up Lucas. He say he stole some money from Mayor Womack. He say the cheriff in San Angelo, he arrested Lucas. He say to told you that."

"Oh, my," said Frances, sagging against the counter. Lucas was not her son, but she felt responsible for him. Ben had been married before, to Matt Baron's sister, Edith. Edith had died before Lucas had had proper mothering. Ben's mother had tried to raise the boy, but she had been active in ranch matters at the time, and had had little time to instill old-fashioned morality in the boy. He had grown up like a tumbleweed, blowing all over the place without any roots.

"I will tell Mister Killian," said Frances. "Thank you, Consuela. Are the children awake?"

"Sì, Señora."

Frances sighed and went into the study. So, that explained why Lucas had written to her. He wanted to make bail so that he could run away again. The boy was almost full grown, nearly seventeen, but he had no more root to him than moss. She sat down at the desk, read Lucas's letter again. Ben would have to know. She wondered if Jane Killian knew. She had probably heard about it on the Zenith she kept in her room. The mayor of Baronsville, Ted Womack, would certainly press charges. Ben wouldn't want Luke to have a criminal record, perhaps go to Huntsville.

A few moments later, Ben came into the study, where she was setting out her day's stack of papers to go through. He carried a brown paper sack tucked under his arm. She pushed Luke's letter under the stack of bills.

The canary in its wire cage hopped to its perch and piped a sharp chirp of annoyance. Frances had named the bird Lady Banana Peel. She called it Lady Peel; Ben called it Banana.

"Ben," she said, "Consuela brought a message from Sheriff Blanchard. About Luke."

"What about Luke?"

"He—he's been arrested in San Angelo."

"What for?"

"Stealing. Money, I suppose."

"Who from?"

"Ted Womack."

"Jesus."

"Ben, please."

"Well, dang it all. Sometimes I think Luke's plumb short of havin' enough straw to make a bale."

"Luke, he's your son. He's just wild. Maybe he's just scared of life."

"Scared of me, you mean. He knows I'll lay the strop to him. Frances, if he needed money, he could have come to me."

"Or me," she said softly. But not Mother Jane, she thought.

"I swear, if you put Luke's brains in a bluebird, it'd fly backwards."

"Do you want me to talk to Roy Blanchard? He's going over there this afternoon to pick Luke up."

"No, I'll go into town when I get back. You just tote up the tally while I'm gone, Sugar."

"We can't let Luke go to prison," she said.

"I'll have a talk with Ted. You keep the bed warm for me, hear?"

Frances blushed, closed her eyes for a moment.

Through the open window, the scent of plum blossoms perfumed the air. Ben stepped close, hugged her with his free arm, pecked her chastely on the cheek. He touched her arm for a second, squeezed it gently above the wrist. She watched him go out the side door to the barn, where the Ford pickup sat under a shed. He took the sack from under his arm, carried it in his hand. He grabbed a slicker off a nail in the shed. He looked up at his mother's window. He didn't wave, so Frances knew Jane was still asleep.

Ben opened the pickup's door, tossed the sack and slicker on the seat, reached in for the crank, advanced the spark after turning on the ignition. She saw him stoop over, fit and turn the crank. The Ford sputtered and coughed as the engine rattled to life. Ben pulled the crank, jumped in the driver's seat, and she heard the motor settle into a rachety rumble as he lowered the spark. A few moments later, he pulled out from under the shed, waved to her as he rattled by. His slow smile burned on her memory for several seconds after he disappeared, leaving in his wake a pall of sun-chromed dust hanging in the still air. She sniffed deeply of the fragrance of apple, persimmon, fig and plum blossoms, looked beyond the clothesline to the orchard, where the trees flowered in bursts of pink chiffon in the tepid glow of the morning sun.

She stroked her arm where he had squeezed her. His touch still burned there, like the taste of fresh crushed mint on the tongue.

She missed him already.

The heady smell of young clover floated through the Ford's open window as Ben drove through the maze of fences that separated the smaller pastures of the Lazy K ranch. Fences and crossfences kept cattle segregated from the blooming fields, the bulls from the cows. The road was ditched now, but he remembered when he and his father had ridden wagons through brush and wild grass to lay out the fields. He had ridden the rocksled to smooth and pack the earth after the brush was cleared. Sometimes, in his mind, he could still hear the chains cracking the mesquite and manzanita as a pair of hands drove a pair of two-horse teams through the tangled *brasada,* the heavy chains hooked to harness between them. It sounded like bones breaking.

He stopped at the first closed gate, shifted into neutral. The gearshift quivered in idle; the cab vibrated with a tinny offbeat hum, transmitting its energy to the pair of long guns slanted across the seat on the passenger's side, a .12-gauge Ithaca pump, and a Winchester .30-.30, both magazines loaded. He filched the quart Mason jar from the paper sack, unscrewed the lid. There was a book inside the sack too, which slid onto the seat. He had just started reading Faulkner's *Sanctuary* last Sunday. It had been published the year before. He liked Faulkner's stories, but he couldn't always unravel his sentences and had to struggle sometimes to comprehend the writer's meaning. But Ben allowed that Faulkner was a powerful writer and damned sure knew his people. He slid the book back inside the sack. It wasn't due back at the Baronsville Lending Library for another week. He didn't expect to have time to read in it, but had brought it along, just in case. He swallowed a mouthful of the corn whiskey, felt it burn his gullet, steam his stomach. He replaced the lid, plopped the jar back into the sack. He looked across the distance, past the barbed-wire fence, the field budding with new clover, to the cattle grazing on mixed grasses beyond. The jolt of whiskey brightened him, crystallized the day. He saw the sun stark and bright against the blue sky, noticed the darkened north like its scarecrow shadow, empty and forbidding, its stuffed arms reaching out to the south in ghostly scuds of clouds. The storm was a ways off, he thought, but it was moving like it had a Kansas wind behind it.

Ben got out of the pickup and slipped the baling wire off the top post, pulled the bottom of the post from the lower loop of wire. He swung the barbed-wire gate outward, let it fall slack and twisted to the ground. He walked back to the truck briskly, got in.

Ben shifted into first gear, let out the clutch. The truck lurched forward, steadied as he engaged the clutch before shifting back into neutral. He set the brake, got out and closed the gate. If there was a big storm coming, he knew he'd have to hurry if he and his hands were to accomplish anything that day. He sniffed the air. There was damned sure a big storm headed their way.

That business about Luke. The boy almost a grown man and still acting like he was wet behind the ears. Luke had run off a month ago and now they had him in the calaboose in San Angelo. Roy was bringing him back in irons. He had been too soft on the boy after Edith died. He felt sorry for him, being motherless when he was just a pup. He thought his mother, later Frances, might take up where Edith had left off, and God knows they'd both tried, but Luke was maverick from heel to topknot.

Ben reached in his shirt pocket and took out a plug of Brown's Mule. He bit off a chew, tongued it into a pouch between his lower lip and teeth. He slid the plug back in his pocket.

The truck snarled as Ben put it into gear, popped the clutch as he smashed the gas pedal to the floor. He had two more gates and over forty miles to go on roads that made the hubnuts rattle and jarred his brains until they jangled like shelf china in a West Texas blow.

Just before he shifted into third gear, he heard the distant rumble of thunder. It sounded like an iron door slamming shut on a hollow basement furnace.

4

ᴍATT FOUGHT THE shudders. He swallowed gulps of air like drafts
of beer from a stein. Tom retched, gasped as he tried to keep his
stomach from bucking like a green bronc. Tears needled his eyes as
he hung onto the saddlehorn, tried to unbuckle his rubber-jointed
knees.

"We'll have to come back for him," said Matt, murmuring as if in
a sleepwalker's trance. "Get him out of that gully, up to high ground.
Rock him over to keep the goddamned critters off him. Goddamn it
all. Jamey. Christ."

Casebolt grunted with the last of the dry heaves, stood wobbly,
lightheaded as a boy sucking his first smoke of cornsilk.

"Be with you, Cap'n, soon's my stomach stops skitterin' around
like water on a hot skillet."

Lou fought back the tears, followed her brother on his grim
errand.

Matt walked down into the gulley, teetering on his bootheels as if
balancing on a circus high-wire. He skidded on a sandy slope,
stopped when his sole hit a clump of salt grass. Pain shot through his
jake leg, but he scarcely felt it. A moment later, Tom made the same
precarious trip. Riding boots were not made for walking on flat
ground, much less sandy slopes. He sidestepped a blossom-studded
cholla, jumped over a prickly pear, heard the spines graze his denim
trousers. Matt and Lou were already down where Jamey lay dead.

Matt's eyes squinched to slits, a ridge of muscle quivering along his jawline.

"I'll help," said Lou.

"No need, Sis," said Matt. "Tom and I can handle it."

Lou stepped aside.

"You get him by the boots, Tom. We'll carry him up to that little knoll back there. Easy."

"Yep. I got him."

They lugged the body up the slope, out of the gully, carried it to a little hump of rocky ground ringed by tenacious manzanita and a lone mesquite bush blasted to deformity by wind, its roots exposed from the wash of floods over the years. Lou followed, prepared to catch the body if they dropped it.

The men grunted as they laid Jamey's corpse down on the bald crest of the knoll. Sweat dripped grime from their faces, spattered on the dry sandy soil. Lou untied her bedroll, draped one blanket over Jamey, tucked the ends under his head and boots. It took the two men and Lou three-quarters of an hour to cover the body with brush they hacked free with their knives and a few rocks to hold it down.

"It'll have to do for now," said Matt. "I don't want that trail goin' cold on us."

"Nope," said Tom, wisely spare with his comments.

Lou said nothing. She was sweating as much as the men. She touched her brother's hand for a brief moment. He looked at her with gratitude.

"It's damn tough," he husked.

"Nothing tougher," said Lou. "A boy like that . . ." Her voice quavered and she knew it would crack if she said another word. She swallowed hard, turned away.

"Lou, better put on your chaps," said Matt.

The three rode into the dry shank of that Wednesday afternoon, baking in their sweat-soaked clothes, legs swimming under the leather kiln of their chaps like bodies in a steam room, eyes burning from the stinging salt oozing from their brows, lips dry as November cornhusks.

The cattle tracks kept angling southwest, paralleling the main swath of brushland, but never getting closer than a thousand yards or so from its jungled edge.

The land changed. Grassland knifed into the sandy barrens, seemed to rise out of the earth, another contrasting pattern in a land of shifting shadows and mottled terrain. Live oaks dotted a stretch of bluestem and gamma grass prairie, a patch left to fend for itself, floating like an island in a cactus-nettled brown sea. Everywhere they looked, the land was like that, wide and endless, huge, bigger than anything on it, stretching to the horizon and beyond, for mile after mile.

"That Box B grass?" asked Matt.

"Have to look at the map," said Tom. "Seems like."

"It is," said Lou. She was older than Matt, had ridden the land with their father, Anson Baron, before he had. She knew it well. "Our pa always thought there was no end to it, until the Aguilars came, and the Killians."

"It sure as hell looks familiar."

"Like one of your daddy's old plots," said Tom.

"That's just what it was," said Lou. "I helped him plant the seeds. Matt was just barely able to walk, back then."

Matt grew silent as he looked at the mirage-like oasis glistening sere and neglected in the sun. Some memory stirred the coals of his senses as if a breeze from his boyhood had sprung up from some summer past, barefoot and innocent, tangy with the smell of blood-bait, and catfish on a stringer, their whiskers curling and twisting like slender worms. He remembered such pastures and how Lou, his father and he would wade through them, burn them off when the wind was down so they would grow again from phoenix-seeds and the ground would hold the grass by the third or fourth year, make its stalks shoot high as a man. But, there were new grasses now, better ones, and these were like the traces of buffalo, a few of them still left here and there, but useless as relics in a museum.

A cannon roll of thunder dissipated Matt's thoughts, shattering the brief spell of nostalgia into scrambled shards. Another sound drew his attention.

"You hear that, Cap'n?" said Casebolt.

Matt reined up, twisted his head.

It was quiet for a moment. Then, they heard the sound again, off in the heat-shimmering distance. It was a terrible, wrenching sound, the disembodied bellow of an animal, or a human, in pain.

"Sounds like an animal," said Lou. "In trouble."

"It's thataway," said Tom, pointing toward a lone oak tree rising from the grassy plain. "Tracks head yonder."

Matt put steel to Esquire's flanks. The horse quivered, bunched up his muscles, bolted to a gallop. Tom strapped Blister's rump on both sides, dug in his spurs to catch up with the rancher. Butterball leaped into motion as Lou raked the horse's flanks with the rowels of her spurs. Boiling air fanned their faces as they rode.

The terrible sounds grew louder as they rode closer.

They all knew an animal was in trouble. They knew it wasn't some old muley cow with its teat caught in a cholla cactus. This was a deep-chested, leather-lunged bull bellowing. To Matt it sounded as if the animal had been spitted over an open fire and was being roasted alive.

Lou's face blanched every time she heard the animal's roar of agony.

The bull was roped to a live oak, sitting there on its haunches, its foam-flecked muzzle tilted toward the sky like a wolf baying at the moon. It sat in a thickening puddle of dark red blood, its curly red and white coat dirty as a bushel basket full of coal miners' dirty laundry. One of its horns was knocked cockeyed and oozing blood into the bull's blinking eye.

"That ain't Dutch," said Casebolt in disbelief.

"The hell it ain't," spat Lou. "Some sonofabitch . . ."

Matt grabbed his Winchester's stock by the pistol grip, jerked it from its scabbard. He swung his game leg over the horn and hit the ground running. Esquire backed away as if he was a roping horse jerking up the slack.

Casebolt sat paralyzed, trying to take it all in as if he didn't understand any of it. He stared bug-eyed as Matt strode up to his prize bull, Dutch Zee, and jacked a .30-.30 cartridge into the firing chamber. Matt didn't even aim. He just put the muzzle up to Dutch's forehead, right under the boss, and pulled the trigger. Lou winced. Dutch stopped bawling in the middle of an ear-mangling note and relaxed all over. Matt cocked the rifle again and fired a bullet behind Dutch's foreleg, straight into his heart.

Dutch's good eye glazed over. The mouth went slack and a last great wheezing sigh heaved from the animal's lungs.

"Jesus H. Christ," said Casebolt. "Dutch, for God's sake."

"Who in God's hell would do such a thing?" Lou asked of no one.

Matt turned away from the carcass, looked at Tom, then at Lou. Tom later reflected that he'd never seen a look like that on a man's face. The closest he'd come was when his folks took him to a tent revival when he was about twelve and the preacher hollered about sins of the flesh and eternal damnation and hellfire for every last sinner on earth.

"They castrated Dutch," Baron said, softly. "Broke his hind legs." He dug a cartridge out of his bulging shirt pocket, thumbed it into the magazine.

Casebolt sucked in a breath.

"Matt, that's a right sorry sight to see."

"It was pure meanness, Tom. Pure damned meanness."

"Matt, we've got to find who did this," said Lou.

"We will," said Matt.

"And cut his nuts off with a dull knife," said his sister.

Baron spoke to Esquire. The horse steadied as Matt shoved the rifle back in its boot. He grabbed horn and cantle, swung into the saddle. He took up the reins. Esquire, ears hardened to cones, stared at the bloody carcass of the bull.

"Let's put some prod to it, Tom," said Matt. "Lou, come on. I might let you do the cuttin'."

"With pleasure," she said.

Lou saw Dutch's sac lying on a rock, then. She knew for sure Matt had seen it right away. Tom followed her gaze and saw the scrotum too. He doubled up, made a sound in his throat.

"Don't go gettin' sick on me, Tom. I'll leave you puking in your hat."

"I'm O.K. Matt. Jesus."

"Swallow it and let's get on," said Matt. He laid the right rein against Esquire's neck, put the horse into a tight turn. He ticked the horse in the flanks and Esquire hit the gallop inside of fifteen yards. Lou and Casebolt caught up to Matt a moment later and the three rode away from the open-air abattoir as if the devil himself was ragging their heels.

The north sky grew fat and dark, like mushrooms under a house. The thunder was almost continuous and the riders saw intricate silver tendrils lace the dark clouds and jagged mercury spears strike the distant earth with blinding suddenness.

"We're in for a gully washer," panted Casebolt, riding up alongside Baron. Lou rode several yards behind them.

Matt nodded, his eyes shimmering with the pulsating glow of anger, like heat lightning on the darkening horizon. The storm was closing in on them, moving fast. They could feel its scouting winds fingering their faces, the cool dankness edging away the heat ever so slowly.

The grassland spun away under the horses' hooves, turned to soft sand and treacherous gravel, thin outcroppings of chaparral breaking up the monotony of emptiness. The dark line of the *brasada* grew larger as they swung almost due east, following the wide trail of stolen cattle, men and horses.

Matt pulled Esquire up when he heard the rales in his throat. Casebolt stopped next to Matt. Both men dismounted. Tom rolled a smoke. Matt pulled on his canteen, looked toward the *brasada* as Lou rode up, dismounted. The stormclouds kept edging in on the sun.

"Tom, you know where they're headed now?" asked Lou.

"I reckon. That slough yonder. Matt?"

Matt nodded. Some called it a slough, some called it brush country. The Mexicans called it the *brasada* and the word had an abrasive sound to it, sure enough. It was part swamp, part mesquite forest, and it was all pure hell if a man had to ride in it. It could tear a pair of chaps to ribbons in no time at all, Matt knew.

"Who could be fool enough to drive 'em in there?" asked Tom.

"Nobody what knows it. No white man."

"That goddamned *brasada*," said Matt, and with the saying of it, the vastness of the brush country seemed to swell in his mind. He remembered when it was even bigger, could still hear the crack of mesquite as the dray horses dragged it with chains and the moldboard plows dug at its roots.

When Matt's pa had begun ranching, his cattle had grazed on open prairie for as far as the eye could see. The land then was covered with a virtually unbroken carpet of grass. There had been small pockets of mesquite thickets back then, but nobody paid them much attention. Within these thickets, sheltered from the elements, grew huisache and small, tough trees, vicious with thorns. But these mesquite stands were few and far between, growing mostly in low drainage places or twisting through the grasslands like scars along the dry creek beds. When Matt had been born, the sea of grass was already losing ground to invasions of brush that grew and spread into impenetrable barriers of thorn. The dry creek beds ran full during the rainy season; sloughs formed in the miniature patches of jungles.

Matt's pa blamed the encroachment, rightly, on the great numbers of horses that grazed on Baron, Aguilar and Killian lands. The horses were mostly responsible for the spread of brush, for they loved to feed on the ripened bean pods of the mesquite. Normally, the bean pods would fall from the trees and never germinate. They died where they fell, and rotted to harmless dust. But when the horses ate the beans, swallowing them whole, along with the pod, the beans survived. As a bean passed through the animal's digestive tract the heat cracked the bean's hull and it began to germinate. When the germinating bean dropped to the ground, it flourished in fresh manure, took root and grew to maturity.

Since men began managing the ranches, they no longer burned off the grass, by intent or accident. In earlier days, Indians and travelers had set fires on the wild prairie. These fires had served to hinder the growth of the thickets, kept them in check. Cattle had contributed to the spread of mesquite, as well. In those places where the grass carpet was eaten away or eroded, the fertile seeds took root. In times of drought, the mesquite thickets ran rampant through all of south Texas.

When Matt was a boy, he ramrodded foot camps of transient Mexican workers for his father. The Mexicans chopped brush and grub roots with axes, grubbing hoes, picks and machetes. The workers were paid five dollars for every acre they cleared. They chopped the mesquite into firewood and were paid fifty cents the cord. If they cut posts for fences, gates, corrals or pastures, they were paid extra, as well. Matt brought in wagonloads of supplies each week, which he doled out to each worker: a pound of coffee, a quart of molasses, seven pounds of *masa* flour, a pound of rice, sometimes barley, two pounds of beans, a pound and a half of bacon, a few ounces of tobacco for chewing or smoking.

But clearing the brush had been a losing battle. Migrant workers came and went. Some worked; some did not. They were paid just the same. Some would draw their weekly rations from the ranch commissary and go back over the border to their families.

Now, this stretch of the *brasada* was part of a belt that stretched from the Nueces to the Rio Grande. It had been contained to some extent, but it still meandered for seventy-five miles, twisting in and out of the grasslands, five or ten miles wide in places, an almost impregnable thicket of brush, slough and mud that sullied the ranchlands of all three families and their hands living in that part of Texas.

"That *brasada* is a damned disappointment," Ben Killian had said one day when they both were chasing down strays that went into the brush.

That it was, thought Matt now, as he realized he'd probably never see his cattle again, might never find the men who had killed Jamey and tortured Dutch Zee out of pure meanness.

The tracks led straight to the belt of brush that formed a large triangle of disputed land wedges, a place where property owned or claimed by the Barons' Box B, the Aguilars' Rocking A, the Killians' Lazy K, well over two million acres of land, came together like tattered pieces of patchwork quilt.

The three mounted up again, kept up their pursuit with grim determination.

"Maybe they'll swing around it," said Tom when they neared the tangle of mesquite and thorn trees.

"They got 'em a purpose, Tom, but damned if I know what it is."

"If they go in there," said Lou, "we'll play hob finding them. I've been lost in there more'n once."

She had gone in there once with Matt and their daddy, looking for strays at roundup. They could hear the lost calves crying for their mamas. They had separated, and she had become lost. She'd started yelling after an hour or so. It had taken Matt and Anson another two hours to find her. She shuddered to think of going in there again.

The tracks turned into single file, disappeared in the brush. Tom stopped, dismounted, studied the tracks.

"The drovers dismounted here, Cap'n. They're a-drivin' 'em on foot."

"Like they know this place," said Lou.

"Ain't this the Rincón?"

"Purt' near," said Matt. Lou nodded in agreement. The Rincón was what they called this corner of brush country. Lands belonging to Ben Killian and Ernie Aguilar converged at this point with Baron range. No one had ever surveyed the *brasada* belt, so they just picked up their acreages on the other side, some ten or fifteen miles beyond, toward the Gulf of Mexico.

The two men and Lou sat their horses. They looked back at the skyline, the approaching storm. The northwest horizon was completely black. Jagged lances of lightning struck the ground intermittently. For a split second the sky looked like silver veining a shaft wall illuminated by a miner's phosphorus flare.

"We could go in there," said Tom, tentatively. "Have to go on foot."

"Hell, they'll split up and go in twenty different directions. We'd get lost inside of ten minutes."

"I reckon," said Tom. "I can smell that swamp in there. Hell on a horse or man."

Lou smelled it too. It smelled of dead things, smelled of rot and decay, of worms working through the rotting flesh of small animals. She could almost see the cottonmouths gliding through the swampy part, seeking prey with their flicking tongues.

"We'll split up, make two halves of a circle, Tom, see if we can find a place not so thick. Maybe they're just going through to the other side."

"Like they want to throw us off."

"Might be they got a truck waitin'. I'll ride north a ways, you go south. Lou, you stay in between. You see 'em, sit tight. We'll get us some help. I just want to know where they're headin' and see if we can't hold 'em for Roy Blanchard."

"Tom'll be crossing Rocking A range," said Lou.

"And some of Ben Killian's, too. Don't pay it no mind, Tom."

"A long ride, Matt. Day's gettin' short and Blister ain't no long horse."

"I want those bastards, Tom."

"I'll ride it short, Matt."

Tom didn't say it, but he wondered about the chance of getting any help this far away from any line shack or ranch headquarters. Everything they needed was a good two days' ride from here. It was another day and a half's ride to the Baron ranch headquarters, an hour's drive to Baronsville to get Sheriff Blanchard. He knew it was none of his business, but wondered why Matt didn't send his sister to town. He knew better than to argue with Matt, though. Jamey's murder and the torture of Dutch Zee outargued anything he might say.

A sound startled the three riders. A crane rose with awkward grace out of the slough with a sacerdotal flapping of gray wings, cleared the mesquite and, once at altitude, headed southwest, leaving a solemn silence in its wake. A pair of mourning doves streaked past, twisting through the air with pinions whistling like muted toy flutes. Then, it grew quiet. It seemed as if every bird went still. Nothing moved. The land darkened as the dark clouds swept toward the sun like a leviathan bearing down on golden prey.

"Meet up with you on the other side, Tom. Lou, you just keep your eyes peeled and listen hard. Once that storm hits, we'll never see another track."

"It's a long hard ride through brush to the other side, Matt."

"Find a spot you can get through quick as you can. Give me three shots if you see anything. I'll do the same. Lou, you think you can find either of us if you hear us shoot?"

"If you hear me shoot," she said, "you can come pick up the meat."

"All right," said Matt.

"You figure they're goin' on through the slough?" Lou asked.

"Dammit, that's what I'd do," said Matt. "Get movin', Tom."

"See ya, Cap'n."

Matt and Lou watched Tom ride off to the south.

"I hope he knows what he's doing," said Lou.

"Me, too," said Matt. Hell, he didn't know what to do at this point. It might be hopeless. He figured the rustlers couldn't stay inside the *brasada* for very long. They'd have to come out to the south or to the east, probably on Rocking A or Lazy K range. They had enough head start to have made it through before he made his circuit around the thicket. He would look for a place to cross through, where the brush was thinner and he could stay on Esquire. If the storm held off, he could track the rustlers well enough once they cleared the *brasada.*

"Well, here goes," said Matt when they could no longer hear Tom in the brush.

"Watch yourself, Matt."

Matt ticked the brim of his hat with his finger. He rode off, alone.

The land went empty as the wind took a breath, or so it seemed. Matt did not hear a single sound. Instead, he heard the quiet pump of his heart, the quick surge of a pulsethrob at his temples. Nothing stirred, as if every creature was waiting for the storm to hit. Even Esquire stood stockstill, rooted to the ground like an equine statue chiseled from granite.

Then, the first winds blew wet and cool; the brasada rattled like a drummer's wagon over rough ground. Trees shook and the grass blew flat, rippled silvery in the gray light as the sun disappeared, blotted out by elephantine clouds that rumbled with thunder. Lightning stabbed the air, charging it with ozone. Matt broke out his slicker just before the rain struck a savage tattoo on every square inch of range along a thirty-mile front.

He drew his Winchester, fired three shots in rapid succession, levering the empty brass hulls out of the firing chamber after each shot. He didn't want Tom to get caught out in the slough. He was worried more about his foreman than his sister. She knew what could happen. A sudden storm like this could flood those creeks in there, turn them into raging torrents.

"Tom! Tom!" he yelled into the teeth of the storm. The wind snatched his words away, swallowed them, spit them out like wet cotton. He knew his voice couldn't have carried ten yards. The rifle shots probably met with the same fate. Lightning flashed, threading silver into the ground a mere two hundred yards away. Thunder crashed overhead; Esquire jolted out of his walk into a skittery lope.

It was dangerous to stay out here in the open. He couldn't wait for Tom. He had to find shelter; high ground if he could. The rain slashed down in slanted sheets, big crystal gouts that turned the hard dry ground into mud, then into a shallow lake. He swung Esquire back to the southwest, bracing his back against the brunt of the storm.

Matt hunkered over the pommel, tried to squint through the curtains of needling rain. The lightning and thunder were almost continuous now, shattering his senses with a cacophonous din that crashed like cymbals in his eardrums. The slashing rain stung his eyes and face when he tried to see ahead. Fifty yards' visibility, he reckoned, sometimes less.

He wondered if Lou had heard the shots. Wondered if she could find him.

He found a rise, followed it to the south, toward Rocking A ranch headquarters. There, he reasoned, he might find shelter until the storm passed. But the rain blotted out all landmarks, and when he came to a stand of oaks on high ground, he headed into them, his dark slicker shining under the whiplash of intermittent lightning so close the ozone tasted like copper pennies in his mouth.

In the howling wind, Matt thought he could hear the bawling of cattle and high-pitched shrieks that sounded like a band of savage Indians on the warpath. At other times, he was certain he heard the deep-throated lowing of his prize bull, Dutch Zee, bellowing in mortal agony.

5

REED PACKER LET out a whoop, slapped his hat against the rump of the last horse trotting into the corral and reached for the latigo tied to the gate. Behind him, he heard the rustle of leather.

Warren Finnerty had too many feet.

Or he always had them pointed the wrong way. Sometimes they turned into clubs. On a horse, he was just fine. On the ground, his legs turned on him, became his enemy.

Finnerty walked up behind Reed, wrestling a handful of bridles with all the awkwardness he could muster. The reins slithered off his shoulders and through his sweat-slick hands like a nest of oily cotton-mouths. One of the reins slid under his boot and Finnerty stumbled. His other foot caught another trailing rein and he pitched forward with the grace and aplomb of a pig on ice.

Warren splashed to the ground with a *whump* that knocked the air out of his lungs, left him sprawled spreadeagled on his flapjack-stuffed belly. He was an angular, bony man, with a long, thin neck, an Adam's apple so sharp it looked as if it would puncture his throat from the inside, offset pale blue eyes, a ragged shock of straw hair and a hooked beak for a nose that never seemed to line up right with any of his other facial features. He wore a little felt hat with a case of the tatters.

"Finnerty, you dumb galoot," said Packer. "You're about as organized as a Chinese softball team."

"I tripped," said Finnerty, struggling to sit up. He managed, with no little degree of natural-born awkwardness, to settle his butt flat on the ground. He sat there, draped in bridle leather, an idiotic grin plastered on his thin, asymmetrical face.

"Reed, don't climb all over me now," said Finnerty, the snaggle-toothed grin fading like gravy on a scraped plate. He fought the reins with jointless scarecrow arms flapping like wind-driven weathervanes, which only served to entangle him further.

Another hand, Jack Bellaugh, came out of the tack room lugging a pair of saddles over his shoulders like dead tortoises, took a look at Finnerty sitting there by the corral, his face empty and homely as a garden spade. Warren's bleak nose was peppered with blackheads like No. 11 lead shot.

"Warren," drawled Bellaugh, "you gangly fuck. You look like a blind man's done gift-wrapped you with cowhide ribbons. Ain't he somethin', Reed?" Jack dropped the saddles on their sides, stirring up two puff-clouds of dust.

Packer shook his head, spoke to Finnerty.

"I swear, Warren, you're dumber'n a day-old nigger. You got too much load to handle in them scrawny arms."

A pair of bits clanked together as Finnerty tried to extricate himself once again. Bellaugh slapped his lean thigh, strode back into the tack room, tweaking one pointed tip of his handlebar mustache.

Charlie Stone, Ben Killian's foreman, walked up, stared at Finnerty with a flinty eye cocked in mock disbelief.

"Warren," said Charlie, "I could damned sure use them bridles when you're through a-playin' with them."

"Mister Stone, I'm a-tryin', I swear. I could use a hand."

"You want a good hand," said Packer, "look to the end of your arm."

Charlie Stone looked away, his gaze on the long dirt road slicing across parched prairie.

"Get a move on, Finnerty. Jack, let's get these horses saddled."

"That Ben?" asked Reed, looking at the dust trail of a fast-moving pickup truck.

"That's him, Reed. Let's don't make him wait none."

Packer grabbed two pairs of reins off the ground, jerked them. Finnerty gagged as a snaggle bit dug into his neck just under the jutting protrusion of his Adam's apple. Reed dropped that set of reins, picked up another. Two bridles broke free. Bellaugh lunged out of the tack room with another saddle, set it next to the corral fence where he'd already draped three saddle blankets.

"Give me that last bridle, Warren," said Jack. He was tall, square-jawed, bowlegged as a horseshoe, with a thick mane of dark, curly hair, a straight, thin, high-bridged nose, piercing hazel-green eyes framed by bushy brows jutting from his wide forehead. "Don't want to keep Mister Killian waiting."

"No, suh," said Finnerty, who had now managed to perch on one bended knee. He still had one bridle bracing his arms, dangling from one ear.

Bellaugh extricated the bridle from Finnerty's clumsy hands.

"Jig time, boys," said Stone, prodding the hands. Reed bridled two of the horses, gave them over to Jack and Finnerty to saddle. He saddled Ben's horse himself, a rangy sorrel gelding with a star blazed on his forehead. By the time Ben's pickup hove into view trailing streamers of dust behind it, three horses stood saddled outside the corral. Charlie's blue roan, Blueberry, shook off horseflies buried in his mane; Reed's bay mare, Lulu, nuzzled Ben's gelding, Red Fox, rubbing his shoulder with her foretop.

Five minutes later, Ben Killian drove up to the corrals at Bandera Creek. The pickup hissed as steam sprayed out of the radiator and the dustcloud folded up and settled back to earth, spread a thin patina on the truck's body and windows. Ben grabbed his rifle and sack, left the key in the ignition. He reached under the seat, pulled out a pair of spurs. The rowels were worn like his stub of a finger, the leather diseased from thorn and brush scrapes over the years.

"You boys ready?" he said, as he strode to Red Fox, shoved the Winchester in its sheath, stuffed the sack in a saddlebag.

"Just about," said Charlie. "Finnerty, bring the grub and our slickers."

Ben looked at the sky, spat a stream of tobacco juice from his mouth. It speckled the ground like liver spots. He furled his lips as he squinted from the sun.

"We could catch it," he said, eyeing the north sky.

"I wouldn't be much surprised," said Charlie.

"Harv come in?" asked Ben. He sat on a nail keg and strapped on his spurs. The tobacco turned tasteless in his mouth as he sucked the last flavor from the packed leaves.

"We'll pick him up in about an hour. He was out before sunup ridin' the creek."

"Dry?" Ben spit out the last of the Brown Mule.

"As a widow's pussy."

"Charlie, this is a sonofabitch. Last I looked, Bandera Creek was springfed, yearlong. Some peckerhead has sure fucked it up."

"Yes sir," said Stone. "I had eight or ten hands drive all the beeves they could up to water in the San Sebastian pasture."

Warren brought the slickers, sandwiches wrapped in oilcloth. Reed and Jack tied the slickers in back of the saddles. Reed put the grub in his saddlebags. Ben mounted first. Reed and Charlie followed suit. All three men carried rifles in saddle scabbards. Charlie packed a Smith & Wesson .38 nickel-plated sixgun on his belt.

"Goodbye, Mister Killian," said Finnerty.

"Warren. Jack." Ben touched his stub finger to his brim, guided a sidling Red Fox toward the creek. Reed rode on ahead at a lope to open the pasture gate.

Ben looked at the buildings that comprised Bandera Creek headquarters. There were a bunkhouse and cookshack, the crumbling remains of a sod line shack, stables, corrals, loading chutes for stock, a pole barn for hay. The tack room was part of one six-stall stable, another could hold up to thirty horses in an emergency. Loose tarpaper flapped on the roof corner of the larger stable with the monotony and mindlessness of black crepe at an outdoor wake.

The sun painted shadow-beards on the faces of the three riders. Their hatbrims shielded their eyes with thin scrims of shade. Reed was already sweating like a laundry worker. Charlie scratched at the hard globules of dried blood that beaded a razor nick in his jaw.

"Ben, it ain't good," said Charlie. "Buzzards so fat they can't fly. We just didn't know that crick had dried up 'til it was too late."

"Must be a hunnert buzzards eatin' cow meat," said Reed.

"Not enough. Charlie, tomorrow you get some boys out there with coal oil to burn the carcasses," said Ben.

It galled him to think of his cattle dying like that, tongues swollen and black as charcoal. Bodies bloating in the sun. The heat of the past several weeks had brought out every kind of pest that could crawl, hop or fly. The flies were bigger than he had ever seen them. Already, the horses were streaked with blood from the bites of horseflies. Their ears twitched and their manes and shoulder muscles shook with the shivers, but the flies clung to their hides like leeches.

Reed's shirt was plastered to his back. Ben could see the moles and freckles through it. Charlie looked like he'd fallen into a creek or walked out of a sweatbath with his clothes on. Grasshoppers crackled as the horses stirred them up and the cowpies were as dry as stovelids, the old ones white-gray as if they'd been sprinkled with powdered sugar.

A white-faced Hereford lay in their path, its russet hide stretched so tight it looked as if it would explode red hair in another ten minutes. Flies crawled in and out of its nostrils, flocked its mouth like black moss. Its glassy eyes glittered green as bluebottles lapped at the frozen lenses, probed the insides of the lids.

"Jesus," said Ben under his breath.

The deaths of these cattle were senseless, he thought. Bandera Creek had always had water in it, ever since he could remember. He didn't blame anyone for not noticing it in time. This was a far range, needed little tending. Until now. There had to be a reason for the creek drying up, but it wasn't something he had expected. But it should have been.

That was one thing Ben's father had told him that made sense. "You got to expect the unexpected when you run cattle," George Killian had said. "Cattle ain't goats. They got to eat right and they got to stay healthy. You got to do everything but curry 'em if you want 'em to fatten up for market. You got to expect hard times ever' so many years."

Ben thought of those words now. Hard times. He knew what they were. So had his father, but George Killian wasn't a man to ride them through. Ben's seafaring grandfather on his father's side had left his fortune to his son George. Ben had been born before the big die-up in 1891 and had watched his father's holdings erode during his boyhood. Now, in 1932, after Ben had bought back much of the land his father had lost, it seemed there was nobody with enough money to buy his beef at any price. To lose so many now seemed ironic. You couldn't ride hard times through unless you could look forward to having something when you got out of them. The man who could hold on, could recover his losses. Someday.

That was something his father hadn't understood. George Killian had finally run off with a young woman after losing much of the land he had bought with Grandpa Roy Killian's money. George had joined the Army, had died of Influenza during the World War. Ironically, he had broken up with the floozie, planned to come back home after the war. Ben's mother had never stopped liking George.

Ben had seen the price of beef climb to $66.41 a head by 1929, but remembered that at the close of the war, in 1918, he was selling beef for $120.03 a head. Yet, two years before, in 1930, beef prices had dropped to $39.83. The numbers stood out clear in his mind. Now, he looked at the dead Hereford and wondered how much the animal would have been worth if it had lived through the drought.

There were more dead cattle the farther they rode. Ben felt like a man with a hole in his pocket. They began to see buzzards five miles from headquarters. The birds didn't even flush when the riders passed by, but worried the carcasses, strutted like ugly and ungainly turkeys, hopped from one cow to get at another. The stench stung the men's nostrils, made their stomachs roil.

Two miles farther on, where the creek made a bend, there was a scraggly stand of cottonwoods, their roots showing like the rib-bones of a cow skeleton. A man rode toward the grove, heading their way. There was something draped across his saddle.

"That'd be Harv," said Charlie, loud enough for Ben to hear. Charlie didn't look back. Reed did, then turned away quickly. He didn't like the look on Ben's face. It made him wince inside as if he'd seen a fresh knife-cut on his own finger.

The four men met in the shade of the cottonwoods. The horses whickered and snorted, tossed their manes, pawed the dry, cracked ground as if trying to dig up water out of the dust.

Harvey Leeds was a big man, standing just under six feet tall, with a jaw square as an iron coal-grate. A pair of moles, big and bluish-gray as cowticks, grew on the left side of his face, one next to his nose, the other just under his left ear. He shaved twice a day, but could have shaved three or four times as much, and the facial hair would still have grown out like weeds. Harvey's beard seemed impervious to the best-stropped razor, grew black and stiff as hog gristles on a scrub brush.

His hair was thick, black, swatched with uneven gray patches. His rheumy eyes seemed to well up continuously and he had a slight tic at the corner of his mouth that made him look as if he was breaking out in a lopsided smile. His hands looked like venous appendages, but were agile and sure as a surgeon's.

Leeds carried a white-faced heifer across his saddle. The calf didn't have the strength to bawl and its eyes were as glassy as agate taws. Its tongue lolled out of the side of its mouth like a strip of veal dropped in charcoal.

Ben squeegeed both of his eyebrows with a swipe of his finger. Sweat trickled down past his right eye. He shook his finger dry.

"That calf just drop?" he asked Harvey. The heifer's hide was dry and curly.

"About an hour ago. Might save her, can I find a cow come fresh with no calf. I counted ten dead newborns by the crick on the way here. This 'un's the least puniest, the onliest one still standin' wobbly on its feet."

Ben dismounted. Charlie and Reed swung out of their saddles. Their saddles were slick with sweat. They pulled at their shirts, the seats of their pants. Ben lifted the heifer in his arms, carried it to the shadiest tree, his limp barely noticeable. He set the calf down. It crumpled to the ground, lay there panting, its ribs showing.

Harvey swung a leg over the cantle, stepped down from his horse, a claybank mare with a square-cut mane, trimmed topknot. The horse couldn't shake off flies from her face much, but she was probably cooler because of Harvey's shears.

Charlie and Reed looked at the calf.

"That'un's so thin, it'd have to stand up twice to cast a shadder," said Reed.

Harvey got a bottle out of his saddlebag. It had a big rubber nipple on it and he'd punched bigger holes in it.

"I milked one cow what lost its calf," he said. He hunkered down, squatted by the calf, stuck the nipple into its mouth. The heifer pulled on the nipple, nudged its boss at Harvey's other hand, which he held over its head. The milk gurgled down the calf's gullet. The bottle drained in less than a minute.

"Harv, how far'd you ride down the creek?" asked Charlie.

"Maybe two, three mile from here." He looked up at Ben as he stood up. The calf tried to rise and follow him. Its legs wouldn't do more than twitch in separate directions. Harvey reached down, patted its boss soothingly. "The crick's fairly lined with roasting cattle far as I could see beyond that. Some of the calves was born dead, lyin' there still in their sacs."

"Christ," said Reed.

"You check any of the tanks?" asked Charlie.

"Bone dry, too. That crick's so far underground the wells don't go deep enough to get at it."

"Hell, we used to get water 'round here at thirty feet," said Packer. He pulled a soggy sack of Bull Durham from his shirt pocket, riffled through the packet of papers to find one dry enough to roll and smoke.

Ben limped over to his horse, pulled the sack out of his saddlebag. He took the bottle out, twisted the cap off and swallowed a couple of ounces. The fumes replaced the milk smell in his nostrils, but not the stench of decomposing carrion.

Ben bit off a chew, tucked the wad between his teeth and gums.

"If nobody's hungry, let's follow Bandera on out," said the rancher.

"Ain't nobody hungry," said Charlie, speaking for the other two men. Reed and Harvey nodded. Reed dropped his butt to the ground, bootheeled it into the dirt.

The men mounted up. The calf bleated pitifully as the men rode off. Harvey looked back. His jaw hardened as his teeth clamped tight together. His chin looked as if it had been smoked with a candle.

Reed Packer rode with his bandanna held over his nose like a crimson flower. Charlie breathed the heavy air through his mouth, his nose squinched up to keep out the stench. Harvey Leeds crushed a horsefly to death on his horse's neck with his thumb, wiped the blood on his reinforced denims bought at Kaufman's Dry Goods and Mercantile in Baronsville. Ben Killian stared at dead cattle and spat tobacco at the ground as if he was spitting out brown nails.

Charlie pulled a crumpled Camel from his pocket, hung it on his lower lip, struck a pophead match on his saddlehorn where the leather had worn away to the gray metal, touched the flame to the end of the cigarette. He blew the smoke out through his nostrils, blew away the smell of rotting cattle. He snapped the match in two, snuffing it out, catapulted the two wooden pieces away with a flick of his index finger. The horses, heads down, plodding on the hard, cracked earth along the creek, nickered to each other like prisoners muttering in a chain gang.

The four men rode along the creek, following its meander, passing the burned carcasses of cattle, setting buzzards to flapping as they hobbled along the ground with bellies so full they couldn't fly. Cows lay so swollen with gases heated by the sun they looked like enormous gourds. Some cattle were still alive and their pathetic moans tore at the men, made Ben shudder with helplessness and anger.

Those sad lowing beeves were only a preview to the sound they heard some twelve miles from headquarters in mid-afternoon. They heard too the rumble of thunder, but they paid it no mind because they listened with surprise to the terrible bawling of cattle they could not see.

"What's that?" asked Ben, riding up alongside Harvey.

"That'd be maybe several hunnert head we ain't seen since the crick went dry."

"Where in Judas Priest's fucking hell are they?"

Leeds shrugged.

"Maybe at the Rocking A fenceline. We're nearabouts right to it."

The bawling grew louder, a huge groaning sound that blotted out all others. The horses lifted their heads and coned their nervous ears, twisted them around like quivering antennae.

"Something's got 'em spooked, but they ain't a-runnin'," said Reed to no one.

"I'll ride on ahead," said Charlie. "Something's not right."

Harvey sidestepped the claybank mare as Charlie urged his mount into a trot. He disappeared around a bend of the dry creek bed.

Fifteen minutes later, Ben, Reed and Harvey rode into the milling herd of Lazy K cattle. The noise was deafening. Herefords crowded the barbed-wire fence that separated Killian land from Aguilar's spread. Charlie, his horse ringed by several dozen head of cattle, beckoned to Ben. Reed looked up and down the fenceline. Cattle flocked to the fence, butting the posts, pawing at the triple strands of wire.

"So, this is where all the missing head have been," said Reed.

"They can damned sure smell water on the Rocking A," said Harvey as Ben and his horse forged a path through the thirsty herd of beeves. Ben kicked cows away with his boots, made his way to Charlie Stone at the fence.

"Looky what we got," said Stone.

Ben saw the dead bull hung up in the barbed wire.

"He die there like that?" Ben asked Charlie.

"No, he's got a bullet hole clean through his forehead."

Ben saw the dark cavity in the center of the bull's skull, just below the boss. Flies swarmed over the caked blood, crawled in and out of the hole like bees at a honeycomb.

"Yonder's a tank," said Charlie, "full as granny's churn."

Ben saw the dam, the tank beyond. And Bandera Creek was running right into the huge pond behind the dam's wall.

"They sure didn't hide it none, did they?" asked Stone.

"Give me your wire cutters, Charlie," said Killian.

"You aim to cut Ernie's fence?"

"These cattle are going to drink, by Jesus. Hand me the cutters."
Charlie dug into his saddlebag.

A clattering of hoofbeats drew the foreman's attention just as he retrieved the wire cutters. Three Rocking A riders pounded into view. Ben and Charlie recognized them.

"Randy looks like he's got blood in his eye."

Randy Connors, one of the riders, was Aguilar's segundo, worked directly under Paco Velez, the Rocking A foreman. With him were Luis Soledad, one of the line riders, and Umberto Iglesias, a wrangler. The hands reined up, opposite Charlie's position on the other side of the fence. Dust rose up to their horses' chests, clung to the sweaty hides like a host of seedticks.

"Charlie, what you aimin' to do?" shouted Randy above the *muo-oows* of the restless cattle.

"Looks like you got some of our water penned up over there," said Charlie.

"Paco's orders. That dam's legal as taxes," said Randy. He was a young buck of twenty-five or so, with dark eyes and sand-blond hair, lean as a quirt-strand, tanned from the sun, wearing a narrow-brimmed felt hat spotted with sweat circles, a light brown shirt, loose-fitting denims. The Mexicans flanked him, wide-eyed and curious as baby barn owls.

Ben rode up to Charlie, took the heavy-duty wire clippers from his hand.

"You step your horse back, Connors," said Killian. "In about two seconds my herd's coming through to that water."

"Mister Killian, you can't cut that fence."

"Like hell," said Ben, dismounting.

"We got to stop you, sir," said Randy.

Ben looked up at the segundo with a look that would have frozen a bowl of hot chili.

Randy looked at Luis and Umberto. The Mexicans avoided his gaze. They looked at the ground as if trying to find a hole where they could disappear.

"I'm askin' you not to cut them wires," said Connors. "Paco, he won't like it none."

"I don't give a good goddamn whether Velez likes it or not. My cattle are parched and dying. I'm cuttin' this fence and then I'm going to have a talk with Ernie."

"I got my orders," said Randy. He stretched his hand out toward the butt of the rifle jutting out of his saddle scabbard.

"You shoot that bull there in the wire?" asked Ben, stepping up to the fence.

"He was fixin' to tear it down, Mister Killian. I had to stop him."

"Charlie, draw your rifle. If any of Ernie's boys make a move to stop me, you pop 'em."

Randy's hand froze, inches from the rifle butt.

Charlie jerked his Winchester from its scabbard, levered a cartridge into the chamber. Luis and Umberto started backing their horses.

Ben snipped the top strand of barbed wire. It released with a singing twang. He cut three more strands and stepped aside. He took off his hat and slapped a cow on the rump, headed it through the opening.

Randy's horse danced aside as cattle streamed through the opening in the fence, clomped toward the pond. More and more cattle clambered after the others, bumping into one another, hooking their horns at one another to get to the gap in the wire.

"Damn you, Ben Killian, you done gone too far!" shouted Randy.

Ben spat a stream of tobacco juice onto the back of a passing cow. One of the fence posts went down under the crush of frantic animals stampeding toward the waterhole. Randy had to move out of the way as three steers bore down on him like a house in a landslide.

Ben grinned as he saw his cattle pour into the pond, scramble along the creek to slake their thirst.

"Okay, Charlie," he said, "let's ride over and pay Ernie Aguilar a visit. Tell Harv to stay here and make sure those cattle stay at the water trough."

"Maybe Reed ought to stay too."

"It's your call."

Ben tossed the clippers to Charlie, climbed back aboard his horse. He unsheathed his Winchester, cocked it. He pulled the trigger, sent a bullet whining over Randy Connors's head. The Mexican hands wheeled their horses, spurred them into a gallop.

Randy swallowed hard and turned tail, chasing the Mexicans' dust.

Charlie rode back past the surging stream of cattle to give Harvey and Reed their orders.

Ben filed his horse into the herd of cattle and rode on through the break in the fence. He levered another shell into the chamber, fired another shot into the air. The smell of burnt powder made him feel good for a moment.

6

ELENA AGUILAR'S SLENDER, magical fingers, delicate as a harpist's, plucked rose petals from her daughter's cheeks. She pinched and kneaded the soft olive skin of Alicia's smooth, unblemished flesh, exciting the tiny capillaries, bringing the blood to the surface until her daughter's face glowed like a mystical southwestern dawn.

Alicia stood dutifully in her white silk slip, barefooted, looking over her mother's shoulder into the shadowy mirror.

"Ouch," said Alicia, a mischievous twinkle in her eye, as her mother slapped her gently on the buttocks.

"That didn't hurt," smiled Elena, a slender, petite woman with shining raven hair, startling sky-blue eyes that bespoke her Castilian heritage, a perfectly shaped face that resembled the Mexican *bulto* of the Virgin Mary that stood serenely atop the small altar-shrine in her bedroom. Indeed, visitors to the Aguilar hacienda who saw the small, primitive statue, shimmering under the light of a flickering votive candle, often asked Elena if she had been the model for the figurine.

"Ah, no," she told such inquisitors. "The virgin was made in my father's village by a *peón* before I was born. The man was a *santero*, a carver of saints, who traveled from pueblo to pueblo with his burro, selling his wares. My mother told me he carved it before their eyes in the patio from the soft root of the cottonwood tree. He made a plaster from gypsum and glue boiled from the hoof of a horse, then painted it with a hog-bristle brush when the plaster dried. He made his own pigments from roots and iron ores, from flowers and fruits and charcoal. I have loved it ever since my mother, God bless her and keep her, gave it to me."

Elena slid to one side on the stool that sat in front of the dressing table, looked at her daughter's image in the mirror. She smiled. The frail coppery light from the lamp glazed the mirror's slightly wavy surface, reflected off their faces.

"Hector teased me at school today," said Alicia. "He was mean. Boys kept trying to spank me. Hector told them to do it."

"He was just being what he is," said her mother. "A boy. A jealous brother. When he has his birthday, you can tease him."

"But he's fourteen, and he said I was ugly," said Alicia, puckering her lips in a mannered pout. "I almost cried."

"You look beautiful, Alicia," her mother said. "Now, let's put on the pretty pink dress Papa bought for you in San Antonio."

Alicia frowned, dissipating the pout. She couldn't take her eyes off her counterpart in the mirror. She was as flatchested as a flapjack griddle. Her shoulders were too small and knobby. Her face looked long and horsey to her and her hair was too straight, too dark. Her eyes were nut-brown like her father's and Hector's, but they looked black now in the mirror.

"I don't like the pink dress," she said. "Mother, can't I wear the blue one so I'll look like you?"

Elena laughed.

"Do you want to look like a grown woman so soon? You'll be so pretty in pink. It is the second of March in nineteen hundred and thirty two and this is your birthday, my daughter, and you are a budding rose. You should look like a flower in your new dress. Besides, you've almost outgrown the blue dress. I will make you another."

Alicia giggled. "Will you make one with lots of pretty colors? I want to look like you."

"Yes. I will make you a dress just like mine. Now, *andale, andale, mì hija.*"

Elena reached over and wiped sweat beads from Alicia's upper lip. The room was warm, balmy, despite the open windows, the late afternoon breeze.

The girl flashed away like a wood-sprite, emptying the mirror of her reflection. Elena sighed and watched her daughter open the wardrobe, stand on tiptoe to pull the pink dress off its wooden hanger.

The distant rumble of thunder made Elena frown. She had been watching the northern skies all afternoon, had seen the far-off clouds turn ashen-gray, then darken to pitch. Now, she went to the north window in Alicia's third-story room, peered through the double glass pane. The sky seemed hung in gauzy dark shrouds, a sure sign of rain. She had never seen a sky so dark, so ominous, and above the torn shreds of cloud-wisps wrenched from the main body of black thunderheads, spectacular lightning displays flashed jagged silver lacework that struck the ground, illuminating miles of misty horizon. The curtains billowed from the breeze, rustled her skirt with invisible fingers. A bewildered fly clung to the lower screen, thwarted from entering the shelter of the room.

"Is it going to spoil my party, Mamá?" asked Alicia, holding the pink dress with tiny blue ribbons tied in bows around the hems of sleeves and skirt.

"If the rain comes here, we will have to stay inside," said Elena.

"Is it coming?"

"I think it is coming," said her mother softly, her heart quickening at something else she saw from the other high window, the one to her left, facing west. There was no mistaking him, even at that distance. She would know Ben Killian anywhere, afoot or on a horse. He and another man were riding toward the house on horseback, making their way slowly down the road that bordered the west pasture. She saw the men stop, shake out slickers, don them as their horses stepped out again.

She could not take her eyes off Ben. He seemed to draw her to him even from so far away. He was magnetic, seemed somehow bigger than the horse he rode, yet somehow part of the animal, like a Centaur. Part horse, part man. Her heart fluttered in her chest like a wild bird in a cage. The blood drained from her brain, made her feel lightheaded, giddy. She moved to the other corner window, stared shamelessly at Ben, wondered why he was coming to her husband's ranch this day. Was it to see Frances? His wife had driven the LaSalle up to the house a while ago, bringing their children, Steve, Connie and April, bearing presents for Alicia.

"What's wrong, Mamá?" asked Alicia, wriggling into the dress. "Is the storm close?"

"Close," murmured Elena, but she was not speaking of the storm.

She seemed mesmerized by the sight of Ben Killian, transfixed, as he came closer.

"Can you help me with this dress?"

Elena shook her head, forced herself to turn away from the enchanted window with its curtains flexing, flapping gently with every puff of breeze.

"What? Oh yes, *mi cariña*," she said. "Be careful not to wrinkle it. Oh, it looks so pretty on you. *Ay de mi*, you mussed your hair."

She straightened her daughter's dress, patted her hair back into place.

"Turn around," she told Alicia. "Did you put flower water under your arms? Did you dab perfume behind your ears?"

"Oh Mamá." Alicia's blushing made her cheeks glow just the way her mother wanted them to without using rouge.

Alicia spun like a ballerina and Elena hooked the loops of wound thread over the pink mother-of-pearl buttons from the waist to the nape of the neck. She straightened a couple of bows at the hem of the skirt.

"There now. You look like a princess. There is a flower downstairs in the icebox. It's in a little cardboard box. I will be on the porch by the patio. Bring it to me and I will pin it in your hair."

"Why are you going there?" asked Alicia. "Is someone else coming?"

"Yes," Elena breathed. "In a few minutes. Do not go into the livingroom. Not until you have the flower in your hair."

"I'm so excited. Are Ethan and Peggy here?" These were the two oldest Baron children. Alicia knew Derek was away at school in Galveston.

"They are here with their mother. There are lots of children here already. More are coming from town. Listen."

They heard the music then, floating upstairs as the mariachis struck up the first chords.

"Hurry," said Elena, pushing gently at her daughter's back. Alicia skipped across the room. Her mother glanced out the west window one more time, saw that Ben and the other man were less than a quarter mile from the house. She heard the first patter of raindrops strike the windows, spatter on the roof. Alicia disappeared through the door. Elena pulled the windows down tight, blew out the lamp, took a deep breath and followed, her heart all tangled up in her mind like a wren in a bramble thicket.

*   *   *

Elena stood under the arched roof of the small front porch that bordered the patio. Raindrops dug doodlebug craters in the dust between the flagstone stepping stones, tinked off the wrought-iron table and chairs that nestled against the adobe wall that sheltered the patio from the wind. This was a little corner of Mexico that she and Ernesto enjoyed, where she had planned to have Alicia open her presents when she and her husband presented her birthday cake to her. Beyond the outer wall, new hitchrails had replaced the old. This was where Ben and his companion would tie up their horses before opening the wrought-iron gate, striding up to the front door.

She wore a colorful cotton skirt with a wide hem of lace, a simple turquoise-hued, short-sleeved blouse with beribboned sleeves. A light lace shawl, white with light blue trim and elegantly simple, nestled around her neck. A white carnation, the petals fringed with pink borders, like the one she had pinned to Alicia's hair a few moments ago, bloomed behind her left ear. She wore a necklace of faceted jade beads. Matching earrings dangled from her earlobes. Her wrists glistened with fourteen-carat gold bracelets. On her left hand, her engagement and wedding rings sparkled with small diamonds.

Elena trembled as she heard the beat of horses' hooves. The faint strains of music interspersed with young laughter seeped through the massive oak door. Ernesto, her husband, was seeing to the comfort of their guests, probably charming the mothers who had brought their children with his boyish smile, his gracious charm.

The hoofbeats went silent and she heard the creak of leather beyond the patio gate.

Moments later, two men appeared beyond the gate's arch. The gate swung open and Ben Killian stepped into the patio, trailed by Charlie Stone, his foreman.

"Elena," said Ben, barreling toward her, his slicker shiny from the rain.

"Ben. What brings you to our home?"

Charlie halted a few feet in back of his boss, tipped his hat politely. Elena smiled at him.

"Come into the alcove," she said. "Both of you."

"Obliged, ma'am," said Charlie, his awkwardness as prominent as pimples on a squeaky-voiced kid's face. His face was damp, a straggle of hair drooping onto his forehead from under his hat.

Ben stepped close to her and she could smell the woody tang of whiskey on his breath. The small hairs on the back of her neck shivered. She remembered. She remembered that taste in his mouth, that breath on her face as thrilling as the fragrance of a good sherry, as heady as her father's private stock of *aguardiente*.

She remembered his strong touch, the way his hands drew her to him, made her melt like burning candlewax in his arms. Such futile memories, she thought. These things had happened long ago, and Ben had probably not thought of her at all during the years since he'd courted her, since she had married Ernesto. Of course he hadn't. Ben was married, too, had three children of his own.

The two men followed her into the little alcove. She wished the whole house was adobe, but some of it was really only a frame dwelling, made of wood. One main section of house was adobe brick, the roof tiled like those in Mexico City. Here, the adobe entrance was attached to the frame section, not as an afterthought, but as a direct link to the original old adobe ranch house of Ernesto's father, which had long since crumbled to dust, much of it blown away over the years by the aggressive, muscular West Texas winds.

"Ben, is something wrong?" Elena searched his face for an expression that would tell her the reason for his visit.

"Ernie in? I hate to bust in on your fandango, Elena, but I got to talk to him."

"Yes, I will get him. Please come inside."

"We'll wait here," said Ben.

She knew he said it out of politeness. His boots were muddy and he was dripping, but there was a rug inside for just such situations. She touched his elbow. Even that small touch spawned a brief shiver of electricity through her fingers.

"There is no need to stay out here, Ben. Please. Come inside."

"I reckon not," Ben said stubbornly. "What I got to say won't take long."

She sensed the tension underneath his words. She knew it was none of her business why Ben wanted to talk to her husband, but she couldn't help wondering. Something was wrong. Ben wouldn't ride all this way on horseback just to talk about something of little consequence.

"We have drinks inside," she said, venturing one last offer before going to fetch Ernesto. "Ernesto would want to show his hospitality."

"It ain't exactly sociable what I got to say," said Ben. She knew he could speak English more correctly than that. He was being Ben the cattle rancher, Ben the throwback to his runaway father. He probably spoke that way because the other man was with him. She had heard Ben speak much better. She had heard him recite poetry and read elegant words from books.

"I'll get Ernesto," she said curtly, then softened it with one last opinion. "But I do wish you'd both come inside and wait."

Ben bunched his lips together, breathed through his nostrils.

A jagged streak of lightning illuminated the figures in the alcove. Three seconds later, a rolling peal of thunder announced a cloud-burst. The rain danced across the patio, rattled the ivy growing on the adobe walls, jiggling the tightly closed honeysuckle blossoms on the trellis.

"We'll wait here," said Ben, stamping out her invitation with the finality of a judge's gavel.

"Con permiso," said Elena, suddenly angered by his stubbornness. It was rude of her to speak Spanish, even that ingratiatingly polite phrase, but it made her feel superior even though she knew Ben understood Spanish as well as any non-Mexican. *"Momentito."*

She opened the door, went inside the house, passing through the wide foyer, with its high, beamed ceiling that connected the main house to the adobe entrance, the umbrella rack, the hall tree bare of coats or hats. The hardwood floor gleamed under the large oval rug that protected its center. She passed the front room, with its arched entrance, the stairs leading to the second story, and entered a narrow hallway that led to the main part of the house. Her dress caught on the doorknob that jutted from the door that led to the basement, the dank rootcellar.

She entered the spacious formal dining room. Beyond, the family livingroom teemed with people, children and their mothers, a bar. The rugs had been taken up and the mariachis clustered in one windowed corner, playing so loudly they drowned out the laughter of the children, the murmured conversations of the adults.

"Where's Don Ernesto?" she asked Silvino Marcos, their handy-man, who had been pressed into service as a bartender.

"Por allá," said Silvino, pointing toward the back porch.

"Stop that," she said sharply to Hector, who was pulling Alicia's hair. Hector dropped the strands quickly, turned sheepishly at the sound of his mother's voice. His mouth opened and he said some-thing that was drowned out by a crashing chord from the mariachis.

The children stood around a long table draped with a cloth

decorated with images of birthday cakes, boxes of gifts, tin horns, streamers and bunny rabbits. The table itself served as a refreshment stand for the children and one end was stacked with gaily wrapped and beribboned presents for Alicia. The large cut-glass bowl held cups around its rim. A chunk of ice floated in the pink punch to keep it cool in the bowl. Most of the children held cups in their hands; most of them sported pink mustaches just above their upper lips.

Alicia shook free of her brother, stuck out her tongue at Hector's back.

Elena hurried toward the back porch, a feeling of dread welling up in her as the musicians went silent between songs. She smiled grimly at Frances Killian and Grace Baron, both of them staring at her in puzzlement, their hands wrapped around glasses suspended in midair.

Kitty Emberlin, Doc Emberlin's wife, was chatting with Naomi Tyler, who owned Naomi's Café, which everyone called "Nomi's," in Baronsville. Naomi was a corpulent women, very tall, possessed of a rich sense of humor and a hearty laugh to match. In Texas, polite folks referred to her as "stout," but up north she would have been called just plain fat. Little Faith Emberlin was tugging at her mother's skirt, trying to get her attention. Faith was only seven years old; her head was festooned with scrolls of blond curls that hung to her waist, bounced up and down every time she jumped.

"Be right back," Elena said to Frances, who was nearest to her. Kitty and Naomi never even noticed her. Little Faith finally plunked herself down beneath her mother's skirt and began to puddle the floor.

Ernie watched the dark stormclouds blow in over the flat pasturelands to the northwest. He looked at the bulging elephantine clouds, saw lightning fork them with serrated veins of fleeting quicksilver.

Raindrops spattered against the screen, filled the tiny squares. Ernesto did not move away from the slight spray, but stood there, rapt in his thoughts.

Maybe an end to the drought, he thought, perhaps the one good thing he'd get out of the day. His meeting with Bone that morning had left him shattered in heart and mind. Besides the anger that wormed through him like an insidious growth, he had been nervous, uncertain all day long. Even his daughter's birthday could not lift him from his depression, or free him from the frustration he felt. He kept seeing the head of his dog, all bloodied and covered with dirt, those unseeing glassy eyes. He kept hearing Bone's chilling laughter echoing over and over in his mind like a maddening Victrola record stuck in one waxen groove.

He heard the porch door open, the click of high heels clacking on the floor. His hand tightened around the glass of wine in his fist.

He turned, saw Elena scurrying toward him, never more beautiful with her dusky gypsy-dark skin, her dazzling blue eyes.

"Ernesto . . ." she started.

"I was just watching the storm," he said quickly. "I hope you were not looking for me, eh?"

"Yes, my husband," she said in Spanish. "There is some trouble, I think."

"Trouble?" He too switched to their second language.

"Perhaps. Ben Killian is on the front porch. He would not come inside. There is another man with him. His foreman, I think."

"Stone?"

"Yes, that is the man, I believe."

Aguilar's face darkened. He did not like the Lazy K foreman because Charlie Stone did not like Mexicans. He called them "greasers," like a lot of other gringos, but in Charlie's case it wasn't just a convenient pejorative. Charlie always gave the Mexican hands the dirtiest jobs, treated them like sub-humans.

As for Ben, Ernesto was always uneasy around him, even though he'd had many previous business dealings with the man. In fact, he had sold Ben back some of the land George Killian had lost because of nonpayment of taxes. Aguilar had bought up the lands and when Ben asked to buy them back, Ernesto had sold them for a good profit. But he did not trust Ben Killian. It had never been expressed, but Ernesto was uncomfortable because Ben had known Elena before he had. He had always wondered how close they had been, but had never asked. Ben had learned cattle from Elena's father when he was very young. Her father had worked for George Killian, but had died of typhoid fever before Ben took over the Lazy K.

"Do you know why he came here, *mì querido?*"

"No."

"I offered them cups, but Ben refused."

"That Killian drinks plenty. I am surprised."

"There is something on his mind. I am sure of that."

"Do not trouble yourself over this visit, Elena, my dear one. I—I will see these men at once."

Elena's lips drooped in a frown. She looked at her husband closely. He avoided her gaze, drank the remainder of his wine. He handed her the empty glass. She knew her husband well. She knew when he was hiding something. She wondered what was between him and Ben Killian. But she knew that Ben's visit was unexpected.

"Do not let Ben spoil this afternoon," she said, twisting the wineglass in her hand.

"No. It is nothing. I will not be long. Please see that our guests are comfortable while I am gone."

"But of course," she said dutifully.

Ernesto strode through the fiesta room, nodding and smiling at the women. His son Hector, a chunky, slightly chubby boy with a mane of russet curly hair, came up and blocked his way, but Ernesto brushed him aside without a word. Hector sulked, a tic wrinkling the left side of his face, making one dark eye wink involuntarily, then followed his father once he was out of sight.

Aguilar carried his forced joviality with him to the front door, grinned wide when he opened it, saw Ben and Charlie standing in front of a curtain of dripping rainwater. He did not close the door. A moment later, Hector crept up, stood there at the crack, listening intently as a cat at a mousehole.

"Ben," Ernie said loudly. "You should come inside, have a cup with us. Your wife and children are enjoying our little fiesta."

"Ernie, you and me got to talk real serious."

"I have a study, Ben. It is private and quiet."

"I got cattle dyin' like flies all along Bandera Creek. You dammed it up and we're dry as a bone on my side."

"I dammed up Bandera Creek?"

"For damned shore," said Stone, belligerently.

"I'll handle this, Charlie," said Killian.

Aguilar's eyes hardened like a pair of Timken ball bearings. He drew himself up straight, stiffened as if a steel ramrod had been spliced to his spine.

"I know nothing of this. I will talk to Paco. Tomorrow. Nothing can be done today. It is my daughter's birthday."

"You've got that creek dammed, Ernie. I won't get any water while you got me shut off. I cut your fence and run my cattle into your tank.

I got calves won't never wear no brand and prime beef feeding a flock of buzzards."

Aguilar looked beyond Ben's craggy face at the dark sky, the rain bouncing off the adobe walls like silver sparks. The thunder was almost continuous and lightning drenched the three men in hot light bright as phosphorus.

"It makes much rain now, Ben. We cannot do anything today about this. Maybe not tomorrow either. There should be plenty of water for both of us if the rains come."

"Ernie, if you don't break down that dam, I will."

"If you cut my fence, you are trespassing on my land. Do not forget that you still owe me money for the Bandera Creek property."

Ben scowled.

"So that's the way it is. You want that damned land back, mean to break me."

"Get your cattle off my land, Ben."

"As long as you got my water bottled up on your side of the fence, I aim to see my beeves get to it."

Aguilar's eyes flashed a sudden warning.

"If I find Lazy K cattle on my land in the morning, I will have my men drive them back on your side. If they do not move, we will start dropping them with bullets."

"You kill one cow of mine, Ernie, and I'll ride you down."

"Do not threaten me, Ben Killian. You are the trespasser."

"We have to listen to this greaser all day, Ben?" interjected Stone.

"Shut up, Charlie," said Ben.

"Go away from my house, both of you. Ben, you are no longer welcome."

Ben nodded curtly. He had said all he was going to say. Aguilar turned on his heel. He stepped through the doorway, bumped into Hector. Ernesto slammed the door behind him.

"What are you doing here, my son?"

"I—I thought you might need me, Papá. I heard Mister Killian threaten you."

"He is a fool. Go back to the fiesta. You have no business here."

"Yes, Papá," Hector said sheepishly. The tic in his face warped the skin, made his eyelid quiver like a nightcrawler with a hook through its middle. He ran across the foyer, shirttail flapping against the seat of his trousers.

Ernesto watched his son disappear down the hall. The boy was a mystery to him. He could not even lie well. Ernesto knew that Hector wouldn't lift a finger to help him, no matter the circumstances. A thundercrack made him jump and the house rattled with rain hard as hail. He held his hands out from his body. They were shaking with silent tremors. But inside, he felt a strange, murderous calm.

1

THE VIRGIN MARY had first spoken to him in a jail cell in Sweetwater, a good dozen years ago, two or three years before he was sent to prison. Bone was just coming off a three-day drunk when she began whispering in his ear, so close he could almost feel her lips brush against his lobe. She had a soft, beautiful voice and she spoke about her husband, Joseph, and about her son, Jesus. She told him about the Father and the Holy Ghost.

"I will send my son Jesus to tell you what to do," she told him and Jack Bone started looking around his dingy dark cell for the Son of God. All he saw was a cockroach.

"Is Jesus a cockroach?" he asked in a loud voice.

"No, he's a Jew," said the transient Yankee in the adjoining cell.

But Bone, in his whiskey-ravaged mind, began to look at the cockroach more closely. It sat there atop a bar of dirty soap next to the lidless toilet, its antennae twitching, its beady eyes glowing, its brown wings pulsing against its long body and Bone knew it was Jesus in another form.

The cockroach spoke to him in a husky, low-pitched voice and it told him it was Jesus. He heard the voice in his mind, telling him his soul was clean, telling him he had been saved.

He had heard lots of voices since then, and he had seen Jesus take many animal forms. Sometimes he heard a heavenly choir and some-times God Himself spoke to him. It was the Virgin Mary, however, who told him, when he first got into Huntsville, that he must go to the *brasada* and live there until Jesus came to take him up to heaven.

The leading edge of the storm slashed into the *brasada,* spearing the brush with lancets of wind-driven rain, rattling the limbs of the mesquite with the sound of clashing sabers, the clack of jousters' lances against helmet and shield. The rain stirred the dust and filled the cracked earth until it swelled shut and boiled into a porridge of mud. The winds whipped through the black chaparral and snapped off limbs in a volley of crackling rifle shots.

The bawl of cattle penetrated the weather's noisy shroud in the wind lull and the goading shouts of disembodied men floated on the sodden air like the hoarse cries of ancient drovers' ghosts.

Bone grinned when he saw Ned Feather, on foot and leading his cowpony, drive the first three head of cattle into the rain-soaked mud-puddle of the clearing where he had been waiting. The creases in Bone's forehead and cheeks, chiseled and leathered from the sun and wind, deepened as his grin widened. More cattle streamed through the opening behind Ned, driven by the others in Bone's band, Jay Black Horse, Virgil Coldwater, Eddie Blue Sky and Barney Whitesides. They were all afoot, like a broken army's stragglers, all leading their horses through the slanting chain mail of rain.

"Whoo boy!" shouted Bone, and he jerked his hat from his head and flapped it at the nearest steer. The cattle slithered on cloven hooves in the mud, skidded, threw up arcing rooster-tails of dirty water, splashing Bone and the others from hat-crown to toe-tip. A cow, swollen with calf, stopped and arched its tail, defecated a steaming pile of dung. It sank like a tiny island in a soupy sea of muddy brine.

"We goddamned sure killed that prize bull of Baron's," said Ned Feather. "Cut his nuts clean off like you said. Goddamned bag must've weighed ten pounds." He was a short, skinny man in his late thirties, wore his black hair long as a feather duster, sported a pair of gold teeth among several that were rotten as wormy corn kernels, looked like fire-blackened pegs whittled down to blunt points.

"You done real good, Ned," said Bone. "How many'd you get?"

"We got us twenty-five head," said Virgil. "We had to put a kid to sleep." Virgil Coldwater was the youngest member of the band, at twenty-nine, with a shock of spikey hair that jutted from under his narrow-brimmed hat like darning needles. He wore a bandanna around his neck to hide the knife scars, one of them deep enough to bury a finger in up to the first knuckle. His long eyebrows fanned out over hooded eyes that bulged from years of malnutrition.

"Yeah? How come?"

"He shit his pants," said Eddie Blue Sky, who was as big as a railroad crate, with hands the size of seed gourds. His round, sloping shoulders and long arms gave him the appearance of a red-skinned gorilla. Tiny, porcine eyes glared out of sockets overhung with caterpillar eyebrows attached to a massive, pockmarked forehead.

Barney Whitesides brought up the rear, ragging a dozen cattle into the sodden clearing with a horse blanket. He was Oklahoma Cherokee, with bony high cheekbones and gristle-hard eyes that seemed to burn with smoldering coals. He had some chunk to him and a slight paunch, but he was almost six feet tall and bowlegged as a set of parentheses.

The cattle herded up and milled, twisting and turning within a narrow perimeter, as if seeking a path that would take them out of the nail-hard rain.

"We got to get them beeves into the corrals we built," said Bone. "Let's cut 'em here, drive 'em yonder."

"Heeeeyaaaa!" cried Ned, and the others picked up the cry. The Indians separated the cattle into two groups, drove them down a hacked-out lane through the brush. They entered another clearing where they had built three pole-corrals, finishing up six weeks ago. Ned and Barney drove a dozen head into one corral; Virgil set the gate poles in place. Bone, Eddie and Jay ran the remaining cattle into another corral. Virgil closed it up. The cattle nosed through clumps of stolen hay under thatched lean-tos, inspected the poles of their new home. They lowed surly as foghorns as the wind-blown rain needled their hides, stung their eyes.

Eddie and Ned gathered up the horses. Jay and Bone struck off through a passage in the brush, the others following like shadows in the mist. None of them wore slickers and their shabby clothes clung to them like sodden rags. Rain flooded from their hats; the flashes of lightning silvered their ruddy faces. The ground shook with the thunder; the brush shook with the constant onslaught of rain and wind as if rattled by a cannonade of grapeshot. Their boots squished as they walked through an inch or so of ground water pooled up on saturated earth.

Bone ducked under mesquite limbs, emerged in a clearing larger than the other one, a place he knew well. It was almost sacred to him, this place of crumbled adobes hidden from the vast grasslands surrounding the *brasada*. Three months ago, he and his followers had cleared out the rats and tarantulas, the snakes and the rubble. They had roofed over the adobe hovels with scrap lumber and parafinned tarps, made them into shelters. The adobes had been built by market hunters who slaughtered ducks and geese by the thousands, stalked the deer and trapped rabbits and muskrats. Bone's father had known of the place and when Bone was a boy, this had been his sanctuary, his secret place where he came to dream, to live in what he called "Apache time."

There were six adobes in a circle, their walls eaten away by the eroding acids of time and weather, the bricks scrubbed smooth over the passing of years, bleached by the sun's blazing forge, reshaped by the wind's harsh bellows. Three or four other structures had once stood there, but flash floods and hurricanes had left little trace. The adobes were all built on mounds and once there had been deep ditches cut around the clearing to keep the high water under control. The ditches were silted up, filled in, but Bone and his cohorts had dug some of them out during the past three months.

They had repaired a large horse corral and now they stripped their horses of saddles, bridles and blankets, grained them under a lean-to made of whip-sawed lumber from live oak that had withstood the weather, but leaked like a colander. Ned, Eddie and Jay hauled the riding gear into one of the adobes used for storage.

Barney and Virgil followed Bone into one of the least damaged adobes. It was also the largest, by a few square feet, and served as Bone's quarters, a meeting place. The one-room hovel was dank from years of neglect and the seepage of rainwater. The gypsum on the walls was cracked and crumbling. The dirt floor had been scraped with a hoe. Much of the rubble had been shoveled outside or raked against the walls. The broken and rusted instrument still stood in one corner, a rake with half its handle gone, a hoe attached to the broken end, which someone had sawed square, making a two-headed tool. Bone's bedroll lay atop a concave mound of dirt. Candle stubs dotted the floor, the windowsills. Burnt matches lay strewn near each candle. A wooden box filled with bootleg whiskey, drinking water in a Mason jar, empty Nehi and RC bottles, soap, a strop and straight razor, a grimy washcloth and an even grimier towel, occupied a position under one window. Rain blew through the open doorway. The door itself, shrunk crooked from age, hingeless, leaned against the wall.

The men began to light candles. Bone rattled the box as he brought out an unlabeled glass bottle filled with clear, unaged moonshine that was better than 100 proof. Eddie came in, followed by Jay and Ned. Ned placed the cockeyed door in front of the entrance. Rain spattered against it like flung rice. Ned snugged the door with a pair of loose adobe bricks set at the bottom corners.

Bone pulled the cork from the bottle, took a long swig before passing it to Barney, who was squatted next to him. The others took their places in a circle on the dirt floor. Bone turned to Virgil as Barney bent his elbow to take a swallow of shine.

"That kid you killed," he said. "Was he a Baron, huh?"

Virgil looked at the others, blinked. He leaned over to take the bottle from Barney.

"Hell, I don't know," he croaked. "He never did tell us his damned name."

"He had plenty of chances, too," said Ned Feather, his eyes glittering oily in the candleflare.

"I think his name was Please Don't," said Barney.

"That's what he kept saying over and over before Virgil cut him another smile," said Eddie.

Virgil grinned and pulled his big imitation Bowie knife from its sheath. He held it up to the candlelight. The blade was rusted dark with blood. He swallowed from the bottle, then began to rub the blade on the inside of his trouser leg. Coagulated blood flaked off, fell to the earthen floor of the adobe, peppered it like dried chili pepper seeds.

Watching Virgil play with the knife reminded Bone of one time when they were in the Monahans jail together, just the two of them in the same cell. Until one night, the cell door opened and the jailer threw a young fish to them, a Mexican kid named Benito.

Benito had a sweet chubby ass and flabby breasts. Bone and Virgil had shared the punk between them. Virgil played with Benito's cock all day long, rubbing it like he was rubbing that knife, in between his legs while they stood in a corner. Then Bone would go up behind the boy and screw him in the ass while the three of them were standing packed together in the corner, Benito purring like a cat, taking all Bone had to give him right in his fat ass and squirming like a woman until Virg dropped to his knees and sucked him off.

Sometimes Bone missed Benito, wondered what had ever happened to him.

None of the men spoke for a time, as the bottle was passed. The candle flames, flickering with the air currents inside the hovel, daubed their faces with sallow light, made little hissing insect noises when they scratched the oil pooling up in the wax.

The storm gathered dangerous momentum as it swept down across the Texas savanna from the north. Its clouds towered more than fifty thousand feet in the air, a gigantic mass of turrets and spires fermenting in the chill, thin atmosphere like a witch's brew.

The castellated clouds brought the cold winds down from the north, from Colorado and New Mexico, a two-day journey begun in the Rockies back of the headwaters of the Rio Grande. The warm Gulf winds boiled into a weather trough, hung there until the blue norther sucked them into its system. High above the rain, the clouds billowed with turbulence. The winds swirled and tumbled moisture-laden clouds like saltwater taffy beaten with a wooden paddle. In the high reaches of the storm, the wind's violent agitation turned the raindrops into tiny frozen pellets. As the ice balls thickened and gained weight, they fell through the clouds, gathering still more bulk as the moisture froze to the gelid mass.

Louise Baron knew she was lost, but she didn't panic. She rode well away from the *brasada,* seeking high ground. The rain blistered her eyes; the wind rapped and tugged at her slicker, trying to snatch it from her body. She knew there was little chance she would find Matt in the downpour, and Tom was somewhere in the brush, probably struggling to find a way out through the maze.

She held Butterball to a track, but she had no sense of direction. She knew she had to get out of the open and under shelter, but the nearest line shack was dozens of miles away. The horse struggled against the shifting wind, kept trying to turn away from it. She rode on, blindly, but the land stayed flat. A half hour later, hunched over in the saddle, she saw a sight that brought her to the brink of despair. To her horror, Lou saw tracks that only Butterball could have made. Despite her attempts to find shelter and stay on a straight line, she had made a circle.

And then, the hail hit.

*   *   *

Baseball-sized hailstones began to pummel the trees where Matt Baron had taken shelter. He heard a limb crack, then another. Hail shot through the trees like white cannonballs, striking the earth with deadly force. A jackrabbit, scared from its cover, bolted across the rain-soaked plain. The hail fell thick, thumping the ground like clubs. One of the stones struck the hare, knocking it senseless. Matt watched as it kicked its hind legs, twitching in its death throes like frog legs frying on a hot skillet.

The wind gusted, staggering Matt's horse, howling through the tree limbs with an unearthly keen. Balls of hail bounced off his saddle, smashed against a tree trunk. Branches fell around him, cracking as they broke, snapping as they hit, littering the ground until it resembled a boneyard.

A hailstone the size of a jawbreaker struck Matt's shoulder. The pain bored through to his collarbone, sent shoots of lavafire up the muscles of his neck, down through the cords in his arm. His arm went numb, and he drew it close to him, involuntarily, grabbed the wrist and snugged it tight to his belly as he doubled over. It felt as if someone had struck him with a ten-pound maul.

He looked at Esquire. The horse was about one thunderbolt shy of going into panic. The Walker had backed down on his haunches until the reins were taut as the strings on a catgut fiddle.

Walleyed as Moon Mullins, thought Matt as distant lightning etched Esquire in a photoflash of light.

"Steady, boy," he said, standing upright. With his good hand, he reached for the reins. He waited for the thunderroll, ticking the seconds off in his mind. Someone had told him once that sound traveled at 750 feet per second and you could tell how far away a lightning strike was by counting in thousands.

He pulled Esquire close to him as the thunder made a sound that was like a hundred keglers all bowling at once in an empty Grange hall. The horse's nostrils quivered, rubbery as a half-filled innertube.

Matt thought of his sister, wondered where she was. He shuddered to think she had been caught out in the open in such a storm. He started calling her name every few minutes, but knew it was futile. It was like yelling into a mineshaft. The thunder and the pounding rain drowned out his words almost before they were out of his mouth.

"Lou," he bellowed, cupping one hand against his mouth. He yelled her name again and again, in every direction. A crash of thunder close by deafened him, made Esquire jump.

In the comparative silence following the dying echoes of the thunder, Matt heard a sharp metallic crack. He turned, so quick he pulled the tendons in his sore wrist, and looked out on the deserted, dark plain. The land was blurred by rain, the earth dotted by over-sized mothballs, but he thought he saw a darker shape against the smudge of brushline that marked the edge of the *brasada*. The shape was moving, dodging the falling hail in slow motion. He saw an orange flash, heard the sound of the rifle a split second later.

Esquire's head snapped up and his ears twisted in tandem, homing in on the sound.

The sky jittered with another flash of lightning, the electrical display masked deep in the clouds, but bright enough to illuminate the approaching rider. Matt stepped to the other side of his horse, patting Esquire's neck to calm him. He jerked the Winchester from its scabbard, stepped away from the tree. He levered a cartridge into the chamber, wincing from the shoot of pain that galvanized the radius nerve in his arm. He pointed the rifle away from the rider, toward the sky. He waited for the thundering to pass, then squeezed the trigger. The rifle bucked in his good hand. Esquire went to a three-legged stance, his eyes still fixed on the dark shape.

"Tom! Over here!" Matt yelled, but the noise of wind and hail and rain swallowed his voice up like a pin falling into cotton.

Casebolt and Blister altered course, came on steadily toward the stand of trees. Matt sheathed the rifle and walked out to meet them. His foreman was bent over the saddle, his slicker torn by brush, hanging in shreds that dripped water like a rusted-out rainspout. Matt noticed that one of Tom's tapaderas had been torn off. It hung there on the stirrup by a single thong, banging against Blister's belly with every gust of wind.

Matt grabbed one rein up close to the bit-ring. Blister seemed docile as a lamb, with all the fight knocked, or soaked, out of him. He looked like an oversized drowned rat, eyes hooded, coat sleek and watersoaked as an otter's.

"Tom? You O.K.?"

Tom lifted off the saddlehorn, shook himself gingerly.

"Can't complain, Matt. Wouldn't do no good nohow."

"You look plumb stove up."

Tom managed a lopsided grin. A trickle of blood, diluted by rain, drooled down the side of his face.

"Nothin' warm or dry couldn't cure."

"We got two foot of tree trunk."

"That'll do," Tom grinned.

Matt led Blister, with his waterlogged cargo, to the tree, helped a groaning Casebolt down from the saddle. Tom sagged against the tree as Matt looped Blister's reins to his own saddlehorn.

Tom tugged his chaps straight, pulled them up over his belt. There were fresh brush scars in the leather. His right boot had nicks in the toe.

"You see anything, Tom?"

Casebolt shook his head.

"Lou's out there somewhere."

"Matt, we got to get the hell out of here. I had to run Blister through herds of snakes, muskrats, jackrabbits and God knows what all. I was a-dodgin' deer and javelina, all a runnin' full bore through the brush. They must have the cattle penned up, maybe on high ground. Else, they got 'em out by truck."

"I don't think so," said Matt. "That storm hit them same as us. I agree we've got to find shelter. I can just see our backtrail running high water. Some of those creeks will flood right out of the *brasada*. We're going to lose some stock."

"Maybe us, too, if we don't—"

"We could double back. Look for Lou. My guess is we'd wind up in the Rio Grande like a couple of drowned rats. Lazy K lies southwest. Twice as far. Closest ranch is the Rocking A, but we'd have to cut through a swath of brush."

"Matt, you 'member that day we chased a hunnert head into the brush? They cut through to Rocking A where it was real narrer."

"I remember," said Matt. That had been two years ago. A cougar had spooked an entire herd of new Brahmins just put out to pasture. The cattle had broken down the fence and more than a hundred of them had crashed through the *brasada* onto Ernie Aguilar's land. It had taken Matt and ten hands three days to round up the herd and drive it back through that cut through the *brasada*. "Can you find the place again?"

"That's why I come back. It's just over yonder. Growed up some, but the narrerest punch through that brush. That's where all them springs are."

"Where Bandera Creek rises," said Matt, nodding.

"Umm. Mighty swampy in there. Downright dangerous."

"Let's climb some horse, Tom. All we're doing here is getting older."

"What about Lou?"

"Hell, Tom, I wouldn't know where to look."

The lightning flashes seemed to be hammering shields of light to the east of them as the storm headed for the Gulf. The thunder sounds took longer to reach them. Matt and Tom mounted up and the wet leather made hardly any noise at all. The hail stopped rattling at their hats, but the rain still came down like it was flung from a five-gallon milk pail. Tom remarked that a man could drown in it just trying to breathe.

The horses spooked at the *brasada* and Tom had to whip Blister on the rump with his reins to get him to break trail. Matt spurred Esquire in sideways through the cut, the water up over the horse's hocks, muddy footing underneath. The horses didn't like it in there, and the men liked it even less. Their chaps weighted on them like lead aprons and the mesquite clawed at them, prodded the horses' flanks so that they were skittery as New Mexican mule deer at a rifle range.

Tom flogged Blister through it and they passed the springs, heard the water rushing below them in Bandera Creek, heard it above the blowing of rain and the occasional pistol shot of hail. It was so dark inside the brush that when they came out on the other side they had to refocus their eyes.

Lou thought she heard her name, but the thunder shattered her ears. Then, she heard what sounded like a muffled shot. She rode toward the sound, her back and arms numb from the pain of being struck by hailstones. She tasted blood on her lips and knew that one of the balls had broken the skin on her forehead. Her lips were swollen where a hailstone had bashed into them.

Then, she saw little bowls filling with water. She followed them, knowing they were horse tracks. She began to look at their groupings and realized she was following two horses. Her heart soared. Butterball high-stepped over dozens of snakes and she saw flashes of animals darting away as she passed.

When the hail stopped, she began calling out Matt's name.

They rode east into the warm rain from the Gulf, the winds rocking them in their saddles with gusts that tore at their slickers and made their chaps flap like batwings. Their waterlogged hats were pulled down so low, their ears stuck out like turnip slices.

"I make it about five mile to the Rocking A," yelled Tom as he leaned into the wind.

"Five easy," said Matt and they spoke no more as they fought for yardage in the flattened pasture grasses, threaded their way past clumps of white-faced cattle bunched up in scattered islands, their rumps jostling like corpulent weathervanes with every shift of wind.

Tom found a wire gate and let Matt ride through to the road. The road was crawling with snakes and the horses danced through them without getting struck. Matt looked down into cottony throats and watched as rattlers coiled and slithered, tongues working like black electricity.

The outbuildings, blurred by the sweat-mist of rain, loomed up on the horizon after better than an hour of riding and the ditches ran full as rivers, drowned rats and field mice bobbing up every so often before they were spattered under again or rolled like meat on a spit.

The cattle were strangely still, clinging to high ground as if they were anchored to rafts. The rain fell even harder and stung their faces, sharp as icicles. It was like being lashed with wet shoelaces, Tom said later, and there was no way to turn your head to get out of it.

"Yonder's the house," said Tom, pointing beyond the bunkhouse with its windows shuttered and dark.

"I see it," said Matt, his eyes aching like neck boils.

Tom opened the gate and they entered the lane that led to the main house. A McCormick reaper sat out by the barn, scrubbed almost free of rust by the scald of rain, and sticking out of one door, a hay wagon, its tongue buried in glistening mud.

Lamplight flickered at the edges of the window sockets where someone had hung blankets to keep the rain out. Nearly every window had been blown out by the hail and the stones littered the ground around like popcorn, melting slowly in the hot rain.

They rode around the house, passed the parked automobiles and headed for the stables. The ranch seemed deserted except for the faint pulse of music coming from the house, the orange rims of wet blankets where the light crept through.

Tom and Matt dismounted and led their horses into the stables. It sounded like a blacksmith shop inside. The wind hammered a thousand nails into every square inch of wood and howled under the eaves like wolves in agony.

They found dry stalls, stripped their horses and gave each a coffee can full of rolled oats from a 100-pound sack.

"At least it ain't as wet in here," said Tom.

Matt made a sound of assent in his throat. His boots squished as he walked on dry straw.

"Let's get on up to the house, see if Ernie can put us up until this mess blows over," said Matt. The other horses in the stalls whickered softly and he heard mice squeak in the loft, terrified by the storm.

They slogged through the mud to the house, saw hands pull the blankets aside, faces appear at the hailed-out windows. They walked through the patio and Elena stood at the open door, smiling at them. Their boots crunched on hailstones, turning them to icy gravel.

"Matt, is that you?"

"Howdy, Elena. What's left," Matt replied.

"Tom? You both come in. Please."

"We don't want to track your house," said Matt as he stepped onto the porch.

"It'll take a tire iron to pry off our boots," remarked Tom.

"It is no matter," said Elena, stepping aside to let the two men enter the house. Matt towered above her. He took his hat off, stood there dripping. "I'll see if we don't have some dry clothes that will fit you."

Tom removed his hat too and stood there awkwardly, wondering what to do with it. Elena laughed low in her throat and took their hats. She hung them on the hall tree as if they were brand new. Then, she glanced out the window.

"Was someone else with you?" she asked.

"Lou," growled Matt, striding to the window.

Elena ran to the door, opened it.

"Is that her?" asked Tom.

"That's her horse. She looks plumb drownded."

Tom and Matt pulled Lou from her horse, got her inside. Elena saw the bruises on Lou's face, took her arm.

"*Pobrecita,*" she said, gently pushing Lou's hair back from her face.

"Elena, you're a sight for sore eyes," said Lou. "And I mean that literally," she added, gingerly touching one of her swollen eyes.

"Come," Elena said to Matt and Tom as she led Lou away. "Do not worry about the floors. We've been mopping since it began to storm."

They followed her down the hall, toward the gabble of voices. The music had stopped and the two men blinked as they saw the crowd of children and grown-ups all gathered for their entrance. Ernie stepped toward them, his hand outstretched.

"So, you come to our party," he said, a humorous leer on his face. "I am honored."

Matt shook Aguilar's hand. He looked around, saw his wife standing with Frances Killian and Naomi Tyler, all three women smiling at him.

"Ernie," said Matt, going along with the joke, "I wouldn't have missed it." He looked at the *piñatas* hanging from the ceiling beams, all brightly colored papier-mâché effigies of burros, roosters, dogs and cats. He found the faces of his children among the other youngsters, their gazes shyly fixed on him and Tom. Some of the children munched on hailstones, their faces bright with glee.

"Ernesto," said Elena, "can we find dry clothes for our guests? I'll take Louise upstairs."

Elena and Lou left.

"Yes. Come, come," said Aguilar. "Would you like some whiskey, Matt? Some tequila?"

"Not now, thanks," said Matt. His and Tom's chaps made puddles on the floor. "The dry clothes sound just fine."

They followed Ernie out to the kitchen, where Aguilar spoke in rapid Spanish to Alberto Horcasitas, a heavyset Mexican wearing a cook's apron. Horcasitas nodded.

"He will bring you some dry clothes from the bunkhouse," said Ernie. Then, his mien became serious. "Matt, I know you didn't just ride out here for the fiesta. I saw you coming down the road and I became worried."

"That's right," said Matt, scooting a chair away from the table. He put a boot up, started unstrapping a spur. "We've been hunting rustlers. They killed Jamey, one of my young hands, and Dutch Zee."

"Your bull?"

Matt nodded.

"We reckon they got away with twenty-five head," interjected Tom. "We tracked 'em to the brush east of here."

"El Rincón?" whispered Aguilar.

"'Bout there," said Tom. "Why? You had trouble yourself?"

"No, no trouble," Ernie said quickly. "You say they killed one of your hands?"

"He was just a boy," said Matt. "They cut his throat."

Ernie cursed in Spanish, and then he said a word that sent spiders scurrying up Matt's back, made the hackles on his neck bristle with an electric chill.

"Bone," he said, and the silence in the room swelled up like a balloon, sucking all the air out of their lungs as they waited for it to burst.

8

CHARLIE STONE WATCHED the earth rise straight up in the air. For a moment, the soil seemed to hang there like a brown shroud. Charlie ducked behind the big live oak for mortal reasons. Then, chunks of rock and shattered brush hurtled through the air with the velocity of bullets and the curtain of earth collapsed, falling back to the ground. Bandera Creek hissed and boiled as loose soil peppered its suddenly flowing waters, exploded as sun-hardened clods splashed out a series of watery bowls and sank like tiny islands into miniature mud seas.

For a time, no one moved. The last of the curtain, the fine dust and the even finer silt, lingered like smoke in an ashen pall that turned brown and yellow in the sun as it slowly settled back to earth.

The dammed-up waters of Bandera Creek on Rocking A land surged across newly blasted dry land toward the rainy runoff that had swollen the creek on Lazy K. The waters boiled for several moments, belching mud and dirt, until they settled, began to flow steadily, between the banks.

"Clear," called Reed Packer, pushing away from the battery pack he had used to set off the charge. He stood up, certain he had done his job well.

"That'll give that greaser Aguilar somethin' to think about," muttered Stone, as he picked himself up from the ground. He looked at Reed, who turned away self-consciously. Everyone knew Charlie's feelings about Mexicans. Most overlooked Stone's bigotry; some shared it. Packer's mother was Mexican.

"Finnerty! Bellaugh!" yelled Packer, reaching toward his back pocket. He yanked a wire puller from his pocket, headed for the fence. Warren and Jack appeared out of nowhere, stalked toward him across a flood-ravaged field littered with fresh clods. Twelve hours of hard rain had done almost as much damage as the drought. Some of the cattle that had been driven onto Aguilar's land had been drowned in a flash flood. Stone and the others had spent most of the day before dragging dead Lazy K cattle onto Killian property, driving the others back through the fence. Harvey Leeds and several hands drove the stock a few miles down Bandera Creek, well away from the blast zone.

"Get the fence repaired and let's get the hell out of here," said Stone. "Finnerty, get your thumb out of your butt."

"Aw, Charlie," said Warren. Jack Bellaugh grabbed Finnerty's elbow, guided him toward the fence. Finnerty was gawking at a blackened hulk, one of the dead steers they had burned the day before.

"Where's Shorty?" asked Stone. Shorty was the powderman, and a damned good one. His name was Earl Robert Coots, but everyone called him Shorty.

"Hell, I don't know," said Finnerty. "Maybe he got blowed up."

The men began calling out.

"Shorty! Shorty!"

"Shorty, goddamnit, where in hell are you?" yelled Charlie.

There was no answer.

"Bellaugh, you seen that little twidget?" called Stone.

"Last I seen, he was a-settin' caps with that kid, Rawlings," said Bellaugh. "I heard him holler they was 'fire in the hole' and I run for cover."

"Shit," said Charlie, walking over to the fence where Warren was gathering up loose strands of barbed wire. He had heard Shorty yell out too and he'd ducked like everyone else. When Shorty hollered "fire in the hole," that meant he had lit a fuse. Shorty had taught them all about dynamite. There wasn't a hand there who wasn't deathly afraid of it. There were men working the Lazy K who couldn't even pronounce nitroglycerin, and who ragged that little powderman something terrible, but when Shorty started handling DuPont 60/40, like today, they treated him with a mixture of respect and admiration. Shorty handled the sticks of nitro as if they were summer sausages and he could turn a man's hair white when he occasionally dropped a stick for effect. He always said dynamite was safe; it was the damned blasting caps that gave a man the stomach ulcers and the chilblains. He said he'd seen a man's arm come off when a cap exploded prematurely, and he had one hand that was all stubs.

Warren dropped a strand of wire and it twanged clear back to the post. Stone jumped a half foot.

"Anybody see Rawlings?" Stone asked, partly to cover up his jumpiness. He hadn't seen the kid, but he knew he had been helping Shorty cut the sticks in half, set them in the earthen dam two inches apart. Rawlings had stuck blasting caps in at least half of the cut sticks. But Shorty always handled the fuses and the main blasting cap. And everyone called him "Mister" when he got to that business.

"He was a-crawlin' over that dam with Shorty, last I seen," said Finnerty, retrieving the coil of barbed wire. It was still jiggling and it took him two passes to grab it by the throat.

"Did you see either of them run back here?" asked Stone.

Bellaugh and Finnerty shook their heads.

"Well, they sure as hell went somewhere," said Stone.

He looked around, tilted his hat forward and scratched the back of his head.

There was a commotion on the other side of the fence.

Paco Velez, foreman of Aguilar's Rocking A, rode out from a clump of cottonwood trees. He carried a rifle across the pommel of his saddle. Seconds later, more men appeared, on foot. All but four of them carried rifles. The four had Shorty and Rawlings braced between them. Shorty was going through his elaborate repertoire of cuss words. Rawlings looked as if he was trying to play tug-of-war with his captors and was just getting his arms stretched for his trouble. He tugged to his right and the man holding his left arm jerked him right back. Shorty wasn't even close to running out of invectives, for he spoke in at least two known languages, English and Spanish. The two men carrying him were big and only occasionally did Shorty's feet touch the ground. He was squirming like a rabbit in a snare, a cigar stub, used to light the fuses, clenched in his teeth at the corner of his mouth.

"You sonsofbitches, you pie-eyed, gaul-fisted, Ethiopian, mother-humpin' *cabrones*," yelled Shorty, and he pedaled his feet as his captors lifted him higher between them. "Turn me loose, you dirty peckerhead bastards."

Paco rode up to the fence, swung his rifle to bear on Charlie Stone.

Charlie looked as if he'd swallowed a prickly pear whole. His face was bellowed up and red as a river sunset. He looked as if every blood vessel in his face would pop like the rivets on a tight pair of Levi's.

"Ho, Charlie," said Paco. "What you do, huh? I caught these men trespassing on Rocking A land. What you think I ought to do with them, eh?"

"You better turn 'em loose, Velez," said Charlie, and his face reddened even more as he went into stage two of apoplexy.

"I think we have a little fun with them, first," said Velez. "Shorty, he likes to play with big firecrackers."

Paco held up four sticks of dynamite he had nestled against the pommel. They were capped and fused. The black fuses looked like miniature rattlesnakes.

Charlie's face lost its color, drained to a chalky whiteness.

"Shorty was just doin' his job, Velez," said Charlie.

"I don't like him much. He scares our cattle and blows up the dam we built."

"You take it easy, Velez. Let Shorty and Rawlings there go."

Velez turned in the saddle and nodded to his men. While some stood guard, the Rocking A hands threw Shorty and Rawlings to the ground. They began stripping them of boots, pants, shirts, shorts, tossing the items aside. Shorty and Rawlings wriggled like lightning-spooked worms. They yelled and kicked and fought, but when they stood up again, they were both naked as jaybirds.

Paco's men laughed.

Killian's bunch bristled at this outrage. Bellaugh and the others stepped toward the fence.

Velez stopped them in their tracks as he set three sticks of dynamite back on the saddle, kept one. He extracted a match from his shirt pocket, struck it with his thumbnail.

The Killian hands took a few steps backward. Shorty continued to curse Paco Velez, running through a list of his dubious ancestors like a litany. Rawlings tried to cover his private parts with his hands. He crossed his legs and that didn't help much. Shorty just let it all hang out as he tried to jerk free and put his fists to work on a couple of Mexican faces.

Paco touched the match flame to the fuse. There was just the whisper of a hiss as the powder caught fire. A plume of white smoke spewed from the end of the fuse. Otherwise, a dead silence descended on those gathered on either side of the barbed-wire fence.

"Holy suffering shit!" exclaimed Shorty. "That's a twenty-second fuse."

Paco spoke to his men. They released Shorty and Rawlings.

"You do not have much time left," said Paco as he brandished the fuming stick of dynamite. "Maybe you better run back to the Lazy K."

Rawlings and Shorty sped toward the fence in an impromptu footrace.

"Ow, ouch!" yelled Rawlings as tender feet encountered sharp, hard stone.

Shorty beat Rawlings to the fence by a fraction of a second. It was the shortest route to freedom, despite the gaping hole in the barbed wire several yards away. He dragged his genitals through the dust as he crawled like a lizard under the bottom strand of wire. Rawlings tried to climb through the fence and the barbs took their toll. He emerged, yowling and hopping about, with several holes in him, each leaking at least a trickle of blood.

If Shorty and Rawlings expected a friendly greeting from their comrades, they were dead wrong. Charlie, Reed, Jim, Warren and the others loped in the opposite direction in a ragtag miniature marathon.

Paco Velez tossed the stick of dynamite onto Lazy K land when it had less than five seconds of fuse. The stick arced through the air in a lazy curve, landed a dozen feet behind Rawlings. He caught up to Shorty and passed him in a brilliant burst of speed.

The dynamite exploded and impelled particles of dust, small stones, dirt and a few broken branches into the backsides of Shorty and Rawlings. Rawlings's scream rose to a thin sliver of squeak before he ran out of air.

The Mexicans laughed and began firing their rifles in the air to punctuate their jubilant triumph.

"We have more dynamite in case you return," shouted Paco, but by that time, he had no audience. When the dust cleared, there was no sign of any Killian hand.

One of Paco's men set fire to Shorty's and Rawlings' clothes before it was time to go back to work. For a long time, the Rocking A hands heard Killian cattle bawling as they lined up along Bandera Creek to drink.

*   *   *

Jane Houston Killian, a prim, wiry woman with savage red hair, fire-crackling blue eyes, sat at the large maple desk that had belonged to her late husband, George. Nancy Fellows, the housekeeper, had brought the ledgers up from Frances's office promptly at nine o'clock when Jane began her business day. Consuela had brought her coffee, salt-rising toast and orange slices at 8:30, cleared the dishes away at 8:50. Jane didn't dawdle over her light breakfast. She didn't dawdle over anything.

She had run the Lazy K ever since George had died, in 1917. She had run it before then, said the older hands, but was smart enough to give credit to her husband. It was the same with Ben. He ran the ranch, was its engine, but Jane was the sparkplug. She knew cattle, she knew horses, and she knew men.

George Killian had been a captain in the Army, but he hadn't died in combat during the World War. He was in the Medical Corps, stationed in Georgia when he fell victim to the influenza epidemic of 1917. Thousands died and George was one of them. Jane still cherished his letters to her, written faithfully once a week from wherever the Army took him during his brief career as an officer. George wanted to be in combat. His letters were full of protests at being left behind when friends of his were fighting in France. Life was full of such sadnesses, Jane reflected as she opened the latest ledger, quickly scanned the figures recorded in Frances's neat hand.

The cost of running a ranch the size of the Lazy K was enormous. Jane concerned herself with the larger issues, cash flow, investments, bank notes, mortgages, the sale of cattle, profit and loss. But she also double-checked the family's expenses: groceries, clothing, liquor, entertainment. The ranch maintained charge accounts in Baronsville, so that the payments could be examined for regularity. Jane's eye was quick to pick up extraordinary expenses, whether it be in feed or seed or supplies. More than once she had caught a merchant padding a bill, and she swooped down on such thieves with all the fury of a chicken hawk.

Frances had organized the Lazy K's various ranch sections into separate accounts. Jane Killian gave the woman credit for that. Jane supervised the grass planting, the grazing and stock sales, while Ben was the husbandman of her domain, seeing to it that her wishes were carried out. They seldom argued, and when they did, it was generally over purchases Ben wanted to make. She knew he resented her tight-purse policy, but she came from hardy Scot stock and watched every penny with a frugal eye.

Jane was born in Lynchburg, Tennessee, in 1857 to Ralph and Doris Houston. Her father had fought with the Tennessee Volunteers, moved to Texas after the War Between the States, in 1867. He went to work for Anson Baron, saved his money, bought cattle and land, started his own ranch, the Bar H. Jane married George Killian in 1877, when she was twenty years old.

Ben Killian was born in 1888, the last of four children, Norman, Theresa, Mercy and Ben. Norman died of typhoid fever in 1882, Theresa developed tuberculosis and died in 1885 and Mercy perished of pneumonia in 1892, when Ben was five years old. Roy Killian, George's father, bought out the Bar H, founded his dynasty on lands purchased from Anson Baron. When Ben married Matt Baron's sister, Jane envisioned enlarging the Lazy K into an even bigger operation than the Box B, but at her death, Edith Baron Kilian's holdings reverted to her brother Matt instead of to Ben.

Jane still rankled at the injustice of Edith Baron Killian's will, and harbored a resentment against the whole Baron clan because of it. That resentment, unfortunately, extended to Frances, who had brought no land dowry to the marriage. Also, Frances reminded her of George's dereliction when he had run off with a younger woman, leaving Jane to run a huge ranch by herself. Frances, in Jane's mind, was a usurper the same as the trollop who had seduced George.

With a sigh, Jane finished her examination of the ledgers, made notations in a tablet she kept for such purposes, dating the entry at the top of the page, signing her name with a flourish, at the bottom.

She stacked the ledgers, tucked them under her arm and left the room. She walked downstairs to the den where Frances was waiting for the inevitable morning concentration.

"Good morning, Mother," said Frances.

Jane put the ledgers on Ben's desk. Frances arched her eyebrows quizzically. Jane sat down in Ben's chair, which had been his father, George's.

"You keep good accounts," said Jane. "We're losing money on the Bandera spread."

"I know. Ben says it's the drought."

"He should move the cattle out of there, split up the herd into smaller groups, get them to grass and water."

"He said we'd lose them even faster if he drove them to another section."

"Wasteful, wasteful," said Jane.

"We've lost only a few cattle. Ben thinks the creek's dammed up somewhere. He's going to try and get water in there," said Frances, without being defensive.

"It won't help. He's liable to lose the whole herd on Bandera Creek."

"Ben disagrees," said Frances flatly.

"I'm going to advise against it. Besides, he's taking too many hands away from the main graze. I'm afraid we'll have more losses and miss the payment for the last bunch of cows Ben bought."

"Is that all that's bothering you, Mother Jane?" Frances knew Jane hated to be called by her first name, but that was what everyone in the family called her.

"Does Ben know about Luke?"

"How did you—"

"Consuela told me, as you should have. That boy. He's full of ginger."

"You spoiled him," said Frances.

"Nonsense. He's a maverick."

"He's a black sheep, Mother."

"Strongest of the bunch," retorted Jane. Frances knew that Jane didn't give her own children the attention they deserved from a grandparent. It was a constant sore point between them. "Edith was a strong woman. Good bloodlines. That's the proof of the pudding, Frances, strong bloodlines."

"Our children are young yet." This time Frances knew she was being defensive. Jane always brought up Edith Baron Killian's name when they were alone. Frances knew that bloodlines had nothing to do with it. Jane still felt cheated by Edith's death, had never quite accepted Frances as a member of the Killian family. Frances drew a secret satisfaction in knowing that Edith had not been perfect. In her case, blood was stronger than water. Jane Killian was blind in that particular eye. She felt sure that had Edith lived long enough, she would have deeded her Box B holdings to Ben.

"And not a piece of backbone amongst them."

"That's not fair, Mother."

"Maybe not fair, but true."

Frances sighed. She won few battles with Jane, and even those she did were Pyrrhic.

"I suppose Ben will bail Luke out," said Frances.

"I'm sure there was some mistake. Ben will take care of it."

"I think Ben's getting wore out cleaning up after Luke's messes."

"Frances, sometimes I think you get your feet all tangled up in your own loop. Ben's a strong, sensible man, much stronger than his father ever was."

"I know he's strong, Mother Jane, it's just that he's got so much on his shoulders."

Jane arose from the chair.

"I'm going to ride out to Querencia and look at that new grass. I'll be back tomorrow."

"Mother Jane, that's forty miles from here."

"And forty miles back. Have Consuela pack me a lunch and some cold chicken for supper. Tell Ben not to worry." Jane left the office before Frances could protest. Not a word about the children. She never asked about them, never showed them any affection. Ben and Luke, they were her world. Frances knew why Jane was riding to that section of the Lazy K. Just to show her up, just to goad her for being a homebody. The truth was, Frances had her hands full and she never rode her horse except on Sundays, with Ben, when they could get away by themselves. Jane was all business, everything for the ranch, nothing for the soul.

Frances laughed mirthlessly to herself. It was a guilty laugh because she remembered what Ben had said once about his mother after Frances had cried over some frightful incident between them.

"Honey," he said, "under Mother's tough shell beats a heart of purest stone."

Sheriff Roy Blanchard worried the grimy toothpick in his mouth, pushing it in and out with his teeth and tongue. His belly hung over the wide Sam Brown belt he wore, drooping like an oversized melon, straining the buttons on his plaid shirt. He was already sweating, although the sun had barely cleared the horizon. His bright brown eyes seemed to take in everything although they seemed not to move in their sockets. He stood on the slope of the hill, a half step in front of Matt Baron, one hand on his hip just above the jutting butt of his .45 Colt Peacemaker holstered on the Sam Brown, the other idly scratching one ball in an itchy scrotum.

Doc Emberlin stood a few feet from the body. Like Roy, he was also watching the two men, Burt and Dave Tyler, father and son, as they removed the stones from the dead body. Deputy Harlan Doakes wore a bandanna over his nose and mouth like a bandit. He stood over the Tylers like the overseer on a chain gang, legs spread wide, arms folded across his chest.

The ground was wet and muddy, the stones over Jamey's corpse dank with residue from the storm. Burt Tyler's overalls were smeared with dark mud, his clodhopper boots clogged with the red clay of the slippery soil. Dave removed the stones from Jamey's head and winced when he saw the torn throat, strangely white and bloodless. He drew back and Burt moved in for a look.

"Quite a gash," said Burt.

"Get the rest of them stones off him," said Doakes.

Burt and Dave scraped the rest of the rocks from the dead body. Blanchard nodded to Doc Emberlin, who nodded back. He slogged through the mud to the body, pushed young Tyler aside. The boy couldn't keep his agate eyes off that cut in Jamey's throat.

Emberlin, a short, thin man in his forties, wearing a dark gabardine suit, knelt down beside the body. He lifted the shirt, undid the belt and checked the dead boy's scrotum. He rolled the body back and forth, checking for contusions. He found several, grunted noncommittally at each find. Sweat beaded up at his hairline, oozed through the prematurely gray swatches of his sideburns. He wore glasses and continually cleaned them with a crisp starched handkerchief of purest white linen. When he was finished, he stood up, walked over to where Blanchard and Baron stood.

"I'd say the wound in his throat killed him," said Emberlin evenly. "The wound is particularly vicious, doesn't appear to be accidental. The knife appears to have partially severed the spinal cord. A person or persons beat him severely, dragged him. His scrotum is enlarged, probably engorged with blood. He's got numerous scrapes and contusions. I'll give him a closer look in town. When they move him, have them take care that the boy's head doesn't come off."

"Thanks, Doc," said Blanchard. "You can go on back to town if you want."

Doc had driven his Ford to within a half mile of the death scene. The others had ridden in on horseback. The Tylers had pulled a Springfield wagon to the site behind a team of Matt's horses.

"Load the boy into the wagon, Burt, will ya? Be damned careful

with his head. Take him on in to Doc's. I'll see you later at Nomi's."
Burt's wife owned Naomi's Café in Baronsville.

"Shouldn't we have some blankets or somethin'?" asked Burt.

"It don't make no nevermind," said Blanchard. "He ain't a-goin'
to feel nothin'."

Dave looked a little sick. His face blanched a doughy white and he
gulped air like a beached catfish.

Burt dropped the tailgate to the wagon. He and his son lifted the
body of Jamey Dobbs and loaded it onto the bed. Burt made sure the
head was still attached.

"Cover his head, Davey," said Burt. "They's a gunnysack under
the wagon seat."

Dave Tyler swallowed. The slash in Jamey's throat no longer fascinated him.

Harlan Doakes strutted over to Blanchard. His .38 Smith & Wesson, nickel-plated, jutted out from his holster at almost a forty-five-
degree angle. He wore black rodeo-cut trousers, black military shoes,
and a dark blue cotton shirt. His felt hat with the silky band had lost
some of its blocking on the crown, but the front brim was bent at a
J. Edgar Hoover angle. Harlan wore a black tie wide enough to
double as a bib. He took sheriffing seriously. His thick eyebrows
seemed knotted out of plump caterpillars and matched his matted
sideburns. He was short and pudgy, with a miniature barrel chest that
swelled up from a narrow waist. He worked out with barbells every
morning and liked his shirts tight in the sleeves.

"Mistah Blanchard, sir," he said as he came to an abrupt stop,
held himself at attention.

"You look around, Harlan, see if you can find anything. A
weapon, rope, shoe prints that wasn't washed away by the rain, ciga-
reet butts, buttons, pieces of cloth. Body was found in that gully over
yonder." Blanchard pointed to the place where Matt and Casebolt
had found Jamey. "That right, Matt?"

Matt nodded. Then he and Blanchard walked over to their horses.
Matt rode a black gelding named Niger, better for the brush than
Esquire. Niger whickered softly, eyed the wagon as it pulled away. The
other horse, a dun with cropped dark mane and black tail, bearing
the Box B brand, was called Dagwood. Both horses were bred to work
cattle. They could turn on a dime and back a rope to take out the
slack.

"Dobbs have any kin?" asked Roy.

"None that we know of. Kid showed up at the Box B one day, asked for a job."

"We'll check it out. I'll look through his stuff at the bunkhouse."

"Tom's got it all laid out for you."

"I don't like this none, Matt. Ground's clean as a egg. Tracks all washed away."

"It's Bone's work."

"I know, you tolt me, but if he's in that brush, he's as good as gone."

"There's a bunch of them, Roy."

"So I got me a case of murder, a case of cattle rustlin', and I don't know what with Dutch Zee."

"We'll help you, Roy," said Matt. "I'll put every hand on it."

"It's nigger work, Matt. Even if we round up them boys, onliest way we'll get a charge to stick is to beat it out of 'em with a ball bat."

"We've got plenty of trees and some stiff rope," said Baron.

"You'd do it, too, wouldn't you?"

"Without batting an eye, Roy."

"Well, let's ride over there, see if we can find out anything."

Matt's leg throbbed with pain as he gained a stirrup. He swung up on Niger, settled into the saddle. The dampness always made the game leg kick up and he had let it stiffen while he stood there watching the Tylers unbury Jamey. He loosened the Winchester in its scabbard.

Dagwood sidled away from Blanchard, made a half circle before Roy could hold him steady. Blanchard whopped the horse on the nose and jerked the bit back on its tongue. He was mounted before the horse could think of another way of avoiding the weight in its saddle.

"God, I remember that wild bresh from when I was a kid," said Roy as the two men rode off toward the *brasada*. "Your pappy did ever'thing but dynamite it."

"He did that, too," said Matt.

"How in hell are we a-goin' to find Bone in that there jungle?"

Matt said nothing. There was no answer to that. Bone could stay in there for a long time. He had a food supply and there were ten thousand hiding places. He could slip out at night and no one would know the difference.

Roy looked over at Matt, when he didn't answer. Roy's gaze lingered on the new lariat tied to a ring on Matt's saddle. The manila hemp had a pearly sheen to it. He had noticed the rope when they had ridden out from the Box B that morning, but it *had* held no significance then. Now, it looked as deadly as a snake.

He crunched the toothpick in half just thinking about that rope and Jack Bone's halfbreed neck.

9

———

STEAM CLOUDED THE windows of Naomi's Café, gauzing the faces of those who sat at oilcloth-covered tables inside. Every time someone came in, or left, some of the vapors escaped, wafting the sugary aromas of sweet rolls, cinnamon, coffee, scrambled and fried eggs, bacon, sausage, donuts bubbling in a deep-fat fryer, chickory and the heady aroma of burning mesquite wood.

Ben Killian smelled the café a half block away, as he passed the Baronsville Bank, not yet open, crossed First and Main, where Lew Pettibone was sweeping the sidewalk in front of his grocery store. Whitewashed lettering on the glass front proclaimed bargains: 1 doz. eggs—30¢, flour, 5 lbs.—16¢, 1 lb. bacon—24¢, 1 gal. milk—42¢.

"Mornin' Ben," said Lew.

"Lew," said Ben. He glanced at attorney Jack Kearney's office next to the Baronsville Land & Title offices. He crossed Main at the tiny public library squeezed in between Dr. Henry Emberlin's office and Willie Powell's Baronsville Drugs & Sundries on the corner. Naomi's Café was next to Ken Loehon's Main Street Barbershop, flanked by a pool hall called Delmer's Pool & Billiard Parlor. Nobody played billiards there, they mostly shot rotation or eight ball, but Delmer Mudd thought the name gave his seedy place a little class. At eight in the morning, the P & B, as locals called it, was already open to accommodate the locals who came in to buy 'shine. Delmer's customers didn't give a hang about buying untaxed liquor. Prohibition was a joke some people hoped would never end. Delmer made more money selling white lightning out the back door than he made up front. Ben Killian was one of his regular customers, and there were others he didn't even know about who sent hands in to buy the illegal whiskey.

The jukebox blared a tinny song sung by a quivering-voiced singer. Ben recognized it as the whining plea on people's lips all across the country, "Brother, Can You Spare a Dime?"

Cater-cornered from the little park square, clotted with tumbleweeds, directly across from Ken's barbershop, stood the city hall, courthouse, sheriff's office and jail. Beyond were dry goods stores, a dress shop, a catalog store, a secondhand store, the post office. The Baptist church was in the next block, on the corner.

The song floating out of the pool hall was annoying. Eastern corruption. Taught people to beg. Downright unpatriotic.

Ben had his own opinions about the Depression. Get rid of Hoover and the breadlines would disappear. Give a man a sack of beans and a shovel instead of a dime and let him grow his own food. Everybody wanted a goddamned handout.

Ken's Model A clattered by; Ken beeped at Killian. Both men waved as Ken turned the corner to park down at the end of the block so he wouldn't crowd out his customers. Ken wore his hair cut short as a kind of advertisement. He made people think their hair was too long. Ben smoothed the hair at the back of his neck, frowned.

Ben pushed the door open, entered Naomi's Café. He shut the door behind him. The smells made him taste the whiskey on his breath. He hated to kill it with a cup of coffee. His eyes narrowed and his glance swept the room. He knew virtually all of the people inside, some better than others. They all knew him. The buzz of conversation only slackened slightly. Ben saw the patterned shirts of the men, the subdued colors of women's dresses, the sea of Stetsons, the balloons of faces, some gaunt, some pudgy, some grizzled, some young and cleanshaven, some powdered and painted, some stark and wrinkled. Some of the stares he saw were aimed at him with suspicion if not downright malice. Jo-Beth Vermeil was there to pick up the latest gossip before she took over the town switchboard, relieving Nancy Hogan, who was the telephone operator on the night shift. Jo-Beth was the eyes and ears of Baronsville. She sat with three other ladies, one of whom was the town tart, Patsy Becker. Patsy leered at him; Jo-Beth winked. He nodded to them as a group, made his way to the long table by the left-hand wall. This was where the ex-officio business of Baronsville took place. Here was where the politicians sat with the business owners, where the traveling salesmen bought coffees for prospects, where Mayor Womack started his day before opening the bank and then going over to city hall to shuffle papers.

"Ben," said Ted Womack tightly.

Mayor Theodore Womack was also president of the Baronsville Bank. He had the look of a giant toad, with his oversized eyes surrounded by wrinkled folds of flesh, his curvaceous mouth, pudgy, sensual lips which he constantly licked and kept wet with his flickering pink tongue. Ted was pudgy all over and he tried to hide it with a long vest and one of the enormous double-breasted worsted suits he bought in Galveston. He wore a large diamond on a gold ring, made to look even larger on the little finger of his right hand. On his left, he wore a diamond-studded wedding band which constantly shattered light in a dazzling display of glittering pyrotechnics.

The pretty waitress, Susy Dillard, glided over to the table, a small apron gripping her long legs and graceful hips. She carried an order tablet in her slender hand, whipped out the pencil tucked into the foldover.

"Coffee, Mr. Killian? Do you want breakfast?"

"Coffee's fine, Susy." Ben sat at the only empty chair, opposite Ted Womack. Next to Ted sat Martin Longerbeam, one of the smaller ranchers, and Willie Powell, the druggist. Ben sat next to Jim Harding, the veterinarian. They nodded to each other cordially. Next to Harding sat Bill Letterman, a used-car dealer who also owned the town's only filling station on the highway. Two other men sat at the table. They wore suits and Ben didn't know them. Transients, he thought. Salesmen or oil prospectors. They looked hungry and one of them had a small pile of coffee chits in front of him which he kept shuffling like a deck of limp cards.

"Marty," said Ben, nodding to the rancher.

"What brings you to town, Ben?" asked Womack.

"You know goddamned well why I'm here, Ted."

The banker picked up the curved bone of a sugared donut, dipped one end in his coffee. He worried it through his lips, suckled it into his mouth.

"Ben, it's in the hands of the law now. I know they've got your boy over in the jail. He'll get a fair trial, I reckon."

"Where in hell's Blanchard? Or one of his deputies? I went to see Luke and the jail's locked up tight."

Martin Longerbeam interrupted. He towered over the others at the table, a tall, lean man in his late forties, with a skull of a face that looked as if it had been sculpted with an axe, pale blue eyes that looked as if they had gathered dust from the room. He wore a plaid shirt and Levi's, Judson boots. A Bull Durham tag dangled from one of his shirt pockets.

"Sheriff and Doakes left early this mornin'," drawled Longerbeam. "Drove over to the Box B. There's been a killin' and some Baron cattle rustled."

"That's right," said Womack, eager to change the subject. "Jo-Beth said one of Matt's hands was murdered."

"Shit," said Ben, as Susy brought a cup of coffee, set it in front of him. To her, he said, "Thanks."

"I can get the jail opened for you, Ben," said Mayor Womack. "We got a new deputy coming in at nine from Galveston. You want to talk to Luke, it'll be all right."

"I want him out of jail," said Ben. He fixed Womack with a withering, accusatory look.

"Who's the new deputy?" asked Harding.

"Ray Naylor," said Womack. "His folks used to live here. Roy hired him last week."

"Wasn't there a Naylor girl killed some time back?" asked Jim, a young, handsome man, light-haired, with a flaxen mustache. He had grown up in Uvalde, where his father, Cecil, owned a small, 1,200-acre ranch. Jim had studied veterinary medicine at Baylor. He liked the outdoors, hunted whenever he wasn't tending to the local ranchers' stock. Matt Baron had enticed him to Baronsville, set him up in business. The two often hunted ducks and geese on the Gulf and sometimes Jim took Matt and Ben up to his father's ranch to hunt deer and javelinas.

"Car wreck," said Longerbeam. "Never did find out who done it."

"Ah, yes," said Jim. "Hit and run. Doc Emberlin told me about it. This deputy must be a relative."

"He is," said Womack. "He's her brother."

"Can't remember the woman's name," said Harding.

"Me, neither," said Longerbeam. "Lacey, Lizzie, Lucy, something like that."

"Ted," said Killian, "I don't want Luke to stand trial. What'll it take?"

"To drop the charges, you mean?"

"That's what I mean."

"Do you, ah, think we ought to discuss this here?" asked Womack. "I'm in a hurry."

"Well, your boy did take money belonging to the bank, Ben."

"How much?"

"More than a hundred dollars."

"How much more?"

"Considerably more, I reckon."

"How goddamned much more?" asked Ben again.

"Two thousand," said Womack.

"Two thousand goddamned dollars? Are you sure, Ted?"

"Absolutely."

"Well, I can take care of that. I want you to drop the charges against my boy."

"I'll have to think about it. There were other expenses. Paperwork."

"Ted, don't try and scatter shit with a rake. Two thousand do it?"

"There's a matter of principle here, Ben. The bank entrusted Luke with the cash. He took it. It was plumb embarrassing. It was a heap more than two thousand dollars just in goodwill. That was money out of my own pocket."

Ben snorted. Ted Womack, he knew, thought in terms of dollars and cents. If he was embarrassed, it was because he had to actually dig in someone else's pocket for the missing money. He certainly wouldn't make up any loss with cash of his own.

"Did you put in an insurance claim?" asked Ben. Luke, he knew, had been a messenger, and had been bonded by the bank.

Womack flushed visibly. His frog mouth widened in a sickly grin as if he'd just swallowed a fly and the fly was stuck to flypaper.

"Well, as a matter of course—"

"So, you may collect insurance on your loss," said Ben. "You'll get full restitution. So now it's just revenge you're after," said Ben.

"Your boy's a thief," said Womack, blurting it out like a tasteless wad of gum.

Ben's face hardened subtly, as if something had ironed out all the shadows, smoothed every wrinkle. He hadn't touched his coffee. Now, he lifted the cup to his lips, sipped it, unmindful of the scalding heat.

His eyes never wavered from Ted Womack's face. They locked on the banker's eyes with unflinching intensity.

Womack blinked four times in two seconds. A little tic began to make a corner of his jaw quiver. The quiver traveled to his lower lip, leaped to his right hand as if the tic had leapfrogged the neural pathways in his brain.

Ben seemed to swell to massive proportions from the waist up. His chest filled out, his neck bulged like a bull elk in the rut. And he seemed perfectly calm, like a storm in lull, like a boulder poised on a precipice, hard and dangerous.

"What'd you pay Luke?" asked Ben, so softly Womack had to strain to hear.

"T-twenty. T-twenty-five."

"Per week?"

Womack nodded and his face took on a ghastly pallor. The tic bounced from jaw to lip and back again, then attached itself to the corner of the banker's right eye. Isolated chunks of flesh trembled with maddening irregularity as the tic performed random assaults with no metric pattern. The paleness of Ted's face fled as he began to blush with embarrassment. He flattened his right hand on the table to stop its trembling, but there was nothing he could do about his facial muscles. They twittered as if tickled by a hog-bristle brush. Womack was an engine running with a broken timing chain. All of his pistons were pumping without any semblance of synchronization and the energy was transferred to his face in erratic surges.

Stricken voiceless with shame, Womack only nodded. His eyes fixed on Killian's hands, the thick wrists, the powerful arms that tautened the cloth of his sleeves drum-tight.

"Christ, Ted. You pay Luke twenty-five bucks a week and send him to deliver nearly two years' pay to someone else? That's like pouring gasoline on a fire. You tempted Luke with that money, and by God, that's a sin, if not a goddamned crime. Same as having a hundred-dollar-a-month maid make your bed and leaving cash on the dresser. Temptation's a mighty powerful thing and you can't blame her for taking a few dollars to feed her kids when you have plenty, just lying around for the taking."

"I—it's not the s-same thing," said Womack, trying desperately to control the rampant tics. "Y—your boy stopped off to shoot a game of pool. He got drunk and spent money entrusted to him."

"Maybe he just borryed it," said Longerbeam. "He was playin' pool with Delmer Mudd for a buck a ball."

"Th-that's no excuse," said Womack, firm in his convictions, if not in self-control. "I—I called Roy Blanchard right away.

"Stovall," Womack continued, "had to pay cash for a shipment of lumber he'd sent over to the dry kiln in Odessa."

"What time did you call Blanchard?" Ben asked.

"Soon as Stovall called me. Right around two o'clock."

"What time did you send Luke over to Stovall's?"

"One o'clock."

"Do you think Luke lost two thousand dollars in an hour of playing eight ball?"

"Might have," said Womack stubbornly. The tic leaped to his upper lip like an invisible worm wriggling under the skin.

"Shit," said Ben.

"Roy didn't go over there," said Longerbeam. "That dumbbell Harlan drove a half a block with his sirene a-blarin'. I was in the pool hall havin' a beer. Delmer, him and Luke, ran out the back door when Harlan came bustin' in, a-wavin' that hogleg around. Hell, I almost ran out with 'em."

"That true, Ted?" Ben asked.

Womack shrugged and looked around the room for an exit. He stuck a finger under his collar as if to loosen it, but his fastidiousness wouldn't allow him to slacken his choking tie.

She came up behind Ben, put her hands on his shoulders.

"Hello, Ben," said Naomi Tyler.

Ben turned and looked up into the cherubic face of the café owner.

"Nomi," he said.

"More coffee?" She smiled angelically. Naomi was what they called a "stout" woman. She was corpulent enough to have to make her own dresses. Yet she was a graceful woman, with dark hair, a peaches-and-cream complexion, a sunny disposition, despite having a lazy husband, Burt, and a lout of a son, David.

"No, Ted and I are going to walk over to the jail," said Ben.

"Well, you boys had oughta eat some aigs and grits before turnin' yourselves over to the law."

Everyone at the table laughed except Womack and Killian. Womack tried, but his nervous affliction possessed him thoroughly at that moment. He just sat there and jiggled in his chair like a man stricken with St. Vitus' dance.

Ben scooted his chair backward and stood up. Naomi squeezed his forearm and glided away to another table, rolling through the room like a giant wake-churning ship easing through a marina of small boats at anchor, making one of her periodic gestures of good-will, just to get out of the sweltering kitchen. Burt did cook occasionally, but he was as reliable as the West Texas weather. When strangers complained about it, people said: "If you don't like our weather, wait twenty minutes."

Womack lurched to his feet. His chair skidded backwards to the wall with a nerve-rattling screech of wood.

Ben put two bits on the table next to his half-empty coffee cup, nodded to Martin and Jim. He headed for the door without a word. Womack left fifteen cents on the table and wobbled along in Killian's wake, the wanness back in his face, the tics temporarily dormant.

Raymond Naylor listened to the police radio crackle as he sat at the long table, looking over a crisp stack of "Wanted" posters. Melba Orr sat in the horseshoe that was the dispatcher's station, part of a small front room with a window much like the ticket booth at the Bijou down the street. There was a little half-moon window on the bottom, a speaker's hole higher up, in the center of the glass.

Melba had her own personal wireless radio on too. She was listening to *Stella Dallas* on the DuMont set, chewing gum with steady precision, buffing her nails with an emery board. Her blond hair was showing brown at the roots and her print dress had too much Argo starch in it. Its yoke was low enough so that when she leaned over to talk to someone outside in the lobby, the tops of her breasts pooched half out of her dress, held back by a pink D-cup brassiere with lacy borders. She kept sidling glances over toward the new deputy, a trim, lean man with his light brown hair neatly cut, his face cleanshaven, his uniform pressed to military smoothness.

"Where y'all from, Raymond?"

"I've been livin' over to Galveston," he said, looking up from the gap in the posters. So far as he could tell no one had ever looked at them before. The faces were predominantly black and Hispanic, but there were some tough-looking white boys in there too. They were wanted for crimes ranging from murder and bank robbery to extortion and passing and uttering.

"They was some Naylors used to live over in them shacks acrost the railroad tracks, beyond the trestle."

"I used to live there," said Ray. His brown eyes never flickered, nor was there any condemnation in his tone. He was merely admitting to fact.

"Oops, sorry."

Naylor went back to looking at "Wanted" sheets. Melba leaned over the DuMont as the announcer for *Mary Noble, Backstage Wife* boomed across the air waves, the theme music wavering up and under in dramatic counterpoint to the dialogue.

The front door opened and Ben Killian entered the lobby of the sheriff's office, followed by Mayor Ted Womack. Quickly, Melba turned the unauthorized radio down, flashed a smile that animated her pudgy face.

"Why, Mister Killian, how ever are you?" she said, her syrupy twang like one of those shit-kicking songs the locals danced to at the Grange Hall on Saturday nights.

"Fine, Melba, fine."

"Well, whatever brings you to my little old jail?" Melba paused, realizing she had spoken before organizing the least bit of thought. "Oh, my, you're here to see your son, Lukey, of course."

Ben cringed at the diminution of his son's name, avoided looking at Melba's ample breasts, displayed behind the glass partition like honeydew melons from the truck farms along the Rio Grande.

"I want to see the new deputy," said Ben as Womack quivered nervously beside him.

"Hello there, Mayor Womack," said Melba pleasantly, turning slightly to offer Ted a view of her bulging chest.

"Melba."

Melba turned to Raymond Naylor, her teeth masticating her gum with unfailing rhythm.

"Some gentlemans here to see you, Raymond. Ben Killian and Mayor Womack."

A puzzled expression on his face, Ray stood up. He walked to the glass partition, looked down on the two men in the lobby.

"Tell them I'll be right out," he said.

"They can hear you, silly," said Melba, giving Ben a lurid wink.

In a few moments, Ray stepped down the short stairs from the jail hallway and opened a door to the front lobby. He entered, halted to face the two men.

"I'm Deputy Naylor. What can I do for you?" Naylor asked.

"I want you to release Lucas Killian," said Ben. "Ted Womack here is dropping all charges."

"Now, wait a minute," said Ted.

"You just take two thousand out of my savings account, Ted."

"Well, I could," said Womack.

"Sir, I can't release any prisoners. Sheriff Blanchard isn't here and I don't have any authority."

"You have a goddamned key, don't you?" asked Ben.

Naylor bristled.

"There ain't no call for you cursin'," said the new deputy. "Whether or not I've got a key don't make no nevermind. I can't release any prisoners."

"You're holding my son in there. The charges against him have been dropped. I'm asking you to let him out, Naylor."

"It's all right, Deputy," said Womack. "I'll vouch for Ben Killian. We'll talk to Roy when he gets back to town."

"Look, Mister Mayor, Mister Killian, I'm new here. This is my first day on the job. But I know I don't have any authority to release any prisoners. I don't even know what your son looks like. I'm just waiting for instructions when Sheriff Blanchard comes back. He called me last night and said he had a murder case to look into this morning."

"Why, you dumb sonofabitch," said Killian. "This may be your last fucking day on the job."

"I can't help that none," said Naylor tightly. Melba turned up the radio. The tips of her ears were scorched to a pearly flame. Mary Noble was talking to a woman who was trying to have an affair with Mary's handsome husband.

"Ben, come on," said Womack. "It won't hurt Luke to cool his heels for another hour or two."

Naylor stood his ground, not flinching from Ben's icy glare.

"Naylor, you're getting off to a real bad start," said Killian. "It looks to me like you've got rooms to let upstairs, sonny."

"Ben, come on," Womack pleaded.

"I'll go, but you tell Roy Blanchard I want my boy out of jail before quittin' time."

"I'll give him the message," said Naylor coolly.

Ben looked at him closely.

"Just who in hell are you, boy?"

"I'm not a boy, Mister Killian. I'm the new deputy."

"Well, you got a lot to tote before anyone calls you mister in this town, sonny."

"I'll do my level best, sir."

"Shit fire," said Ben and turned on his heel. Womack shrugged and flashed a look of sheepish apology at Deputy Naylor. He waddled after Killian, reaching out to keep the front door from slamming in his face.

Ben reached the sidewalk that ran along Main and stopped. He turned to Womack.

"When I get Luke out, you'll get paid," he said to the banker.

"Maybe we ought to take care of that matter first, Ben. While you're in town."

"You heard me, Ted."

Ben stalked down the street, back to where he had parked the DeSoto. As he passed Naomi's Café, Martin Longerbeam looked at Killian through the window. Martin spoke to Jim Harding, who was still there too.

"Ben's a-smokin'," he said.

"I didn't see Luke with him."

"Luke ain't no damned good, you ask me," said Longerbeam.

"He's good and wild," said Harding.

"He'll bring Ben to grief sooner or later."

"Looks like he's headed that way," agreed Harding.

Ben got in the car, twisted the ignition key savagely. He pressed the electric starter down to the floorboard. The engine roared to life and screeched until he let his foot off the starter. He backed onto Main, narrowly missing old man Phipps in his Reo.

Ben drove toward the Box B, the closest ranch to town, some twenty miles away. He knew he couldn't go home and face Frances or his mother without bringing Luke home. He needed to talk to Roy Blanchard and it was likely he'd be at Matt Baron's sometime during the day. He didn't want to miss him. He had come close to knocking Deputy Naylor down and he didn't like that feeling inside himself.

Ben reached across the seat and grabbed the paper sack with the bottle in it. He set it between his legs as he unscrewed the cap. He tipped the bottle up and poured whiskey into his mouth. He sighed and swallowed slowly. He took another drink and started to feel good.

A jackrabbit burst from the brush alongside the dirt road outside of town.

Ben pushed the accelerator to the floor and gunned the engine.

The DeSoto lurched ahead, rear tires grabbing at gravel, spitting it out behind the car in a cloud of West Texas dust.

"Missed the sonofabitch," he said, as the jackrabbit appeared in his rearview mirror, bounding through the barbed-wire fence that bordered the Box B Ranch, graceful as a gazelle.

Ben didn't let up on the gas and he left a dust trail hovering above the road for a full quarter mile in his wake.

"Goddamn Luke anyway," he muttered, the tang of his whiskey breath strong in his nostrils.

10

———

SHERIFF ROY BLANCHARD braked his wheezing '29 Plymouth just outside the fence around Matt Baron's house. When the car stopped, he set the handbrake, daubed his sweat-oiled face with a red bandanna.

Although it was early, the heat from the sun had already turned the inside of Blanchard's car to an oven. The backs of his trousers were wet, plastered to his skin. His armpits had shed sweat through his shirt. He shoved open the door, climbed out of the car, still mopping his face. He did not close the door and it hung there with its white faded letters proclaiming "Baronsville Police" on its black surface. Roy looked toward the sprawling house, wondered if anyone had seen him drive up. He had tried to call before leaving Baronsville, but the telephone lines were out, something that occurred more often than not. He looked toward the outbuildings as if searching for someone, or something. His forehead wrinkles deepened and he snorted air through his nostrils in disappointment. He sucked air through his teeth and he worried the toothpick to the other side of his mouth. He took off his hat, swabbed the hairline with the bandanna. His badge of office gleamed dully on the front of the Stetson's crown.

Roy had been to the Baron house before, but it never ceased to fascinate him. They still called it *La Loma de Sombra*, Shadow Hill in English, although Grace hated the name, Roy knew. Old Anson

Baron had named it that because of the many large oaks and box elders he had planted that grew tall and threw shade over the huge grass lawn. The house was a collection of frame houses that Matt had dragged from the other ranch sections he owned. He had joined them together with their porches, then closed those in, except for those on either end, so that he had a rambling home with privacy for everyone in his family, plenty of room for guests, the foremen of his other ranches. There was a brick house that was better built than the main house. Anson had built that as a school and playhouse for his children, and Matt's kids used it, as well. Roy knew the Barons kept Shetland ponies, Great Danes, goats for their children's amusement. Matt had had little wagons made for them, and Blanchard had often seen Ethan and Peggy riding in one of them, pulled by a goat when they were small, by a Shetland when they got older. Little Derek had done the same thing, but had no one to ride with him since Ethan and Peggy were so much older than he.

The dairy herd grazed on the big fenced meadow beyond the milking barn, some at the hay bins, others on new grass that was fetlock-high. There were Holsteins and Jerseys, a half dozen of each, a few young calves that had not yet been weaned. The air was thick with the smell of manure, threaded with the faint waft of honeysuckle that climbed the cistern high above the watering trough on stilts.

Roy walked around the police car and opened the gate. He ducked through the trellis with its wisteria vines thick on the latticework. Hummingbirds worked the blossoms of the morning glories that lined the brick path, seemed impervious to the sheriff's presence, so intent were they on sipping nectarous dew through their long beaks.

When he was halfway up the walk, the front door opened. Matt Baron stepped out onto the porch. He walked stiff-legged to the edge of the porch, pushed his Stetson back, exposing his sun-burnished forehead.

Blanchard stopped at the bottom step, put a boot on it, looked up at Baron.

"Roy."

"Matt."

"You get that boy over to the mortuary?"

"You can bury him tomorrow. Coroner from Corpus signed him off last evening."

"We will, then. You need anything?"

"Matt, I got Harlan and Dave Tyler goin' down to look over that corner of brush at the Rincón. You said if I needed any hands, you'd lend me a couple."

"You make Dave a deputy?"

"He's swore in."

"We're late to roundup, but I could spare maybe Hank Janss and Rudy Fritch. Be over there myself after the funeral."

"Good enough. Where can I find 'em this time of day?"

"I sent 'em over to La Plata with a wagonload of cottonseed cakes for José Perez to put out for the stock. Told 'em to keep their eyes peeled, do some cow-scoutin' for us. They might be ridin' that corner today, carryin' Winchesters. You could maybe call down there and tell José, my fence rider, to find 'em for you, if they haven't ridden out yet."

"Much obliged."

"Anything else?"

"I got your nephew in the *juzgado*. Ben's probably goin' to raise hell about it."

"Luke's in more trouble, then."

"I reckon."

"Damn phone's out."

"I know. Matt, that boy Jamey didn't die easy. They dragged him a ways. Coroner said he died quick once his throat got cut."

Matt winced. "I figured. Soon as we get the tally and head some beeves for the meat packer's, I want to get after Bone."

"I better be there, Matt. Man deserves a trial."

"Bone likely won't see it your way, Roy."

"Just the same. We want it all legal."

"I'll let you know."

"Fair enough. Well, I'll go back to town, give José a jingle. Much obliged, Matt."

"See you at the funeral," said Matt.

"'Nother thing," said Roy. "Had a break-in last night. Nobody knows about it yet. Chandler's Feed Store."

"What's that got to do with me, Roy?"

"Boy who minds the store, Andy Erickson, sleeps in a loft up in Chandler's, said he saw some Indians come in. They broke into that locker where Merle keeps the wolf poison. Took a passel of strychnine."

"What the hell . . ." said Matt. "Bone and his bunch?"

"Looks like. Andy said he knew Bone from before. He didn't know none of the others."

"What in hell would Bone want with strychnine?"

"That's just what I was wonderin'," said Blanchard.

"Goddamn Bone," said Baron. "You tell Hank I said to give you all the help you need, Roy."

"Much obliged, Matt."

Baron stalked back into the house, his one boot ringing on the hardwood louder than the other. Roy turned back to the car. He hadn't told Matt that someone had spotted Bone and some unknown Indians or greasers in town the night before. They had broken into the pool hall and stolen some 'shine. Blanchard got back in his car, slammed the door and threw his bandanna on the seat. The sun blinded him as he turned the car and headed back down the lane to the main road back to Baronsville.

Jamey Dobbs was buried in the Baronsville cemetery the next day. Matt paid for the simple stone, had a stonecutter in San Antonio inscribe the kid's name on it. Nobody knew when or where Jamey was born, or who his parents were. Roy Blanchard could locate no relatives. There was nothing in the deceased's effects to help solve the mystery.

"I hope they catch the sonofabitch who killed Jamey," said Lou.

"Vengeance is mine, saith the Lord," said Grace.

"Horseshit," replied Lou. There was no love lost or misplaced between the two women. Lou thought Grace was a citified piece of furniture on the Baron ranch and Grace thought Lou was a crude, foul-mouthed spinster with the manners of a cowhand.

Matt ignored them and set his Stetson straight, pursed his lips in thought. Death's quirt flayed people in different ways, and families bore the scars for the rest of their lives. Some just got cut deeper than others.

Ted Womack dropped the theft charges against Luke Killian and Roy released the young man from jail that same afternoon. Frances was thrilled to have her son home, but she knew he would probably not stay.

There was a lot of talk around town over the killing of Jamey Dobbs and the slaughter of Matt Baron's prize bull, Dutch Zee. Naomi's Café buzzed with talk for days, and, gradually, the news about Jack Bone living in the *brasada* with a bunch of renegade

Indians leaked out. For the next several weeks, people in town complained to Sheriff Blanchard that they had heard prowlers, and several reported break-ins, food missing from storm cellars, kitchen cupboards. The thefts were blamed on Bone and his gang, at least by the habitués of Naomi's. Sheriff Blanchard took no official stand, at least not publicly.

Matt Baron, Ben Killian and Ernie Aguilar all had their hands full with spring roundup, so they put away their differences for a time, like hunting guns put on the racks until the next season. Paco Velez told Aguilar that Killian's men had dynamited the dam Paco had built on Bandera Creek.

"A shame," said Aguilar.

"I will build another one," said Paco.

"Don't shut the Box K off of water completely," said Don Ernesto.

"No, I will find another way to keep some of the water on the Lazy A," said Velez.

"There will be trouble anyway," said Aguilar.

"Por seguro," agreed Paco, and walked back to the bunkhouse to pick men to ride with him that day. He, like the other ranchers, had to tend to the roundup, to the gathering and feeding of weak stock, to getting the cows heavy with calf, or with calves, to the green pastures.

Ernesto stood on the porch a long time, his hands in his pockets, listening to the sounds of another morning, but not hearing them. There was already trouble. He didn't have to wait for it. You could change the course of a creek, he thought, dam it up, divert it, but you couldn't change a man's heart so easily. Ben Killian would not like any tampering with his water supply on Bandera. Matt Baron had practically accused him of rustling Box B cattle. Not in so many words. Matt, he was sure, thought Bone was working for the Lazy A.

Bone. He was the trouble. He was the big trouble. But, he would not give Bone any land. He would just want more. More of everything.

Ernesto cursed softly in Spanish, and went back in the house. The General crowed and Ernesto bristled as if someone had laid a cold surgeon's knife against a raw nerve. He wanted to wring that rooster's neck.

No, he thought. He would like to wring Bone's neck. He would like to squeeze the life out of him until the Indian's eyes popped out of their sockets, until his face turned blue and his lungs collapsed for want of air.

"Pinche cabrón," he muttered to himself. But the cursing did not help. When, moments later, he joined Elena for breakfast, he was still clenched up like a fist.

"You are not hungry, my husband?" Elena asked when he picked at his eggs.

"No," he said. "I do not feel like eating."

"Then that is when you should," she said. "It will put your mind on something else. And maybe I won't have to wash out your mouth with soap."

Ernesto looked startled. Elena's smile was conspiratorial. She passed him a basket of sweet rolls. She turned back the napkin that kept the heat in.

"You heard me swearing?"

"I have not heard those two words since I was a little girl," she said.

"I'm sorry."

"Eat," she said, and Ernie reached for a sweet roll. He ate two bites before the dryness of his throat made him choke. He swallowed coffee and pushed away from the table.

"I have much work to do," he said lamely, without looking directly at her.

"Do you not wish to tell me what is making you so angry?"

"Everything," he snapped and saw her face draw up as if he had slapped her. He leaned over, stroked the back of her hand, kissed the side of her neck. "I'm sorry," he breathed into her ear.

"I am sorry too," she said after he had left the dinette. She watched him cross the yard to the stables, his shoulders hunched, his head bowed. Then, she began to weep softly and the morning was spoiled like all the other mornings since Bone had returned.

Jane rode her favorite horse, Bravo, a five-year-old sorrel gelding, over the gently rolling green land. She wore polished riding boots, a soft denim skirt and poplin blouse, a Stetson lady's hat, a silk kerchief around her neck. She carried her belongings in a hand-tooled set of saddlebags, and, as always, a rolled-up slicker was snugged down behind the cantle. The pastures were irrigated along a hundred-mile stretch that was twenty miles wide. She took pride in an accomplishment that represented years of planning and back-breaking work. While the Barons had been pioneers in bringing electrification to that corner of Texas, the Killians had introduced irrigation. They had

widened the creeks, diverted the rivers, built the ponds, the stock
tanks, husbanding the watershed, achieving a delicate balance in a
harsh land where rainfall was often scarce. The Lazy K took advantage
of the extremes, storing water when the severe Gulf storms struck,
guarding it when the land was parched.

La Querencia was her favorite section of the ranch. Its boundaries
were days apart, even by motorcar, and it encompassed the best
topography that part of Texas had to offer, emerald-green hills, vast
expanses of grassland benches, sweetwater streams, bottomlands,
desert pockets that had changed very little in hundreds of years. This
was where she came when she wanted to think about life and death,
forget the daily demands of ranch operations and be with men and
women she had known for years. Only a few lived at the main ranch
now, since the younger generation preferred town and the company
of people, but Old Silvero and his family still lived there, and Lew
Carmody, who must be nearing ninety, and generations of Balcoms,
who knew no other way of living than what the Lazy K provided.
Lester Balcom, the patriarch of that silent, stiff-lipped clan, had
roamed the coastal plain above Matagorda Bay, had worked the
ranches, with their deep grasses and Siberian clover, around Palacios
Point, Matagorda and Trespalacios. It was said he had sailed with
Jean Lafitte on the brig *Pride,* and learned cattle from Captain Richard Grimes who settled Palacios Point in 1840.

Lester's sons, Dean and Jim, had grown up working cattle, had
married quiet, hard-working southern girls and fathered sons and
daughters who stayed on the land, spreading out beyond the Matagorda, with its salty Gulf breezes and sea-storms that razed the land
with hurricanes that were still remembered by the grandchildren and
their children. The Balcoms had married Reynoldses and their offspring married Sheplees and theirs in turn married Longerbeams
and Austins and Loves and Sanchezes and Rodriguezes until they
were a swarm over the land like all those begats in the Bible. Jane kept
track of her families and knew their histories, their trials and tri-
umphs, and had become a kind of matriarch to all of them who had
worked, or were presently tending, the vast acreages of the Lazy K.

She passed the herd of Guernseys that gave the milk the Lazy K
' all over Texas to various companies and smiled with satisfaction.
\d been the first to corner that market in Baronsville and now
'huge industry, giving the ranch a vital and steady cash flow.
'ere fat and many of them gave ten gallons or more of milk

a day. From that sweet milk came butter, cheeses, buttermilk and cottage cheese, the finest in the land.

She opened the far gate and closed it, holding onto Bravo's reins and her hat at the same time. There was a warm breeze blowing now and it raked off the heat and brought a coolness to the air. She could smell the far-off Gulf marshes, the tangy scent of the sea.

Bravo followed the road to Querencia without drifing from his path. A little after noon, when the sun was straight up overhead, Jane stopped under a live oak, one of her favorites, and ate the light lunch that Consuela had fixed: half an apple, two prunes, a thin sliver of beef on salt-rising bread, lightly patted with fresh butter. She washed the food down with sweet lemonade that was slightly warm from being in her saddlebag, even though it had been wrapped by Consuela with cool wet handtowels.

Jane dozed and fell asleep against the tree. When she awoke, the flies were at the leftovers and she shooed them away, packed her saddlebag, slung it over Bravo's rump. Her bones creaked when she stepped into the saddle. Her fingers had stiffened during her nap and she flexed them to bring back their springiness. Tonight, she thought, she would rub them with the Jergen's she had brought along.

She opened the gate to Querencia, breathed the air. Somehow, it seemed different here, older, more stable, comforting. She could almost smell the olive trees she had planted around the old ranch buildings when she was a young woman. Ahead, spread all over in bunches in the glowing grass, cattle grazed contentedly. She started counting all the new calves although they had already been tallied and branded, she knew.

Twenty miles later, she rode into the main complex of Querencia, saddle-weary and sweat-soaked. The breeze had died off and the sun beat down like Vulcan's hammer. Bravo's sleek hide was rivered with blood from the horseflies and she took him to the water tank, removed the bridle, slipped the bit from his mouth. He would not go anywhere, she knew.

"Hola, Señora," called a voice.

Jane turned to see Silvero walking bowlegged toward her, his gait a little slower than the year before, the lines in his face slightly deeper, his hair thinner and grayer.

One of his sons, or grandsons, ran out of the stable to catch up

Bravo and take him to a stall, where he would pour grain and rub the gelding down.

"Silvero, how are you, my friend?"

"Bien, bien," he said, grinning wide. His tobacco-stained teeth, what few were left, did not darken the warmth of his smile. "I am happy you have come. The olive trees they have many fruits and the garden she has many tomatoes and chili peppers."

Jane laughed. She put her arm around Old Silvero's shoulder and they walked toward the main house, where it would be cool and she could sit in a rocking chair and Silvero's daughter, Magdalena, would pamper and spoil her with sweetcakes and apple cider. Silvero would tell her how the roundup was going and where everyone was and that night they would drink wine and brandy and stay up late listening to Silvero's sons play *son huastecos* and the girls would dance and sing for her pleasure.

"It's good to be home, Silvero," she said.

"It is good to have you home, *Señora,*" he replied. *"Bienvenido a Querencia."*

"You don't look a day older."

"You look younger than before."

Jane gave Silvero's shoulder a squeeze and the weariness seeped out of her. She tripped up the steps almost like a young girl and now she could smell the olive trees and the apples ripe in the orchard, the heady smells of things growing in Silvero's magnificent garden just beyond the cluster of box elders and sycamores at the edge of the yard.

She stepped into the house and Magdalena rushed up to her and hugged her, screeching in happiness.

"Mother Jane, welcome, welcome," she said. "How is Ben? How are the children?" A thousand questions in a split second. "Give me your hat. Do you want slippers?" Magdalena took Jane's hat and disappeared without one question having been answered.

And Jane smelled the cakes and pies baking in the kitchen on the old wood stove and heard the radio crackling with Mexican music.

"This is truly a land of plenty," she said, as she sat in the rocking chair and heard its familiar song on the hardwood floor. Magdalena turned the radio off in the other room and it was peaceful and quiet and cool.

"What did you say?" asked Silvero.

"Oh, I was just thinking out loud."

Then, Magdalena brought the apple cider and a tray of sweet-cakes and a fan which she waved gently to one side of Jane's face while she sat on a hassock and looked up adoringly at this goddess with the flame-red hair who had come to earth to bless her children.

"Bienvenido a Querencia." Silvero's words echoed in Jane's mind. The welcome. *Querencia,* she had learned from Old Silvero, was a bullfighting term. When a bull faced death, he picked a spot for his last stand. That was his *querencia.* The English translation was "preference," but it did not carry the weight of the Spanish. To Jane, the word meant what it meant in Spanish, a special place where a person could face death unafraid.

Hank Janss pulled the wagon into the barren yard at José's adobe line shack. Rudy Fritch rode his grulla under the big oak tree that was the only shade for six hundred yards in any direction. The weathered windmill by the corral creaked and groaned as it twisted to pick up the listless, heavy wind. The water in the stock tank was green with slimy algae. The pens and corrals were empty of stock. Horses whick-ered from the stables.

"Perez!" Hank called, as he set the brake, wrapped the reins around the handle.

José Perez opened the door of the adobe, stood there, rubbing the sleep out of his eyes.

"Brung you feed you got to get out," said Janss, swinging down off the buck seat. The flatiron springs twanged with the release of his weight.

"Gottam Mexican," grumbled the German, Fritch. "Sleep all de gottam time like de pig." Rudy swung out of the saddle, ground-tied the grulla. He took off his battered and sweat-rimed hat, swatted at a horsefly that was gnawing a hole in his horse's rump. Blood streamed from the bite. The horse's hide rippled convulsively at the blow. The fly dropped dead to the ground.

Janss, a big, rawboned man, with a square face, square jaw, walked to the back of the wagon, untied the reins of his horse, a skittish sorrel quarterhorse gelding with three white stockings. A Winchester jutted out of the boot, its stock worn and gouged by years of use in brush. Hank's high cheekbones were laced with red and purple spider tracks; his eyes seemed to droop like a bloodhound's in sockets pulled by fatty bags of flesh underneath.

"You better get to crackin', José," said Hank, as he swung the sorrel away from the wagon. "Tom figgers to finish roundup over here next week."

José blinked at the sudden intrusion, stood in the doorway, wearing only dirty shorts and limp socks. He grinned idiotically, his half-carious smile mottled with gold caps.

"What you gonna do?" asked José, the slightest of Spanish accent tingeing his Texas drawl, as if he was struggling to keep the Mexican out of his English.

"Me'n Rudy's goin' to work the Rincón. You get them cakes out pronto, hear?"

"I was up all night," said Perez. "Son'thin' was out yonder. I heard hollerin' and cattle bawlin'. Couldn't esee nothin'. I took me a 'lectric torch. Didn't esee no goddamn thin'."

"Where was dat?" asked Rudy, walking up on legs bowed out like a pair of ice tongs. He stared at José as if he had never seen a man in his shorts before, or maybe he was still baffled by this further example of a Mexican cowhand. He neither understood Mexicans nor liked them much. He thought José was worth more dead than alive. He often said if José died, he'd pick the gold out of his teeth and cash it in for greenbacks and "spend the money on a heathen woman."

"Yonder." José pointed toward the southwest.

"We'll ride on over," said Janss. "You get them cakes out, José."

"I'll put the cakes out, Hank," said José, amiable as a cub bear in the berry patch. "I surely will. I ain' esloppy no more, I mean esleepy."

"You 'bout set, Rudy?" asked Janss.

Rudy Fritch continued to stare at Perez as if the Mexican had just stolen Rudy's favorite horse.

"Yah, we go," said Rudy and he squinted his flat, blue eyes at Perez, scrunched up his Teutonic face in a scowl. "Dey eat too many frijole beans," he muttered under his breath.

José grinned as the two men mounted up and rode away to the southwest. He went back inside just as the phone on the adobe wall began to jangle with a throaty, off-key ring of its bell.

"Hallo," said José, holding the alien instrument to his ear and speaking into the mouthpiece. "This is José."

"Sheriff Blanchard."

Static crackled in Perez's ear.

"Cheriff, hallo."

"Let me talk to Janss or Fritch."

"They are not here, Cheriff. They rode off."

"Can you find 'em? Tell 'em to wait for my deputy. Doakes will be there in a spell."

"I can try and find them, I think."

"You do that, José."

José heard a click and the line went dead. He took the earphone away from his head and looked at it for a long moment. Then he put it back in its cradle. He dressed quickly, his stomach growling. He left the door open as he walked toward the stable, tucking his shirt inside his cotton trousers. His spurs, with their worn blunt rowels, rattled in the stillness like little bells.

He saddled a dark cowpony named Pattycake, a fleet little mare that could work brush like a ferret. He looked at the wagon as he rode out. The two horses were standing hipshot in the shade. When he was a half hour gone, José remembered he hadn't brought his rifle. He knew Matt's orders. He thought about going back for it, but he knew he wouldn't be gone long. Hank and Rudy had left clear tracks in the dust. He ought to catch up to them soon. When he told them what the sheriff had said, he would ride back and take the wagon out to the scattered herd. It would take him the better part of the day to set out the cottonseed cakes. He would carry the rifle as Tom Casebolt had ordered.

But José Perez never found Rudy and Hank.

A few minutes later, he heard the moan of a suffering cow and veered off the track of the two cowhands.

It was a serious mistake, but José didn't know that at the time. His first instinct was to find the cow and see if he could help it.

José knew where the hurt cow had to be, and that puzzled him. There was a waterhole and a windmill he had checked a week ago. There was enough wind to work the blades of the windmill, but he didn't hear their creak as he rode closer. He skirted clumps of brush and wind-gnarled mesquite trees, came up to the waterhole. It was bone dry and the windmill was down. Suddenly, he knew what some of the racket had been the night before. Someone had pulled the rig down and it lay in the mud of the waterhole, its frame twisted and bent, one of its blades crumpled like crushed tin.

He didn't see the cow at first. But he heard it bawl again, and rode cautiously toward the thick clump of stunted trees that grew beyond the waterhole, clinging to life through their deep roots.

A few yards beyond, four men straddled a cow. The stench of burning flesh ragged at José's nostrils. He didn't recognize any of the men. Several hobbled head of cattle milled inside of a makeshift rope corral. José noticed these were wearing the Rocking A brand.

Jack Bone stepped out of the brush and brought a battered rifle to his shoulder.

"Hello, José. Remember me?"

José's face drained of color, turned pale as sand.

"What you doin' here, Bone?" The quaver in his voice made Bone laugh.

"Workin'."

"Those are Rocking A cattle."

"They'll be Box B right quick." Bone grinned. "Too bad you come along. Best you get down and come on over here. We'll all of us take a ride when we finish up."

"I ain' goin' nowheres with you."

Ned Feather stepped out of the clump of trees. He too brandished a rifle. Virgil Coldwater came out right behind Ned, spears of hair shooting out from under his hat like bladed wheat standing in unruly shocks. His cyanic eyes sent a chill through José. He had a yearling cow on a rope and a knife in his hand. That was the cow that had been doing the bawling, decided José.

Virgil's knife was bloody. The yearling had been grubbed, its earmarks removed altogether. There was just a pair of bloody holes where they had been. The cow's wounds were oozing blood into its pain-glossed eyes. José felt his stomach roil with fear, as if someone had ticked his own throat with a straight razor.

Virgil shaved off a piece of the cow's shoulder brand with his big knife and the animal bleated in pain.

"It ain't easy to make a Box B," said Bone. Eddie Blue Sky and Barney Whitesides led a string of horses out of the brush. They were all saddled. José swallowed air and still couldn't breathe.

The men working the running irons didn't look up. Bone pointed to them.

"We cut some of that rocker off, then lay a straight iron across the bottom, square off the right side of the A, and put B on top, and we got a fair Box B. Virgil here, he does the grubbin'. He likes cuttin' with that frogsticker."

"'Sus, Maria,'" the Mexican swore.

"Light down, José. We got one more to do and then we'll have a drink. You want to drink with us, José?"

"No. I got to put out feed."

"Light down," said Bone and the grin disappeared from his face.

And that's when Perez made his mistake. He dug his spurs into the cowpony's flanks and jerked the reins over to turn the horse.

José got the pony half-turned before Bone pulled the trigger. The rifle bucked against his shoulder. A spray of sparks spat out the muzzle and there was a smack as the lead projectile from the old Henry .44-40 struck José's left shoulder blade.

It felt like a hard slap to José. He heard the rifle's report, but didn't think it had anything to do with him. Then, he felt something pull at his chest and he saw a cloud of blood spray out in front of him. When he tried to breathe, he felt only a hot wind against his face, as if he'd opened the door of a potbellied stove at full heat. He gasped and crumpled in the saddle. The sky and trees began to spin around and then he lost his bearings. He felt a jar when he hit the ground, but he thought he was still on his horse, riding away.

José stared at blurred pebbles and stones, a clump of nopal, the flowers faded and withered, the spines scintillating in the sun.

Bone stepped over to the dying man.

"You are still going to ride with us, José," he said quietly. "Dead or alive, you chili-pickin' sonofabitch."

11

HANK JANSS RODE up to the crumbling adobe line shack warily. His eyes squinted in the hollows above his beefy cheekbones. The eyes shifted in their sockets as he noticed the wagon still standing in the yard, flies swarming over the cottonseed cakes. A few head of cattle ragged at the wagon, trying to get at the feed.

"José!" Janss called, and his voice sounded hollow in the silence. He knew the minute he said the name that Perez wasn't inside the shack.

Rudy Fritch was still out on the grasslands. He and Hank had split up that afternoon, agreeing to meet back at the line shack for supper. Now, he wished Rudy was there. It was then that Janss noticed the police car parked down by the barn. He breathed an audible sigh of relief. He rode down to the barn, dismounted.

Swatting at flies, Hank led his horse inside the barn. Squinting in the darkness, he found an empty stall, tied the reins to a post. Then, he started counting heads. José's little cowpony was gone, and two more horses that he knew Perez kept there. Casebolt wouldn't be down with the remuda until next week. There was one horse in the far stall on the other side of the barn. The animal whickered when Hank walked up to it. He looked in. Its feed trough was empty. The door to the tack room was wide open.

He wondered whether he ought to strip his horse and wait for José and the sheriff, and whoever else was with him, to return. Or should he ride out and try to find Rudy?

Hank walked out of the barn, unable to make up his mind. He walked to the shack, humming to himself as if to fill up the silence. Something just didn't set right here, he thought. José gone all god-damned day and a couple of Roy Blanchard's deputies riding around La Plata. Why? What in hell was going on?

Hank stopped just in front of the line shack, stared at the open door. The hum died on his lips. José was sure acting peculiar, to leave his place open like that. A cow could get in there and make a wreck of things.

"José?" he called again, feeling stupid about it.

There was no answer.

Janss looked all around, then stepped inside. When his eyes had adjusted to the light, he took in the room. It was messy, he expected that. But something on the table in the middle of the room jarred him. He walked over, looked at the set of running irons. He picked up two of the irons, held them up to the light coming through the windows. Puzzled, he turned them around in his hands. One iron was bent to produce a straight line. The other was a B, like the one used by the Box B. But it was slightly different. The bulges were rounder.

"Damn, José. You doin' hot-iron work?" he said aloud.

Hank heard the sound of hoofbeats out in the yard. He dropped the irons as if they were still hot and blind-bolted for the door.

He squinted at the glare as he stumbled outside. Riding up were Rudy Fritch, Louise Baron, Deputy Harlan Doakes and Dave Tyler, Burt's boy.

Janss raised a hand to wave, then pulled it back down quickly. By the expression on Lou's and the three men's faces, they didn't have anything pleasant on their minds. Janss strolled slowly into the yard, wondering why he wished he was anyplace else but right there.

"Where's dat bean-eater?" asked Rudy. "Doakes here wants to ask him some questions."

"José ain't here," said Janss.

Harlan Doakes reined up and slid out of the saddle. Hank could see he was stiff from the ride. Davey sat his horse, chewing a wad of bubble gum. Rudy and Lou dismounted.

"I got some questions for him," said Doakes.

"What kinda questions?" asked Janss.

"He thinks Perez might be in with that bunch of Indians," said Rudy. "Rustlin'."

Lou rolled her eyes in disbelief. She stood there with her hands on

her hips, glaring at Doakes. The deputy was puffed up with righteous-
ness and didn't even notice Lou's disapproval. Doakes had the bit in
his teeth and he was running with the wind.

"Jesus," said Janss. He cocked a thumb back toward the line
shack.

"What?" asked Harlan.

"I found some runnin' irons inside. Just a few minutes ago. But,
hell, I—"

"We'll just damned see about that," said Harlan, strutting across
the yard toward the shack. Janss exchanged glances with Rudy.

"What'd you find?" Janss asked.

"Some cows fresh-branded," said Dave Tyler. "Looked to be
Rocking A once't. Now wearin' Box B marks. Lou here seen 'em."

"Hell, Dave," said Lou, "anybody can blotch a brand. José's not
that stupid."

"Lou's right," said Janss, "that don't make no bit of sense. Man
rustlin' cattle for hisself ain't goin' to put his home brand on 'em."

"I never thought of dat," said Rudy. He tilted his hat back on his
head and scratched his scalp. "We found José's fire, a bunch of horse
tracks, three or four head of rustled cattle. No sign of anyone. Somebody pulled de windmill down into a stock pond." He pointed off in
the direction from which they had come.

"What's Doakes doin' out here, anyways?" Hank looked at Dave.

"Perez was supposed to meet us here and we were going looking
for Bone."

"Why, that's plumb crazy," said Janss.

Harlan Doakes emerged from the line shack, carrying the running
irons. He wore a smirk on his face.

"Well, by golly," he said, "Sheriff Roy's just goin' to have seven
kinds of fits when he sees these. Lou, you better tell Matt Baron he's
got some 'splainin' to do. These here are illegal irons."

"What in the hell are you drivin' at, Harlan?" asked Lou. "My
brother doesn't know a goddamned thing about them irons. And
neither do any of our hands here. That includes me, peckerhead."

Doakes's face puffed up, turned rosy, as blood suffused his capillaries.

"Plain as glass," said Doakes. "That Mex worked for the Box B
and he was damned sure rustlin' Aguilar beeves. Got the goddamned
evidence right here."

"You've got shit," said Lou.

"Now, Miss Louise, I don't want to get in no argument with you. We got evidence and we got to turn it in."

"What you have, Harlan," said Lou, "is shit for brains. José is as honest as the day is long. Somebody put those running irons in the bunkhouse because they knew you, or someone with your Neander-thalian mental capacity, would be sure to find it and jump like a blind mendicant, hearing his tin cup clank, to the wrong conclusions. You don't have coin of the realm here, you've got lead sinkers in your goddamned cup."

Rudy said nothing. Dave smiled wanly.

Harlan hadn't the least idea what Lou had said.

"We'll just see about that, Miss Louise. Come on, Davey, let's get the hell out of here. Boy oh boy, rustlers. And I got 'em cold."

Lou stared at Harlan as if he was a bug. Janss looked at Rudy.

"Well, you just gonna sit there and say nothin'?"

"I don't know," said Fritch. "The man found the irons in José's kip. And we did find those three head. He even grubbed the earmarks off. Today, Hank."

"Well, shit, that don't mean nothin'," argued Janss. "José, for all his goddamned faults, was as loyal to the Box B as Matt Baron hisself, or Lou here."

"Why, thank you, Hank," said Lou. "And I saw the same things Rudy saw, but I don't put José in this business."

"Come on, Davey," said Harlan, clinging to his theory like lint on a wool blanket, as the boy dismounted. "We got to see the sheriff right away." He turned to Fritch. "You put them horses up for us, Rudy."

Rudy nodded. Janss kicked at an imaginary can. Lou smoldered fiercely, her lips pressed together tightly. She watched as Doakes and Tyler got in the police car, a '29 Plymouth, virtually a twin of Sheriff Blanchard's, and slammed both doors. A moment later, a grinning Doakes roared past them, stirring up dust.

When it was quiet, Janss sighed and took the reins of the two horses Doakes and Tyler had used.

"It don't make no sense, Lou. Rudy, what do you think?"

"Ah, it makes sense," said Fritch. "Perez took up with Bone. You just can't trust a Mexican."

"Rudy," said Lou, "you're as full of shit as a Christmas goose."

Rudy laughed good-naturedly and climbed out of the saddle.

"Looks like we got to put out those cakes, Hank. José, the innocent one, the one who does not rustle cattle, who does not own a set of running irons, is not here. Casebolt won't like it if we don't take up the slack."

"Piss on you, Rudy. You put these goddamned horses up. Lou, O.K. if I call Matt?"

"Sure," said Lou. "Call him. Tell him I'll be in this afternoon. You boys can put out the cakes and I'll tell Tom you're both hard at work."

Janss hurled the reins down on the ground and stalked across the yard toward the shack.

Rudy chuckled to himself as he watched him disappear inside the shack.

"Rudy," said Lou softly, "as a friend, you'd make a good enemy. José didn't rustle those cattle any more'n I did."

Fritch gave a Teutonic snort and Lou mounted her horse and left him standing there blinking stupidly. She heard him fart as she rode off and took it as the feeble insult he meant it to be.

Randy Connors, Ernie Aguilar's segundo, could read tracks as well as any man.

He could count too. There were eight head of cattle missing from the corral where he had penned them two days ago. He had notched their ears the day before. Now, they were gone, the gate to the corral strangely closed. That puzzled him until he began looking hard at the tracks.

He counted eight unknown hoof-tracks, another familiar to him. The eight tracks followed the cows' hooves, tracked over them. The familiar hoof-mark turned back toward the Aguilar home.

"Now if that don't beat all," Randy murmured to himself.

Bone took the bottle of whiskey from Eddie Blue Sky, swigged until he had to catch his breath.

"Ah, good," he said.

"Jack, what you do all that work for?" asked Eddie. "We don't get the cattle, we leave them good runnin' irons. We don't get nothin'."

Big Eddie and Bone rode ahead of the others, back toward their camp in the *brasada*. The body of José Perez, neck-roped, bounced along behind Ned Feather's horse. Every so often, the corpse got caught in the brush. Ned and Barney would free it up, then follow along again.

"Eddie," said Bone, "you got the brains of a horny toad. Kickapoo brains. Now, me, I'm a Lipan, and we never did sign that goddamned Treaty of Council Springs. My daddy told me that. We were southern Lipans and we lived in Mexico and raided the shit out of Texas."

"When was that?"

"Hell, I don't know. Damned near a hunnert years ago."

"My daddy never told me nothin'. He just drank all the barley whiskey he made up in Waco."

"'At's right," said Bone, feeling the whiskey glow in his guts. "So, we're raidin' Texas, see, Eddie? We got them cows from Ernie Aguilar, took 'em over to Matt Baron's. You changed them brands so's it looks like Baron done rustled Ernie's stock. We get Baron and Aguilar and Killian all fightin' like range dogs and they forget about us. We can take what we want. Blame who we want."

"We coulda sold them cows acrost the river," said Eddie.

"There's plenty more. We'll get to Mexico when it quiets down."

Eddie said nothing. Bone laughed. Eddie would think about this for weeks and still not know any more about Bone's plans than he did before.

"I ain't no Kickapoo," said Eddie, after a while. "My daddy was a Tonkawa. Said he was."

"Well, hell, Eddie, then we're all Apaches. And the goddamned white man is the fuckin' enemy."

Eddie grinned idiotically and grabbed the bottle back from Bone. It looked small in the big Indian's massive hand. He drank generously. The bottle neck disappeared in his mouth.

"Your daddy ever tell you about the Thunder Beings or Coyote or White Painted Woman, Eddie?"

"Nope," belched Eddie, as he took the bottle from his mouth. "My daddy never talked much to me. Kicked me a lot."

"Thunder Being is why I purify myself before going on these raids. You ought to do it, too. My daddy told me to always purify myself before a fight, if I could, and if not, to pray to Thunder Being."

"I ain't never heard of no Thunder Being," said Eddie. He handed the bottle back to Bone. Bone drank until his eyes watered.

"There's a bunch of them. Thunder Beings make the storms and they look out after animals, make them move at certain times. They got a lot to do with sickness, too. You can get real sick if you don't keep them in mind, talk to 'em once every so often."

"Yeah?" Eddie Blue Sky was fascinated. He had never heard such things before. "How do you talk to 'em?"

A blue heron grazed the skyline, routed from the marsh by some animal. Mourning doves flushed from a storm-shattered juniper tree ahead of the riders and their wings whistled as they knifed the air, heading northwest. Here, the grass fought with the nopal and the Spanish bayonets for dominion. It was neglected land, border land that might one day be taken over by the mesquite. Unless Matt Baron claimed it with grass.

"Inside your head, sometimes," said Bone. "Or out loud when things start to look bad. You ask 'em to make you well, guard you against bad things. Like Coyote."

"I heard about him, I reckon," said Eddie. "Plays tricks on people."

"Coyote is big trouble, Eddie. Coyote fucked up everything around. A long time ago. He's the one who made day and night, winter and summer, fall and spring. He just likes to keep you humpin', keep you off guard. He's the one who brought death to us. Wasn't no death a long time ago. A man could live forever."

"Be damned," said Eddie. "That so?"

"That's what my daddy told me. And his daddy before him. He said Coyote was bad business. But Coyote could be a white man."

"Huh?"

"That's right. Coyote can be anything and I been thinkin' that Coyote might just be Aguilar sometimes, and Ben Killian sometimes and Matt Baron, too. The sheriff. I been thinkin' a lot about that and I talked to some others, Kickapoos and Lipans and Mescaleros. They told me that they thought some white men are really Coyote."

Eddie started looking around him as if he thought Coyote might jump out at him.

"Yeah," said Bone, "I think we got us a Coyote problem here." He laughed and it sent shivers up and down Eddie Blue Sky's spine.

The two men didn't speak for a long time and they could hear the dead Mexican dragging across rocky ground, rustling through brush.

"Why did you shoot that greaser back there, Bone?" asked Eddie.

"Hell, the poach had it comin' a long time."

"You knew him?"

"He used to work for Aguilar when I did. José bossed me before he quit and went to work for Baron. Me'n Virg, and a coupla other Lipans what ain't there no more."

"I wouldn't let no Mex boss me," said Eddie.

"Well, I didn't like it none. José, he done it mostly when nobody was around. Him and me did all the outhouse work, forked shit in the barns."

"Where you takin' that dead greaser?"

"Back to Ernie Aguilar's." Bone laughed dryly. "Ernie knew I didn't like Perez none. And maybe he'll get blamed for his killin'."

"I don't savvy a hell of a lot what you're doin', Bone."

"I'm givin' back and I'm takin' back, Eddie. This was Apache land and it's about goddamned time we got it back."

"Ain't worth much. Not that mesquite brush."

"We'll get better. We'll have these white ranchers on the warpath 'gainst one another damned quick."

"You think so?" asked Eddie.

"I think so. Old Matt's goin' to think José was rustlin' cattle from Ernie Aguilar. And Ernie's goin' to think Matt rustled his cattle."

"How'd you know them cattle would be in the pen just a-waitin' when we rode up there to the Rocking A?"

"Ernie's kid, Hector. He done it for me. He don't like his old man none. 'Spec he'll be joinin' up with us." Bone looked back at the dead man. José's face was worn off from being dragged. He had long since ceased to bleed. "Yeah, Eddie, we got a lot of surprises for Killian, Baron and Aguilar. Maybe we'll get the tribes back together."

"You think so?" asked Eddie.

Bone's eyes blazed.

"Damned right," he said. "Poaches. That's all they are. White poaches. Worse'n ghosts."

"Ghosts?" asked Eddie. He knew that Bone, when he got mad, always called whites "poaches." He had wrestled with that word a long time. He knew what ghosts were, but he never thought much about them. Ghosts were for children. They were not real to Eddie Blue Sky.

Jack Bone had feared death and ghosts all his life. His father had told him that death, lying, theft and anger, as well as other sins and crimes, created disharmony. And if a person died, the ghost of the deceased must not be allowed to harm those still living.

"You ever wonder, Eddie," asked Bone, "why we Apaches don't have no Indian names no more?"

"We got Indian names."

"First names, I mean."

"No, I just figured we got civilized."

"That ain't it at all, Eddie. The fuckin' white poaches, the god-damned Mexican scalp hunters, killed so many of us that we run out of names."

"Huh?"

Bone was thinking back and he wasn't listening to himself. Just talking out loud. Talking to Eddie, but talking to himself more than anything. Remembering things his father had told him. Things his grandfather had talked about, too. The old ways. The old things that had happened. Bone hadn't paid much attention to such talk when he was a boy, but now he remembered it.

"When somebody died, or got killed," said Bone, "you didn't say their name once you buried 'em and finished up the mourning time. If somebody had a name that sounded like yours, you had to change your name."

"I never heard nothin' like that," said Eddie.

"The Apaches finally run out of names. White poaches and Mexican scalp hunters killed so many of us, we had to use Mexican names and then we run out of those and started using white names. Just so we wouldn't have no trouble with the ghosts of the dead."

"Aw, you're just makin' that up," said Eddie.

"No, I ain't," said Bone. "My daddy told me it and he got it from his daddy."

"Well, I don't know," said Eddie and Bone ignored him and took another shot of the whiskey. Whiskey was good. It made him remember things he had forgotten.

"It's all true, goddamnit," said Bone, but he didn't want to talk to Eddie about these things anymore. Eddie wouldn't understand about White Painted Woman, who had created all the animals and was the shaper of the earth. Or Killer of Enemies, who had taught the Lipan Apaches how to hunt, how to make clothes from the skins of animals, how to protect themselves from ghosts. Killer of Enemies also destroyed monsters and giants and had given them two animals that gave the Lipans much power, the buffalo and the horse.

Bone handed the bottle back to Eddie.

"When we goin' to sell off more cattle over in Mexico?" asked Eddie.

"Soon's Matt gets done with roundup. They'll be a bunch down this way next week. Let things settle down some."

"Good," said Eddie and he said no more. He just listened to that body scraping through dirt and cracking brush, sliding over Spanish bayonets and whacking into nopal. José made a hell of a sound.

12

MATT SAT AT the cherrywood desk in his den looking at the rain-smeared windowpane. Rain or no rain, they would continue the roundup. Tom Casebolt knew he'd be a little late. Lou was with him. They had saved the roughest bunch, the herd on La Plata, the range that bordered the *brasada,* until the last. They had finished the gather on the other ranches: Santa Magdelena, the largest acreage lying to the west; La Paloma, down near Ben's Lazy K; and La Golondrina, which lay like an island to the east of the house. His game leg throbbed, as it always did when the weather changed. It had stiffened up on him during the night and now it just ached like someone had hammered the bone with dozens of faint taps. Beyond, the hay barn glimmered a dull red and needles danced on its tin roof. The sound of the rain thrummed through the house, brought a soothing peace to the large room that Grace insisted on calling a "study."

This room was Matt's favorite. It had been his father's favorite, and his grandfather's favorite. There were strong memories in the room. On a rug-padded sawhorse sat his great grandpa's old Santa Fe saddle. Leaning against it, as if Jethro Baron might return at any moment, was a Kentucky rifle, made in Lancaster County, Pennsylvania, in 1810. On the wall, beyond the saddle, hung his grandfather's old Sharps, and there was the Henry 44.40 with its yellow metal receiver, its massive lever action. Underneath the Henry there was a succession of Winchesters, the latest manufactured in 1894. His father's muzzleloading plains rifle stood in a glass and teak cabinet, along with various shotguns collected over the years, including a genuine Greener that Matt's pa, Anson, had told him once belonged to Zane Grey.

Someday, Matt thought, his sons would look at things he had owned, things not handed down from father to son, but acquired since the death of Matt's father. Some of his guns were already in the room, but the ones he used every day were out in his ranch office, locked up in a plain pine cabinet. This room, however, contained part of the history of the Baron family and Matt drew comfort in knowing his lineage as a Baron man. There were no doilies in this room, no female bric-a-brac. This was a man's room and it smelled of tanned cowhide and wood polish and pipe smoke, straight bourbon whiskey and gunmetal.

He reached across his desk, took out the gnarled briar pipe, grabbed the leather tobacco pouch with his little finger and scooted it across the desk. He was just filling his bowl with Prince Albert, when Grace Baron entered the room, carrying a silver tray. The fragrance of coffee mingled with the aroma of tobacco as Matt lit his pipe. He knew he shouldn't smoke; it just aggravated that other problem he had, those stomach pains. They had started shortly after finding Jamey's body and the loss of his prize bull, Dutch Zee. Doc Emberlin had wanted to check him out, but he'd put the man off until after roundup. Sometimes it hurt like fire, and sometimes he didn't even feel it. But it worried him whenever it kicked up. It made him feel sick all over and he didn't know how long he could ignore it, or hide it from Gracie.

Grace Baron set the tray down on a table near the desk as Matt drew on his pipe and looked out the rainwashed window at the hazy silhouette of the hay barn. The rain made a dull tattoo on the pane as the wind shifted.

"I'll be glad when school's out," said Grace, a stately beauty in her new maternity outfit. She wore a skirt with the midsection cut out, an elastic band to hold it up. Her blouse was soft and dainty, flared out to cover her swollen belly.

She was twelve years younger than Matt. Her delicate hands fascinated him. They seemed like marble sculptures, perfect, soft white, yet cold as stone.

Grace Baron wore her blond hair cut short and kept it marcelled in the style of Jean Harlow. She was a slender, willowy woman, stood five feet eight in her bare feet. The haughty look was practiced, the aloofness part of her nature. When women said that Grace thought she was better than anyone else, they were not far from wrong. They did not know that the haughty expression she wore on her face hid a terrible secret she was determined to protect.

"Tomorrow?"

"Yes. Ethan wants to help you. He said he could skip school, drive down from Austin early tomorrow. Peggy and I have plans."

"And Derek?" Derek was the youngest of the Baron clan. He was attending a private school, where it was hoped his tutors would take some of the starch out of him. The school was limited to thirty children of wealthy families and was run by a stern schoolmaster named Bernard Redford Huff, who also taught history at Lamar University in Beaumont three times a week. He ran a no-nonsense operation and paid for the services of two equally stern female teachers.

"Derek will be home from Beaumont next week, Lord willing." She rattled one of the bone-china cups as she lifted it to a manageable level. She poured the cup nearly full, handed it to her husband.

"Nervous about it?" he asked.

"A little," she admitted. "Matthew, I don't know what we're going to do with that boy. He's wild."

Matt's laugh was a low rumble in his throat. A vagrant spark flashed in his left eye, but it was only a reflection from a bolt of lightning splashing the pane with a brief coating of silver.

"Casebolt will put some tame in him," he said. He laid the pipe in the large glass ashtray that nestled inside a mahogany frame. He brought the coffee cup to his lips as Grace poured her own cup half full and sat in the big leather chair nearest her husband. The light from the window made her face seem almost translucent, like the thin china of her cup and saucer. There was a thin blue vein next to her temple that Matt found fascinating. It gave her a look of delicateness that belied her pioneer sturdiness of will and character. Her soft hair caught the light, too, and spun webs of delicate filagree in her blond locks. The marcelled wave was losing some of its spunk, but it still curled over one side of her forehead like the froth on a lemon meringue pie. He liked the way she kept it curled on the ends, cut short enough that it showed her beautiful neck in all its grace and elegance. Her neck, like her hands, showed the delicacy of her flesh and bone. The veins showed beneath the skin, blue as royal blood, delicate as fine bone china.

She glowed with the life in her belly. Odd, he thought, how such a cold woman could make a man catch on fire. Yet, she could be passionate, when it suited her. That was what kept him interested. He couldn't stand her when she was cold and that usually meant she wanted something, or had been drinking. When she turned cold she refused him his privileges as a husband. There was iron in Grace and it didn't show. Only at night, when he wanted her and she stiffened him away, the taste of mint on her breath masking the whiskey smell.

Thursday was their morning to talk business. Grace went over the accounts with him, listened to him talk of things they must do to keep the ranch running at a profit. He relied on her. She kept his mind straight on business, when he thought only of the livestock and the land that sustained every head, every manjack who tended it like a garden. Ever since the Revenue Act of 1924, their Federal taxes had been brutal. The rates, applicable to net estates in excess of $100,000, had been substantially increased. Matt had had to borrow money to pay taxes in 1929. They owed creditors more than $2 million in that year, but Matt had cut the debt down to size since then. This year, 1932, would be crucial to their survival, however. Matt had been trying to expand ranching operations, without going further into debt, and so increase overall earnings. Many of the other ranchers had cut back, and it was costing them dearly. Matt's idea was to improve his stock by experimenting with better grasses, and by upgrading the cattle through breeding. Grace placed a great deal of importance on their Thursday meetings. This was the time when they could speak privately about the more complex aspects of cattle ranching. They rarely talked business at any other time.

First, they would have their coffee, then they would go over the paperwork and she would take notes.

This morning, Matt did not wait until he had drunk his coffee.

"I've been thinking of gettin' rid of that brush once and for all," he said. "Lou and I talked about it."

"And what brush is that, Matthew?" She made a point of setting her coffee cup back on the tray. She got up and went to the tall wooden file cabinet against the wall, sliding the top drawer open. She took out a notepad and a pair of sharpened Eberhard-Faber pencils.

"That big strip over at El Rincón. It's been growin'. Should have burnt it off last winter."

She knew he was talking about more than fifty thousand acres of land. The *brasada* itself slashed down through ranchland all the way from the Nueces River to the Rio Grande, crossing hundreds of thousands of acres of good pasture.

"You can't burn mesquite that easy. My granddaddy had to pull five acres of stumps when I was a little girl."

"I know," said Matt. It would cost a fortune to eradicate the Rincón of the mesquite trees once and for all.

"What did Lou say?"

"You know Lou. She'd fight the devil if you asked her to. She thinks it would be a lot of work."

"But not impossible?"

"No," said Matt.

Grace sat back down, crossed her legs. She opened her notebook. She set one pencil on the edge of Matt's desk, poised the other over the large notepad with its clean white pages. She looked, Matt thought, much the same as she had when he first saw her. Grace Lorraine Richmond had just graduated from Dallas Business School when she applied for a job on the Baron ranch. Matt had advertised for a clerk-accountant after he had taken over the Box B following his father's death in 1918. He had interviewed a dozen men, liked none of them, when Grace was ushered into his office den. She had carried a notepad and two sharpened pencils. He'd questioned her closely, learned that she was not only an accountant, but a stenographer. She wrote in Gregg's shorthand during the interview, read him back what they both had said.

"When can you come to work?" Matt had asked.

"From the questions you've asked me, I'd say we ought to get started right away."

None of the men he had interviewed had been so brash. None were as smart. He hired her on the spot and three months later, he married her. He had never regretted either decision. It wasn't until much later that he learned Grace had come from a prominent Fort Worth family. Her mother, Georgia Lee, was a Love, and her father, Kenneth Austin Richmond, was an engineer and builder, a graduate of Texas A&M.

She had come to a small house, supervised its growth over the years. From three rooms, not much more than clapboard framing them, she had hired carpenters to tear it down, build a two-story house with gabled windows, a wide front porch. Since then, they had built onto the back and sides until the house covered almost two acres of land with its L extensions on either end, giving them six bedrooms, two and a half baths, a sewing room, a large hall with a dance floor for entertainment, a dining room, large kitchen, livingroom, a den, twenty-five feet by thirty feet, an office, a sewing and quilting room, a playroom downstairs just off the side porch, storerooms, pantries and linen closets, all strategically placed within the hull of the enormous home.

"It would have been a disaster," said Grace, bucking him back to the present.

Matt nodded somberly.

It had been Matt's practice to cut some mesquite and burn off brush during the winter when the ground was wet and grass roots would not be damaged by fire. But this had been a dry winter and an even drier spring.

"That section of the *brasada* has been a thorn in the Baron family's hide for better'n a hunnerd years," said Matt. "I remember my pa makin' me and Lou and the men pile dead wood around the trunks of those mesquite trees. Then, we would fire it."

"Did it work?"

"It worked, but it was slow."

"And expensive," said Grace.

Matt smiled. After he had married Grace, he had asked her why she had wanted to work for him.

"You were the biggest rancher in the state," she told him frankly. "And the richest."

"You were a gold digger?"

"I still am," said Grace, and she had toyed with her wedding ring, held it up to the light. "I can help you run the ranch, Matthew. It's a dream I've had since I was a little girl. I spent the summers on Grandpa Love's ranch in Uvalde. He used to talk about your ranch. He admired your father very much."

"You set out to marry me?"

"How else would I get a ranch this big?" she had replied, and Matt fell in love with her all over again. "Almost two million acres. So big it would take a year or more to ride over every inch of it. A whole lot of expensive real estate."

"Yes, too expensive," said Matt, letting out a breath that was almost a sigh. "Pa bought a stump puller, oh, around 1910, I think. It was made by the Hercules Company of Centerville, Iowa, I remem-

ber. We'd find a patch of mesquite, get ahold of the biggest tree in
the stand. Then we'd attach a cable to that tree. That was our 'dead
man,' and we anchored a drum to the cable. Pa hitched two mules to
the drum. I'd whip the mules and they'd turn that drum. The winding
cable pulled out the tree slick as you please. Slower'n hell, though."

"Tedious, too, I imagine," said Grace, soothing him the way she
always did. Her voice touched him like a soft hand, made him swell
with pride. Grace made him feel like a man should feel. He loved her
for it.

"I hated it."

"You can't beat Mother Nature when she wants to hold on."

"No," said Matt. "A few years later, when pa was ailin', he bought
a couple of Buffalo Pitts traction engines. These were big old iron-
wheeled tractors. He had Larry Davis, he was just a pup then, weld
him some plows in his blacksmith's shop. The plows were heavy, had
to be. I recollect they were three-bladed moldboards."

"Grandpa Love came out and watched you clear with those tractors," said Grace. "It was all he talked about one whole summer."

"We drew quite a crowd. We'd all get behind a tractor and follow
it through the brush. We'd pull up and stack the mesquite roots. They
used those to run those tractors, burned 'em to make steam. Those
tractors weighed ten tons apiece and I'd see 'em strain and puff, their
slick iron wheels slipping on the mesquite. They were always breaking
down."

"Not very efficient."

"When Pa died, I bought two Twin City gasoline tractors. They
didn't break down as much and were easier to run. I think now we
should buy some of those Ford iron-wheeled four-cylinder tractors.
What do they call them?"

"Fordsons," said Grace immediately. "They're expensive. You'd
have to buy plows, too. Larry told me he'd never build another
three-bladed moldboard."

Matt laughed.

"Look into it, will you? See what's the best price you can get."

"Matthew, before we buy tractors, don't you think we ought to
find out who actually owns El Rincón? Seems to me that these were
always disputed lands."

Matt frowned. Grace was right, of course. That corner of the
brasada had always been a no-man's land. That was why it had grown

so much. Nobody claimed responsibility and everyone had been too busy to check out who owned what.

"Will you check the deeds, Gracie?"

Grace scribbled a flurry of notes on her pad. When she was finished, she looked over at her husband.

"You didn't sleep well last night," she said. "You were moaning."

"Moaning?"

"Almost screaming."

"Naw," he said.

"What's wrong, Matthew? I've noticed that sometimes you bend over as if you're in pain and when you straighten up, your face is drawn up hard as a prune pit and sweat breaking out on your forehead."

"I don't know what you're talkin' about," he said quickly.

"Should I buy more Milk of Magnesia?" she said, and he knew that she knew about his taking slugs of that chalky-tasting medicine.

"Sometimes my stomach kicks up," he said.

"Doctor Emberlin wants you to have a physical," she said. "You should. Shall I make an appointment?" She poised her pencil over the pad.

"I'll get to it," he said.

She leaned toward him.

"When?" she asked.

"Gracie, sometimes you're so damned practical it plumb galls me."

"One of us has to be," she said, persistent as a cowtick behind a calf's ear.

"What about those deeds?" he asked, knowing she had the upper hand.

"I've already looked them up," she replied. He had often thought she could read his mind. She often did things before he even asked her to, and it prickled him because she was so efficient when he might have been worrying over something for days before he said anything about it. How did she do it? She was positively uncanny sometimes.

"And?"

"It appears we may own that slough, or a portion of it. It will take a surveyor to determine the exact boundaries. The mesquite has grown so much, no one's been in there since 1920 or so, to determine which part is Box B, Rocking A or Lazy K land. As for El Rincón, it appears we do not own it."

"Does anyone?" he asked.

"I'm going into the courthouse today to find out for sure."

"Gracie, I don't know what I'd do without you. This damned legal stuff. I don't understand it."

"I do," she said softly and he took in a breath and held it like wine in the mouth. Grace understood it all. She kept him free to do what he liked to do. The books, the accounts, the legal documents, he hated all of it, and Gracie thrived on it like the Mexicans on corn and wheat flour.

"Good. That damned corner. Nobody wants it, but if we don't do something, it might eat us up."

"Do you remember what you told me when you first took me out and showed me the *brasada?*"

"That was a long time ago. I wanted to show you what wild was."

"You told me that until you went into the *brasada,* you thought you owned the land."

"And after I saw it, I said the land really owns us," he finished.

"Do you want me to hire a surveyor?" she asked.

A sudden pain gripped Matt's innards, fastened on his abdomen like the steel jaws of a wolf trap. He rode it out, refusing to double over and grit his teeth.

"No, not yet," he said, as the pain passed. "First, I'd like to know if Ernie or Ben own any of that corner. If they don't, we may have to file on it."

Matt recovered from the pain quickly. He tapped his fingers on the desk to keep them from trembling.

But Grace noticed the beads of sweat that broke out on his forehead. She rose from her chair and dropped her pad and pencil on the desk. She came around behind him, put her arms around his shoulders.

"Matthew," she said. "Do you want something for the pain? We have some Bayer's. We're all out of Bromo."

"No," he said. "It's done passed."

"I'm calling Doc Emberlin this morning, Matthew."

"Next week," he pleaded. "I want to take Ethan out to check the grass roots tomorrow."

Grace sighed. She began to rub the sweat on his forehead, smoothing it into his skin. She was glad he could not see her face. There was fear in her eyes, she knew, because she was afraid, terribly afraid.

But Matt knew.

Grace's hand trembled against his forehead. It began to shake so hard, he reached up and enclosed it in his own. He squeezed it gently, trying to reassure her.

And now, with everything else, there was this between them, this mystery that both of them feared.

Matt was superstitious. If he went to Doc Emberlin, he might find something bad wrong with him. If he stayed away long enough, maybe whatever was hurting him would cure itself.

Matt put away his pipe and fished his pack of Camels out of his shirt pocket. He would not light a cigarette until Grace had left the room, but this was his way of telling her that the business meeting was over and that he wanted to be alone.

The rain whipped against the window and Grace took her hand away from his forehead. She gathered up her notes, tore off the top sheet, set it on the coffee tray. Later she would sit at her own rolltop desk upstairs and make her telephone calls. Only after Matt had left the study would she return to dust and add to the files for next week's meeting.

"I'm worried about you, Matthew," she said, as she glided toward the door.

Not so cold now, he thought. But she could be cold. At night, when he wanted her. Some mornings. Mornings, she was always cold.

The door closed and he was alone again. He looked out the window at the gray rain, the needles dancing wildly on the barn's tin roof.

What was it his father, Anson, had said? "If it ain't broke, don't fix it."

As long as Matt could sit a saddle, swing an axe, rope a steer, there was nothing broke. If he had an ulcer, as he believed, it would go away.

He got up from the desk slowly. Time to go. Like always, everything important had to wait until after roundup. It looked to be a long, hard week. Harlan Doakes and Dave Tyler hadn't found a damned thing in a month of looking, and he'd had to pull all the hands off Santa Magdalena for this last gather on La Paloma. He had saved this one for last, in hopes that they might run into Bone and his bunch. Maybe, he thought, Bone had moved on, gone somewhere else. The moment he thought it, he knew it wasn't true. Bone had something in mind. And maybe he was in with Aguilar. It sure looked that way. Well, if so, Aguilar had made a poor choice. Matt took his favorite Winchester, a '94, from the gun case, scooped a handful of shells from the drawer and stuffed them in his pants pocket. Ever since Jamey had been killed, every man on the Box B carried some kind of weapon. Matt had given orders to shoot Bone on sight.

Roy Blanchard be damned. No use trying to lasso a mad dog.

13

HECTOR SLIPPED OUT of the house before dawn, creeping through the darkness on soundless feet. The air was heavy, smelled of rain. He froze at the sound of his father's voice calling him inside the house.

"Hector. *Levantasé!*"

The boy smiled in the dark as he hugged a corner of the house. In the east, the sky began to open. A pale light bled through the rent in the dark fabric. He saw the high, thick clouds, then. He was sure it was going to rain.

"Where is that boy?" called his father. "Elena."

Muffled voices from inside the house. His mother, then his sister. Lamps flickered with flame, painting one window, then another, with orange smears, glittering yellow scrawls.

Hector edged around the back corner of the house, dashed across the yard toward the barn. His heart thumped, drowning out the sound of his boots thudding on the ground. He reached the barn, stopped short, his breathing hard and ragged. Someone inside the house lit another lamp. The lamp in his sister Alicia's room flared bright, then dimmed as she turned down the wick. A cowbell clanked out in the pasture. He heard the murmurs of the chickens in the chicken house, faint clucks that told him they were stirring on their shit-spattered roosts. He saw his mother as the lamp in the kitchen began to glow.

He stood there, panting, trying to quell the rush of fear that drenched his nerves.

He did not want to see the man who pretended to be his father. Hector was sick and tired of him, but more than that, he was curious about the man his father kept speaking about in whispers. Bone. He was in the *brasada* and his father was afraid of him. That was enough to stir Hector's curiosity, roil his thoughts into a bubbling broth of conjecture. That was why he had ridden over there the other day, waited around until Bone rode out of the *brasada*. They had talked, but Bone had not told him much. He had wanted a few head of cattle. Hector had run them into the corral and now they were gone. Taken where? And why?

Who was Bone and why was his father afraid of him? He had overheard only snatches of conversation between his mother and father and when they knew he was near they fell silent, their faces stiff and blank as cardboard.

Hector knew that Bone had once worked for the Rocking A. He remembered him vaguely. Now, Bone was back and his father was angry. Tough aggies. Hector was glad he'd put the cattle up for Bone and that Bone had taken them. It was one more way to express his anger at Ernesto for keeping secrets from him. Well, he had a hunch who his real father was, and he had made up his mind to find out once and for all.

One thing sure. Hector did not want to live with a man who was not his real father. He would rather live with Bone. There was something exciting about a man who lived in the *brasada* and had some kind of strange power over Ernesto Aguilar.

Hector had made up his mind. He was going to do something and if it made Ernesto angry, then it would be worth it. His hatred had gone so deep he fed on it, devoured it as if it was a necessary sacrament.

There would be more hog butchering today, and Hector could not face another morning like the past two. His stomach bucked at the thought of another long day spent slaughtering and dressing out hogs.

Hector Aguilar harbored secrets like most boys his age collected marbles. And he toyed with his secrets, stacked them, put them in rows, mixed them up, and hid them in secret pockets of his mind. He loaded his daydreams with secrets and he spun fantasies from the mixture, spun them with the dark coils of shadows, threaded them with sombre strands gathered from wide-awake and sleeping night-mares.

At fourteen, Hector was a very troubled young man. He brooded in his room instead of studying, and he pretended he was invisible when he followed the spoor of suspicion along his own private trail of fears. He had long suspected that Ernesto Aguilar was not his real father. He thought, from things he had overheard, or imagined, that Ben Killian was his real father. He kept these thoughts to himself, and at times, they rambled and became tangled into Gordian knots that he could not separate.

The smell of butchered hogs was still in his nostrils. The images of death lingered long after the gutted hogs, their bellies slit so surgically neat, had drained and their hollow corpses been cut down from the trees. He still smelled the acrid stench of burning bristles and the stomach-wrenching stink of hog intestines as the men stripped them of shit and dropped them like deflated bicycle inner-tubes into an empty tub, later to be boiled and cleaned and stuffed with sausage. He could still see the dead hogs hanging from the trees in the clearing where they were slaughtered by Paco Velez, who shot them between the eyes with a .22 single shot. The smell, Hector could not rid himself of the smell, though he drank RC Cola and Orange Crush and scrubbed his face until it was raw and blew his nose until it bled.

In the silence of morning and in the fog, Paco shot the pigs and the men came in with their long knives, sharpened like razors stropped to a fine edge, and cut their throats. The live pigs squealed and screamed like children, and they snorted and grunted in fear until the sounds mangled Hector's senses and he wanted to yell at his father to stop the killing, stop killing the children, stop cutting them to pieces and hanging them from the trees like hideous Christmas-tree ornaments. But Hector held his tongue and watched it all like a dreamer standing on the edge of his own nightmare and he couldn't eat sausage anymore because he couldn't stop thinking of those three-hundred-pound hogs, all dead and cut open, the hairs boiled from their hides, hanging there like fat children, turning slowly on the manila ropes and the smell of pigshit and boiled hog bristles making him sick, sick as a dog, sick with all of it, and sick inside and way inside, in his mind and in his bones and belly and brains.

Hector slipped inside the barn. Fog was beginning to form in the meadows, along the creek. The sky paled even more and he adjusted his eyes to the dimness as he sought his horse. He found the little mare, Ginger, saddled her, listening for any alien sound. When he was finished, he cautiously led the horse from the barn. The eastern sky was aflame and he knew he had to hurry.

Voices from the back porch drew his attention.

Hector's mother was already at work, making sausage with his sister, Alicia. He heard his father clumping through the large adobe brick and frame house, with its Spanish tile roof covering two stories and fourteen rooms, calling his name. The stupid bastard! As he led the horse past the chicken house he could still hear his mother and sister on the back porch, banging the washtubs, chattering like a pair of magpies.

Hector started to mount Ginger, when his blood froze. A rooster crowed not five feet away. Hector felt the fear rush through him like a cool fire. He turned, saw the banty rooster flapping its wings. *Whapwhapwhapwhapwhap!*

"You bastard," cursed Hector.

He stood there, watching The General, his right hand clenching and unclenching. He felt like wringing the rooster's neck.

The General herded his flock of four bantam hens into the pigpen, standing guard as each ducked under the bottom rail of the fence. The hens started for the nearest trough, but The General scooted under the rail and headed them off. His golden eyes widened and his neck feathers bristled. He strutted around them until they were again aware of his domination. Then, he led them to the trough, his feathers once more sleeked down flat, his gold epaulets brilliant in the sun. He cocked his head, fixed a single blaring eye on the caked mud around the pig feeder. He found pieces of corn, flakes of shorts, wheat chaff, which he pointed out to his concubines. The hens began to feed on the morsels their chief diligently discovered for them. The hens scratched the mud clods and clucked contentedly. The General strutted around them, ever on guard lest one of the Poland China hogs rouse from its sleep and lumber over to the bantams' dining table. After a few moments, The General flapped his wings and hopped up on one side of the trough for a more commanding view of the pen. He froze for a moment, a gaudy weathervane in the breezeless summer air.

Hector mounted Ginger and rode off toward the Lazy K, his heart still pumping wild in his chest, little tremors of fear still coursing through his veins.

An hour later, the rent in the sky disappeared and it began to rain.

* * *

The La Plata range lay against the southwesternmost border of the Baron ranch holdings. It covered nearly three hundred thousand acres of grassland, fed by meandering creeks and the spastic rainfall. Through its southern edge ran the thick *brasada* that came to a halt at El Rincón, the corner where the Box B, the Rocking A and the Lazy K all came together. It was the oldest of the Baron spreads and the main ranch compound consisted of a crumbling adobe house, a newer, frame bunkhouse, a barn made of both adobe and pine, and several holding corrals and loading chutes.

Tom Casebolt had been there since early morning, having driven forty horses in from Santa Magdalena, helped by Billy Bob Letterman, Louise Baron and Umberto Iglesias. They were met by Troy Davis and Hank Janss, who had come in the night before from two line camps at opposite ends of La Plata. Several other hands had come in by truck from the other ranches during the night. It had been raining in brief spurts since before dawn and was raining still, although not so heavily. It was a sporadic hot, dripping, spattering rain that did little good for the land.

Rudy Fritch rode in, grumbling in a thick German accent about the weather, his slicker torn in a half dozen places by brush. Casebolt, Lou and Billy Bob ran the horses into the barn, where Hank and Troy were already forking hay and breaking out the saddles for the day's ride. The other hands were currying the horses, gentling down the skittery ones. They spoke to the animals and among themselves in low, gruff voices.

Rudolpho Algodon, whom the hands called "Cotton" to keep from confusing his first name with Fritch's, and Alberto Horcasitas drove up in the Reo, which had been converted to a chuckwagon. Carpenters had constructed a small boxlike structure on the bed of the truck. The little house had four small windows, a tin smokestack sticking up from the sloping, shingled roof. Heavy crates lined the truck bed, loaded with utensils and food staples. The two cooks looked sleepy.

A few minutes later, Matt Baron drove up, hauling a stock trailer and two working horses behind his '29 Ford pickup. Casebolt was there before Matt got out of the seat, unbuckling the hasp on the trailer. He whistled to Janss and Fritch.

Matt got out of the truck slowly. He walked kink-legged around to the back of the trailer.

"Is Ethan coming?" Lou asked.

"He got his belly full last week," said Matt. "Casebolt ran him so ragged his butt's got saddle sores."

Tom laughed. Lou did not. She had her own ideas about succession, the duties passed down from father to son. Ethan, as the eldest of Matt's children, should be working harder than any of them.

"If he's not careful," she said to her brother, "Derek's going to pass him on the far turn. Ain't that right, Tom?"

"Derek's a pistol, all right," said Casebolt.

Lou let the matter rest there. She knew she had made her point with Matt. Ethan was soft. He had no feeling for the land, the cattle. Not like Derek. The trouble with Derek was that everything came easy to him. He could learn in a day what took most men a year and he could learn in a year what many men couldn't learn in a lifetime.

"Help you unload, Matt?" Lou asked.

"I'll get it." He paused, then looked at his sister. "Ethan will make his own way," he said, so softly only she could hear it.

"I know he will," she said. She bit her tongue to keep from saying more. She wanted to tell Matt that Ethan would never make a rancher. Sometimes she wished that she had married and had children, but when she saw the grief the youngsters visited on their parents, she was not sorry she had remained a spinster. Still, she wished she had a son like Derek, or Ethan, even. Matt was the last of his breed, and she wanted him to have someone to carry on in the Baron tradition.

Matt took the bolt out of the eye running through the hasp, pulled the trailer door wide. The horses thumped their rumps against the sides as they shifted the weight on their hind hooves.

"Which one you wanta ride, Matt?" asked Casebolt.

"Better saddle up Dingus, Tom." Dingus was a sorrel gelding with a pair of white stockings up front, a small star on his head just above his eyes. The horse had good bottom, was quick in rough country. He was only fifteen and a half hands high, with a clipped mane and bobbed tail to keep him from getting tangled up in brush. The other horse, a muddy grulla mare, Matt called Smoke.

"Get Matt's saddle out of the truck, Hank," ordered Casebolt. "Rudy, you take the mare over to the barn, grain her."

"Right, boss," said Rudy. Janss was already opening the pickup door on the passenger side.

The pickup was spattered with rain-pelted dirt. It had stopped raining forty minutes before. But Matt knew it would hit them again within the hour. Lou and the men cast no shadows under the dark sky. Matt took in everything with a sweeping glance.

"Any word on José, Matt?" Hank asked.

"Blanchard couldn't find shit in a pigsty."

"Mighty peculiar."

"There's a lot of peculiar goin' around," said Matt. When Hank finished saddling the gelding, Matt checked the cinches.

"Whenever you're ready, Captain," said Tom.

"You got the ground laid out, Tom?"

Casebolt jerked a sack of Durham from his pocket, built a smoke. During roundup, the foreman didn't use tailor-mades. They got sweaty and crumpled.

"We work the middle, to El Rincón, two bunches a-circlin', then cross back and forth in big X's 'twixt the corners. Chuckwagon's going out when you give the word."

"Reps here?"

"No, and I ain't gonna wait for 'em. Ernie and Ben both know we're workin' La Plata."

"Everyone packin' rifles?"

"Yeah. Even your sis."

Lou grinned.

"Well," said Matt, "Lou's pretty salty."

"Salty as corned beef hash," said Tom.

"Peppery, too," said Matt, winking at Louise. She had boxed his ears more than once when they were growing up and she had cold-cocked many a lad who thought she was easy pickin's.

"You make me sound like something on the chuckwagon," said Lou.

Casebolt laughed. It was a good way to start a day that was going to be all bad and then get worse. They'd probably all be cussing each other before the sun set.

Matt walked over to the pickup, reached in for his gunbelt and slicker. He girded his waist, buckled up. A Colt .45 Peacemaker jutted from the hand-tooled leather holster. He'd had a gunsmith reblue the barrel and cylinder, but he hated to do it. It was like wiping a man's name off a slate. He jerked the Winchester rifle from behind the seat, rammed it into the boot attached to his saddle.

"What you got on Daddy's old Colt for?" asked Lou.

"Snakes," said Matt, without mirth.

"I'll keep a lookout," said Lou.

Matt drew a breath. Nothing felt right to him. His leg was hurting from the long drive over to La Plata and he'd drunk a quart of Bromo Seltzer that morning. His gut felt as if it was lined with barbed wire. He had been puzzling over José Perez ever since Sheriff Blanchard had called him a few days before. José used to work for Aguilar, but he'd been a loyal line rider for a half dozen years. His family knew nothing of his disappearance. His wife was like a stone, holding back her worry, but Matt knew she was hurting. He had assured her that José was on the payroll for as long as he was missing. But, he knew, that was little comfort to Felicita Perez and their five children.

"Boss?" asked Casebolt.

Matt looked at his foreman.

"We're ready."

"Let's get to gettin', then, Tom." Matt pulled on his slicker, smoothed it around the Colt.

Tom made a sign to Algodon. The cook got in the truck and started it up. The engine shook the cab, jiggled the bed as it lumbered into motion.

"They know where to go," said Tom, grabbing up his reins. "We'll meet 'em at Sand Creek 'round noon. We should end up at El Rincón by this evenin'."

A quail piped from a distant lookout perch and Lou and the men mounted their horses. Frogs growled and belched from all around. Matt swung up into the saddle with difficulty. He almost groaned as the sudden pain in his leg fought to overpower the pain in his gut. The slicker rasped a loud whisper as he slipped the tail over the cantle.

Lou noticed her brother wince, but said nothing. Now was not the time or place. But she had something to worry about the rest of the day besides cows in the brush.

The riders fanned out in pairs, flanked the tracks of the chuckwagon. Matt and Tom rode together, headed toward the first waterhole. Lou rode with the rest of the men, even though none would have thought less of her had she ridden with her brother. There wasn't a hand on the Box B who didn't know that Lou pulled her own weight and did her work better than most men. A light rain began to pepper their faces, tattoo their hats.

A half hour later, Casebolt came across a dead cow wearing a Box B brand. The animal had already begun to swell and stink. Its mouth gaped open and the flies had already discovered a feeding ground in its maw.

Tom slid out of the saddle so quick, Matt didn't notice him until he walked up to the dead cow and circled it. He bent down and looked into its fly-swarmed mouth. He picked up a stick and pried its jaws apart, peered at the swollen tongue.

"I'd say strychnine," he said to Matt.

Matt's jaw hardened.

"I'd say Bone," Baron said softly.

Paco Valez swore.

"Who in hell is it?" he asked Mendoza, who had a bad case of the shakes. Rafael Mendoza was one of the riders who was supposed to rep the Rocking A at La Plata. The other wrangler, Alfonso Serrano, had crossed himself a dozen times since Perez had come out to the shed where Ernesto Aguilar's old town car was parked.

Alfonso's flea-bitten dog, Carrajo, was slinking around the shed sheepish as a thief. Paco lunged at the dog, shooing it away.

"I don't know," said Mendoza. "He don' have no face."

"*Jesus, Mari'*," muttered Serrano. Alfonso crossed himself again.

Paco squatted down to look at the corpse. The body was stretched out, flat on its back, snug against the front wheels of the Hudson.

"Somebody," he said in Spanish, "went to a lot of trouble here."

Mendoza was right. The dead man was faceless. The nose was gone, the lips. There were empty sockets where the eyes had been. Paco stood up, kicked one of the legs.

"Stiff," he said.

"He stinks like a skunk," said Mendoza. "The man was dragged in here. He does not hardly have no neck no more."

"*Jesus Cristo*," said Serrano.

Paco, annoyed, turned to his suffering hand.

"*Vete, Alfonso, a la casa. Digale a Señor Aguilar que paso' aqui. Digale a el que necesita a venir pronto.*"

"*Si, Paco. Me voy.*"

Serrano ran from the shed toward the house, the tail of his slicker flapping behind him.

"The body is not wet," said Paco to himself. It was raining outside. The men should have left for La Plata an hour ago.

"We were afraid when we saw him," said Mendoza. "We did not know who he was."

The wrangler had ridden all the way out to the hog pens, where Paco and some men were cutting out the hogs to be butchered that morning. Wisely, he had not spoken in front of the other men. So far, only three of them knew about the dead man. It was not a good thing, this. Ernie would not like it, but he had to know.

"Why did you come in here?" asked Velez.

"That dog of Alfonso's. He was barking. Alfonso, he wanted to see what was in here."

Paco said nothing. He thought this was a funny place to put a dead man. Ernie had not driven the Hudson in a long time. Paco wondered why he did not sell it. Ernie was always washing it, even though he never drove it. He washed it at least once a month, and he wouldn't let anyone help him. He just came out to the shed by himself with a bucket and soap and wax. He kept it waxed and Paco could see the dust on the hood. Ernie did not wash it so much during roundup and hog butchering. But the car looked like it had been washed recently. And waxed.

"They are coming," said Rafael Mendoza.

"I hear them. You keep that goddamned dog of Alfonso's out of here."

"I would like to shoot it," said Rafael.

"Alfonso would shoot you."

Ernie entered the shed. He was dressed in his old clothes, ready to butcher hogs. He wore the Big Boy overalls, the old Sears & Roebuck boots, a bandanna around his neck, another dripping from his back pocket. He had on the tattered straw hat, speckled with dried hog blood.

Alfonso wore a look of perpetual sadness and suffering on his face.

"You put that dog up," Paco told him.

"*Si, Paco,*" said Alfonso obediently.

"What is it you found?" asked Ernie.

Paco pointed to the body. He watched as Ernie squinted, froze.

"Who is it?"

"We do not know," said Velez.

"He does not have a face," said Rafael.

Ernie stepped closer to the body. Paco saw his shoulders shudder as if he was trying to keep from vomiting. Ernie did not move for several seconds.

Then, the rancher turned and looked at Paco.

"What are these men doing here? Are they not to be at La Plata?"

"*Sí, Patron,*" said Paco.

"I don't want them to say anything about this, Paco."

"They will not talk of it."

"Send them to the Box B. Right away."

Paco barked orders to both men in Spanish. Rafael and Alfonso left the shed as if they had been banished from a forbidden place.

"What do you want me to do, Ernie?"

"I—I will take care of it, Paco. Go. You go to the butchering. I—I will be there later."

"Are you going to call the sheriff?"

"No," said Ernie quickly. "No. I do not want anyone to know about this."

"What will you do?"

"Bury him."

"Do you know who he is?" asked Paco.

"No."

"Or who put him in here?"

"Paco, you ask too many questions. Go."

Paco turned his hands palms up in a gesture of helplessness. But, he didn't leave.

"There is a shovel in the barn, and some lime," he said. "And the ground is very soft around that old well we closed up last summer."

"Yes, yes. Go, Paco."

Paco turned to leave.

"Have you seen Hector?" asked Ernie.

"No," said Velez.

"That bastard," Ernie said.

Paco left without another word. He sure didn't feel like butchering hogs this day. He could not drive from his mind the picture of that faceless man, snug against the wheels of the old Hudson, staring sightless into eternity.

Paco headed toward the bunkhouse to wash his hands. He felt contaminated. He heard Ernie cursing inside the shed. He sounded very angry in two languages.

14

———

LUKE KILLIAN MOPPED his lean, chiseled face, sopping up fresh rainwater and sweat in his bandanna. He rode a rock-jawed gelding full of morning ginger. The damned horse had tried to run out from under him twice, had balked at every stray calf, every wall-eyed steer that had come bucking through the brush.

"You miserable sonofabitch," Luke growled. The horse, which everyone called No Balls, snorted as Luke pulled on the reins, pulling the bit hard up against the back of its tongue.

"Luke," one of the hands called. "Cut that brindle calf out of the brush 'fore he gets down in the slough."

"Shorty, cut it out yourself. No Balls is trying to swallow me for breakfast."

It had been that way all morning. In and out of the thick brush that bordered both sides of a large slough, thick with mist and slippery with mud. The rain, light as it was, made it worse. Noble, for that was the horse's actual name, didn't like either surprise or mystery. The gelding's hocks were covered with wet clay, its hooves packed tight with swamp mud.

Shorty C rode up, swatted No Balls on the rump with a coil of manila rope. The gelding bunched its haunch muscles and bounded four feet forward. Luke's back whipped as he was thrown off balance. He lurched to sit straight and dragged the reins hard toward him. The horse jerked to a jolting halt. Luke almost flew between its ears.

The saddlehorn dug into his gut with the force of a ten-pound maul.

Luke wheezed as the wind emptied from his lungs.

Shorty laughed.

"You short-legged little peckerhead," said Luke as he put a bow in the horse's neck with the bit.

"You can kid me about bein' short, Luke," said Shorty amiably, "but us little hombres is the last to be rained on."

"Uh-huh," said Luke as he brought No Balls under control. "And, come a flash flood, you're the first ones to drown too."

Luke Killian was a tall young man, dark-haired, with hazel eyes. He was lean and lanky, with a devilishly handsome face, long eyelashes, smooth features, a strong straight nose that was more Baron than Killian. Some said he looked like his dead mother, while others said he resembled Matt Baron as a boy.

They were working the circle on the left flank of the roundup herd. Ben Killian was somewhere up ahead riding toward them. Charlie Stone and Harvey Leeds were on the bottom end of the circle, taking the cows and calves up to the herd. Jim Bellaugh, Reed Packer and Warren Finnerty were holding the herd for the tally, while on the other side, a bunch of men were riding circle. Some of the men were cutting the strays back into the main herd.

For the past three days Luke's bunch had been riding this last stretch of country for the most elusive cattle on the Lazy K range.

That morning, Luke and Shorty had been dropped off a mile apart by Charlie Stone, who was leading the drive. But the cattle were thick in the brush, feeding on lush grass that grew in the bottoms and Shorty had come up to help Luke get them all out. Their faded yellow slickers and leather chaps were shiny with rain, their hats soggy wet.

"Settle down," said Luke to No Balls.

"You ready?" asked Shorty. "I saw four cows with calves down yonder."

"I saw 'em too, and so did this pea-brained iron-mouthed sonofabitch."

"Luke, your daddy would tan your hide to hear you call a good horse anything but Sweetie Pie."

"My daddy wouldn't get in but one lick."

"Well, here he comes now and he don't look like sunshine."

Luke looked up and saw his father riding toward them. Ben's face was dark and glowering as the rain-spitting clouds overhead. He wove his horse through the chaparral, across patches of glistening grass, around clusters of nopal and clumps of prickly pear.

Ben's temper had been as short as a two-second fuse since Luke had gotten out of jail. He'd been on Luke's back like cockleburrs on a spaniel's ears. Luke complained that he always seemed to draw bad horses on this gather. His griping did not sit well with his father. One night at chuck, Ben told Luke that whatever horse he picked was purely the right choice for his contrary nature.

"You're always on the short end of the stick, Luke," said Ben. "That's because you want everything easy."

"Who broke these horses, Dad? Warren Finnerty?"

"They're broke and broke good. You're the one ain't broke," said Ben.

"I broke them horses," said Lazurus "Ike" Ikert. "They're all good cowponies. Gentle as lambs."

"Yeah," said Luke angrily, "I know how you break horses, Ike. With a cuss and a hickory stick."

"You lay off Ike," said Ben. "A horse won't work for a man who don't work him."

"Luke," said Ike, "you'd gripe if somebody gave you a new rocking chair to ride."

It had been that way ever since Luke had come home from the Baronsville jail. Ben had been keeping the rope short and snubbed up hard. Luke would rather be in town shooting pool or sparking that gal he'd met up in San Angelo a few months ago. Trouble seemed to follow him like his shadow. The gal had been married and Luke had gotten caught by her husband. But Luke knew that if he'd stuck around, she would have run off with him. Now, though, Ben was making him work off the money he'd "borrowed" and it was like paying for a dead mule as far as Luke was concerned.

"Oh, shit," said Luke, and thrummed spurs in No Balls's flanks. "Let's get them cows outta there, Shorty."

Shorty Coots, all muscle, bowlegged as a claw-foot andiron, with a mop of russet hair that appeared to have been electrocuted continually since birth, was twenty-five, but looked forty. He had sad, droopy eyes and deep lines in his face. The men teased him because he was no bigger than a minute, but he pulled his own weight. Shorty was an expert powderman, and Ben Killian said he was the best all-around cowhand he had, and that only made the men rag him harder. Shorty also had a chip on his shoulder that was twice his size. Today, thought Luke, he was in a fairly good mood.

"You better hold up, Luke. Your daddy's giving you the high sign."

Luke watched his father prod his mount into a canter.

"He's sure in some kind of hurry," Luke admitted.

Ben closed the distance. His gray slicker flapped at his legs. Shorty and Luke sidled their horses, held them in check.

"Luke," said Ben as he halted Sombra, a steeldust gray, mottled with shadowy dark circles, "what in hell are you doing to Noble there?"

"Pop, I'm tryin' to get him to go down there in the slough and not try to rub me off on ever' danged tree he passes."

"Well, all you're doing is making his mouth sore. You give him his head and he'll work cows."

Luke snorted. Ben fixed his oldest son with a look that could wilt turnip greens.

"Shorty, what in hell are you doing?" asked Ben. "You got your thumb up your butt?"

"I was trying' to help Luke get old No Balls off a balk," said Coots.

"Well, the two of you are holding up this drive. And who's that following you?"

Luke and Shorty twisted in their saddles, looked back over their shoulders. Several hundred yards away, a lone rider walked his horse back and forth as if holding back.

"Beats the crap out of me," said Coots.

Luke squinted. In the drizzle, he could not make out the rider clearly, or identify the horse.

"Not anyone I know," said Luke, with a lazy shrug.

"Maybe one of the Box B reps," said Shorty.

"Well, you boys go on and finish up," said Ben. His whiskey breath washed over Luke. "I'll ride over there and see who we've got among us."

"Might be a Rocking A rider," offered Luke, as he glanced once more at the restless rider. "That horse looks some familiar."

Ben said nothing as he reined his horse past his son and started toward the unidentified man. Luke put spurs to Noble's flanks and Shorty hung his coiled rope on the saddle horn and headed for the slough.

Luke knew what Shorty was doing. He would drive the cattle out in the open. No Balls just might start working if Luke could keep him out of the mud.

"Thanks, Shorty," Luke called.

"Don't get wet," Shorty replied.

Luke laughed. No Balls stepped out in a stately walk along the edge of the brush. He snorted a couple of times, but didn't try to perform any circus acrobatics.

"Hold up there," called Ben as he approached the mysterious rider.

The man stopped pacing his horse and waited.

Ben rode up, tilted his hat back on his head as he halted his horse.

"You from Rocking A?" the rancher asked.

Hector Aguilar nodded, looked up nervously at Killian. Ben saw his face for the first time.

"Heck, that you?"

"Yes sir," said Hector.

"You repping for your papa?"

"No sir."

Hector fidgeted in his saddle. He squirmed against the cantle, shifted his buttocks from side to side. He looked everywhere but straight at Killian.

"Why'd you ride all the way over here in the rain?"

"I dunno."

"Well, we're smack dab in the middle of roundup. You go on back home, hear?"

"No sir. I gotta talk to you."

Ben rubbed the stub of his finger against the top of the saddlehorn. He heard Luke and Shorty yelling at cows down in the slough. A cow bawled, ragged, throaty.

"What about?" asked Ben.

"I—it's hard."

"Well, son, I can't help you none. What you got in your craw is yours 'til you spit it out."

"I reckon."

Ben waited a few minutes, watching the boy. He looked some like Elena. Had her coloring. His face was soft and boyish, his hair some lighter. A strange boy. Acting strange, too.

"Well, son, I ain't got all day," said Ben.

"No sir. Well, I—I just wanted to ask you something."

"Go right ahead."

Hector swallowed. He opened his mouth, but no sound came out. He looked as if he wanted to ride away.

"Spit it out, Heck, goddamnit."

Hector's eyes widened in a wild flare. He looked, then, straight at Ben, and swallowed again. When he spoke, his words rushed out in a high-pitched squeak.

"I wanted to ask you, sir, if you were my real father."

"Are you asking me that?"

"Yes sir."

"What ever gave you that notion, Heck?"

"Things my mama said. Things my papa, Ernie, things he said too. A long time ago."

"What things?"

"Just things," said Hector.

"Well, now, that don't tell us much, does it?"

"I know, though."

"You know what?"

"That you're my real father. I've seen the way my mama looks at you. I know you were, were sweet on her before Ernie."

"Well now, that don't mean nothin'."

"It does to me. I've been figuring when I was born and when you and mama were courting and my papa, Ernie, he thinks I'm your son, too. And I asked Mama about it and she looked at me real funny."

"Son, all that don't amount to a hill of *frijole* beans. You're just makin' something out of nothin'."

"No sir, I'm not. I got to know. I got to know now."

Ben drew in a deep sighing breath. The rain made a light drumming sound on his hat, a sputtering whisper on his slicker.

Killian had wondered, at the time Hector was born, if he might be the boy's father. And, at times, he had sensed that Elena had wanted to talk to him about something important, something deeply urgent. But, like other matters in his past, he had buried the thoughts, had turned them into foolish fancies. Now, the notion had arisen again. This boy, Ernie and Elena's boy, had brought up the past, had opened an old wound.

"Why do you want to know something you can't do nothin' about, son?"

"I know it's true. I—I just can't live with it anymore. Ernie is not my real father."

"Heck, you're treadin' on dangerous ground. You could hurt your mother."

"I don't care," snapped Hector. "I'm tired of being lied to."

"Nobody lied to you."

"Are you my father, Mister Killian?"

Ben tasted rainwater on his lips. He fixed the boy with a hard look, a scathing rake of flint eyes.

"No, Heck. I ain't your father. Now, go on home and forget about all this hogwash."

"I'm not going back home, Mister Killian." Hector's voice quavered. "Not never."

"You'll break your mother's heart."

"She broke mine."

"No. That's not true."

Hector jerked the reins hard, turning his horse's head.

"I'm leaving, Mister Killian," he said. "I just wanted to know if you'd tell me the truth."

"I don't know the truth, Heck. But I know I ain't your father. You're the son of the man who raised you and that's the long and the short of it."

"Goodbye, Mister Killian."

"Where are you goin', Heck?"

"To live with Bone," said Hector. "He's the only one who'll stand up to Ernie. Ernie's scared of him."

Hector tapped his heels into his horse's flanks. He wore no spurs. The horse stepped out, shaking raindrops from its eyes.

"You'll be makin' the biggest mistake of your life if you go with Bone. He's wanted by the law."

"Mister Killian, you just don't understand. I don't have no home."

"Ernie's been a good father to you," said Ben.

"He hates me," said Hector. "And I hate him."

Ben dug spurs into his horse's tender flanks. He rode up to Hector, grabbed his coat lapels, pulled him half out of the saddle.

"Son, I ought to horsewhip you right here. Bone is seven kinds of sonofabitch. Either he'll get you killed, or he'll kill you himself. And if that don't happen, you'll kill him. Either way, you're headed for trouble. Think of your mother. Think of your father."

Hector glared at Ben. Ben felt the heat of the boy's anger, the withering steam of his hatred, his contempt. He shook his hand clenching the boy's lapels. But he did not break the stare between them. He opened his hand and shoved Hector back in the saddle.

"Go on back home, boy," he said again.

"Where?" asked Hector, and kicked his horse hard with both feet. "Where is my home?"

Ben wanted to ride after him, chase him down and knock him off his horse. Instead, he watched as Hector disappeared in the rain, the mist. One moment, he saw the boy's back, the next moment, he was gone.

The stock pond was littered with dead cattle. Some had fallen into the water; others had dropped in their tracks a few yards away. The twisted wreck of the windmill lay like a broken metal tower across the center of the pond. The stench of rotting flesh rose up, assailed the two riders' nostrils, even in the drizzling rain. Matt's jaw hardened like something chiseled out of black granite. Tom covered his mouth, fought down the bile that rose in his throat.

"Come on, Tom," said Baron. "You'll have to send some hands to pour coal oil on these carcasses and burn 'em before we all get sick."

"Jesus," said Casebolt. "No tellin' how many cattle them sonsof-bitches poisoned with that strychnine."

The two men rode away, following a parallel course to the chuck-wagon. As soon as they had left the scent of dead cattle behind, Matt spoke.

"Tom, when we get through with the brandin', I want you to put every goddamned man you can spare to huntin' down Bone. I'm goin' to bring in a crew and cut, stomp, burn and tear out every goddamned mesquite tree in that *brasada.*"

"Matt, you can't hardly do that," said Tom. "It would take forty years and more money'n the Klebergs and Kennedys have."

"I don't give a damn what it costs," said Matt. "A man who'd poison cattle and cut a boy's throat, castrate a prize bull, deserves to be hunted down and shot in cold blood. If Bone's in that *brasada,* I'll burn him out. He's by God not going to kill another head of my stock nor any man who rides for the outfit."

Tom shook his head, but said nothing. He thought he could get a good tan in the glare of Matt's temper that morning.

"I'll get that bastard," said Matt, "if it's the last thing I do. If it takes every cent I have. I'll get him. And you tell the men I'll pay one thousand dollars to the one who brings Bone to me, dead or alive."

"Christ," said Casebolt. "Sheriff Blanchard hears about that, he'll be spittin' twentypenny nails."

"You just keep this in the family, Tom. Don't even say anything to Lou."

Matt said no more as they rode through the soft rain. Soon, they drifted apart, scouting out cattle in the ghostly morning.

An hour later, the two men met again, closing an imaginary circle they both knew by heart.

Matt drove six head of Santa Cruz cattle, cows and calves, into the old corral, closed the gate. A few moments later, Tom Casebolt herded another four head of cows and calves up to the corral. Matt opened the gate, helped Tom run them in.

"Still holding up," said Tom, as Matt closed the wire and wood gate.

"I remember when we built it. You and me."

"I remember," said Casebolt. "Dozens of 'em."

"My daddy built 'em too, taught me how." Matt built a smoke, offered the makings to Tom. Tom shook his head. The rain had stopped, but the sky was overcast. It was hot. The grass seemed to be steaming.

"They ain't as wild as them ones we used to hunt down in here," said Tom.

"We've got a good breed here, Tom."

Matt shook one of the corral posts, testing it. The green cowhide had long since rotted away, been replaced by baling wire. He looked down at the ground, at the packed earth that had hardened over the years. He and Tom had dug trenches three feet or so deep, joined them in a large square. Then, with a dozen men helping, they had set ten-foot posts on end. The men had come along and tromped the dirt around the posts. Matt and Tom had lashed the posts together about halfway up their height with long strips of green cowhide.

The Box B still had wild cattle on it when they had built the new corrals on La Plata. Longhorns hid in the brush, holdouts from Matt's breeding program.

"What was it, Tom? Fifteen, sixteen years ago when we rounded up those wild longhorns?"

"More like sixteen, Matt. More like huntin' 'em, though."

"You didn't think decoys would work."

Tom grinned sheepishly.

"I still don't," he said.

Matt and Tom had acted as spotters. When they found wild cattle in the dense thicket of chaparral and mesquite, they whistled in the roundup crew. The men led the decoys into the brush, domesticated longhorns, some mixed breeds of shorthorns and Herefords. Then, the men surrounded the *brasada* and began singing. They sang the songs they used on nightherd, odd off-key melodies about cattle and cowboys and heartbreak. The Mexicans sang *son huastecos,* those mournful dirges of lost love and broken men, the songs they sang in *cantinas* and at lonesome campfires on long drives across deserted sandy stretches of Baron land.

"You changed your mind when you saw those cattle coming out of the brush," said Matt.

"Damndest thing I ever saw," admitted Casebolt.

Matt recalled the first time he had used the decoy trick. After a time, some of the cattle had begun to wander out of the brush. He saw some of his own breeds, then a few of the wild longhorns. When the wild ones saw a rider, they bolted. But, everywhere they turned, there was another rider. They ran the wild and domestic cattle into the corrals. After a few days, when the feral cattle had settled down, and mingled with the domestic cows, it was fairly easy to drive them to the main herd.

"Good-lookin' calves," said Matt now.

"Them are old Pinteros all right."

"They got the red in 'em," said the rancher.

Matt's father, Anson Baron, had started building up the Box B herds, adding shorthorn and Hereford bloodlines to the original longhorn stock. But he had worried about the new breed as he watched them fare poorly in the subtropical coastal grazing lands. The beef had a better quality, but the herd lost its hardiness under the blistering Texas sun.

Then, Anson heard about the Brahmin cattle from India around the turn of the century. These were tough, fast-breeding cattle. Their meat was poor-tasting and they were mean as bulldogs, hard to handle. But they had one thing in their favor. They could stand the heat. Besides, they also had a high resistance against ticks and other pests. Like the Longhorns, they could live on coarse grass and puny pasturage.

Anson tried for years to introduce Brahmin blood into his Shorthorn and Hereford stock. But government import regulations restricted the number of these cattle and Texas stockmen found it difficult to obtain purebred Brahmins for their ranges. It wasn't until 1911 that Anson bought a Brahmin Shorthorn bull from a man in Falfurrias. He put the bull, Victoria, in with the other Shorthorn bulls in a pasture with 3,000 purebred Shorthorn cows.

He castrated all of Victoria's male offspring except for a single promising bull calf with red hair. He turned all the heifers back with the Shorthorn bulls. By the time Matt was old enough to handle ranch responsibilities, the experimental breed had improved the herd, producing the best range cattle for hardiness, size and beef quality.

Matt had continued to improve the herd and was still experimenting, trying for a better beef producer. He hoped to pass along his knowledge of cattle breeding to his sons, Ethan and Derek.

By mid-morning, the corral was almost full. One of Ben Killian's reps rode up, waited for Matt and Tom.

Harvey Leeds was looking at the cows and calves when Matt drove in four unbranded yearlings.

Lou rode in a few moments later, driving three bulls and a heifer.

"Hee-ya," she yelled and her horse stopped the cattle in their tracks, held them fast, ranging back and forth, blocking every attempt to escape. She held a lariat in her hand, just in case, the loop ready to throw.

"Missed some last year," said Leeds.

Matt was out of breath. Harvey opened the gate. Matt ran the yearlings into the corral. Lou backed her horse off and her four cows bolted into the enclosure.

"Whew," she said, grinning. She hung the lariat on her saddlehorn, stood up to stretch in the stirrups.

"The yearlings you brought in, Matt, are as wild as jackrabbits," she said.

"No mistakin' the breed, though, with that red hair," said Leeds.

"I appreciate you sayin' that, Harv."

Leeds offered Matt a store-bought. The name on the cigarette package was "Piedmont." Matt and Harvey lit up, waited for Tom.

"You got a herd shapin' up," said Harvey.

"You been up yonder?"

"I come through, dropped Jared off on the other side of the chuckwagon."

"Lord, I can smell the beans," said Matt.

"Me, too," said Lou.

"Purt' near."

The two men were nearly finished with their smokes before Tom rode up, driving three head of cattle that Matt knew were not his. Harvey jerked up straight in the saddle as if he'd been poked in the rump. Lou sat in her saddle, gaping.

"Well, looky there," said Leeds. Both men knew the cattle belonged to neither of them.

"Strays?" asked Lou.

Tom's horse cut off the three beeves, held them until Matt and Harvey rode up.

"What you got there, Tom?" asked Matt.

"Somebody's been cute with a runnin' iron."

"That's the funniest Box B I ever did see," said Harvey.

There was no mistaking the blurred edges of the Rocking A brand beneath the ragged, lopsided Box B burned into the hides with an arrogance that made Matt wince.

"You know what we got here," Tom said. "Pure trouble."

"Let's drive what we got up to the herd," said Matt. "Let Ernie's reps take a look."

"What's a-goin' on here?" asked Harvey.

"I'll give you three guesses," said Matt, without a trace of humor. He turned to Casebolt.

"Soon as brandin's done, Tom, you get the men right to work on that brush job."

"Sure, Cap'n," said Tom.

Lou said nothing, but she knew something was up. Well, maybe he would tell her. And maybe not.

Harvey rode up to Casebolt.

"Whoo boy," he said. "We got us some big trouble here or what?"

"Shut up, Harvey," said Casebolt. "Just shut your doggoned trap."

Lou looked hard at her brother.

Matt looked the other way before she could make eye contact.

"Well, fuck me a-runnin'," she said under her breath. Matt seemed a hundred miles away, although she could have reached out, almost, and touched him.

"Lou, you just never mind," said Matt.

She crimped a nasty smile at him. Sometimes, she thought, little brothers were a pain in the ass.

15
—■—

THE GENERAL LED his hens out into the fallow field where winter wheat had been harvested two months before. Grasshoppers began to leap into the air. The General bristled until his feathers added inches to his bulk. His golden eyes scanned the ground ahead and when the next hopper jumped, the bantam rooster leaped up to intersect its flight path. He caught the grasshopper in midair, clamped his beak on its body neatly. He hit the ground, turned and carried the insect to one of his hens. He waited patiently as she took it from his beak, munched it into her craw, ass first. The grasshopper's head disappeared and The General sidled away after more prey. The rooster caught one grasshopper after another and fed them to his hens. They followed after him like proper ladies on a nature hike, clucking in subservient gratitude. Every so often, The General singled out one of his small flock and mounted her frenziedly. He pecked the back of each hen's head as he copulated and they presented themselves to him, wriggling their cloacae, hiking them up, their feathers drawn back like layers of petticoats, exposing them so that he could penetrate their sex with ease.

The chickens traveled across the field, crisscrossing the flailed land like scavengers roaming an empty battlefield. The General ate a grasshopper or two, and killed a small garden snake that was unlucky enough to catch a glance from his jaundiced eye. They would not return to the coop until just before dark, when Silvino would have scattered chicken feed on the ground for the domestic chickens. Then, The General would herd his charges inside the wire and into the coop, seeing to it that each took to her roost before he joined them. If there was an alien, full-sized chicken on his roost, he would knock it violently off its perch, drive it away, leaping into the air and hurling his weight at the intruder, jabbing the hapless bird with thrusts of his spurs like a fighting cock going for the kill.

Following the raid on the grasshoppers, The General led his flock to the manure pile down by the old well. That was where Ernesto Aguilar had buried the body of José Perez. Ernie had directed Silvino to haul manure from the stables to that spot. As far as The General was concerned, it was an excellent place to find grubs and earthworms. He didn't mind that Ernie went there every day to look at the manure pile and measure, with his eye, its height and width. The chickens had become accustomed to seeing the man walk down into the bottoms every day and look at the steaming mound of cowpies and horse manure.

Silvino wondered about Ernie, though. He thought it was odd to haul manure that far and he had not failed to notice the fresh-turned earth when he first went there, the traces of white lime mixed in with the clods. But it was not his place to question his employer. Aguilar had told him to pile the manure as high as he could and to continue hauling the offal there until further notice.

Silvino thought the silent, heat-generating mound was a waste of perfectly good manure.

Roy Blanchard knew there was trouble brewing among the ranchers.

"We're a-settin' on a goddamned gee-haw powder keg," he told his deputies, Doakes and Naylor, after two months of frustration. They sat in the "coffee room" of the city jail, a cell that Roy had converted to a combination lounge, interrogation and conference room. The jail was empty, anyway, that day late in May when the rain had started up again with less malevolence than the previous March, when the drought had been in full bloom.

"How come?" asked Naylor, who was several notches brighter than Harlan Doakes.

"Matt doesn't tag Bone as a lone rustler and murderer. He thinks Bone's workin' for Aguilar."

"Is he?" asked Raymond.

Blanchard shrugged.

"Could be. Baron found several of his cattle cut into Aguilar's herd after findin' some of Ernie's amongst Box B stock. Ernie denies Bone works for him, but he's hidin' somethin'."

And Roy had left it at that, but he knew there was tension between Ben Killian and Ernie Aguilar, as well. There was visible animosity between the two men. Whenever he questioned either of them, he sensed a deeper hostility because of the way they spoke of one another. There was a remote possibility of a range war, he knew. After all, this was 1932, not 1832, but Blanchard knew men. The most kindly of them could kill if pushed hard enough against a wall. Ben didn't push much, and neither did Ernie nor Matt.

Then, too, there was the white-sheeted specter of the Ku Klux Klan, with Delmer Mudd stirring up people against Bone and Aguilar. Delmer was some kind of bigshot in the KKK, was recruiting all the time. Roy didn't give a damn one way or the other, as long as nobody caused any trouble. Let them parade around at night in their costumes and burn crosses out on the little hill north of town once a month. Delmer Mudd had shit for brains. Roy had warned him not to trespass on any of the ranches or hold his cross-burning meetings in town. So far, there had been no trouble. So far.

"Yep," he told Naylor privately, "we're a-settin' on a powder keg all right. You have any luck out there at the *brasada* the other day?"

"Roy," said Naylor, comfortable enough in his job to call Blanchard by his first name, "that there's a jungle out there. I found horse tracks and man tracks around the edge, but inside, it's all swamp now. You couldn't track an elephant in there. Baron's men and some outside hires have been cuttin' and burnin' that brush, but they ain't even dented it."

"I know," said Blanchard, and he frowned rather than vent his frustration in a string of invective. "It's a red bitch, ain't it?"

Matt Baron was spending a lot of money trying to clear that stretch of brush that slashed through the center of his holdings, meandered down to Aguilar's Rocking A. Some of his hands thought he was crazy and they hated working down there. There was still no trace of José Perez and his horse was still missing. But there had been no more killings.

"I've talked to them ranch owners. They all seem like reasonable men," Naylor said.

"Except when it's hard times," said Blanchard.

"None of 'em seem to be feelin' no pinch," said Naylor.

"Well, they all are, Ray. What with the gee-haw drought a-killin' stock, and this danged Depression of Hoover's, their pockets are feelin' the shorts same as ours."

"Not the same as ours, Roy."

"They think so."

Blanchard was curious about Raymond Naylor. The man spent a lot of time at the courthouse, looking at records. He had learned this from Betty Swaine, who worked there. And Roy had noticed that his own files had been gone through more than once. He knew Naylor was the one, because he always noticed the shuffled papers, the files out of sequence, after Raymond pulled night shift. He didn't know what to make of it, but he was keeping his eye on the deputy. It might be that the young man was just eager to learn all he could, but if so, he was going about it in a mighty secretive way. Naylor didn't say much. He didn't ask a lot of questions. He did his job and kept to himself. But he was looking for something, that was for damned sure.

Matt heaved a self-indulgent sigh as he strode through the door of the building next to the stables that served as ranch headquarters. He entered his office, the largest of the cubicles. It was quiet. The late-summer winds had not yet begun to blow. But Matt had been expecting them since early July. Next door was his foreman's room. Tom Casebolt's office was small, but larger than the rooms used by the foremen of the other Box B ranches. Matt left the door open, glanced at the knotty-pine walls. He wondered if he should have the walls varnished. The wood still smelled new to him every time he came inside. The panels fit snugly and there wasn't a nail in a single board. They were all doweled. One of Larry Davis's touches. Larry was Matt's head blacksmith, but he was a fine carpenter, as Grace Baron had discovered when she'd decided to build Matt an office away from the house. Grace did not like Matt tracking into the den, working in there. Instead, she had Larry and his son, Mark, construct the small frame building, put in a long L-shaped table that snugged against two walls and a corner. She brought in a big desk, put in wooden filing cabinets, tacked maps of the Box B ranches to the walls. She had hung a framed corkboard on the wall by the door, for notes. On his desk, she had put two spindles for bills and purchases.

Matt knew why Grace didn't want him doing ranch work in his den. She had gradually assumed dominion over that room, making it her private suzerain. Except for their Thursday talks in his den, evenings, and Sundays, Matt felt that he was not welcome in his own home. When he had business to do, he conducted it in the ranch office, where even the tangy aroma of horse manure could not quell the scent of the planed knotty-pine boards that walled him in.

Now he sat down at the big table, picked up a wooden box.

He set the box on its end. The box was divided into labeled compartments. In each compartment there was a small sack filled with dirt and grass. Each sack was tagged. There was writing on each sack.

Once a week, the foremen of the various Baron ranchos used a small garden shovel to extract a portion of grass and soil from the larger pastures. They sent this to ranch headquarters for evaluation. The day before, Matt had sent his oldest son, Ethan, to collect the sacks.

Now, he looked them over, pouring their contents into little piles on a piece of cardboard that someone had set out for him. Herds had to be rotated or they would chew grass down to the roots. Matt chose the healthiest fields on which to run his stock.

A moment later, Ethan entered the room.

"You got the diggings?" he asked. Ethan was tall, resembled his mother. He had light hair, nut-brown eyes, a pear-shaped face. His voice was soft, like Grace's. Unlike his brother, Derek, Ethan was shy, introspective, serious.

"Just lookin' at 'em, son. You bring 'em up?"

"Yes, sir," Ethan said proudly.

"Let's check 'em together."

Ethan grinned, pulled up a chair. He sat next to his father. Matt picked up a clump of sod, rolled the roots through his fingers. He studied them for color and density and thickness.

"The fescue looks good," he said.

Ethan nodded. His grin widened.

"Yes, sir. Looks good. Lespedeza's poor over at La Golondrina."

"We're going to look into some foreign grasses, Ethan. See what they'll do. You got some plots staked out, son?"

"Yes, sir. Whenever that whatsitcologist gets here."

Matt laughed.

"Horticulturist. Porfirio Martinez. Hard man to track. Last I heard from him, Lasater had him up at Falfurrias."

"Well, when he shows up, I'll take him to that good bottomland at the south pasture." Ethan pulled a sack from the box, handed it to his father. Matt poured the sod onto the cardboard.

Matt remembered his father taking him to a pasture that had been cleared of brush, root-plowed and seeded with new grass. The earth smelled rich and loamy; the ground manicured with a loving hand. Anson told his son, Matt, "I've done all I can do, now it's up to the good Lord and the sun and the rain."

Through the years, Matt had waged a battle against the brush, trying to increase the available pasturage for the stock. He'd had his men build retaining and spreader dams and had started a program of pasture terracing. His men had fertilized large areas with phosphates to enrich the soil and grass. They had plowed and sowed huge tracts of pastureland with new and hardy range grasses. The hands had planted prickly pear along miles of fences and in broad, fallow fields for stock feed during periods of drought.

"Good place to start," Matt told Ethan, holding a clump of sod in his hands as tenderly as if handling a baby bird that had fallen from its nest. "That's what we got here, you know. A kingdom built on grass from the ground up. Can't ever let the land take anything back. Keep seeding it; keep trying new breeds of grass and the stock will thrive. You done good, son."

"Thanks, Daddy."

Matt was proud of his eldest son. He wished his other son would take the same interest in the ranch as Ethan did. The two boys were different. Ethan liked to work in the office with his father. Derek was more at home on a horse, working with the men, sweating, cursing, horsing around.

"Where is Derek this mornin', anyway?" asked Matt.

Ethan snorted through his nostrils.

"He left real early this morning to drive over to El Rincón with Tom and Aunt Lou."

Matt frowned.

"Tom ought to know better. Lou, too."

"Took my twenty-two with him," said Ethan. "Didn't even ask."

"Well, Derek will want to come back once he starts chopping mesquite. Tom will work him alongside the others."

"Tom spoils Derek and so does Aunt Lou, I think," said Ethan, surprisingly mature for his age. His voice had changed, was deepening. Ethan was twenty-two. Derek was sixteen, would be a senior in high school that fall. Ethan attended the University of Texas at Austin, studying law and politics on the side while obtaining a liberal education in livestock management as an undergraduate.

"I reckon he does, some. But he works him too."

"Not like he worked me," Ethan said, with some resentment.

"How's your mother?" asked Matt abruptly.

"She's mad at both Derek and Tom. She doesn't like all the money you're spending on clearing that brush over at the Corner."

"She told you that?"

"She wasn't talking to me. Daddy, I think Mother's got some liquor hid away."

"She might," said Matt, then turned his chair around so that Ethan couldn't see his face. He had suspected that Grace was drinking again when he got up that morning. She had avoided him, made herself look busy. She had shooed him out of the den, saying she had to go over the books. She hadn't said a word about El Rincón. But he knew that she was angry that he was tending more to that than the ranch work. She couldn't see that they'd never have any peace as long as Bone was living in the *brasada*.

Matt could never smell the liquor on Grace's breath. But he always knew when she had been secretly drinking. Her mouth tasted of the fresh crushed mint that grew beneath the cistern. She took her hard liquor in juleps and chewed mint after she brushed her teeth. So he could never tell for sure. Grace was clever about her drinking when she didn't want him to know. He never drank during the week, and when he took alcohol on weekends, just before supper, he was obliged to allot Grace her share for the mint juleps.

But Grace couldn't stop there. The bottle would go down drastically by Sunday night or else disappear. She would accuse him of drinking it all, and, over the last few years, he had lost every argument. She took away his weapons with the ferocity of her accusations. He was often so stunned by the force of her conviction that he had drunk all the liquor that he doubted himself. Truth in Grace's mouth twisted and looped like a kinked lariat.

The problem was, when Grace was sneaking her liquor, he could never catch her at it. Her speech didn't slur; she was always composed and regally beautiful, like a goddess.

That was the hell of it. Matt never had any proof that Grace was drinking by herself. He did not know where she got her liquor. Not from his bootlegger, Delmer, he knew that. But she got it from somewhere, for damned sure. She always turned cold on him at night when she was drinking alone and in secret. If they drank together, she was loving on Friday night and on Saturday night. But by Sunday, she would turn into a sour bitch, as if the alcohol had drowned all traces of the beautiful woman he had married.

When she was sober, she rejected his advances in bed. Sleeping with her was like sleeping on a cold slab with a frozen woman.

"Daddy," said Ethan, "Derek says he doesn't want to go back to school in Beaumont next year."

"Why?"

"He's got too many demerits, he says."

"The trouble with Derek is he always wants to be someplace where he ain't. Casebolt's been tryin' to tame him."

"Derek can't be tamed," said Ethan ruefully.

"There ain't a horse what can't be broke," said Matt, as he opened another sack.

"Except Derek. He'll always be wild. He hit Peggy last night. In the mouth. Made her cry." Peggy was eighteen, in the middle. She was going to business school in Dallas, and, like her brothers, was home for the summer.

"I'll box his ears for that," said Matt.

"You'll have to catch him first, Daddy."

Matt laughed. Ethan laughed too.

Together, they looked over the soil samples for the next hour. When it came to lunchtime, Matt looked at his watch. Ethan drew in a deep breath. They looked at each other for a long time without speaking.

"Why don't you holler at Peggy, see if she wants to ride out to El Rincón with us? We can grab a bite to eat along the way. We got a good cookie over at Santa Magdalena."

The Santa Magdalena was fifty miles away, covered 800,000 acres. Wedged between Santa Magdalena and La Loma de Sombra, Martin Longerbeam's Flying M took up more than 100,000 acres, small by Box B standards, but prosperous enough to keep the Longerbeams fed and clothed.

"Gee, Daddy, we won't hardly get there much before dark."

"Well, you want to go?"

"You bet," said Ethan, grinning again. That smile, Matt thought. It would take Ethan a long way in politics. That was his son's dream and Matt, despite Grace's protests, encouraged him. He wanted his sons to get out in the world, make something of themselves.

"You go call Peggy out. I'll put this stuff up, get the car ready."

"Sure," said Ethan. He scraped his chair as he got up. "I'm getting hungry."

"Hurry, then."

Ethan left the room, the thoughts between them unspoken.

Neither wanted to go to the house for lunch if Grace was drinking. And they sure as shoot didn't want to suffer through supper with her.

16

BEN KNOCKED ON his mother's door.

"Come in, Benjamin."

Jane sat in her rocker, looking out the large window Ben had put in for her. From there, she could see the pastures and fields to the west of the main ranch. In the evenings, the sky was a fluid painting of constantly changing colors, gradually blending into the fabric of night.

"Mother," he said, closing the door. "You didn't come down for supper tonight."

"I know. I wasn't hungry."

Ben snorted.

"Set, Benjamin, and don't be snorting at me."

The sky outside her picture window was ablaze with orange, gold and russet clouds, the fields were blotched with shadows. Ben sat on the settee where he could see his mother and she could see him. She continued to look out the window, ignoring the concern in his eyes.

"We were worried about you when you were over at La Querencia."

"I was at home there, Benjamin."

"You said you'd be back the next day. I had to send Jack Bellaugh over there right in the middle of roundup."

"Oh pooh, Benjamin. I'm a grown woman. I don't need caretakers and such."

"Why didn't you come down for supper? It's not like you to miss Sunday at the family table."

She turned, then, to look at Ben. Her red hair was almost as bright as the western sky.

"I'm feeling the years, Benjamin. I had to see Silvero and his family, find some peace of mind. I declare, I think Old Silvero will go on forever."

"He's older than you are."

"I know. Lately it seems we're the same age."

"You try to do too much, Mother. I don't like to see you ride that far all by yourself."

"I've ridden farther in my day. A person gets old, they miss things. Miss doing things like they used to. If I couldn't ride, I'd probably just wither away and die."

"Mother, don't talk like that."

She was silent for a moment, stole another glimpse at the sunset. Ben put his hands together, started to rub his fingers, stroking the calluses, the deeply etched lines of his own age.

"The closer you get to it," Jane said suddenly, "the more appealing it seems."

"What?"

"Dying. It doesn't seem so bad when your old body starts giving up on you."

"Your body isn't giving up a damned thing."

"Oh, I can feel the changes, Benjamin. I've been feeling them for a long while now. It's not just the slowness, it's little aches and pains and sometimes you can't seem to get enough breath and you pee more than you used to."

Ben squirmed on the settee, coupled his big hands, started working them in earnest, making the knuckles snap softly in the quiet of the room. The sunset grew richer, playing light against the darkening windowpane, daubing the sky with variations on the colors already smeared there on the horizon. It was as if the dying embers in the sky were pressing against the pane, trying to leave lasting impressions before their vibrancy was gone.

"I hate to hear you talk this way," said Ben. "I wish there was something I could say or do . . ."

"There isn't, so you just don't need to pay it any mind."

"I do, though."

"I was happy at La Querencia," she said. "I think that's where I want to go to die. Those people, the Mexicans, they don't fear it like we do."

"That's a long way off, Mother."

Jane turned away from her son, looked out the window again. For a moment, Ben thought she was crying.

"See that sunset out there, Benjamin? That's what I feel like. The colors are fading and soon it will be dark. I look out there every afternoon at this time of day and I know night is coming. But lately, it seems different, more final, somehow. It's as if God is telling me something, writing a message to me in the sunset, telling me my time on this earth is short and that I should get my house in order. That's what I feel, Benjamin, and I'm not sad about it. I've had a good life and I cherish each day even more than the one before. Yet, I know there won't be many left."

"You sound sad," he said lamely. "You make me feel sad."

"It is sad," she said. "I will miss you. And you will miss me."

"Mother, I wish—"

She turned to him again.

"We'll talk in the morning," she said. "Leave me be, now, before I start to moping and feeling sorry for myself."

Ben stood up. He seemed to be trying to shake off a heavy burden as he unclasped his hands and straightened out.

"Good night, Mother," he said, and started for the door.

"Ben?"

He stopped, turned to face her. She looked small and old in the dying light.

"What are you going to do about Hector Aguilar?" Her voice was sharp and crisp, no longer somber.

"Not a damned thing," he said.

"That's good, Benjamin. Good night."

He closed the door softly and stood there for a long moment. Why in hell, he thought, did life have to get so goddamned complicated?

Bandera Creek turned tame in late summer. High upstream on Aguilar land, Paco and some of the Rocking A hands began to plan the building of the dam. When the stream had been flowing full, Paco had measured its flow rate. He and Randy Connors had chosen a point in the stream where the bed was smooth and the water had a clear run of forty feet. Paco stepped off thirty feet and stood at that point downstream. Randy, upstream, tossed a chunk of wood at the starting point and looked at his watch. When Paco yelled out that the scrap of wood was exactly opposite him, Randy marked the time on his pocket watch, a battered Waterbury.

The two men then erected posts on both sides of the bank at those points, using four posts in all. They connected the two upstream posts with a rope. Using a carpenter's level, they tautened the rope until it was perfectly level with the stream. They did the same with the two downstream posts. Then, they divided the stream into equal sections along the ropes and measured the water depth for each section.

Once they had the cross-sectional areas of the stream marked off, Paco did his calculations to determine the flow of the creek. He had learned the formula from an old man who had worked on river dams to bring power to small towns in Mexico. Paco used the man's simple formula to calculate the maximum flow of Bandera Creek: stream flow (cubic feet per second) equals average cross-sectional flow area (square feet) times velocity (feet per second).

For two days, he and Randy had taken turns helping the hands bring in material to build the dam. Each of the men had been sworn to secrecy.

"How are you going to get away with this?" Randy asked him, when all the materials were stored at the dam site.

"I'll build a gate that we can open or close. Ben Killian doesn't have to know about this. Ernesto, neither."

"Paco, you're just a half a bubble off plumb."

Paco laughed. Sweat rimed his brows, splotched his shirt. His brown eyes, the whites mottled with coffee-colored stains, glittered with a conspiratorial light.

"Randy, get some hands and start building a cofferdam about fifty yards upstream. Cut some pilings and drive them in across the dry part. You can build an embankment there, and then we'll cut the other half over."

"You know how to build these things, don't you?"

"Maybe yes, maybe no. I am trying like hell to remember."

Work on the dam continued over the next several days, with Paco writing figures on wrinkled paper and scratching his head every so often. Randy supervised the construction of the headrace and tailrace, while Paco figured the hydraulic radius, referring to a dog-eared book on dam-building he had gotten from his father.

Paco built most of the dam with earth, to save on concrete. He and Randy built a spillway to carry off the excess water. They lined it with boards to prevent erosion and seepage.

"How come?" asked Randy.

"The earth can hold still water," said Paco. "Moving water will wear the dam away. We can't let the dammed water run over the crest."

They built the crest just wide enough to walk across. The gate could be lifted easily by two men, one in a pinch. When the dam was completed, Paco and Randy worked the gate to show all the men how they could control the flow of water into Bandera Creek.

"We'll have to keep an eye on it, make sure nobody crosses the fence from the Lazy K," said Randy.

"*Seguro que sí*," said Paco, grinning. "I cannot wait to see it work when the creek's running full."

"Boy, ol' Ben Killian would throw a striped fit if he saw this baby."

"Well, he ain't gonna see it," said Paco. "The trick is to let him have a little bit of water when we got plenty, so he don' worry none."

"Jesus, I hope it works. I wouldn't like to fight them boys again."

"Me neither," said Paco, rapping his muddy gloves against his legs.

A week later, it rained and the dam held. Paco said a prayer of thanks in Spanish as he and Randy let water through to run on Killian land. Paco had built the gate so it could stay open as long as he wanted it to, and he could control the amount of water passing through the opening.

"Nobody would ever guess," said Randy.

"*Ojalá que sí!*" exclaimed Paco. "I hope so."

And he crossed himself just to make sure.

Bone had all summer to brood, and the heat to goad his hate, the hot dry winds to fan the flames of his madness. He drew away from the others living in the *brasada* for long periods of time. When he returned to their company, he came armed with slings of schemes, quiversful of fervent plans to torment the cattle ranchers, arrows tipped with resentment.

He wanted to use Hector Aguilar in some way against his father. But he hadn't made up his mind yet what to do with the strange boy. Hector seemed eager to steal Ernie's cattle and run off all his stock, but that was getting them nowhere. The ranchers were not fighting each other as Bone had expected. The only thing different was that

Matt Baron was trying to cut away the *brasada,* burn and destroy every mesquite tree for miles. But he wasn't getting anywhere. Bone's camp was still in the same place. None of Box B's hands had even come close to it.

Some days, when the wind was right, Bone could hear the Baron hands yelling, cursing the heat, the dust. At night, he could see the sky aflame with the burning mesquite, could smell the faint aroma of smoke. It gave Bone satisfaction to know that Matt Baron was spending so much time and money on the *brasada,* trying to cut away something that had been there for longer than anyone could remember, and would be there always. He sat in the shade of the old adobe that was his dwelling. Eddie Blue and Virgil had gone to Baronsville the night before to steal grain for the horses. They had not yet returned.

Bone's father used to talk about the *brasada* as if it was a living thing. He did not hate it like everyone else did. For most of his life, Bone did not understand his father's affection for the thick, impenetrable stand of mesquite that once had held dominion over hundreds of thousands of acres. You could not hunt in it, you got lost in it.

Bone remembered that when he was a boy, one of his jobs was to work with the hands clearing the brush, chopping, digging out the mesquite. He had hated the job until he had found that he could hide in the *brasada,* sit in its shade for hours and look at the sky with none to bother him in his reveries. But for a long time, Bone had hated the *brasada.*

Bone's father had talked of it with affection.

"These white men came to Texas to get rich," he used to say. "They spoiled the land. They took from it. They drove us Indians off like we were wild dogs. They hunted us down, paid bounties for our scalps. They cut down the mesquite, burned it, piled it up. And the mesquite comes back, always. It keeps coming back and they'll never get rid of it. The minute the white bastards turn their backs, the mesquite comes back and if they don't watch out, it will grow right back up to their porches and spread all around their houses and knock the glass out of their windows. That stuff will finally just grow right through their houses and swallow them up. God, I'd love to see it."

But that had never happened. Still, there was that stretch of mesquite that grew right through all three of the big ranches. And it wouldn't go away. It was, Bone thought, a sacred place. His father had believed that.

"White men can't live in the mesquite. They tried it. They built their 'dobe line shacks right in the path of the *brasada,* in a clearing, and the mesquite grew right back and cut 'em off. A white man lives like the rabbit or the deer. He's got to be out in the open where the sun can burn his eyes and the wind blow dust in his face. But the Indian can live in there. Forever. If the Indians wanted to come back up here to Texas and take the land back, why they could just live in that *brasada* and the stupid whites wouldn't even know they were there."

"Why don't the Indians come back and live there?" Bone had asked his father.

"They got us all scattered, boy, and ain't no one to lead us. Now, if we had a man who was brave enough, who could gather up all the old Apaches and come up here and live in that mesquite, why we'd take the land back and drive the whites out same as they drove us out."

Bone remembered his father talking about that. He remembered it after the Virgin Mary came into his jail cell and spoke to him. If he could just get Ernie to give him some land, he and the other Indians could live in the *brasada* and raise some cattle. Pretty soon they could just take more and more land and push the other ranchers off, make them go someplace else.

Bone wondered what progress the Baron hands were making. He had not seen them, only heard and smelled what they were doing down at El Rincón.

Hector watched as Bone worked the leather thongs. Bone made it look so easy, the braiding. Hector held three separate strands of leather in his hands, but he could not tame them, make them interlace with smoothness. He would make two or three crossovers and then he would form a knotted joint that interrupted the flow.

"You got to do it without thinking," said Bone.

"Where did you learn how to do this?"

"From my pa. I used to make watch fobs and key holders. My ma would take them to town and sell them at the bus station. Pa taught me how to tan cowhide and deer, make both buckskin and rawhide from the deer. He always said a deer had just enough brains to tan its own hide."

Hector had watched Bone curing the hides from the cows they

had butchered for food. Stirring the pot full of ashes and water, making sure the hide was thoroughly soaked. He had helped with the scraping, but he didn't like doing that much.

"I get mixed up," said Hector.

"That's because you think about it too much. Once you start making your braid, you just let your fingers do all the work and pay 'em no mind."

"I tried that."

"Maybe you ought to just make short fobs."

Hector laughed.

"For short watches?"

Bone looked up from his braiding. There was not a trace of humor in his countenance.

"To shove up your butt," said Bone.

"I was just joking," said Hector.

Bone stopped braiding the watch fob and looked at the thin, dark face of Hector Aguilar. Hector was always so serious, but now he was trying to make jokes. Maybe there was something to the kid besides some kind of blind hatred for his father. Bone never could get it out of the boy, but he knew Hector wanted to make Ernie Aguilar suffer. Maybe, he thought, Hector was queer. He had known a boy like him in jail once. The other prisoners had used him like a woman. Bone used to hear the boy scream at night and smile in the darkness. Once, he even thought about trying out the boy himself, but he didn't want to give the other convicts the satisfaction of knowing he was just like them.

Thinking of these things reminded Bone of a story his father had told him. Or was it his grandfather? Well, maybe both of them had told him different versions when he was very small. The story had made a great impression on Jack Bone. And now he thought of it again.

"Heck," Bone said, "did your daddy ever talk to you about women?"

"No, never."

"You ever humped a girl?"

Hector's face darkened.

"No," he said sullenly.

"Scared of 'em?"

"No. Hell, no."

Bone laughed.

"I used to be. Everybody used to be."

"I never was."

"Well, you ought to be, maybe. Ever hear of Kicking Monster? Killer-of-Enemies?"

"No. Sounds like a fairy tale."

"Ain't no fairy tale. True as anything."

"Indian stuff."

"True, anyways."

Hector struggled with his braiding, thinking Bone was finished talking.

"You listen, Heck. Maybe you'll learn something your daddy never told you."

"I don't have a daddy, Bone."

"Everybody's got a daddy."

"Go on, tell your old story."

"I aim to once you stop fiddlin' with that damned fob."

Hector let out a sigh, put the tangles of leather thongs down on the ground.

"You go right on with your fairy tale, Bone. I'm all ears."

"You mind your mouth, boy," said Bone. He leaned over, resting his elbows on his knees. He spoke in a low voice, his eyes opening and closing like the cowls of hawks' eyes.

Hector leaned forward too, so that he could hear.

"They was once't a murderous bein' in the world what was call't Kicking Monster," said Bone. "He had him four young daughters and they was the only women in the whole world what had pussies. They were 'pussy gals.' And they lived in a house that was full of pussies."

Hector's face darkened still deeper as he flushed with embarrassment.

"These pussies looked like real women, but they was really only pussies. They was pussies hangin' on the walls, a-settin' in chairs, a-lyin' about all over. But these four gals they had legs and could walk around.

"Now, everybody heard they was pussies in that house and the men used to walk down the road to get there and get 'em some pussy. Whenever a boy or man come up, Kicking Monster met 'em at the gate and took 'em up to the house. He kicked 'em inside and they was never seen again. They just never come out of that house full of pussies.

"Then our boy hero, Killer-of-Enemies, he heard about all these disappearin' men and boys, and he come a-lookin' for Kicking Monster. But Killer-of-Enemies was smart and when he come up, he didn't turn his back on Kicking Monster. He made like he was a-fixin' to leave and then he come back and snuck into the house.

"When he did, these four gals come up to him and begged Killer-of-Enemies to fuck them. He asked them where all the men had gone to that had been kicked into the house. They tol't him that they ate them up. He ast why and they said they just liked to do that. Eat up the men and boys. Them gals tried to put their arms around Killer, but he pushed them away. He hollered at them, 'Stay away! That's no way to use your pussies!' "

Bone paused, looked over at Hector. The boy was listening raptly, his eyes wide.

"Well, sir, then Killer tol't them he was a-goin' to give them some medicine. He said they ain't never tasted it before, but it was made of sour berries, four kinds of wild berries. He said if they ate this medicine, he'd let them gals fuck him as much as they wanted.

"So, he gave them gals the four kinds of berries and said that they would make their pussies real sweet. Well, them gals chewed and swallered them berries until their mouths got plumb puckered and they couldn't chew 'em no more, they could only swaller them. They liked the sour berries. They said they made 'em feel like Killer-of-Enemies was fuckin' them. They got so giddy with pleasure and such, they just giggled like they was getting fucked. They thought he was really fuckin' them, but Killer wasn't doin' nothin'.

"Now, what happened was that when Killer-of-Enemies came to their house, these gals had real strong, sharp teeth. That's how they come to eat up all those men and boys their daddy had kicked into the house. But that medicine he gave 'em plumb dulled their teeth, and ground 'em down to powder, until they was all toothless as hags. So, after that, anybody could fuck a woman and not get his peter chewed off."

Bone leaned back and picked up the fob.

Hector stared at him for a long time, digesting the story.

"It doesn't make any sense," said Hector, finally.

"Well, it does. It tells how women used to be and how they got them soft little pussies."

"Oh, Bone," said Hector. "It's just a story."

Bone laughed. He looked over his shoulder and beckoned to Feather.

"Ned, come over here," Bone called. "Jay, you too."

Hector had toughened up in the *brasada*. He was mad that Bone had not let him go with Virgil Coldwater and Eddie Blue Sky the night before. He was restless, Bone knew. Did not like the confinement of the brush camp. Ned Feather was throwing his hunting knife at a mesquite log. Jay was gnawing on a cold biscuit, drinking the last of the grounds-filled coffee. Hector was sitting there on an old nail keg moping, trying to make the leather braid right.

"You boys want to ride over to where the Box B's burnin' that brush?" asked Bone.

"What for?" asked Jay Black Horse.

"See what useless looks like."

"I've seen enough of that right here."

"Don't you get smart now, Jay."

"Well, we ain't doin' nothin'. Ain't no women here."

Jay looked sullen. There was a flash of defiance in his dark eyes. Bone ignored the look.

"There'll be plenty to do when Eddie Blue and Virgil get back."

"When will that be?" asked Hector.

"They'll be here when they get here. They got a lot to tote."

"I could have helped," said Hector.

"I ain't a-goin' to argy with you," said Bone. "I'm fixin' to ride over and take a look-see. What about you boys?" He tossed his braided fob onto a weathered piece of two-by-four.

"I'll go," said Jay. "Nothin' else to do."

"Them boys are carryin' rifles, Bone," said Ned Feather.

"Well, we got rifles, too," Bone said.

"Yeah, I'll go," said Ned.

Bone looked at Hector.

"You can stay here and wait for Virg and them," said Bone.

"Naw," said Hector. "This place gives me the heebie-jeebies."

"You can always go back home, kid," said Feather.

"No I can't," said Hector.

Bone smiled mirthlessly.

"Let's get to goin' then," he said.

A half hour later, the four men rode out of camp, headed for El Rincón. They threaded their way through the mesquite trees toward the black smoke in the sky, the dark column that marked the spot where the Box B hands were cursing the heat, sweating, slapping at flies and mosquitoes.

Grace Baron sat at Matt's cherrywood desk in his den, groggy with self-loathing. Naomi's son had brought her another bottle of un-taxed whiskey the day before. She had been secretly sipping the contents since starting out that morning with a jiggerful in her coffee. The figures in the ledger swam before her eyes like tadpoles in a quivering pond. The numbers bobbed up and down like corks in a stormy sea.

I hate myself, she thought. Hate myself for being so weak. She clamped her teeth together; her jaw hardened and set. Resentments boiled up in her; resentments against Matt, against Peggy and Derek. Ethan, her oldest, was still the first in her affections, the child she most cherished. She hated herself for loving Ethan more than Derek or Margaret.

She tried to make sense of the numbers in the ledger. She looked at the stack of bills in front of her and wondered how she would ever be able to begin to set them down on paper in her condition. There were extra wages for the men working in the *brasada*. There were charges for equipment, for repairs, for gasoline, tools, cable, dyna-mite, kerosene, an endless list of costly items that were draining money from the Baron coffers.

That was another thing she resented: Matt's wild spending on clearing the *brasada*. It was costing the ranch money that they could ill afford. Ever since 1925, she dreaded having another year like that and the year after, when cattle prices fell alarmingly.

Now, instead of using the money for necessities, Matt was spend-ing a great deal on clearing that brush out of El Rincón.

She pulled open a drawer of the desk and looked at the small glass filled with a gin-clear liquid, the 100-proof sour-mash whiskey that Dave Tyler had brought. Grace looked around the room furtively, then closed her delicate fingers around the glass. She sipped the whiskey, felt it burn her tongue and throat. A rush of pleasure infused her senses, a heady surge of pleasure and guilt, all tangled together, all storming and swarming through the feather-edged nerve ends of her brain.

It had always been that way, ever since she had tasted her first drink of whiskey when she was twenty-one. Even then, she knew something was wrong; that she was different. The alcohol was beguiling, and it was not her slave, but her master. A demon in disguise. She hated the taste of it. She hated what it did to her. Yet she could not control her thirst for it, the craving, the incredible, overwhelming craving.

She heard Peggy moving about the house. Fear stirred the nerve-ends in Grace's brain. She had a dread of being discovered indulging in her secret passion. She put the glass back in the drawer and closed it, quickly, but gently so as not to spill it.

There were places all over the house where Grace had small portions of liquor hidden. Some places she had even forgotten. At times she would discover a flask or a bottle and, if she was sober, be filled with a deep sense of shame. She took a small sprig of mint from a small sachet she carried in her waistband, the sash that went around her dress. She put the mint in her mouth, crushed it with her teeth, felt it wash away the fumes of alcohol, fume up into her nostrils with its aromatic scent.

Oh, she hated herself. Why couldn't she stop? She could at times, of course, sometimes for months. But the craving was always there, the need, the endless need, the insurmountable desire to take the poison into her, to drink of it, to feel it flood her flesh and her senses, make her veins tingle, tingle with electricity.

Now, of course, she had been drinking for days. She had lost that glittering edge, that razor-sharp sensation of power. Now, there was only that infernal wallowing in torment. The wind, the interminable West Texas wind, blew hard against the house, rattling the window-panes, filling the sills with silt and grit. She hated the wind. She hated the heat of the summer, the desolation she felt inside.

The alcohol dulled some of her senses, but not all of them. She could still hear the wind, could feel it tearing at the house, razing it with dust blown from fallow, grassless pastures.

"Mother," Peggy called.

Grace's throat constricted and she leaned over the desk, tried to make sense of the figures in the ledger. She felt woozy, but swallowed a gulp of air and tried to clear her senses.

A moment later, the door to the den opened.

"Mother, I'm going with Daddy and Ethan over to La Plata."

"Did you finish the breakfast dishes?"

"Yes, Mother," said Peggy. She was a slender young woman, fine-boned like her mother, with small, budding breasts, light ashen blond hair, soft brown eyes that with her penetrating, open gaze, gave her the look of a startled doe. She was not as delicate as she looked, could ride with the best of her father's hands. Grace thought she was too thin, but Peggy thought she looked like Jean Harlow. She often wore huge beaded necklaces and loved patent-leather shoes, silk stockings. Now she was wearing riding togs, boots, the flared trousers, a loose-fitting blouse. Her hair was combed straight, tied in back with a brown silk ribbon. "I did everything you told me to."

"Why are you all leaving me?" asked Grace, sitting with her back straight as a cigar store Indian's, as if summoning up her haughty dignity as a weapon. "Maybe I'd go along, too."

"No, Mother. You wouldn't be able to sneak your whiskey," said Peggy, her voice petulant with sarcasm. "Besides, Daddy doesn't want you to come."

"Don't you talk to your mother that way," snapped Grace. "I'm your mother, and don't you forget it."

"Mother, you're slurring your words. Goodbye."

"You come back here, young lady. Come back here right now."

Grace stood up on wobbly legs. But Peggy was gone. She heard the door to the kitchen slam. A few minutes later, she heard the burred growl of Matt's car engine. Grace sat down, slumped over the ledger and began to weep. Then, the sobs racked her body. Her shoulders shook. Her chest quivered with short, gaspy breaths. This was a stage of her drinking she dreaded, when she lost control.

"Oh, I hate you!" she screamed. "I hate you all!"

But Grace hated herself most of all.

And the house grew suddenly silent as she closed her eyes and stopped weeping.

17

━■━

THE LAND WAS his, all of it. And he owned the sky, every majestic white ship-cloud that sailed its vast ocean, the whole blue sea of it from horizon to horizon, and the sun; the wind, too, with its grit wave and taste of dry alfalfa and blossomed lespedeza, velvet green clover, its tang of salty Gulf air and dank tidepools on driftwood beaches swarming with fiddler crabs and shrieking killdeer.

The horse he rode was a part of him, like extra legs and muscles and sinew, dancing through the smoke from the *brasada,* gliding graceful at the touch of his knees, the soft graze of his spurs along quivering tender flanks. Sugar was her name, and she was a one-man pony, sleek with her sweating summer skin, proud as any thoroughbred show mare, quick on her feet, trained to the rope, the best cutter in the outfit, with five good strong gaits and a show-horse spirit that belied her small size. She was quick and intelligent, with big sad brown eyes, and a quirky temperament. She was hard to catch and hard to rope, but she was a sucker for the sugar lumps Derek carried in his shirt pocket and would only surrender to the halter when he coaxed her across the pasture with the sweet bribes in the palm of his hand.

"Frisky, ain't she?" said Tom Casebolt, riding Thunder some thirty yards away.

"She's always got to have her morning ride," laughed Derek as he took Sugar out of the singlefoot and into a fox trot. The saddle became like a rocking chair, the ride smooth as silk, even and steady as a clock's tick.

"Don't go ridin' off now," warned Casebolt, but Derek Baron paid him no heed, and Sugar broke into a gallop at the delicate touch of his spurs, laid her ears back and braced the wind like a champion.

Derek rode through the battle streamers of smoke toward the sound of the steam tractors and the ringing chains, the angry growl of fire eating the stacked brush of the *brasada*. He was a great Civil War general, riding at Shiloh, rallying his troops, brandishing his imaginary sword as the brush rattled with grapeshot and unseen cannon boomed from the Union line.

He wheeled Sugar, felt her surge under him in a tight turn, surefooted as the eagle's hold on the sky, dodging brush, bounding over the scattered mesquite bushes, angling hard over like a sailboat beating to windward on a close reach. And Derek's laughter floated through the dark smoke, fluttered above the clank of machinery, the lashing crack of the flames gorging on green wood.

Sugar shied at a blazing faggot that popped into the air from a burning mesquite and Derek lurched in the saddle. The pony humped up under him and kicked with both hind legs as she hesitated for a moment to do battle with the sparking enemy. Her hind hooves hit the ground with a jolt, jarring Derek's butt against the cantle. Then, she bunched her muscles and raced away from the smoke and the crackling noise of the brush, the bit in her teeth, the reins slack in Derek's hands.

Derek gave Sugar her head, let her run until they cleared the smoke. Then, he hauled in on the reins, wrestled her for control until the bit shook loose. He hauled the iron hard against the back of her mouth.

"You little basket," said Derek, imitating his father's baby talk.

Sugar snorted and slowed to a lilting single-foot under Derek's expert prodding. He brought her to a walk, suddenly winded from the ride. The noise of the machinery seemed to ebb and mute as he and Sugar rode farther away from that part of El Rincón.

A sparrowhawk leaped into the air twenty yards in front of Derek and Sugar, a grasshopper in its beak. The horse spooked and veered toward the *brasada,* heading eastward. Derek laughed and watched the bird catch a current of air and soar over the mesquite trees until it disappeared.

Sugar galloped a zigzag pattern along an old wagon road that paralleled the *brasada*. Derek, shirtless in the heat, slackened his grip on the reins, let her run. The boiling sun lost its molten grip in the brisk rush of air fanned by the pony's headlong dash away from the noxious fumes of the burning green brush.

Derek exulted in the ride, feeling a part of Sugar, his muscles melded to hers, his face washed by the same warm clean air that blew her mane and topknot. Freshets of slough-scented dankness tingled his nostrils and he drew the faint tang of the sea, wafted on vagrant zephyrs, into his lungs.

Some movement, some shadowy presence caught Derek's eye as Sugar sped in aimless crooks and turns over grassy patches of earth strewn with the detritus of dead tree limbs, the flotsam of spring gully washers and windstorms. He twisted in the saddle, unsure of what he'd seen. Sugar bolted at an acute angle, and Derek knew she'd seen the same alien presence, the same dark figures afoot just outside the edge of the *brasada,* their horses tied to scattered willows that gave them shade.

He heard a yelp, then a high-pitched scream that died so quickly he thought he imagined it.

At first, Derek thought the men might be Box B hands, tending to a stray calf, but as he hauled in on Sugar's reins, he realized that they were not.

"Whoa, Sugar, whoa up girl."

Sugar slacked her pace and stumbled over a bent tree limb blown to the patchy sward by some long-gone wind and slowed to a jolting, stiff-legged halt.

Two men stood, their backs to Derek, watching something on the ground. Derek heard the sound of a man, or a calf, groaning. He rode up to see what the men were doing.

He knew now that they were not Box B hands.

"What's a-goin' on here?" Derek drawled.

One of the men turned around, glared at Derek.

Derek saw that the man was an Indian, someone he'd never seen before. Someone, something, on the ground moaned and he heard a soft slapping sound. Derek's throat constricted; he tried to swallow. For a moment his mind swam with confusing thoughts. He knew of no Indians who worked on the Box B. It took him a second to arrange the jumbled thoughts bobbing aimlessly in the swirling sea of his mind.

The other standing Indian looked around, stood up straight.

"What you got there?" Derek asked, rising up in the stirrups, trying to see past the two strangers. He saw arms and legs on the ground, but no faces. One of the men on the ground seemed to be lying on his belly.

Neither Indian said a word. One turned back to watch the two men on the ground. The other swung his rifle around, pointed it in Derek's direction.

"Somebody hurt there?" Derek's words sounded foolish to him. One of the men on the ground was moaning pitifully, as if in pain. "Fall off his horse?"

The words sounded false in Derek's ears, all hollow and empty like the strained questions you ask in the dark when you think you heard something, when you think someone you can't see has entered your room at night.

"Better get the hell out of here, boy," growled the Indian who was still looking at Derek.

The other Indian looked around again. He stepped aside, grinning.

Derek did not know what to make of what he saw. There were two men on the ground. They seemed joined together. Both were facing downward, one atop the other, as if they were wrestling. The man on top was another Indian. His trousers were down around his ankles. The man on the bottom was stark naked, except for his socks.

The Indian on top looked over at Derek. His eyes glittered with a glazed look. He grinned crookedly.

The bottom of Derek's stomach plunged downward with a sickening rush. He recognized the Indian. This was the man his father, and every Box B hand, was hunting.

"Criminy," breathed Derek. "You—you're Bone."

"Y'ant some white meat, sonny?"

Bone grabbed the man on the ground by the hair, jerked his head around.

"Go on, Derek. Get out of here," bleated Hector Aguilar. There were tears in his eyes; dirt streaked his face. His lips were crushed and bloody; they looked as if he'd been eating raspberry jam and it was smeared all over his mouth.

"What's he doin' to you, Heck?" asked Derek.

"Puttin' the rod to him," said Bone, grinning. The other two Indians smiled widely, nodded in agreement.

"Go away, Derek," said Hector.

"That Matt's young'un?" asked Bone. He moved his hips and Hector closed his eyes, winced in pain.

Derek saw what was happening to Hector, but he didn't know what was happening. His mind screamed for him to shut it down, lock out the terrible sight he saw, but it wouldn't shut down. He could not stop looking either. He watched helplessly as Bone did those things to Hector. He watched Hector squirm and heard him moan and cry out when it hurt him. He saw the naked flesh of the two men and he imagined what he could not see. And that was the worst thing of all.

Derek could not stop his mind and it roiled with dreams that had come alive, dark dreams that became stark images in the glaring sunlight. And he saw the faces of the other two Indians, saw them leer and saw their eyes glitter like the eyes of stalking snakes. Derek shuddered inwardly and tried to look away. But he could not tear his glance away from Hector and Bone. He could not stuff his ears to silence. He could not breathe and yet his heart slammed thunder in his chest and his eyes glazed with the horrible sight of Bone pinning Hector to the ground and doing an unspeakable thing to the helpless boy.

Derek's mind raced with thoughts that had no anchor, no tie to anything he had ever known or ever dreamed. They swarmed up in confusion like startled moths, like deformed insects hatching, taking wing, flapping awkwardly in circles, burning in the light like streaking comets, like dying fireflies gone mad.

Derek could not put words to what he was seeing. He could not put meaning to any of it, and for those few dire moments he was unable to look away, or to help Hector. Time seemed not so much to stand still as to become warped, distorted like a wavy image in a tin mirror. The images of Hector and Bone drifted in and out of the crumpled mirror and they were locked together in a kind of primitive timelessness.

There was both something unnatural about the act and something shatteringly normal. In his mind Derek knew he had seen such things before, or thought them, or dreamed them, or imagined them, or lived them in some dark corner of his mind. It was, he thought, in a moment of brilliant lucidity, as if he had come upon two animals in the wild, caught them unawares. One was fierce, the hunter, the other was frightened and weak, the prey. And, somehow, Derek knew for that single diamond-cut instant that Bone was killing Hector, that he had run him down and was sinking his fangs into his neck and disemboweling him with something Derek could not see, did not want to see. It was a killing, something wild and strange, an animal killing another and devouring its kill while the creature was still alive.

April Killian shrieked as the rubber ball with a picture of a clown on it sailed past, just out of reach of her hands. She turned helplessly and watched it strike the ground, bounce through a clump of alder bushes and roll downhill.

"You dummy," cried her sister, Connie. "That was an easy catch."

"It went into the berry patch," said April. "I'll get it."

"You better not go in there, April. No tellin' what's down there."

"Oh, you old fraidy-cat."

Twelve-year-old April and her sister, Constance Paige, who was fifteen, were playing in the fallow field near the house. The ground was bare from the tread of their feet over the years. The croquet gates had long since rusted and sagged out of shape. Here, they had played jacks and marbles with Steve, their older brother, had laughed and run after one another at tag, played hide-and-seek and "prisoner." There were horseshoe pits along one side, their pegs leaning disconsolately in four-inch-thick dust. The badminton net hung loosely on two cast-iron poles near the pony track, littered with dried horseapples and remnants of worn-out leather halters, the D-rings long since lost and rusted in the thick dust. At one corner were swings and slides that had not been used in years, a sandbox where the children used to play with toy shovels and pails.

April stepped cautiously down a short, steep path into a gully choked with blackberry brambles. Connie ran up to the top, stood there, unwilling to go any farther. April reached down and tugged on one of her knee-high socks, smoothed her green calico skirt. She was wearing soft canvas shoes and a yellow jersey blouse. Her sandy hair was tied back with a green satin ribbon.

"I don't see it," said Connie, who was wearing khaki shorts and argyle stockings, leather sport shoes, a plaid Western shirt. Her hair was auburn, her eyes blue.

"It can't be far."

An ocotillo waved in the soft breeze. Dotting the border of the path were Spanish daggers and small cholla, a few dried clumps of nopal. April swiveled her hips to avoid the daggers and was careful not to brush her feet against the deceptively beautiful cholla with their fine needles.

The girl disappeared into the thicket.

"Dang you, April," swore Connie. "You come back up here right away."

"Oh fudge," said April. "I can't find it."

Connie stood on tiptoes to try and see her sister.

"Where are you?" she called.

There was no answer.

Connie bit her lip, started down the path.

April winced as she brushed against thorny berry bushes. She reached down, touched her leg. She looked at her fingers; they were smeared with blood.

"Darn," she said. She felt slightly dizzy, looked around for something to wipe away the blood. She didn't want to get her clothes dirty. Her mother would be upset if she got blood on her skirt or blouse. "Oh, shoot," she said, and started to go back. Then, she heard something that gelled her veins.

A clatter sounded in the brush that sounded like a thousand wooden castanets. Then, she heard another and another, all around her, a chattering chorus rattling louder and louder until her senses shrieked at the cacophonous fugue.

April looked down at her feet, saw the blur of motion as the first rattlesnake struck. She felt a sharp slap on her leg, saw the writhing snake coiling up to bite her again. She felt a searing pain, saw blood and a yellowish puslike fluid oozing from a pair of holes in her flesh. She kicked at the snake and another struck, from a different direction.

Connie screamed, ran back up the path.

"April, come back," she called.

April heard her sister's voice, turned, feeling weak and nauseated. Her stomach tipped in a queasy whirl. She felt other slaps against her legs, but she couldn't look down. She tried to find the path, stumbled through bushes that raked her legs with bloody scratches.

"I'm going to get Mother," yelled Connie.

"Help me, help me," called April, her voice faint. "Snakes."

Connie hesitated, turning in different directions. She didn't want to leave her sister, but she was afraid.

"Run, April, run," screeched Connie. "Come on. Hurry."

"I—I can't," said April, woozy from the rattlesnake bites.

"You want me to run for help?"

April stepped on a rattlesnake. It whipped up, sank deadly fangs into her kneecap. She batted it away with a swipe of her hand. She found the path, tried to climb it. The bushes scratched her hands, lashed at her legs. She did not feel the Spanish daggers prick her skin. She stepped in a clump of cholla and needles stung her through the canvas of her shoes.

"Ow, ow," she whispered, unable to summon her full voice.

Connie heard the noise of April's passage up through the thicket, the soft whisper of her voice sounding far away.

"Hurry, April, hurry. Did you get bit?"

"Oh, oh, oh," moaned April and this time she sounded closer.

Connie, afraid of snakes, started to go back down the path, but couldn't uproot her feet. She began to weep, uncontrollably, a fear rising in her until it gripped her throat, sandpapered it raw. She stood there in helpless dread, waiting to catch sight of her sister.

April began to falter. Dark blots floated in front of her eyes. Adrenaline rushed through her veins, giving her strength. Her heart pounded fast, hammered blood at her temples, and the ocean roared like a storm-surged tide in her ears. She no longer saw any snakes, but their images were indelible in her mind, twisting, striking, coiling, whipping at her like quirts in a gauntlet.

Connie saw the top of her sister's head.

"Oh, April, come on," she said, her voice suddenly back. Tear tracks streaked her face, but she was unaware of them. Her eyes brimmed with moisture, but she felt a rush of grateful relief. "Hurry, hurry."

"I'm—I got bit," gasped April, looking up, seeing her sister standing there. "I feel funny."

"Oh my God," said Connie.

April hove herself up the last few feet, then collapsed. She fought against the darkness folding over her like sudden nightfall. A wave of nausea engulfed her. She vomited, spraying bile and half-digested pancakes, bacon and biscuits into the dust. Spittle oozed from the corners of her mouth. She began to shudder with convulsions.

Connie saw the fang holes in April's legs, recoiled at the sight of the vomit flowing from her sister's mouth. She smelled the acid tang of the vomitus and her stomach rippled with an involuntary spasm.

April's body undulated in a convulsive seizure. Her eyelids fluttered, batting open and closed, revealing the vacant stare of a person in shock.

Connie turned and ran, screaming, toward the house, four hundred yards away.

"Mother, Mother, oh God," she yelled.

Frances Killian heard Connie's cries, got up from her desk in the den and raced to the window.

She saw Connie running across the playground, flailing her arms, her face bleached white.

Where is April? howled through her mind.

Frances rushed to the kitchen, banged through the back door at a run. She caught Connie in her arms, felt the girl surge against her, sobbing and gibbering incoherently.

"April, she got bit. Snakes. Quick. Mother, help me."

"Where is she?" Frances asked calmly.

Blubbering and whipping her head back and forth, Connie pointed back toward the playfield.

"Now, you just calm down, young lady," said Frances. She took her daughter's hand and they ran back to the field to find April. Connie resisted her mother's pull on her, but Frances jerked her along.

"There, there," sobbed Connie, pointing to the crumpled body of her sister.

Frances released her grip on Connie's hand, dashed to April's side and knelt down. She saw the ugly dark holes in the girl's legs, all puffed and blue around the edges, still oozing creamy venom mixed with blood. She turned April over, wiped her mouth with her hand. She bent over, listened for her breath. She opened both of April's eyes, saw the vacuous stare.

"She's still alive," said Frances. "Connie, run to the house and call Doc Emberlin. Quickly."

"Oh God," said Connie, her eyes fixed on her unconscious sister.

"Right now," Frances said calmly. "Go right now. Then, find Consuela, have her meet me."

Connie shook off her fear and numbness, ran toward the house.

Frances listened to April's shallow breathing for a moment, then picked her daughter up in her arms. She held her tightly, speaking softly into the girl's ear.

"Stay with me, April, honey. Mommy's going to make you well."

April's mouth was slack and every few seconds her body shook with faint convulsions.

Frances knew the poison was racing through April's veins, toward her heart. She prayed silently that she could save her life.

"Consuela," she said to herself, "please be there to help me."

She heard a door slam at the house, looked up. Connie was inside. But April was dying slowly in her arms.

18

———■———

A T FIRST, THERE was nothing in Derek. There was no fear, no hate, no judgment, no conclusion. There were just the mystery and the ghastly wonder, the awesome fascination, the thrill of discovering something unknown and forbidden, of seeing something no one else in the world had ever seen. He did not see Hector in pain. He did not see Bone impaling him. He could not fathom such things during that first moment of shock. Instead, he saw nameless specters, faceless beings performing a strange, slow dance on the ground, a primitive ritual that only a few had ever witnessed.

Hector moaned and Derek felt something tug at his senses, a ripple of electricity that coursed through his spine and stung his brain. He did not know if Hector was groaning in pleasure or in pain. He saw the look on Bone's face and recoiled from it. The Indian wore the savage, mindless mask of the conqueror, the gloating smirk of the victor in an ancient rite of combat. It was a chilling look, a look that struck deep chords in Derek, a look that stirred up hidden primordial fragments of thoughts, as if he remembered being naked himself and dancing around a fire in a deep, dark cave, with obscene paintings on the flame-smudged walls.

And then, Derek knew he had to stop it. Had to stop it before he was drawn into it, drawn into the hurt and the thrill of it. Before he became like Bone and the other two Indians.

"You leave Hector alone," said Derek, his voice squeaking with an adolescent whine.

"That one looks tender," said Bone. "Virgin, too, I bet."

Jay Black Horse and Ned Feather swung their rifles around and started toward Derek.

"Yeah," said Ned. "You get down off that horse, boy."

Hector tried to squirm free of Bone's grip. Bone smashed a fist down hard on Hector's head, driving his face into the dirt. The ground pinched off Hector's scream as his mouth flattened against it.

Sugar started to back away. Jay dashed forward, grabbed the bridle close to the bit and jerked hard.

Derek leaned over Sugar's withers, threw a roundhouse swipe at the Indian's face.

"You sonofabitch," yelled Ned, rushing up to grab Derek, unseat him from the horse.

Bone stood suddenly, pulled his trousers up.

"You stay," he said to Hector. Hector shivered with the sudden release, lifted his head to see what they were doing to Derek. Bone buckled his belt, took three steps to retrieve his rifle. The weapon leaned in the crook of a mesquite tree.

Hector saw Bone pick up the rifle. He turned over, pulled his legs up to his naked belly, tucked himself into a ball. He began to sob and to rock with fear. Tears streamed down his face.

"Don't kill me," Hector whimpered.

"Shut up," said Bone.

Jay and Ned were trying to unseat Derek. Derek kicked Ned in the face with the heel of his boot. Jay had worked himself around to the other side and was trying to grab Derek's stirrup. Sugar's eyes flared like a pair of peeled boiled eggs and she tried to rear up.

Bone cocked the rifle, brought it to his shoulder. He took a bead on Derek's horse, set the front blade sight square on the middle of Sugar's chest. When the horse's forefeet struck the ground, Bone squeezed the trigger. The old Winchester bucked against his shoulder.

Hector screamed in terror.

As soon as Bone had pulled the trigger, he heard the pound of hoofbeats. A split second later, he heard a rifle report. It sounded like the crack of a twenty-foot bullwhip. He saw Derek's horse stagger under the impact of the hundred and fifty-grain bullet.

"Somebody's comin'," Bone shouted.

Ned and Jay jumped backwards as Sugar fell back on her haunches, blood streaming from her chest. They too heard the sound of a horse coming fast. Ned heard the spine-tingling *whuz* of a bullet streaking over his head. Both men scrambled into a ragged run for their horses. Bone was already climbing into his saddle by the time they reached their mounts.

Tom Casebolt fired his rifle again. A puff of dust spun up from the earth as the bullet plowed a furrow under Jay's boot just before he swung into the saddle.

"Let's get the fuck out of here," yelled Ned, whipping his horse with the reins, banging his heels into the animal's flanks.

Casebolt shot on the run, levering the shells into the chamber of his rifle as he closed the distance.

Bone headed straight for the *brasada,* disappeared into a clump of mesquite trees, leaving a trail of broken branches and torn leaves. Ned and Jay followed close behind, vanishing out of sight at different angles. A bullet whipped through the brush, whined like a snarling badger.

Sugar crumpled. Her forelegs collapsed. Blood flecked her rubbery nostrils, blew out in a cloud of rosy spray. Derek slid out of the saddle, staggered to one side as Casebolt rode up, the barrel of his rifle smoking.

"Derek. You O.K.?"

"O.K." said Derek.

"Who's that yonder?" asked Casebolt, pointing with the barrel of his rifle.

"It's Hector. Jesus, Tom, look what that bastard Bone done to Sugar."

Sugar fell over on her side, her eyes glazing over with the frost of mortal agony.

Tom left his saddle as he reined up. His horse was still moving as he dismounted, hit the ground running. He gripped his rifle, used it to keep his balance.

"He shot Sugar, Tom," said Derek.

"Goddamned Bone."

Tom scanned the edge of the *brasada* for a long moment before he knelt down to see what he could do for the injured horse.

Derek stared at the hole in Sugar's chest. It continued to pump blood, dark freshets that stained the sand, the stones.

"It looks bad, Tom."

"She's a goner, Derek. Sorry."

"Can't we do anything?"

Tom started to shake his head. He never finished. There was a rattle of brush and three shots shattered the stillness. Derek heard the dull thud of lead smacking into flesh. He thought, at first, that the bullets had hit Sugar, but she didn't move. Instead, Tom made a low sound in his throat, stiffened for a moment.

"God, oh God," murmured Tom as he pitched forward. Derek saw the tears in the back of Tom's shirt, reached out to grab him. Tom quivered, gurgled, and reached out with a single arm. Then, his hand dropped limp, fell on Sugar's neck.

Derek turned him over, saw the blood bubbling from Tom's lips.

"Tom, Tom," Derek called softly. Tom's eyes fluttered and the sound in his throat died as air from his lungs pushed a bloody bubble through his lips.

Derek turned around quickly.

"They're gone," said Hector. "I heard 'em run away after they shot their rifles."

"They killed Tom," said Derek, his voice hollow and sounding far off in his ears. "They killed him dead."

Hector said nothing. He lay there, curled up into a ball, his eyes wide and sad as anything Derek had ever seen. He looked back at Tom's face. He leaned over, put his ear to Casebolt's mouth. Tom was not breathing. Derek pulled the foreman close, held him in his arms.

"I'll get them, Tom," he whispered. "I'll get ever' damn one of 'em."

It was dead quiet for several moments. Sugar heaved a last sigh and startled Derek. He twisted around, looked over his shoulder. The horse's eyes were closed. A froth of blood clung to her lips.

Just like Tom, he thought incongruously and fought back the tears.

"Sonsabitches," he muttered.

Hector got up from the ground slowly. He did not try to hide himself from Derek.

Derek watched Hector stand up wobbly as he held Tom Casebolt in his arms, holding him even though he knew his friend was dead. Tom was no longer bleeding. And he wasn't breathing. And he didn't move. But Derek held him and looked at Hector.

Hector gathered up his scattered clothes and put them on, first his torn underwear, then his Levi's, his boots, and finally, his shirt. He moved as if he was in great pain. Then, he walked over to his horse, ground-tied to a mesquite bush.

"Hector?" said Derek.

Hector looked at him as he grabbed the saddlehorn with his left hand. He put his right foot in the stirrup, swung up into the saddle.

"Where you going?" asked Derek.

"Home," said Hector.

"We got to take care of Tom," said Derek idiotically.

"He's dead, isn't he?"

"Yes, but we got to do something."

"I'm going home, Derek."

There was something about the way Hector said it that made Derek realize how important it was to Hector. To go home. Derek knew he had run away. Run away to live with Bone. Well, that was over now. Bone had done something to Hector. Something bad.

"Well, just go on then," said Derek.

Hector rattled the reins, turned his horse. He rode over to where Derek was sitting on the ground with Tom in his arms. He looked down at Derek and his eyes were dead and cold and empty. They were filled with a sadness that Derek could feel all through him, something deep and hard and chilling that was like cold in the bones, but all through him, under his skin like frost, like ice.

"Don't you ever tell anybody what Bone did to me, hear?"

"Well, I wouldn't—"

"I mean it, Derek. If you tell anyone, I'll break your neck."

"Cripes, Heck, come on."

Hector said nothing. Instead he looked away, dug his heels into his horse's flanks and rode off, to the west, to his home.

Derek watched him go and felt that chill run through him again, that emptiness that filled him and made him sad, and then he looked down at Tom's dead face and started to cry. His sobs began building until he could no longer control them and he tightened his grip on Tom and rocked with him and then he began to curse and pray at the same time.

"Oh, Tom, goddamnit, why did you let them kill you?"

Frances slapped Connie across the mouth, firmly, but gently, snapping the girl's head to one side, rattling the pupils of her eyes into erratic orbits.

Connie did not cry out, but the blow sobered her, brought her back to her senses.

"Yes, Mother."

"Go up the stairs to our washroom and bring your daddy's straight razor. Do you know where he keeps it?"

"I don't know. Yes." Frances sensed her daughter's confusion, but she was so tense she could not manage to be indulgent. She knew April's condition was grave, that she might die.

"Hurry up, honey. Please."

Connie waggled her head to shake off the daze that clung to her thoughts like shaggy Spanish moss. April lay on a pile of blankets on the dining room table, her face ghostly white, her limbs jerking spasmodically as though she were being electrocuted. Connie choked back the tears, stumbled from the room.

"I should have never let April go down there," she muttered to herself.

Frances pulled April's shoes and socks off, shuddered at the sight of all the puncture wounds. Her eyes burned with an intense, sad light, a fierce determination to make her daughter well. But she could not shake off her anxiety, the dread she felt in her heart. Yet her hands were as steady as her resolve as she steeled herself to view all of the snakebite holes on April's body.

"Consuela," called Frances, her head turned toward the kitchen. *"Andale, andale."*

"I am coming, *Señora.*"

The *criada* emerged from the kitchen carrying a large pot of boiling water and several clean dishtowels. She set them on a rattan mat on the maple table at April's feet. There were more blankets piled on the glassed-in maple hutch, larger towels, just in case they were needed. The dining room was spacious, all in maple furniture, knotty-pine walls that were doweled. There was a hearth, a large stone fireplace for cold winter evenings. Now, to Frances, it seemed in disarray, cold and heartless with April lying atop the table, not even conscious.

"Do you want me to bring the soap?"

"No," said Frances. "Just go and find Connie upstairs in my washroom and see that she has Ben's razor. Bring the razor strop."

Frances dropped one of the dishtowels into the pot of boiling water, holding onto one corner. She pulled it free, let it drip for several moments. She wondered if she had forgotten anything. She had seen a boy get bitten by a rattlesnake when she was a young girl and had watched as his father cleaned the wound, cut deep into it with a sharp pocketknife and sucked the poison out. She had not recoiled at the sight, but had watched the whole thing in rapt fascination.

"This is going to hurt, honey," she said to April. Then, she grabbed another corner of the hot wet towel and slapped it on one of her daughter's legs. April never moved.

Frances swabbed the leg gently with one hand, draped another towel over the edge of the pot, half of it in the steaming water. She cleaned the holes of blood and venom until they stood out in stark relief on April's legs, swollen puncture wounds that made her mother wince with empathetic pain.

Connie entered the room with the straight razor. Right behind her was Consuela, carrying Ben's razor strop.

"What do you want me to do with this?" Connie asked, offering her mother the razor.

"Give it to Consuela. Strop it sharp, Consuela, then take the razor into the kitchen. You have another pot boiling on the stove?"

"Sí, Señora."

"Put the blade in the water and let it stand for a minute or two. Then, bring it back to me."

"What are you going to do, Mother?" asked Connie.

Consuela took the razor and strop into the kitchen. They could hear her raking the blade across the smooth leather. It sounded as if she was slapping human flesh.

"Never mind. Did you reach Doc Emberlin?"

"Yes, ma'am. He said he'd come right away."

Frances bit her lip as she gently turned April's leg over and saw more puncture wounds. It would take the doctor the better part of two hours to drive to the Lazy K, another forty-five minutes or so to reach the house from the gate. Time was precious, so precious she couldn't even fathom it.

"Did you tell him your sister was bitten by rattlesnakes?"

"Yes, ma'am."

"What did he say?"

"Keep her warm, don't let her walk around. He said to tie a turn-a-key or something like that around her legs above the wounds and keep her head higher than her feet."

"A tourniquet," said Frances, pulling April's skirt up to see if there were any other snakebites. She slid her daughter's panties down her legs, rolled her to one side, then the other. She breathed a long sigh of relief.

Consuela brought the straight razor. She handed it to Frances, then forced herself to look at April's legs. Her hands went to her mouth and a look of shocked surprise contorted her bronze face.

"*Ay de mi,*" Consuela gasped. " *'Sus Mari—*"

"Consuela," said Frances steadily, "I am going to cut an X in each of those bites and suck the poison out. I want you to take a clean hot towel and wipe away the blood. Constance, bring me a large bowl to spit in." She set the razor on a clean towel she had laid out for that purpose.

"Ugh," said Connie. But she left the room, and Frances heard the dishes in the cupboard rattling and clinking.

"But first, I'm going to tie tourniquets around her legs, high up," Frances said to Consuela. "Bring me two wooden spoons."

Frances wiped a strand of vagrant hair away from her sweating forehead, where the worry lines had deepened into quivering furrows. She folded a dishtowel into a thin rope, slid it under April's right leg. Connie set the bowl on the edge of the table, watching her mother in fascination. Consuela brought two short-handled wooden spoons. Frances pulled the towel tight, tied a knot, leaving a loop for the spoon handle.

"I want you to twist these tight every few minutes, Consuela," said Frances, "then loosen them for a moment. You'll have to remember to do it or April could lose her legs."

Consuela nodded, her face a pale mauve.

Frances tied another towel around her daughter's left leg and inserted the other spoon handle. She twisted it until the tourniquet was tight.

Consuela tightened the other tourniquet.

"Are you staying, Constance?" Frances asked. She placed the rolled up tablecloth under April's head, elevating it.

"If—if I can help."

"You can. You can take another wet towel and help Consuela."

Frances picked up the razor, chose the highest puncture wound and sliced two cuts in the shape of an X. Blood and venom flowed from the cuts. She bent down and placed her mouth over the fresh wounds and sucked until her mouth filled with fluid. She grabbed the bowl Connie had brought and spat into it.

"Ugh," said Connie again.

"Keep quiet," said Frances, barely moving her lips. She continued to suck at the wound until there was only blood. Then, she cut into the bite right next to it.

For what seemed like hours, Frances sucked out poison and blood until her cheeks and lips were numb. Consuela and Connie worked the tourniquets. April continued to have mild convulsions and once her eyes opened, but she did not cry out.

Doctor Emberlin arrived two and a half hours later, came into the room unannounced.

"You've done fine, Frances," he said, after lifting April's eyelids and taking her temperature. "Do you have rubbing alcohol?"

"Yes," said Frances. "Consuela."

"*Si, Señora.*"

"Frances, take all of April's clothes off. I want you to rub her entire body with alcohol. She's running a high fever. I've called for an ambulance. It should be here soon."

"Will she . . . ?"

"I don't know," said Emberlin. He took off his coat, loosened his tie and rolled up his sleeves. He removed his stethoscope from his black bag as Frances removed the rest of April's clothing. He draped a towel over the girl's pubic area and listened to her heartbeat. He moved the stethoscope to several different places and listened for a long time at each spot.

"She's in shock," he said.

"Is that bad?" asked Frances.

"It could be, but I think it's a blessing at the moment. She's breathing fairly well. Her heartbeat's slow, but that's in our favor. If we can get her to the hospital in Corpus, she might have a chance. She will probably need a blood transfusion, maybe several. Do you know her type?"

Frances shook her head.

"They'll type it at the hospital. In the meantime, get as many people as you know over there who give us their blood and we'll try and save this little girl."

"I wish Ben were here," said Frances.

"Where's Mother Jane?"

"She went into town with Steve. I don't know when they'll be back."

"Try and find her. April will need as many of her friends and relatives as possible around her when she comes out of this."

"Connie, get on the phone. Call all the ranches and ask for volunteers to give blood."

"Yes, Mother," said Connie. She went into the den as Consuela brought a bottle of rubbing alcohol into the dining room. Emberlin began swabbing April's legs, her chest. He rubbed her back as well. "This will help bring down her temperature. I'm going to give her a couple of shots to help lessen the fever and to ward off infection." He looked at the bowl on the table. "You got all that out of those puncture wounds?"

"Yes," said Frances.

"You did a hell of a job, Frances. Has she had convulsions?"

"Yes."

"Many?"

"Quite a few."

"Strong?"

"Not very strong," said Frances.

Emberlin gave April another shot.

"This is an anticonvulsive drug," he said.

"Doc," said Frances. "I'm scared. Real scared."

He took her hands in his, squeezed them.

"We'll do all we can to pull her through. Make some coffee, take it with you to the hospital in Corpus."

"Can I ride in the ambulance?"

"Of course," he said. "I was going to insist on it."

He loosened the tourniquets on April's legs. An old white ambulance, a Buick, drove up into the yard. Consuela let the attendants in. They carried a World War I Army stretcher into the dining room. Emberlin gave them instructions.

The two men put a smock around April. They seemed to know what they were doing. Connie watched their faces as they looked dispassionately at April's naked body.

"Can I go too?" she asked. "In the ambulance?"

Doc Emberlin looked at the chief attendant. The attendant nodded.

"I'll leave now," said Emberlin. "I want to get everything ready."

"I wish you were going with us, Doc," Frances said.

"These boys know what to do," he replied. He put his stethoscope away, closed his bag and waved goodbye.

Frances, Connie and Consuela watched as the ambulance attendants lifted April from the table, placed her on the stretcher. They
wrapped her tightly with blankets and carried her through the living
room and out the door. Connie and Frances followed after.

"Tell Jane and Steve where we are," Frances said to Consuela.
"Tell Ben if he gets in."

Consuela nodded, too stunned to talk.

"Mother, do you want to take along a pot of coffee?" Connie
asked.

"I'd probably burn myself to death," said her mother and then
hated herself for saying the word.

As they walked toward the ambulance, Connie noticed, for the
first time, that there were tears in her mother's eyes.

19

—■—

DEREK FINALLY STOPPED crying when he heard the rumbling growl of a motor and recognized the metallic clank of his father's car. He waited until it drove up, then swiped the wet tears from his face with the back of his forearm.

His father and his sister, Peggy, lanky as a colt, got out of the car and came over.

"What's the matter with Sugar?" asked his sister. "Oh my God, she's dead."

Matt ignored his daughter, stalked over to Derek. Derek looked up at him, his face smeared with streaks of dirt and tears.

"Tom got shot," Derek said.

"Was it Bone?"

"I reckon."

"Get up, boy."

Derek glared at his father. Peggy squinched up her face, looked down at Tom. She crinkled her nose.

"Whoo boy," she breathed softly.

Peggy was wearing her hair shoulder-length, braided, the ends tied off with brown silk ribbons. She wore a loose ranch shirt that emphasized her wide, boyish shoulders, tight trousers that revealed the lean hips that flared out in graceful curves. Her ankles, hidden by cowhide boots, were trim as a racehorse's, her arms and legs lean, without a trace of fat.

Derek glared at her, then pushed Tom away, laid the head gently on the ground. He got to his feet. His knees felt like they were full of jelly and he was lightheaded. He wasn't as tall as his father, but he stood as straight.

"Let's take Tom home," said Matt. "Derek, you get his legs. Peg, open the back door of the car."

Matt grabbed Tom by the shoulders. As he lifted Tom, Derek raised the feet. He couldn't look at Tom's scuffed boots. He felt sick inside. They carried him to the car. Matt climbed in, pulled Tom across the seat. Derek had to let the dead man's feet dangle to the floor. Matt turned Tom over so that his face was turned toward the back of the seat.

"Close your door," Matt said to Derek.

Derek closed the door. His father closed the other side. Then, Matt doubled over in pain, staggered to the back of the car. He held on to the rear fender, his face drenched in sweat, contorted in pain.

"What's wrong, Daddy?" asked Peggy, coming around to his side.

"Damned gut," said Matt. He was wondering what his sister, Lou, would say when she found out Tom was dead. "Can you drive, Peg?"

"Sure," she said.

Derek walked around, stood next to his father, watching helplessly.

"Let's go," said Matt. "Damn, I hate to tell Lou about Tom. It'll hit her hard."

"Aren't you going to send anyone after Bone?" asked Derek.

"Not now," grunted his father through gritted teeth.

"Maybe I better get after him myself," said Derek.

Matt straightened up. His face, blanched, looked ghastly, Derek thought.

"No, you stay out of this, Derek."

"Well, damn, Daddy. I mean we can't just let him get away with what he done. He can't be far. We could catch him and shoot him like he done Tom."

"Not now," growled Matt. "Get in the car. Both of you. And quit talking like a damned field hand, Derek."

"Well, shoot," said Derek.

"Drive over to where the men are working, Peggy," said her father. "I want to see Ethan before we go on back to the house."

"We ought to take you on home, Daddy," she said. "You're looking mighty peaked."

"Do what I say," Matt said, his face scored with tight deep lines. He slumped, then, and his shoulders started shaking as he fought back the tears.

Peggy sat there, unable to move. Derek stared at his father, his lips quivering as if he wanted to speak, but unable to summon up the words.

"Goddamn, Tom," croaked Matt, and he let the tears come, let the grief wash through him like a rain, like a mighty Gulf tide sweeping across the stagnant marshes, rattling the cattails, shaking the driftwood and tangled dead plants loose from their moorings.

Peggy looked at Derek. Derek looked at Peggy. Both sat there, stunned, as Matt shrank in the seat, doubled up with pain and the first crush of mourning.

"I'm really sorry, Daddy," squeaked Peggy.

"Best get on," said Matt, sitting straight, pawing at his face, the tears, blinking his eyes. "Derek, you get Tom's rifle, tie Thunder to the back bumper. We'll drive real slow. One of the hands can ride Tom's horse back to the stables." Matt's voice sounded weak, strained.

Derek got out of the car. He returned a few moments later, tied Tom's horse to the back bumper of the car. He put the rifle in the back seat, on the floor.

"Let's get out of here," growled Derek. He didn't look at his father, but Matt seemed to have a grip on himself.

"Well, all right," said Peggy with a sigh of relief, shifting the car with a grinding of gears.

Derek looked back at the *brasada* as Peggy drove away at a crawl. He wished he could go in there now and find Bone, drag him out and punish him in some way. He looked at Sugar lying there and a sadness engulfed him like a smothering tide. He thought of Tom Casebolt, alive until a short while ago, now dead. Tom would never ride with him again, never rouse him out of sleep early in the morning and take him along as he did his work. They would never sit down at the table again and complain over Cookie's sonofabitch stew, nor rave over his flapjacks. He would never see Tom tie a knot, burn a brand, bulldog a steer, shoot an empty tin can tossed in the air. Derek had learned so many things from Tom, so many they blurred in his mind, like fluttering spring leaves through a rainy windowpane.

Derek fought back the tears welling up in his eyes. He turned to look out the front window as Peggy spun the wheel in a tight turn to go back the way they had come. His father was looking at him.

"We'll get Bone," said Matt. Sweat streamed into his eyebrows, scudded down his cheekbones. Derek could hear his father's teeth clack together.

"I bet he'll run now."

"We'll still get him. No matter where he goes." Matt let out a sigh that was like a groan. He was thinking that Lou would be the first to take up a rifle. She would cry, privately, but she'd find that steel in her and go after Bone, same as the others. In some ways, she was more like their father, Anson. Very quiet, but deadly when cornered. And with no qualms about killing a beef-eating coyote or a cattle-stealing man. Or a murderer, like Bone.

"We saw Hector," said Peggy suddenly. "We stopped, tried to talk to him, but he just rode off."

"What did Hector have to do with all this?" asked Matt.

"Nothing," said Derek.

"He was with Bone, wasn't he?"

"I don't know. Maybe. I guess."

Matt was silent. He held onto the dash as Peggy straightened the car. She drove slowly, churning up spools of dust, cracking dry brush, mindful of Thunder following behind.

Derek looked away, bitterly lost in his own dark thoughts.

Elena Aguilar saw Hector ride in, just at dusk. At first, she thought she was seeing things. The sun was just going down over the western horizon, leaving a few tattered salmon and lavender clouds hanging in the sky like shreds of colored flour sacks.

The kitchen smelled of mashed corn and molé, sliced tomatoes and chilis, the steamy aroma of boiling frijoles.

A few moments before, Elena had seen the General prod his flock into the henhouse as long shadows striped the yard, daubed the empty pastureland with soft smudges of charcoal. There was a kind of sadness to the land at this hour, Elena thought, as if nature was shutting everything down, shuttering off the sun, pulling the night over the fields like a shroud.

Through the kitchen window, she saw Hector rein in his horse, dismount. When he touched the ground, his knees seemed to give out on him. He reached out, grabbed the tapadero to keep from falling.

Elena wanted to rush to him, but a sudden thought warned her away. She watched helplessly as Hector led the horse inside the stables.

A few minutes later, her son reappeared, walked gingerly across the yard. Elena's heart seemed not to beat, as if it was suspended from all activity, holding her breath on its own accord. She held a sharp knife in one hand, an onion in the other. She had not yet sliced into the onion. She was glad that Ernesto was not here, and Alicia, as well. Alicia had gone to the Killian ranch to spend the night with April. She would not be back until the day after tomorrow. Ernesto had gone into town with Jesus Roxas to buy supplies for one of the line shacks.

As Hector drew close to the house, Elena set down the knife and onion. She wiped her hands on a towel, left the window, walked quickly to the hall. She opened the back door to let Hector in. Her heart thrummed in her chest like muffled castanets.

"Hector, *que pasa?*"

"*Mama, 'stoy muy cansado.* Very tired."

"*Tienes hambre?* I can fix you something to eat. There are beans and tortillas, the good *salsa casera.*"

"*No tengo hambre. Yo quiero dormir.* I just want to sleep."

"Son, let me help you," she said, switching to English. "You are limping."

"Mama, I hurt. All over."

"Come, I will take you to your room. It is all ready for you."

"I am ashamed," he said. His eyes looked hollow in the light. There was a gauntness to him, as if he had aged since last she had seen him. A distance seemed to lie between them, an eerie gulf that wrenched at her heart.

"Do not have shame. What has passed, has passed."

"Oh, Mama."

Hector fell into her arms, sobbing. She embraced him, caressed the back of his neck, stroked his hair. Just touching him made her feel better. She could feel his heat, his heart beating against her breast. She led him to the bedroom, laid him on the bed. She began to undress him. She said nothing about the stink of him. But she turned him over when he was naked and he winced when she touched his bruised buttocks. He lay there, shivering. She saw the blood, the dried blood on his legs, on his backside. She stifled a scream of anguish, swallowed the choking catch in her throat.

"You wait," she whispered. "I will be back to bathe you."

"Oh, Mama." Hector sniffled, tried to choke back the sobs that welled up in his throat. His eyes glistened with a misty wetness.

"Weep," she said in Spanish. *"Llora, mi hijo.* Weep all you want. We will say nothing of this to your father. You do not have to tell me anything, my son. I will take care of you."

"Thank you, Mama," he sobbed. "I hate for you to see me."

"Shush, now, *mi Hectorito."*

She bathed him gently with warm soapy water and put salve on his bruises. She soothed his feverish forehead until he fell asleep. She covered him with blankets and closed the door when she left the room.

When Ernesto came home that night, she spoke to him. He reeked of dry oats and corn, oil and fried foods, and there was the tang of whiskey on his breath. She loved the smell, usually, but tonight it seemed a sacrilege.

"Our son has returned," she said.

"I want to see him. He has some questions to answer, *por Dios."*

"No. He is asleep. Do not disturb him. Do not scold him for leaving."

"But I am his father. I have a right to—"

"No, Ernesto, you will not harm the boy. He has been hurt more than you can ever punish him."

"What do you mean, woman?"

"I mean it is time to open your heart to him. Do not ask questions. Someday, maybe, he will tell us both what he wants us to know."

"I do not like this," said Ernesto, as she set a plate before him. "He was with Bone." The stove smelled of chilis and corn tortillas, beef and beans. Even though they, like the others in the county, had electricity, they still cooked on a wood stove. The room was warm and dry, the air pungent with the smell of burnt mesquite.

"It does not matter. Our son is home. That is enough."

She served him supper before he could protest further and that night she was very warm and loving to him when they went to bed, so that he did not question her about Hector, but plundered her body until he was exhausted. Later, Elena went into her son's room and kissed him on the cheek.

The nightsounds swelled up around her, the sawing orchestras of crickets, the *arump-whump* of frogs booming deep notes in the bass clef. Elena stood up, listening to the creak of the house, the comforting familiar noises of a Texas night.

"My son," breathed Elena, "sleep, rest. Tomorrow will be another day."

Hector did not awaken.

Only a few hands, those not scattered so far away on the Baron ranches that they would lose a day or two of work, came to Tom Casebolt's simple funeral. J. D. Brown, the stableman, was there; Billy Bob Letterman, limping around from a broken leg gotten when he tried to run one of the steam tractors into the *brasada* and a mesquite broke off and slammed a limb into his leg just below the kneecap; Hank Janss; Larry Davis, Matt's blacksmith; Ora Cornejo, the maid; and Ethan, Peggy and Derek. Matt stood there, bent over, favoring his gut, but trying not to show the pain that gave his face a stony cast in the shade of the dogwood tree that shadowed him like an umbrella. Grace was standing next to him, holding onto his arm, but she had started in on the liquor early that morning and was not too steady herself.

The old Baron cemetery was tended to twice a year by Hervé Cornejo unless there was a burial. He cleared the brush and mowed the grass on Armistice Day and Memorial Day. Derek had helped him once, but when the rattlers started streaking out of the high grasses, he had climbed a tree while Hervé scythed as if he was blading wheat.

The graveyard was fenced, but the fence had broken down over the years. The wide gate hung disconsolately off its leather hinges, made from scraps of shoe soles or saddle leather. Derek hated the cemetery and was no longer curious about the gravestones, the sunken plots that had once been mounded with dirt. Buried there were his father's parents and his great-grandparents, one of his uncles, a few trusted hands who had worked for Anson Baron, a stillborn child who would have been Matt's brother.

There was no preacher, no church. Tom had wanted to be buried on Box B land in the old Baron cemetery.

Matt spoke the words in the simple ceremony. Aunt Lou stood a few feet away, her face a hard mask, her lips clenched tight. The lines in her face seemed all smoothed out, the skin drawn taut over the bones of her skull. She wore a black skirt and blouse, polished riding boots, a black, narrow-brimmed hat. Only her eyes betrayed the seething emotions she kept locked inside her like a cache of gunpowder.

"We are here today to bury a friend. I've known Tom Casebolt for twenty years or more. He was honest, a hard worker, and he knew cattle. We'll miss him some. Goodbye, Tom." Under his breath, Derek heard his father mutter, "Goddamnit."

Derek looked at his father's weathered face, the deepening lines carving craggy fissures into the granite jaw. He looked at the sky, the deep clean blue of it, felt the warm late-summer breeze wash against his face, bringing with it the scent of rich grass and the pungent smell of cattle. Far off, he watched an airplane carve lazy arabesques in a series of acrobatic maneuvers. His eyes glowed as he punched Ethan in the side with his elbow.

"Looky, Ethan. I'll bet that's a Waco."

Ethan looked up, as Derek pointed to the airplane.

"*Shhhhhhhh,*" warned the older boy.

"One of the these days I'm going to ask Daddy to give me flying lessons."

"Be quiet, Derek," whispered Peggy. Aunt Lou shot them all a dark look.

Derek gave Peggy an ugly face and she stuck her tongue out at him. The airplane dove low over the horizon and disappeared.

Derek watched as two men lowered the pine box into the open grave with manila ropes. The box made a crunching sound as the men pulled the ropes free. It all seemed so final, thought Derek. He felt hollow inside; uncomfortably mortal.

"So long, Tom," said Derek softly. Ethan shrugged self-consciously. Peggy sniffled. Aunt Lou cleared her throat, let out a sigh. Grace Baron hiccoughed.

As the Baron family walked back toward the car, they saw Sheriff Blanchard drive up, stop some distance away. He got out, stood there with the door open.

"Wonder what he wants," said Matt.

"Nothing good," said Lou.

"Better find out," said Ethan.

"Peggy, put your mother in the car," said Matt. "Ethan, you come with me. Lou, you want to come along?"

"No," Lou growled, and headed for the family car.

"I'm going too," said Derek.

Matt looked at Derek in surprise, but said nothing.

Roy Blanchard walked out to meet Matt and his two sons. His tan uniform was wrinkled, dirty. His hat looked as if it had survived a game of kickball. As they drew closer, Derek noticed that the sheriff's eyes were red-rimmed, with dark smudges underneath, as if he hadn't slept in days.

"What you got, Roy?" asked the elder Baron.

"Bone's done lit out."

"The hell you say."

"Me'n my deputies got together a posse, rode into that brush where he's been hid out. 'Member those old 'dobe shacks your pa built?"

"How'd you find it?" asked Matt.

"We caught a couple of his boys a few nights ago. Greaser Indians. Eddie Blue Sky and Virgil Coldwater. Know 'em?"

Matt shook his head.

"That Virgil, he's tough as a hickory nut. But we worked on Eddie some."

"How so?"

Blanchard's mouth widened in a humorless grin.

"He don't like that nightstick much. 'Specially laid up against his balls. Virgil, he took it until he passed out. But that Eddie now, he can scream like a danged woman in the labor."

Ethan winced. Derek's eyes glittered in narrowed slits.

"Well, now," said Matt, "this Eddie done told you where to find Bone. How come you didn't find him?"

"Oh, we found out where he's been hidin', all right. But he lit out and we follered his tracks clear to the Rio Grandy. I 'spec he's in Mexico."

"Well, that's a sonofabitch," said Matt.

"Thought you'd like to know. Old Bone won't be botherin' you no more."

"What about those two Indians you got in jail?" asked Matt.

"Judge'll send 'em to Huntsville, I reckon. Caught 'em stealin' grain, carryin' firearms. They won't bother you none neither."

"All right," said Matt.

"Somethin' else you oughtta know, Matt."

"Let's hear it."

"Bone stopped off at the Rocking A before he rode off. I seen tracks goin' in and out from Ernie's place, too. Figured there was somethin' goin' on."

"You going to chew on it all day or spit out it, Roy?"

"Ernie, he filed on El Rincón the other day. He told me he put the deed in Bone's name, gave him the land."

"The hell you say."

"Fact, Matt. He up and made Bone a goddamned landowner. Now, don't that beat all?"

"Why, for Christ's sake?"

"Said he owed him."

"Well, shit," said Matt. He looked back at the car. Lou was staring at them. She'd throw a conniption fit when she found out about all this.

"That settle it then?" asked Roy.

"Not by a damn sight."

Matt turned on his heel walked back to the car, his two sons trailing him. Roy took off his hat, scratched his head. Then he too turned back to his car.

"Daddy," asked Derek, "what did you mean?"

"I mean Bone will be back," said Matt.

"Will you kill him?"

"I'll sure as hell try. And Ernie's got some explaining to do. I don't think he owns El Rincón."

"Boy, I'd like to be there when you kill Bone."

"Killing's wrong," said Ethan. "Against the law."

"Oh, what do you know?" challenged Derek. "Bone deserves it. He killed Tom."

"The law has to do it," said Ethan stubbornly.

"Shut up, both of you," said Matt. "Get in the car and don't talk about this anymore today. Especially around your Aunt Lou."

"Aw, shoot," said Derek.

"Yes, Daddy," said Ethan.

The three Baron men climbed into the car. Peggy started the engine, shifted into low, turned back toward the ranch house.

"What'd the sheriff say, Daddy?" she asked.

"Bone's gone to Mexico."

"Good riddance," slurred Grace.

"Well, Daddy's going to kill him if he ever comes back," said Derek.

Matt clapped a hand hard against Derek's ear. Derek winced, but did not cry out. His face hardened and the ringing did not go away for a long time. He opened his mouth to say something, but quickly closed it.

"Not if I kill him first," said Lou, so softly they almost didn't hear it. "That goddamned swine."

Matt's jaw flickered with a rippling muscle.

That night, Derek went to bed without any supper. He told his parents he wasn't hungry. He stayed awake a long time, listening to his father and mother argue about her drinking. Before he went to sleep he thought about Tom Casebolt and Hector Aguilar. And Bone.

Maybe, he thought, he'd kill Bone himself one day. If his daddy didn't do it, he would.

He hated Bone now too. Hated him more than he had ever hated anything in his life. He hated him for killing Tom and he hated him for what he did to Hector. A man like that was bad. He made everybody feel bad. He wished he could go to Mexico and kill Bone himself.

Derek touched his ear. It was no longer sore, but he felt the stinging even so. His father slapping him like that—that hurt worse than anything. And in front of Peggy and Aunt Lou. It just wasn't right, damnit. He was too grown up to be whacked like he was a baby in shit-stained diapers. Damnit, he was a man, same as Daddy.

And Derek began to sob in the darkness, the hurt in him so deep he was sure it would never go away. And he knew the weeping was not for himself or his pride, but for Tom Casebolt, the best friend a boy—no, a man, ever had.

20

THE SMALL PRESBYTERIAN hospital in Corpus Christi, Good Shepherd Infirmary, was surrounded by cars and trucks, people chatting in small quiet groups. At a side entrance that led to the basement, people stood in a long line, waiting to go inside. The Baronsville ambulance was parked nearby, its doors open. The two attendants inside were serving orange juice and cookies to the people who came out of the basement of the hospital, men and women, some slightly dizzy, others walking on wobbly legs.

Inside, Doctor Henry Emberlin, assisted by Doctor Richard S. Wheeler, a tall, snowy-haired man with a rugged, kindly face, supervised two women nurses who carefully stabilized April Killian with oxygen and isolyte fluids slowing dripping into her veins. A male nurse, using a strong suction device, drew blood and venom from each of April's snakebite punctures.

A pint bottle hung on a stand, its tube attached to one of April's arms, gravity feeding blood into her vein at a slow, steady pace. Doc Emberlin had enlarged each of Frances's cuts, packed the wounds with sulfathiazine powder.

"In the old days," said Wheeler, "we'd have poured gunpowder in those bites and set them afire."

"I once hooked a woman in snakebite shock up to a Model T, set the spark advance and cranked it until the electricity jolted her out of it," Doc Emberlin said.

Wheeler laughed softly. One of the women nurses smiled.

*   *   *

Ben Killian stalked into the hospital five hours after April's arrival. His face was gaunt with worry, his eyes cloudy with an inner pain. Behind him trailed his mother, Jane, and his son Steve, looking like bewildered barn owls caught napping by the morning sun streaming through an open window in the loft.

"Where's my wife and daughters?" Ben roared, and the late-afternoon shift nurses at the reception desk scurried like barnyard chickens running from a hawk's shadow.

Down the hall, Emberlin and Wheeler strode alongside Frances and Connie, each of them speaking softly. Wheeler's hands moved like an orchestra conductor's when he told of the procedures they had used to save April's life. Frances kept nodding in disbelief. Constance walked along like a somnambulist, drugged by the total experience of that nightmare day.

Ben saw them coming, swept past the nurses, bowled his way down the hall.

"Ben," said Emberlin congenially, "glad you could make it."

"How's April, Doc?"

"She'll be fine."

"I want to see her."

"A little later. She's resting."

"Bullshit," said Ben.

"Ben," said Frances, "calm down. There's nothing you can do. These two good doctors saved little April's life." Her drawl was so sweet she took all the snort out of Ben's bellow.

"Well, I'm damned glad to hear it," said Ben. "Did you see all the folks out there? From Baronsville, the Lazy K, all over. What in hell are they doin' here?"

Frances smiled.

"I guess when Connie was calling all the ranches, asking for the hands to come over and give April some blood, Jo-Beth Vermeil was listening in. She called just about everybody in town."

Emberlin chuckled.

"That Jo-Beth. If she wasn't the switchboard operator, she'd be the town crier."

"I always thought she listened in to our calls," said Ben.

"In this case, I'm glad she did," said Frances.

"Maybe you'd better go out there and thank 'em all, Ben," said Emberlin. "You need some fresh air."

Ben started to protest, but Frances took his arm, turned him around and marched him to the front entrance. When she saw Jane, she gave her and Steve a hug.

"My baby's going to be all right," she said. "Connie can tell you everything that happened."

Frances took Ben outside. They walked to the ambulance, spoke to the two attendants, to some of the folks they knew. Word passed quickly through the blood donor line about April's condition and a cheer rose up from every throat.

Frances choked back tears, then let them flow. Ben squeezed her hand.

"Some mighty good folks here," he said.

"Ben, I want you to burn that berry patch and kill every snake in it."

"I already told Reed Packer to do it. When I left there was so much smoke in the sky I figured nary a snake could live through it. I heard shots, too, and that was Jared and Harvey killin' any what tried to get away."

"You're a good man, Benjamin Killian."

"And you're a mighty fine woman, Frances."

They waved to the cheering crowd as a nurse came outside and tried to shush them.

"This is a hospital!" she yelled.

"You're goddamned right," said a tipsy blood donor who took his orange juice and cookies in 100-proof fermented grain spirits.

The Good Shepherd Infirmary took in 300 pints of blood that day when April almost died. Some of it they could pack in dry ice, refrigerate and actually use on other patients. They also discovered two cases of syphilis, three people with serum hepatitis, and from some of the men, two dozen pints so laced with booze they could have bottled it in bond and sold it as eighty-proof whiskey.

21

<hr>

THE LEGEND ON the opaque glass panel read: JOHN P. KEARNEY, ATTORNEY-AT-LAW. And underneath, in smaller letters: *Abogado*, Baronsville, Dallas. Matt Baron opened the door, entered the outer office. A young blonde woman looked up from her Royal typewriter.

"Howdy, Georgeann. Jack in?"

"Good morning, Mr. Baron. Yes, he's expecting you. Just go right on in. May I take your bag?"

Matt hefted the canvas valise in his hand. He had borrowed it from Derek to carry his shaving gear and personal belongings.

"No, thanks. I'll hang on to it."

Georgeann Sinton smiled and batted mascara-laden eyelashes at the tall rancher as he swept past her desk and opened the oak-paneled door marked "PRIVATE" in gilt lettering. The typewriter clattered in his wake.

Jack Kearney bit the end off the Havana cigar, spat it into his wastebasket. He thumbed the wheel on his Dunhill lighter, pulled smoke through the Corona Corona just as the door to his office opened. Matt Baron strode through the door, his clean Levi's and Western-cut shirt contrasting sharply with the wood and leather decor, the fancy trappings of success. His boots made no sound on the soft Karastan rug. His gray Stetson shadowed his rugged face until he tipped the brim back. Jack, wearing a sharkskin suit, white

"I know," said Jack. "Ben's already signed with Sherco Oil."

"You handle it, Jack?"

Kearney never batted an eye.

"Might be in your best interest, Matt. These leases are tricky. We wouldn't want Ben tapping into one of your pools, would we?"

"Ben's running scared, like all the rest. Ernie Aguilar, too. They think Roosevelt's just as bad as Hoover."

"Well, he isn't," said Jack, a staunch Democrat, like Matt. "Getting us off the gold standard and buying up all that silver will get us around a corner."

"We're all still hurting, Jack."

"Look, Matt, I just talked to Keith Sherwood in Houston this morning. We both have Frank Anthony's report on our desks. The Baron ranches almost certainly harbor vast oil reserves. One of these days, that oil is going to mean big money. I've talked to Senator Deane in Washington and he tells me the same thing. There's talk of trouble with Japan. They don't like us much after we terminated the Anglo-Japanese Alliance in 1922 and hated us for the Immigration Act of 1924, which barred all Orientals from our shores. Others say we might get into war with Germany again."

"What the hell's all that got to do with me?" asked Matt.

"War means oil, Matt. Lots of oil. And after those wildcatters in East Texas struck oil and the state got in a fight with the federal government, we want to be sure all of your leases and agreements are in order."

"So, what do you want to do, Jack? Sell me down the river?"

"You know better'n that, Matt." Jack rose from his chair and walked to the window, puffing gently on his cigar. He looked out at the smoke-smudged skyline of Dallas. "I think you know that I've always had your best interests at heart. Remember the drought?"

Jack turned away from the window, sat on the edge of his desk nearest to Matt. Jack acted differently in Dallas than in Baronsville. Here, he seemed more sure of himself. Matt rubbed his game leg.

"Too damned well."

"That was in 1925, when Ethan was seventeen. The cattle industry went belly up. You saw the cattle market go down like a goddamned stone in a well. Ninety-five percent of western cattle loan companies went into liquidation. Thousands of men lost their ranches. You started losing money. I saved your ass then and I'll save it now if you'll give me half a chance."

Matt remembered that Jack had urged him to send Ethan to the University of Texas to study law and politics on the side while obtaining a liberal education in livestock management as an undergraduate. Later, Jack had arranged for Ethan to cut his teeth on politics, got him a job as an aide and adviser to James Ferguson, later to Governor Jimmy Allred. Jack had staved off the creditors, saved the Baron ranches from bankruptcy. But they still had not recovered. Times were still rocky.

"Do we need the cash, Jack?"

"There'll be some cash, but that's not the only reason I want you to sign with Sherco Oil." Jack blew a perfect smoke ring, slid off the edge of his desk, went back to his chair. "Keith called me this morning, Matt. He said that he thinks you're sitting on a lake of oil that will make Spindletop look like a mud-puddle. Even Killian's land doesn't look as rich as yours. Frank says he thinks every acre around that brush section will yield oil. He predicts between seventy-five and eighty thousand gallons a day to start, and no end in sight. Sherwood's so damned excited, he's willing to lay out hard cash to sign you up, long term, pay you monthly even if he doesn't drill."

"It sounds almost too easy," said Matt. But he knew they were cash-poor. Grace had gone over the figures again before he had flown to Vickery with Cameron. That business of trying to cut away the *brasada* at El Rincón two years before hadn't helped any. And, they were in the middle of another drought. The old grasses weren't holding up. Matt needed to do something and he didn't have the cash to do it.

"Well, we're going to make it hard for Sherwood to get away with anything," said Kearney. "Ethan and I went up to Monahans two weeks ago and met with those wildcatters I told you about. They're selling oil for a nickel or a dime a barrel and running from the sheriffs and federal marshals like a pack of rats on a sinking ship. I think oil's going to go to fifty cents a barrel or more by the time Sherwood gets a well down and I think it'll go to a dollar or two before Roosevelt is out of office."

"Ethan said something about that," said Matt. He hadn't really paid any attention. Grace's drinking had gotten worse after they lost the baby in October of 1932 and he had been worried that the Box B would become a dust bowl like so much of Texas. Good grass was the only thing that could save him and he'd been experimenting with a number of breeds that he hoped would work. But there was still a long way to go and his creditors were getting noisy.

"I suggest we give Sherco a five-year lease, with a stipulation that they develop a producing well, or so many producing wells, within that length of time. And I will drive a hard bargain on oil royalties, force Sherwood to a bottom at which he can't sell. That will take care of the goddamned wildcatters. Look, Matt, word of this has already leaked out and I've gotten calls from Texas Fuel and Humble, and Lone Star Gas wants a peek at your land. Anthony thinks you're loaded with it. We've already got natural gas here and in Fort Worth, all piped in, neat as you please. Take a look at this map Anthony marked up for me."

Matt looked at a large sheet of drafting paper that Jack laid out across his desk. All of the Baron ranches were plainly marked. There were boundaries that showed where the Rocking A and Lazy K ranches butted up against Baron land. Slashing through most of the Box B was a wide dark swatch of charcoal. The *brasada*. There was one section where the Box B, Lazy K and Rocking A all came together in a point, like a jigsaw puzzle, marked in red pencil.

Jack stabbed the red markings with his right index finger.

"There's the baby," he said.

"That's El Rincón," said Matt.

"I know. Frank says that may be the big one."

"I don't own it. Ernie does. Or says he does. And I think he gave it to a goddamned murdering Indian named Bone."

"Get it back, Matt. Have Grace send me up all the papers on that section. We won't be able to move until we clear title to all of it."

"Hell, I don't know."

Kearney rolled up the map, fixed Baron with a steady eye.

"Leave it to me, Matt. Your original boundaries show that property as Baron land. I think Aguilar pulled a fast one on you. And if we don't move pretty quick, one of the big oil companies will get to Ernie and he'll suck up all of your oil while you're standing there with your finger up your butt. Killian, too, unless I can stop him. He's using another geologist, name of Larry Braden. A smooth customer."

"Why you sly sonofabitch. Is that why you signed up Ben Killian? Never mind. I don't want to know. This is pretty much over my head, Jack."

"Well, Ethan's a pretty smart boy. He understands it. He's going to make you a fine manager someday. By the way, who's running the ranch for you now? I haven't been to my office in Baronsville for a month of Sundays. Hard to find a man as good as old Tom Casebolt."

"Ethan doesn't have much of a feel for cattle or ranching," said Matt. "I expect Derek will make a good foreman one of these days. He took to the new man like he took to Tom. I put Billy Bob Letterman in charge of La Paloma after we buried Tom. Then I hired a man away from the King ranch last year, Johnny Bell. He cracks a good whip; knows cattle. He's already made Derek a section foreman on La Golondrina during the summer."

"Bell didn't come cheap, Matt."

"No," said Baron ruefully. "Bob Kleberg didn't much like it, but I needed Johnny in the worst way."

"Good choice." Jack set his cigar in the ashtray, let it fume to ash. "Derek's how old now?"

"Eighteen. He's like a young colt, not broke yet, but wanting to run. Johnny says he's smart."

"A little young, but he'll be there when you need him. I always thought Ethan, as the oldest . . ."

"Ethan's soft inside, too much like his mother. Practical, but doesn't want to get his hands too dirty."

"Well, maybe he'll be a help in other ways. Politics."

"That seems to be the way his twig is bending," admitted Baron.

"Well, Matt, let's go over these leases together. If you like what you see, sign them and I'll take them up to Houston tomorrow, get Sherwood's John Hancock on them. And a check to boot."

Jack grinned. Sometimes, Matt thought, Kearney looked like a mischievous leprechaun.

"I know," said Matt. "You want to get back to your secretary before the day gets too long in the tooth."

"Now, Matt, come on. What do you think keeps me young and in full vigor? It sure as hell ain't my gold-digging wife." Pilar Kearney, Matt knew, spent money like branch water.

"Let's get it done," said Matt.

"Good. I've got some prime Kentucky bourbon in that cabinet over there."

"The only way I could drink it would be in a glass of goddamned sweet milk," said Matt wryly.

"Well, I'll drink it for you, then. Want me to have Georgeann pull your chair around behind this desk, so we can go over this stuff?"

"I'll do it," said Matt, and Jack laughed in that booming courtroom baritone of his. "If I got Georgeann into bed, I wouldn't know what to do with her."

"That's the beauty of young pussy, Matt. You don't have to know what to do with Georgeann. She'll prime your pump and fire your boiler with just a wiggle of her sweet little ass."

"Jesus, Jack, what do you do now? Train 'em?"

"At my age, I've learned a great secret, Matt."

"What's that?"

"You can have anything you want. There's a hitch, of course."

"There always is."

"A small hitch."

"All right. I give up, Jack."

"You buy it. Cash is king. Presents are the way to a girl's heart. And the young ones all like fancy clothes. Georgeann graduated from secretarial school, came up here looking like one of the Jukes family. I hired her, took her to a beauty parlor, to a dress shop, and she was just too grateful for words."

"You can be arrested for that kind of crap. Pilar might shoot you, to boot."

Jack never even blinked at the mention of his wife. "Oh, she's of age, Matt."

Matt looked at his attorney, shook his head.

"I wonder if you are, Jack."

Jack slapped Matt on the shoulder.

"Buck up, Matt. You're still a young man. If we put some cash in your pockets, you'll brighten up. You've been working too damned hard. A little strange poon wouldn't hurt."

"Jack, it's all strange to me," said Matt wryly. "Now, let me see those goddamned oil leases and keep that little brood mare out there to yourself."

Matt moved his chair behind the desk as Kearney laid out the drafted leases with all the blanks filled in. Matt took a deep breath to ease the uneasiness he felt. Jack had been after him for a long time to open up the Box B to oil exploration. Matt's father had even talked to a Shell geologist before his death. The geologist had told Anson Baron: "Whatever you do with this land, Mr. Baron, keep the mineral rights."

But Matt was a cattle rancher. That was all he knew, all he cared about. Oil was something used to settle the dust on roads, something used to grease machinery. And gas? Gas was dangerous. He had smelled it in the quicksand seeps in the *brasada,* and it had made his stomach queasy. He had seen oil too, and grass wouldn't grow where it oozed out of the ground.

One thing he did know. The grass on the Baron ranches had been losing its vitality for years. Maybe oil could be used as a tool to try new seeds, test the foreign grasses he had heard about. He just didn't know and suddenly he felt weary. The pain in his gut began to creep back, strangle his thoughts.

He looked at the papers Jack spread before him and winced as a jolt of pain wrenched at his senses. He shook it off and forced himself to read the words that would change the way the Baron ranches worked—perhaps forever.

22

STEVE KILLIAN TWITCHED violently at the sound of cut wire. The loud *twaaank* made his horse jump. The animal started to back up on his haunches as Steve dug the bit into his mouth to hold him steady. Three wild turkeys, startled by the sound, took flight, their wings beating thunder as their pinions strained to clear the copse of trees where they'd been feeding. The horse spooked at the turkeys too, his muscles bunched to leap away from the threat of anything else alien in his world.

"Whoa-up-air, Sonny," Steve said to the gelding. He tightened down on the reins of Luke's horse, Dandy, as he balked in unison with Sonny. Two more turkeys scuttled from the trees, but did not fly. They raced away like ungainly women holding up their skirts, their long, spindly legs awkward as stilts.

"Shut up," said Luke, standing at the wire, the cutters poised over the second strand.

"Hell, Luke, you're makin' more noise than me. You're scarin' Sonny."

"You'll think scared if we get caught."

Luke snapped the second wire as he clamped the wire cutters on the twisted strands. The wire whipped like a snake, *whurrrk, whurrrk*, as the tension gave way. Quickly, Luke bent down and cut the last two strands of the four-wire fence.

"Tight sumbitch," said Luke.

"Godamighty, Luke," breathed Steve. "I am scared. What if we get caught?"

"You think Ben gives a damn? Or Charlie? Hell, they'd probably laugh if Ernie caught us cuttin' his damned fence."

"Do we have to do this?" Steve's voice was still changing and it squeaked in the high register. He ran sweating fingers through his wavy, thick roan hair, streaked with strawberry veins. He still seemed to possess his baby fat, in his cheeks, his butt, especially. At five feet eight, he was considerably shorter than his half brother Luke. He looked at his horse through hazel eyes bracketing a strong, straight nose.

Steve brought Sonny under control and Dandy settled down, stood hipshot, his tail swicking at horseflies the size of pinto beans. Sonny shook his head, rattled the bit in its fastenings. The noise made Steve twitch again. He didn't like this, going on another man's land, sneaking around. Now it was so quiet, even that made him nervous.

Luke picked up the bottom strands, moved them out of the way. He crammed the wire cutters into his hip pocket, strode toward Steve and his horse. Luke had thick dark hair, blue eyes, a square jaw, slightly rounded shoulders. He was lean and tall, a bare half inch over six feet. Luke's eyes seemed to be perpetually narrowed, except when he laughed, which was often. He drew a Lucky Strike from the familiar green pack, stuck it between thin, sensuous lips. He fished a match from his shirt pocket, struck it on the heel of his boot. When the tobacco caught, he blew the match out, left the cigarette dangling from his mouth.

"Now, we'll see just how come Bandera Creek dried up so all of a sudden," said Luke as he grabbed his reins from his half brother. He hauled himself into the saddle with no effort, something Steve always marveled at. Everything came easy to Luke. And he didn't take anything seriously. Maybe that was why Ben and Charlie Stone, his daddy's foreman, had sent them to check on the reason Bandera Creek had gone dry again.

"Daddy told you not to cut the wires, Luke. He said to just pull them down."

"Pullin' 'em, cuttin' 'em, what's the difference?"

"He said he didn't want any trouble with Ernie."

"Hey, Stevie, Ben's had trouble with Ernie ever since I can remember. If Ernie's dammed up that creek again, there'll be more trouble. Come on, let's go and get it over with."

"You think that's what Ernie done?"

"Did, Stevie, did. Christ, didn't they teach you English at Baronsville High?"

Steve's face flushed red as the inside of a pomegranate. He hated it when Luke made him feel foolish. He admired Luke so much, looked up to him. It hurt when Luke treated him like a kid.

"Well, do you think Ernie dammed the creek?" Steve asked, recovering his composure.

"I wouldn't put anything past Ernie Aguilar," said Luke. "He's just a damned greaser, like every fruit-picking, bean-eating, tortilla-gobbling Mexican I ever saw. And I saw plenty of them in Fort Worth, Dallas, Houston, San Antonio, San Angelo, Waco, El Paso. Christ, El Paso's pretty near all greaser."

"You've been around," said Steve lamely. He envied Luke his travels. His mother and father were always talking about Luke running away, always wondering where he had gone. But Luke never talked about his travels whenever he came back. The only way their parents knew where Luke had been was from the sheriff. Luke was always getting into trouble, and Steve had always wondered why. Today, there was something different about Luke. He didn't know what it was, but he sensed that Luke was getting ready to run off again.

"Going again," said Luke, as if reading Steve's thoughts.

"You are? Where this time?"

Luke laughed, slapped Sonny on the rump.

"Let's do Ben's dirty work for him and I'll tell you," Luke said.

They crossed the broken fence, rode onto Rocking A land. The creek was dry on Aguilar's side too. Luke followed its meandering path, ducking under the branches of trees, looking at the creek bed now and again. The dry sand at the edges was crisscrossed with tangled wedges, like Phoenician cuneiform, of turkey, quail and dove tracks.

"Where you goin'?" Steve asked again.

"Houston. I met up with a fellow lives in Needville once and we got to talking. Oh, this guy is a pip. He plays guitar, sings, and he's got big ideas. He's an artist, knows how to draw and everything. Well, we talked about a lot of things at a little old honky-tonk speakeasy down by the Houston stockyards one night and got to be real good friends."

"What's his name?" asked Steve as they crossed the creek at an open place where the brush had thinned. A covey of quail flushed fifty yards ahead of them, fanning out, hugging the ground low, until they disappeared over a cactus-studded knoll.

"Jim Goff. Sings those old cowboy songs, plucks guitar, always smiling, laughing. Makes you feel good. Well, he's got this idea about advertising, wants me to go in with him."

"What's advertising?"

"You know. Those announcements in papers and catalogs for cigars, automobiles, clothes. And you hear them on the radio all the time."

"Well, I know that," said Steve, "but I thought the owners did all that."

Luke laughed. "The owners?"

"I mean the people trying to sell the goods."

"Jim says a man can make a lot of money in advertising. He wants me to write the copy and he'll do all the drawing."

"Boy, that's punkins," said Steve. "Did you tell Daddy yet?"

"Soon as we run this creek and get finished, I was going to say *adiós.*"

"What about Mother? Oh, I'm sorry."

Steve's face flushed again. He knew Luke had a different mother and that she was dead. He just kept forgetting.

"Oh, I'll tell your mother. Tonight. I'm leaving early in the morning."

"Can I go with you?"

Luke laughed again. He reined up his horse. Steve hauled Sonny up short, wondering why Luke had stopped.

"Stevie, I don't want you to take this wrong, but I think it's time you learned your P's and Q's. If you ran off with me, Daddy'd haul you back in handcuffs and have me arrested for kidnapping. Our daddy thinks that goddamned ranch is the world. You and Connie and April aren't ever going to get away from him. Your mother feels the same way. Frances, sweet as she is, worships Ben. Whatever he says do, she does. I'm just a bastard. He knows it and I know it. So, I don't count for much. But you and the girls, now, he's not going to let you out of his sight."

Steve snorted, but he couldn't get Luke's words out of his mind. There were differences between them, he knew. Luke got away with things that would have gotten Steve a strapping. He had never understood his father's attitude toward Luke. Ben worried about Luke all the time, whether Luke was at home or not.

"Daddy likes you a lot, Luke."

"You're wrong, Steve."

"But he worries about you—all the time. So does Grandmother Jane."

Luke laughed more loudly than before, but there was a wry, twisted cast to the tones, as if he had forced the laughter through a mouthful of bitter fruit.

"Ben hates it when one of his calves runs off. He'll chase a maverick down until it drops dead, rather than lose it. Our dear old pappy loves branding time best of all, because that's when he puts his mark on what he owns, or claims to own. Grandma Jane's the same damned way. She says 'shit,' you automatically squat."

"Jeepers, Luke, I never knew you thought like that."

"Don't you think the same?"

"I—I never really thought much about it."

"You're growin' up, Stevie. 'Bout time you started using your head for something besides a hatrack."

"Yeah, I 'spec," said Steve, trying to sound grown-up. "Say, what are you going to do in this advertising business?" he asked, to change the subject.

"Jim thinks I have the makings of a writer. I showed him some of the stuff I wrote in jail."

"What kind of stuff?"

"Stories, poems, some little tunes I made up."

"I didn't know you did that sort of thing," said Steve.

"Well, it was something to do. You know your daddy and your grandma. Always reading. Well, I guess some of it rubbed off on me. Then, I met a guy in jail who gave me some good advice."

"What was that, Luke?"

"One day I was looking out one of the little windows and this guy, I don't know what he was in for, but he rode an Indian motorcycle. He said to me: 'When you get out of here, just remember what it's like.' I asked him what he meant and he said: 'You're on the inside looking out.' Well, I thought about that a lot and realized freedom was just about the most important thing in the world."

"What's that got to do with writing?"

"Well, this guy told me something else. He said: 'Just look at these cons in here, these hard cases. None of 'em have a brain. They drink and fight and steal and fuck up. If you have to do any time in Huntsville or jail, don't mix with these bums. Get a book and read it. While they're beating their meat, letting their brains rust, you can be learning something. Everything you want to know has been written down in a book.'

"I thought he was a pretty smart guy, on the level. I didn't have any books, so I started writing, thinking of little stories, things that had happened to me, people I'd met in my travels. I just wrote them down on scraps of paper and I got me a notebook after I got out and started writing all kinds of things."

"Well, I don't know," said Steve. "Seems to me you have to be pretty smart to write. I mean books and things."

"It was amazing, all right. Something just seemed to pour out of me. I think you just have to sit down and start writing. Jim Goff liked my stuff. He's pretty smart."

"Well, maybe I'll try it sometime myself," said Steve.

"You do that. You might like it. Well, let's ride on up this dry creek and see where it goes."

"All right," said Steve, pensive as he clucked to his horse.

The two young men continued riding up the creek, following its serpentine course. Four quail burst from cover, fanned out with a staccato whirring of wings. Luke laughed.

"What kind of stories do you write?" asked Steve a few moments later.

"One I wrote was about that guy I met in the Odessa jail," said Luke. "I never did find out his name. So, I called him Gabe in my story."

"Gabe?"

"Yeah, short for Gabriel. Nobody knew his name; nobody knew why he was in jail. I thought the guy must have been an angel."

Ben Killian worried the tip of his nose with the stub of his short finger. A flask of legal whiskey—he was drinking *Old Crow* instead of white lightning since Prohibition had been repealed the year before—jutted from his hip pocket. At mid-morning, the container was not quite half empty. He watched as Larry Braden, with gloved hands, poked primers into half a case of dynamite.

"You going to bury that?" asked Ben.

"We use a surface charge," said Braden, a sandy-haired man eight years out of Colorado School of Mines with a degree in geology. He wore starched khaki trousers and shirt, field boots, a John Deere cap. "When this charge goes off, we'll be looking at that seismograph we set up five miles away."

Ben glanced nervously at Charlie Stone, who had the motor running in the new 1936 Dodge pickup with the legend "KILLIAN ENTERPRISES, INC." painted on each door panel. Harvey Leeds leaned against the bed, one leg cocked back against the tire. He would set off the charge twenty minutes after Charlie drove them to the place where Braden had set up his instruments.

"I'm using DuPont sixty-forty dynamite, Mister Killian," said Braden. "Should be enough here to give us a good subsurface reading. Best thing I've ever seen to find out what might be down below."

"What can you tell from all this?" asked Ben.

"Well, sir, after Leeds there sets off this charge, that seismograph will record the speed of energy waves between here and the instrument." He attached a two-minute fuse to one of the caps, laid it out on top of the sandy ground. "The whole formation down below this point and where I've set up the seismograph will register. If the shock waves are slow, then it'll tell me the energy is traveling through soft beds, sand or shale. If the waves come pretty fast, I'll know we're going through solid rock."

"So, what are you hoping for?"

"Slow. That's mean it's likely you've got oil in that shale and sand. We'll keep going as far as we can past that five-mile point, then take readings at various points from north to south and east to west."

"I have to take your word for it," said Ben. "Machines."

"Sir, my first job was with a geologist who discovered Dad Joiner's East Texas field in 1930. We defined that field by instruments as forty-two miles long, four to eight miles wide and covering two hundred square miles."

Ben whistled. C. M. Joiner's field was a legend in Texas. Dad had drilled a thousand wells in the first six months and drawn a hundred million barrels of oil out of the ground. There was oil on virtually every acre of land in that field.

Braden finished his work, beckoned to Leeds. Leeds slouched over to them.

Braden stood up, pointed to the fuse.

"As soon as we're past that big oak tree over there," said the geologist, pointing, "you start your time on that stopwatch I gave you. Give us exactly twenty minutes, then light that fuse there."

"I got you," said Leeds.

"Then, you run like hell to that ditch over yonder and lie flat behind it. You might get peppered some, but I don't see anything big here. That's sand underneath."

"Sonny," said Leeds, "I've blowed dynamite before."

"Yes, sir," said Braden.

Ben saw something out of the corner of his eye, walked toward it. He stooped over as Braden was checking the charge, the fuse and dynamite caps. Leeds started to walk back toward the pickup.

"Charlie," Killian called out. "What the hell is this?"

Charlie Stone got out of the pickup. He and Leeds walked over to where Ben was standing. Killian stared down at a wooden stake with numbers marked on it in blue chalk.

"Looks like a survey stake to me," said Stone.

"I know what the hell it is," said Ben. "Who the fuck put it here?"

"Damned it if I know, Ben. Maybe that college boy."

"Braden, did you drive this stake?" Ben called.

Braden shook his head. He too walked over.

"No, sir, I selected this site because my calculations show this to be a prime spot to look for oil. Three miles from here your neighbor, Baron, has three wells pumping, another six farther on, all in a direct line with where that dynamite sits. You've got all that brush over there, coming to a point, sandy soil, a good likelihood we'll find shale and sand underneath. I figure we're over the same pool that Baron tapped into last year." Braden pointed to the section of the *brasada* that lay a thousand yards beyond. Ben followed the line of sight from the tip of the geologist's finger to the abrupt end of the mesquite grove. There were three more stakes in a line.

Killian scoped the surrounding terrain with a quick eye-scan.

"Christ, there are stakes all over this goddamned place," he said.

"Sure as hell are," said Stone. "Weren't here before."

Killian reached down, grabbed the stake in a tight fist. He shook it from side to side, jerked it free.

"We'll damn sure find out who the hell surveyed my property," he said, handing the stake to Stone. "Braden, you ready to shoot?"

"We're all set, Mr. Killian."

"Then let's get to it. Charlie, drive us the hell out of here. Harvey, you start your time after we get going."

"Right, Mr. Killian."

"Shit," said Ben, stalking angrily toward the pickup.

* * *

Fifteen minutes later, Charlie Stone pulled up at the line shack, a frame dwelling set on square blocks. It had electricity, a telephone, four bunks, a small kitchen, a hot plate, cupboards, a supply room, a table and chairs. The shack was simple and functional, with no porch, a flat slant roof, small windows, only a single door in front.

Inside, tin cups hung on hooks attached to the wall. There was an icebox, but there hadn't been any ice in it for two years or so. Cupboards and bins held staples: beans, flour, sugar. The stove served as an oven and heated the shack in winter. There were storm lamps and battery-operated flashlights, a single bulb hanging from the ceiling in the center of the room.

Ben Killian and Larry Braden stared at the silent seismograph, the array of instruments laid out on a table in the line shack. Five minutes after entering the shack, Ben looked at his watch. At the same time, Braden's stopwatch buzzed an alarm.

"I don't hear anything," Ben said.

Braden picked up his stopwatch from the table.

"That charge should have gone off when this buzzed, Mr. Killian. I pushed the button on my stopwatch when we passed that oak tree. Your man Leeds should have done the same."

Charlie Stone sat on one of the bunks. He looked up as Killian turned to him.

"Start that pickup, Charlie," said Ben. "Braden, you stay here in case that dynamite goes off. We'll find out from Harvey what went wrong."

"Could have been a defective fuse," said Braden. "Or the main cap. But I checked everything thoroughly."

"Well, we're going to check it again. Maybe you got a box of wet dynamite."

"That wouldn't make any difference, Mr. Killian. But it was dry. Dry as a bone. Fresh out of the box."

Stone headed for the door.

"You keep those instruments humming, Braden. We've got plenty of dynamite, fuses and caps. We'll set off that charge for you."

"Yes, sir," said Braden, but Ben was already out the door.

Braden stared at the seismograph for a long time. And he listened for the distant sound of an explosion.

But he heard only the empty ticking of the shack as the wood frame warmed in the sun.

23

L UKE REINED DANDY up, reached out and grabbed Steve's shirt.
"What's the matter?" asked Steve.

"Listen," said Luke, as the last quail disappeared in a clump of scrub cottonwood trees. A silence rose up as if the birds had never flushed.

Steve held his breath. Luke twisted his head as if straining to pick up the softest sound.

"I don't hear anything," said Steve.

"Something spooked those quail. It wasn't us."

Steve stood up in the stirrups. His saddle leather creaked under the strain.

"I still don't hear anything, Luke."

"Maybe somebody doesn't want us to hear anything."

The hairs on the back of Steve's neck prickled his skin as they stiffened. It felt as if a daddy longlegs was crawling up his back.

"What do we do now?" Steve whispered.

"Just ride real slow and listen. We'll go on. Keep looking all around. I think somebody's up ahead of us."

But they saw no one.

The stream angled to the south through more scrub cottonwood, then took a lazy bend to the west. As Luke and Steve ducked under the branches of a tree, Steve's horse, Sonny, whickered. Steve hauled in on the reins. Dandy's ears hardened to a pair of cones, twitched. Sonny's ears did the same, twisting to snatch up any sound.

The horses gingerly picked their way around a cluster of rocks. Luke rode ahead of Steve, crossed the stream bed. The trees thinned, the land opened up, rose gently. A hundred yards upstream, something glinted in the sun.

"Well, there it is," said Luke, pointing.

"What?"

"A little old dam, Stevie. No wonder Bandera Creek's dry as a widder's tits on our side of the fence."

"Daddy blew that dam four years ago," said Steve. "I thought."

"Not this one, he didn't. That other dam was just this side of the fence I cut. Old Ernie's pulled a fast one on us."

"What are you going to do, Luke?"

"Have a look-see, Stevie. Looks like a pretty good dam, by golly. That's concrete, not dirt. And I can hear water running."

The horses smelled the water as the two young men rode up to the impoundment.

There was a different smell to the air as if the dryness and heat had fled, leaving a tangy coolness, a lull in the tropical heat.

The horses stepped up to the near bank, shook as they arched their necks and lowered their heads to drink. Water stood behind the dam, forming a small pond. A second spillway released water into a fork that took the creek in another direction. Cattle drank upstream and two of them stood belly-deep in the pond.

Luke's jaw hardened as he looked at the condition of the Rocking A cattle. The pond was like an oasis in the middle of a blazing desert.

"Easy enough to fix," said Luke, surveying the dam itself. "Just pull that gate up and the water will go where it's supposed to, back on Lazy K land."

"We better not do anything, Luke, you reckon," said Steve.

"Haw," Luke snorted. "Stevie, just think. For the past two years we haven't had enough rain to fill a thimble or make a pot of coffee. Two years ago this country dried up like a prune. You could chunk a rock at every cistern in the county and hear a hollow clang. Now, we've got bald spots all over the Lazy K where there used to be strong green grass. They're calling Oklahoma and Texas the 'Great Dust Bowl.' And here's a goddamned Mexican stealing our water while our grass withers and our land blows away in the wind. I'm going to open that gate. You keep a lookout, just in case."

"Just in case of what?"

"In case somebody comes up on us."

"Luke, I'm scared."

"Shoot," said Luke, with a grin. He swung out of the saddle and slapped his half brother on the back. "Won't take but a cotton-pickin' minute."

Steve watched as Luke took a last look around, then walked to the concrete dam.

"Mighty nice dam," said Luke. "Maybe we should go swimming first."

"Luke, hurry up," said Steve.

Luke laughed. Holding his arms out like a tightrope walker, he stalked out to the gate. The cows in the pond stared at him with listless eyes. Luke grabbed the gate by the handles on both sides, pulled it upward. The water began pouring through the spillway, back into the old creek bed. He noticed that there were two gates, but he left the other one in place. He threw the panel in his hands out onto the ground, walked back across, skipping lightly this time. As he reached the embankment, he and Steve both heard a noise. Two men walked out of the trees. One of them carried a rifle.

"Uh-oh," whispered Steve. "We got caught."

"Hold on there!" Paco Velez called. "You there, get off your horse."

"Just sit right there, Stevie," said Luke. "I'll handle this."

Steve's palms began to sweat. His butt itched.

Paco advanced toward the two Killians, brandishing his double-barreled scattergun. The man with him seemed less aggressive, held back a few paces, head lowered so that neither Luke nor Steve could see his face. He did not seem to be carrying a weapon.

"What if he shoots?" husked Steve.

"He won't shoot," replied Luke.

But the two men strode closer, and Paco held the shotgun with both hands as if ready to bring it to bear on the two Killian men.

"Paco, you sumbitch," said Luke, recognizing the foreman of the Rocking A, "why don't you put that popgun away and let us go on about our business."

"You shut your fucking mouth, Luke Killian," said Velez pleasantly. "Hector," he said to the young man following a few steps behind him, "put that gate back where it was."

Steve's eyes widened as he recognized Hector Aguilar. The Killians hadn't seen him in two years, but there had been a lot of talk in Baronsville and at school. People said he had run away and lived with an Indian named Bone and Bone had made a queer out of him. Steve didn't know there were such people as queers, but the idea fascinated him. Steve just didn't believe that men did things to each other like other boys said they did. It was just too unnatural, too disgusting to think about. He just couldn't picture such behavior in his mind. He knew that other boys played with each other and jacked off to see who could make jism first, but that wasn't queer. But it was difficult, even, for him to picture normal sex between a man and a woman in his mind, for although he was twenty years old, he had never done anything with a girl.

He had listened to other boys at school brag about the girls they'd pumped, and he'd lied about his own experiences so they wouldn't think him odd. But the truth was that Steve got tongue-tied around girls. He was, in fact, although he wouldn't admit it to anyone, afraid of girls his own age. They seemed so much wiser, so much more complicated than boys. Once a girl in school had teased him, saying, "Steve, I heard that you slumber in your sleep." His face had turned red and he had run away, thinking she meant something dirty. And, later, he had accused April of telling on him. One day April had surprised him in the bathroom playing with himself. He had been suspicious of her ever since. Later, when he found out that "slumber" was just another word for "sleep," he was deeply embarrassed. But he didn't trust girls. They were so secretive, so smug, so smart-alecky.

When he first heard some boys talking about what their parents did to make babies, Steve had become very angry. He was ashamed of his reaction now, but he remembered it clearly. He had told the other boys, "Well, maybe your folks do that stuff, but mine don't!"

Now, he knew better. Just like dogs and horses and cattle, men and women did it to each other. The man got on top and put his thing inside a woman's pussy. But he still had trouble picturing his daddy and mother doing such a thing.

Hector walked over to the gate and picked it up. He carried it to the dam while Paco, Luke and Steve watched him. Hector rammed the board down hard, shutting off the flow of water into Bandera Creek.

Luke kept edging toward his horse every time Paco's attention was diverted. Steve didn't notice it right away, but Paco did right after Hector walked off the top of the dam.

"You just don't move no fucking more, Luke," said Velez. "I am not fucking kidding you. I will shoot you for trespass, *por Dios.*"

"Paco, don't be a damned fool," said Luke evenly. He slid his left boot a few inches toward his horse.

Velez stepped closer, swung the shotgun barrel until it pointed in Steve's direction.

"You are both trespassing and I'm going to call the law," said Paco. "Get off your horse now, Steve."

Steve started to swing out of the saddle.

"Stay right there, Stevie," ordered Luke. "Goddamnit, Paco, put down that gun before it goes off."

"It will go off in your fucking face if you do not both come with me," said Paco. He leveled the twin-barreled shotgun at Luke. Luke's face darkened. A muscle quivered along his left jawline. Steve settled in the saddle, his face frozen in a querulous squinch.

"I'll shoot if you don't get off that horse," said Paco to Steve. "Hector, you get their horses."

"You get them," said Hector.

Luke realized two things, then. Paco was running scared and Hector didn't like to take orders from his foreman. That, he decided, gave him the advantage.

Steve shrugged. Paco brought the shotgun to his shoulder.

Luke made his move, then.

"Hey!" he shouted, then whirled, ran toward Steve. He jerked the reins of his horse out of Steve's hands.

"Get moving, Stevie," he said. "Ride like hell out of here."

Luke slapped Sonny's rump and yelled at the horse. Sonny bunched his muscles and leaped forward as if he'd been bitten. Steve grabbed the saddlehorn to keep from being hurled out of the saddle. Luke jumped behind his own horse, whacked him in the ribs and jerked the reins to the left. The horse bolted toward Paco Velez.

Paco cursed in Spanish, touched one of the triggers on his shotgun. The charge flew over Steve's head as Sonny raced toward the pond, out of control.

Paco tried to aim the shotgun at Luke, but Killian was following his horse from behind, ducking low to stay out of sight.

Hector ran toward Steve, threw himself at the left stirrup as Sonny tried to scramble out of the way. Hector grabbed Steve's boot by the ankle and was jerked off his feet. He held on until the horse stopped at the lip of the pond, turned to look at Hector.

Steve jerked his boot loose from Hector's grip, tried to kick Hector. Hector lunged, grabbed Steve's belt, jerked him out of the saddle. Steve leaned over, off balance, tried to lean the other way. Hector's weight was too much for him. He tumbled out of the saddle, fell into Hector's arms.

Luke's horse, at the last moment, veered to avoid running into Paco. Paco, confused, tried to get out of the way. Unfortunately, he broke the same way as the horse took. Paco stumbled, and his finger ticked the other trigger. The shotgun roared and a load of buckshot dug a hole six inches from where Paco halted. At the sound of the explosion, the horse bolted in the opposite direction, toward the dam, a dead end route.

Paco looked around as the horse galloped away, only to see Luke charging toward him as if Killian's boots were fleet track shoes.

"Ay de mí!" shouted Velez, but neither his voice nor bracing himself with the shotgun held in front of his chest could stop Luke's headlong rush.

Luke hit Paco full force in a tackling dive, driving Velez off his feet. The shotgun flew from Paco's hands, skidded through the dirt like a starched snake. Paco grunted as the air left his lungs. Luke pinned the Rocking A foreman's legs to the ground just like he'd done at the Baylor gridiron when he was in college. Paco kicked like a mule with the fits to free himself.

Meanwhile, Hector and Steve waged a free-for-all tussle on the ground, each trying to lay serious fists into the other's face while lying in awkward positions. Steve acted instinctively. He was not much of a fighter, although he had fought a boy once at Baronsville High. He had lost, but still remembered the satisfaction in hitting back. Hector, a more experienced fighter, kicked Steve square in the groin.

Lights exploded in Steve's brain and the pain seared his loins with a sickening fire that spread to his stomach, made it boil to a queasy swirl.

"Damn you, Hector," gasped Steve.

Hector scooted away, got to his feet. He clenched his fingers into fists and waited for Steve to get up. The younger Killian doubled up in pain, glared at Hector with pain-glazed eyes, his scrotum swelling like a sudden neck goiter. He cupped his hands over his groin to protect himself from another kick.

Luke clawed his way up Paco's legs, grabbed the Mexican's belt with his left hand, swung a roundhouse right into Paco's kidney. Paco pumped his legs in a series of quick scissor-kicks, trying to find a target. The blow to his kidney didn't even phase Velez.

"*Chingon!*" hissed Paco.

Luke knew there hadn't been much steam in his punch, but he wanted to keep Paco busy until he could find a piece of face to pummel. Paco squirmed, trying to get away, but Luke grabbed Velez's shirt collar and twisted it as he climbed still higher up Paco's frame.

Steve got to his feet, started to bring his arms up to a boxing position.

"Owww!" yelled Steve as Hector drove a fist into Steve's gut with pile-driving efficiency. The blow exacerbated the pain in Steve's testicles and if he hadn't gotten mad, he would have folded right then. Instead, he started after Hector, kicking at him like a girl. Hector retreated, his fists balled up for the next strike.

Steve, blood in his eyes, stalked after his prey.

Paco lashed out at Luke, trying to jab Killian's eyes out. Luke crawled into a crouch, trying to pin Velez at the waist. Paco knocked off Luke's hat, grabbed for a handful of hair. Luke swept the foreman's arms aside and rammed a fist into the soft flesh of Paco's mouth.

"*Cabron!*" shouted Paco, humping his chest out to dislodge Luke. Luke pitched off to the side as Velez swung a leg in a half arc, driving the toe of his boot into the left cheek of Luke's ass.

Luke braced his fall with stiffened arms, but the force of Paco's kick drove him forward so that he almost performed an involuntary handstand. Paco rolled the other way and crabbed to his feet, giving Luke a chance to recover. Luke bounded to his feet and twisted around to face Paco. Both men went into fighting crouches and began circling each other warily, each looking for an opening.

Hector didn't wait for Steve to attack. Instead, he waded into the fight with both arms flailing. Steve backpedaled to escape Hector's rush, holding his arms up to ward off the blows. Steve stumbled over the fallen shotgun. Hector pounced, grabbing Steve's arms, encircling them with his own. Steve panicked in a sudden blind fear.

"Let loose of me!" he shrieked.

Hector forced Steve to his knees, released his grip. Steve gaspd for air as Hector stepped back, started pumping fists into Killian's face. The blows stung and Steve tried to duck under them.

Hector seemed to go into a frenzy, hammering Steve's face, smashing him in the eyes and mouth until Steve's senses started to teeter. Shooting stars flashed in his brain; black shadows blotted out the light and he left himself falling backwards under the furious onslaught.

"Don't, don't," cried Steve, but Hector kept bashing him.

Luke reversed his stalk, caught Paco with a wild left that banged into the Mexican's ear, staggering him. Following up his advantage, Luke slung a hard right to Paco's chin. He heard a sharp crack and Paco's legs buckled at the knees. Luke hit him twice more on the cheek as Paco's rubbery legs crumpled underneath him. Paco's eyes rolled backward in their sockets, and he hit the ground with a sodden thud.

"Chingaso," sighed Paco.

"Give it up, Velez," said Luke, panting. He rubbed sore knuckles as he gulped in air. His side ached from the exertion.

"You win," breathed Paco.

Luke turned, saw Hector beating Steve to a pulp. He ran over, grabbed a handful of Hector's hair, pulled him off his half brother.

"That's enough," said Luke softly, still trying to draw in a full breath.

Blood streamed from Steve's nostrils as he got to his feet, stood on shaking legs.

"Hector," said Luke, "you better take care of Paco. Steve and I are going to get the hell out of here."

"We're going to call the law on you, Luke Killian," said Hector. "You're in big trouble for coming onto our property."

"Hector, you don't even know what trouble is. When we get through with your father, you'll be lucky to have a ranch."

"You damned queer," said Steve, spitting a gob of blood out of his mouth.

Hector's eyes widened, then narrowed to slits.

"What did you call me?"

"Steve, that's enough," said Luke. "Let's get out of here."

"Everybody knows he's queer," said Steve.

Hector lunged for Steve, but Luke stepped between the two young men and backed Hector off.

"Steve, you shut up," said Luke. "Hector, cool down."

Hector said nothing. But he didn't take his gaze off Steve. The sparks of hatred burned in his dark eyes. It had been a long time since Bone had done those terrible things to him. He had hoped he wouldn't have to remember what had happened four years ago. But now Steve had brought the memories back. At that moment he wanted to kill Steve Killian.

Steve saw the look in Hector's eyes and averted his own gaze.

Luke pushed his younger brother away. He too had heard all the talk, but this was not the time to humiliate Hector Aguilar. There had already been enough trouble for one day.

"Get our horses, Steve," Luke said softly.

Steve glared at Hector, then wiped the blood from under his nose with a rake of his sleeve.

"You'll be sorry you ever hit me," said Steve, as he walked away.

"I'm not afraid of you," said Hector. "I just hate to fight with my own brother, that's all."

"What the hell, you ain't my brother," spat Steve.

"I'm just as much your brother as Luke is," said Hector, the hatred burning in his eyes like distant fires.

"You bastard," said Steve.

"That's enough," said Luke. "Both of you. Steve, get your horse."

Steve did not look back. He climbed on Sonny, retrieved Luke's horse.

"You're going to be sorry, Luke," said Hector. "You're both going to pay for this. Someday."

"Aw shit, Hector," said Luke, as he turned to walk toward Steve, who was riding toward him on Sonny, leading Luke's mount, "we all pay for everything we do, one way or another, now or later."

"Steve hadn't ought to of called me what he did."

Luke sighed heavily, shook his head.

After Luke was aboard his horse, he rode over to Paco, who was now sitting up, holding his head with both hands.

"There'll be another day, Paco," said Luke.

"For what?"

"To take care of this dam, once and for all."

"Fuck yourself, *Chingon,*" said Paco.

"Hell, I wish I had the time," said Luke with a grin.

The two Killians rode off toward the cut fence, following the still-dry stream bed. Neither spoke for several moments, although they had much on their minds.

"What was Hector babbling about back there?" Steve asked. "He acted like he was kin to us."

"Maybe he is," said Luke.

"Hell, he's just a Mexican."

"Well, he thinks Ben is his daddy anyway."

"You mean Daddy and Hector's mother—"

"Steve, I just don't know. Hector came to see Ben one day and they had words. I guess it's possible our daddy might have sown some oats about nine months before Hector was born."

"Well, I just can't believe anything like that," said Steve.

"No? Well, stranger things have happened."

Steve chewed on that for a long time, but the puzzle was too big for him. He rode in silence, hurting from the blows Hector had given him. And all he knew was that he hated Hector Aguilar—not so much for hitting him, but for saying what he did, and for being a queer to boot.

Luke knew something had been started back there at the dam. Something that might not be finished for a long time.

24

―■―

BEN SLAMMED THE door of the pickup. Charlie pushed the gearshift lever into first gear, let out the clutch.

Ben shifted in his seat, unable to sit straight until he reached behind him and pulled the flask from his pocket. He unscrewed the cap, offered the pint to his foreman.

Charlie Stone shook his head.

Ben tilted the bottle, took a hefty swallow.

"Sonofabitch," he breathed.

"Bad whiskey?"

"No, I was just thinking of that goddamned Sherwood. Here I been waitin' for Sherco to strike oil and Matt Baron's pumping yay many barrels a day from a dozen wells. That's why I hired young Braden back there. I think there's a dark gentleman in the proverbial woodpile."

Charlie eased the pickup through the gears until he was in fourth, then he pushed the pedal to the floor with the heavy sole of his riding boot. The pickup jounced over the grassy soft soil, slithered past vacant-eyed cattle, scooted through dry ruts that marked the ranch road.

"Sherwood ain't been here often enough to dust off the welcome mat 'tween times," said Charlie.

Ben looked at his foreman, wedged the flask in between the seat and the door. Charlie was a range-toughened third-generation cowhand. He had grown up on a Palo Duro homestead, run cattle along the Brazos when he was just a freckle-faced kid, drifted from place to place as the West shrank up. He had once told Ben Killian that he was most comfortable on a big ranch like the Lazy K, where he had acres of land and thousands of cattle to manage. He did not like cars, town, pantywaists or slackers. He'd done everything for Ben, from stringing fence to branding cattle and doctoring for the pink eye and blackleg. He thought anyone who didn't eat beef once a day had something wrong with him. Charlie loved to hunt and he was particularly fond of shooting bobcats, skinning them out and making rugs out of them. He was a quick wing-shot, and talked now and again of Fort Worth in "the old days." He treated the new pickup like a maverick, seemed bent on wearing its engine out before the tires lost their treads.

"I think Sherwood's been favoring Matt's holdings over my own interest," Ben said.

"I 'member them two college boys he sent out to do like Braden's doin' and both seemed light in the head. One of 'em couldn't roll a rock down a steep hill."

"I should have paid more attention," said Ben, with a rueful undertone to his voice.

"That one son of a buck, Liggett, not only didn't know a whole hell of a lot about oil, he didn't even suspect much."

Ben laughed wryly. The road took a turn and Charlie managed to make it on all four wheels, but Ben had to hold onto the dashboard to keep from impaling himself on the floor shift as the pickup hit the straightaway at fifty miles per hour. Ben looked back and saw a funnel of dust rising in their wake, fanning out to powder the blackjack scrub that dotted the flat, parched grassland.

"What about Braden?" asked Ben. "You think he's working for me or is Sherwood paying him to lead us around like a couple of blind geese?"

"Braden's his own man, I reckon," said Charlie, which Ben knew was a high compliment. "I seen him takin' measurements and studyin' and he sure enough worked for the Klebergs and did a job for them."

Ben didn't need to ask if Charlie had checked. Stone was born suspicious. And, he could size a man up in five minutes. Charlie, in fact, had warned Ben about the geologists who worked for Sherco Oil, saying both of them had rooms to let upstairs. Ben was pretty sure Keith Sherwood had told those geologists not to test the ground at El

Rincón. That would be tapping into Baron's field, even if the drills were on Killian land. Ben had refused to sign the new leases and had hired Larry Braden before going to another oil company. Money was so tight, the drought so bad, that he needed another source of income or his creditors were going to grab a lot of cheap Lazy K land.

"Fact is, near as I can figure," said Charlie, "oil just ain't ever'-wheres. I talked to a Shell gee, gee . . . whatever it is . . ."

"Geologist," offered Ben.

"Yeah, one of them, and he said he doubted like hell there was enough oil under West Texas to grease a sewing machine."

"He said that?"

Charlie nodded.

"He said one place could be dry as a widow's pussy, the next have a lake of oil that could pump for a hundred years and never miss a lick."

"Well, it's damn sure hard as hell to find on Lazy K land," said Ben.

Braden had worked for Sherco Oil, but he was really an independent geologist, or claimed to be, so Ben had to trust him until he found good reason not to be confident in Larry's findings.

Charlie slowed the pickup. Ben straightened up, looked through the windshield.

"Uh-oh," said Charlie. "Looks like Harvey's got him some unwelcome company."

Ben saw the dark silhouettes of two men standing on one side of the dynamite, Harvey Leeds standing on the other as if they were playing a game of mumbly-peg or arguing over who was going to go first.

"Looks like ol' Roy Blanchard's got Harvey in a standoff," said Charlie. "Don't know who that other jaybird is."

"Ernie Aguilar," said Killian. "But that's Blanchard's police car."

"Looks like we done stepped in a pile of shit."

"Well, somebody has, maybe," said Ben. "You got a permit for that dynamite, right?"

"Ben," said Charlie wearily, "I got enough papers to start a bonfire."

"Well, something's up," said Ben. "We'll find out what soon enough."

"Likely," said Charlie and gunned the motor as he jammed the gas pedal to the floor. The pickup leaped ahead as its tires dug down into sand and hit hard bottom.

As they drove closer, Ben leaned forward in the seat.

"Charlie, there's somebody else there."

"Where?"

"Standing just behind Ernie Aguilar. See him?"

Charlie changed course.

"Son of a buck," he said. "You're right. Can't make him out, though."

"Neither can I," said Ben, but he felt a sudden queasiness in his stomach. "But that's Ernie Aguilar sure as shootin'."

"The ol' greaser grandee hisself," said Charlie sarcastically.

Charlie swung the pickup toward Harvey in a wide circle. He hit the brakes, skidded to a dusty stop.

"Somebody else is sitting in Roy's police car," said Ben.

"He's a-gettin' out," said Charlie.

"That's Ray Naylor. Looks like Ernie called out all the troops."

"Goddamned greaser," muttered Charlie as he switched off the ignition.

"Steady now, Charlie," said Ben as he pulled at the door handle to get out.

He knew that many of his hands hated Mexicans. In fact, a lot of white Texans were prejudiced. Ben had wondered if he was, many times, and had decided that he was, although he considered himself more tolerant than most. But even that bothered him. He and Frances had talked about it more than once. She was a liberal and didn't like the jokes the men made about Mexicans. She especially didn't like hearing them called "greasers." Ben had told her that he didn't like it either, and she had climbed all over him about tolerating it. "You ought to say something to your hands," she'd said. Ben had said that would not only be useless, but he'd likely have a mutiny to put down, or worse, all of the born and reared Texans would walk off and go to work somewhere else. But Frances had a point. Ben didn't like Ernie Aguilar, but he told himself it wasn't because he was a Mexican or because he had married Elena.

Charlie climbed out the driver's side, bristling like a dog coming across a rattling sidewinder. Harvey Leeds walked away from the group, headed toward Ben.

"What's up, Harvey?" asked Killian.

"Roy there says we're a-settin' on Rocking A land and if I set off that charge, he and Naylor are going to take me off to the calaboose."

"He's full of green calfshit," said Charlie Stone.

"Hold on, Charlie," said Ben, "I'll handle this."

"Whatever you say, Ben. But if Roy gives you any cause, I'll be glad to tangle assholes with him."

"Harvey, what happened, exactly?" asked Ben, ignoring Charlie's offer.

"Ernie and Roy and them come up on me just after y'all left and jerked the fuse out of that dynamite. I told 'em you'd be a-roarin' back here when that blast didn't go off and they said they'd just wait 'til you did come back. I swear you could have plumb scraped the smug off old Ernie's face like it was dried calfshit. Roy, now, he just grabbed that fuse and walked away like he was a-goin' to wait until you come back and whup your ass with it."

"Well, let's just see what Roy has to say," said Ben softly. He tickled the side of his nose with his stub finger, but his face did not change expression.

Harvey, Charlie and Ben approached the sheriff, who held the strand of dynamite fuse in his hand as if it was a snake he had just killed. Ernie stood stiff and silent as a post, the man behind him taking up Aguilar's shadow so unobtrusively Ben had to squint hard to see part of a shoulder and leg.

Killian fixed his attention on Roy Blanchard. The rancher slid his gray Stetson back on his head, reached into his pocket for the pack of Camels. He shook one out, stuck it in his mouth, but did not light it. His right hand crabbed over his shirt pocket, as if looking for a match and in no particular hurry about it.

Deputy Ray Naylor, for some reason, went back to the police car, climbed in and sat there looking through the windshield. He left the door open on the passenger side, however. Ben noted his behavior with mild curiosity. He could feel the nervousness in Aguilar if not in Blanchard. The sheriff had his brick-wall face, though. He was a pretty good poker player.

Ben glanced at Ernie once more for a brief moment and nodded before gazing at the fuse in Blanchard's hand.

"Roy," said Ben.

"Ben."

"What you got there?" asked Ben.

"Ben, I'm just upholdin' the law."

"I know you are, Roy. Harvey here tells me you pulled that fuse. We were fixin' to make a little test for oil over yonder."

"Well, that's just what the problem is, Ben."

"I've got a permit."

"I know you do, Ben, and you can sure blow off them sticks of dynamite."

"Then, why don't you just hand me back that fuse and we'll start Harvey all over again."

"Well, Ben, you can't set it off exactly where Harvey was a-fixin' to."

"Why is that, Roy?" Ben found the match and worked it out of his shirt pocket. He put a fingernail to the sulfurous head.

"See those stakes there?" Roy asked.

"I see them. Not mine."

"No sir, I reckon not. You see, this has done been surveyed and Ernie Aguilar, he owns this section of land. That is, he used to own it. He's done deeded it over to Bone there."

Ben's thumb dropped away from the matchhead. He looked over at Ernie. Ernie shuffled his feet and stepped aside a pace. Jack Bone stood there, staring owlishly at Ben Killian. No one said a word for several seconds. Charlie Stone made a choking sound in his throat.

"Ernie, what the hell is this?" asked Ben, finally. "You're giving my land away to a thief and a murderer."

"Now, Ben," said Blanchard, "there ain't no call for you to jump all over Ernie. I've done checked the papers and everything's all legal and Bone owns this part of El Rincón just like Ernie says. I don't want no trouble."

Ben felt a sudden surge of anger boil to the surface of his brain. Jack Bone wore a smirk on his mouth that was like a red flag to a fighting bull. Roy's meat-bone face darkened with a red flush and his neck swelled against his sweat-soaked collar until the veins stood out like blue garter snakes. He could play some hands of poker better than others, Ben thought.

"I thought Jack Bone was wanted for murder and stealing," said Ben softly.

"We ain't got no evidence on him, Ben," said Blanchard quickly. He reached in his back pocket and pulled forth a sheaf of legal documents. "These here papers are all legal and show boundary markers and everything, Ben. So, you got no cause to get mad or start any fight with Ernie or Bone. I'm here to see that you go quietly back to your own property and let well enough alone."

"Well, I'll be a pluperfect, ring-tailed sonofabitch," said Ben, as Roy walked over and handed him the papers. "You're telling me that land I've owned since my daddy died, land my daddy owned and his daddy owned, is now the property of that no-account piece of trash there? Ernie, you haven't got the brains God gave a piss-ant."

Ben looked at the plat marks, the property descriptions. It looked to him as if he had lost a few dozen acres to a surveyor's string.

"Ben," said Blanchard, "it's all legal. You just made a mistake, that's all. Your daddy or your granddaddy never owned this corner. That's what the papers say."

"I know what the goddamned papers say," said Ben. "Ernie, you better pray to sweet baby Jesus that your survey pans out because I'm going to check every fucking plumb line and marker before this is over with. And if I find one goddamned line off the bead, I'll be all over your ass like yellowjackets on a mudhole."

Ben cracked the unstruck match in half and turned on his heel.

"Come on, Charlie, Harv. Let's get the hell out of here before I do something that'll make Roy draw his gun."

"Ben, don't take this personal," said Blanchard.

Ben didn't answer. He walked over to the cluster of dynamite sticks, picked it up. Then, he looked back at Ernie and Bone and tossed the bundle up in the air, caught it with one hand. Then, he crumpled up the papers in his hand and dropped them to the ground. He ground his bootheel into the mass of crumpled papers as if putting out a fire.

Ray Naylor got out of the sheriff's car and walked over to stand beside Roy. He carried a sawed-off double-barreled shotgun in his hand.

"Put that goddamned thing away," said Roy.

"Well, you told me to stand by."

"It's over with," said Blanchard. "Go on back to the car and mind your own business."

"Yes, sir," said Naylor sheepishly.

"It's not over with," said Ernie.

"It better be," said Bone, grinning.

Ernie looked at Bone and closed his eyes. Naylor caught the look as he was walking back to the car. He opened his mouth to say something, but kept on going without uttering a word. It bothered him that a man like Aguilar would take up with Bone. Ernie obviously disliked Bone, but he had sure enough deeded him some land. Land that might be soaked with oil. It seemed strange to Naylor and he was a man to worry over things like a dog gnawing on tough leather.

Roy watched as the three men climbed into the pickup. Charlie drove off. The dust spooled out from the tires and hung there in the boiling air for several moments.

"Ernie, was I you, I'd stay clear of Ben Killian for a long spell."

"Sheriff, thank you for coming out," said Ernie. "I knew Ben would not like to see those papers. He took it hard."

"Hard ain't the word."

Blanchard turned, started back toward his car.

"Sheriff, if you don't need that fuse, I could use it," said Bone.

Blanchard stopped in his tracks, looked at the fuse in his hand and then at Bone.

"Bone, you just keep your mouth shut. You're lucky I don't turn Naylor on you with that sawed-off and have him blow your nigger ass all over your fucking property."

Bone's eyes narrowed and he went back inside himself as if the clouds had suddenly swallowed up the sun.

Ernie Aguilar stood there a long time after the sheriff and his deputy drove off. He stared at the trail of dust marking Ben's path as if hoping Ben would turn around and settle everything once and for all.

"Well, that didn't mean so much," said Bone, chuckling. "Killian got his ears pinned back."

"Bone," said Ernie, "if there's anything Ben Killian hates, it's to lose. I don't know if that deed Blanchard had is as good as the paper it's written on."

"You said it was."

"Ben might not think so when he looks very close."

"It had better be good, Ernie, or you'll go to prison."

Ernie sighed inwardly.

"I might go anyway, Bone."

"What you mean?"

"I might just go to prison for shooting you dead."

Bone laughed, but he did not like the odd look in Ernie's eyes as he walked away. Aguilar had left his car parked at Bone's shack, one the Indian had built at the edge of the *brasada,* right where the three points of El Rincón came together like wedges holding together an entire empire on a single shaky fulcrum.

"A deal's a deal," said Bone, following after Aguilar. "Killian won't be no trouble."

"I would not bet on it, *amigo.*"

As he walked toward Bone's shack at the edge of the *brasada,* Ernie felt lower than he ever had in his life. Bone had cut him off from the company of his neighbors just as if he had thrown a fence around the Rocking A. Bone was as free as a bird, while Ernie was a prisoner. When Matt Baron found out that Bone was a landowner and owned a part of El Rincón, he was sure to throw a shoe and get to bucking.

Aguilar's shoulders sagged as he drew in sight of his car. A great weariness seeped through him like a slow poison. He had lost the respect of his son Hector, he knew, and Elena looked at him sometimes so hard that he felt he could read the loathing in her mind. His daughter Alicia was quiet, and while she didn't say much, Ernie knew that she felt the tension at home the same as they all did. But he knew no way of getting rid of Bone without admitting his guilt to something that had happened a long time ago. If he did that, he would be sent to prison and he would lose everything. He hated himself for being so weak, but he couldn't deliberately kill a man. That other thing was an accident. An unlucky accident.

But he had never confessed to his priest, and he knew he never would. Sometimes he could fool himself into believing that it had never happened. But not with Bone. Bone kept prodding him with it, jabbing him with the sharp end of it so that the wound in his mind would not heal.

"Bone," said Ernie as he opened the door to his DeSoto, "don't ever ask me for another thing. I don't want to see you or hear from you. Do you understand me?" He looked at the small shack. It had been built with scrap lumber, with some of Ernie's own lumber and nails. He knew Bone had stolen from him since he came back, but he was powerless to stop the thievery. He took Bone's threats seriously; hated himself for it.

Bone smiled that oily, smirking smile of his.

"Why, sure, *amigo,*" he mocked. "I won't ever ask you for nothing. After all, you have been good to me, Ernie. You are a real good Mexican. Just like a brother to me. *Hermanos,* eh?"

Ernie climbed into the car and slammed the door. The window

was open. Bone leaned down, rested his arms on the door and stuck his head inside the car.

"Aren't you going to say goodbye to your good friend?" Bone asked.

Ernie twisted the key in the ignition. He heard Bone's laughter long after he left El Rincón, driving too fast, wanting only to shower and wash off the stink of . . . he started to say Bone, but it was the stink of himself, strong in his nostrils, like something that had died and rotted, like carrion in the furnace of the Texas sun with the hot winds blowing the stench in every direction for all to smell.

25

ETHAN BARON FELT uncomfortable in Henry Emberlin's office. He sat stiffly in the leather chair, his long legs stretched out, boot-heels cocked at an angle against the worn carpeting. He had lost the awkward, gangly look of the college boy, was now filling out at a shade over six feet tall, four years after graduating from college. The clinic smelled of disinfectant, rubbing alcohol, infection, disease. A baby squalled in the waiting room, impervious to its mother's whining pleas. Doc Emberlin seemed oblivious to the phone ringing on his desk. Alicia Luz Aguilar, his nurse, came in and gave the doctor an exasperated look. Emberlin ignored her and she started to open her mouth to speak.

"Shut the door, will you, Alicia?" said Emberlin.

"Doctor, the waiting room's full; Mr. O'Neil is doubled over with stomach pains; Mrs. Hartman's baby boy has the colic; Junior Collins has a broken arm."

"You do what you can, Alicia," Emberlin said patiently. "I'll be out directly."

"Ethan, Derek wants to know how long you'll be," she said to young Killian.

"I—I don't know," Ethan stammered. "Alicia, is that you, all grown up?"

"It sure is," she said, her voice chromatic, lyrical as a songbird's. "Didn't you recognize me?"

"Not at first. It's been a coon's age, since I've seen you. You've grown up."

"Why, I'm eighteen, Ethan. Didn't Derek tell you we've been seeing each other?"

"Uh, not exactly."

"That will be all, Alicia," said Dr. Emberlin.

"'Bye, Ethan," said Alicia, looking at him coyly. Ethan flushed. She had filled out, was really a beautiful woman, with her olive skin, her dark eyes, raven hair. He had last seen her when she was fourteen, and that was four years ago. He had no idea his brother was dating her. But he was not totally surprised. Derek, from what Peggy had told him, had chased every young lass in Baronsville, Galveston and Corpus Cristi.

"We won't be long," said Emberlin, as Alicia glanced at the doctor with a stern look on her face.

The phone stopped ringing a few minutes after Alicia left the office. Ethan, dressed in a conservative suit, had lost the look of the young graduate of the University of Texas who had studied law and politics on the side while obtaining a liberal education in livestock management as an undergraduate. His hair was neatly combed and pomaded, the straw hat he wore balanced in his lap. He had no idea why Dr. Emberlin had called him into the office. Derek had wanted to come along, but Emberlin said he only wanted to talk to Ethan. Now, Ethan knew why Derek was eager to visit Emberlin's office. Little old Alicia Aguilar. Wasn't that something?

"Doctor, is there something wrong with me?" Ethan asked.

Emberlin chuckled, shook his head. He had gained little weight over the years, but his hair had turned snowy at the temples, the lines in his face deepened, and Ethan noticed the wattles on his neck had grown flabby. His clear blue eyes looked large and watery under the strong lenses of the horn-rimmed spectacles he wore.

"With my mother?" Grace's drinking had gotten progressively worse the past couple of years. She still tried to hide it, but Derek said that she often passed out and treated Peggy, their sister, like a field hand, cursing her, hitting her, for no reason.

"That's not why I called you into town, Ethan. But how are you doing? Did Miriam Ferguson treat you well?"

"She did," said Ethan. "I learned a lot from her and from James, too." In his spare time he had worked as an office boy during Miriam Ferguson's successful attempt to unseat Governor Sterling in the democratic primary, had worked for her during her second term, when the state's annual deficit rose to $14 million. "I learned more from Jimmy Allred, though." Allred had been elected to the office of governor four years ago, in 1934. His second two-year term was about to expire.

"Good. What's next for you, son?"

"I'm going to work with W. Lee O'Daniel. He's going to win the election."

"Oh, he is, is he? Well, I hear him on the radio all the time, singing and making a fuss. I expect Texas can withstand him just as easily as we did Pap or Miriam Ferguson."

Ethan recalled the day Allred quit and eleven candidates rose up out of the bushes to vie for the governorship. Each man said he wanted the job because there was so much graft in Texas. Each one promised to put an end to the corruption.

W. Lee O'Daniel had a popular radio program that boomed out early every morning all over the state. Poor people listened to him faithfully and so did many of the rich. Ethan was intrigued by O'Daniel, a down-home, seemingly simple soul who sang songs with a country twang, spoke from the heart, seemed to inspire a genuine intimacy with his listeners.

April 21, San Jacinto Day in Texas, was traditionally the day on which all gubernatorial campaigns were opened and the candidates announced their intentions. None did in 1938. Instead, the candidates began sporadically to enter the race a few days later. Ethan told his father that it was like listening to a dog bark at night. Every dog in earshot took up the chorus until they were all chasing after each other in a mindless pack.

Ethan listened to the garbled oratory over the radio. He listened to the sulfurous words of each man denouncing the other candidates. Each one called himself an honest man and branded the others as outright thieves. The voters were confused.

"If each one called himself honest," Matt had told Ethan, "and the other ten thieves, it was ten to one against any of them being honest."

"What about O'Daniel?" Ethan had asked his father.

"Go see him," said Matt.

Ethan didn't have to do that. O'Daniel sent for Ethan. From the first moment they met, he was intrigued with the politician.

"Texas," O'Daniel told Ethan, "is a land so corrupt no real Christian would want to live in it."

"What do you think of the candidates for governor?" Ethan had asked O'Daniel.

"Somethin' sure stinks here," said Lee, sucking on a stick of straw. "Texas needs better."

"You got anyone in mind?" asked Ethan.

"We had four years of Dan Moody, two years of Ross Sterling and four of Jimmy Allred and not one of 'em made a crooked dime. But, damnit, they all just about killed Texas politics. No one cares who gets into office. Everything in Austin is cut and dried. Nobody's even listenin' to these charlatans. You come in with me, boy, and we'll set the voters' hearts to thumpin'."

"I'm in," said Ethan, fascinated by O'Daniel's approach to grassroots politics. But he'd talked to his dad about O'Daniel's crazy campaign.

"Hell, son," Matt had said, "it's a damned circus. You might as well be the ringmaster."

Emberlin cleared his throat, jarring Ethan from his brief reverie.

"Yes, Doc," said Ethan, "well, politics is funny. Is that what you wanted to talk about, sir?"

"No, Ethan, not really, but I wanted to see how you were situated, find out what your plans were. And Derek? He's doing well?"

"Daddy says Derek is a big help to him. When he's not flying that Waco, he's out in the oil fields, or tending to the new breeds of cattle Daddy brought in, working the horses. We're developing some new breeds. He and Johnny Bell do most of the work running the ranch. Daddy, he seems to be fighting with John Nance Garner on the phone all the time, or fighting with Mother over the accounts. Roosevelt's New Deal didn't work too well for Texas."

"Yes, last year the Supreme Court cut Roosevelt's legs out from under him. At least he didn't have to buy a wheelchair."

"Oh, I get it," said Ethan, "the polio."

"Not a very good joke, I'm afraid, Ethan. You boys have done well. I know Matt's proud of you both. You might wonder why I didn't talk to you when I was out there last week seeing your father."

"I didn't think anything of it. I know you and Daddy are old friends."

"Yes, I don't know which of us is more stubborn."

"I can guess, sir."

Emberlin chuckled again. The laugh was forced.

"Well, son, I looked at your father again last week and this morning I got back the reports from Dallas. I sent some tests up there."

"Tests?" asked Ethan. He felt very odd, his senses honed to a keenness by something in Emberlin's voice. The smells in the chamber seemed more acute now, although the sounds in the next room were subdued, faded into the background as klaxons rang in his brain.

"Matt likely has stomach cancer," said Emberlin.

"What's that?"

"A growth. A very large one. But it's spread, to his colon, maybe, will probably spread to his liver and at least one kidney if my hunch is correct."

"Can you cut it out?"

Emberlin shook his head.

"Too advanced. He's probably had it for years. I warned him. He wouldn't listen. Now, it's too late. We could open him up, but he won't go to a hospital. Wouldn't do any good if we did. X rays and blood tests give every indication that he has a cancer, maybe a whole bunch of them. I did all I could by probing and taking pictures of his organs. A radiologist up in Houston said it looked like cancer spreading all through his innards."

Ethan felt as if all the oxygen had been sucked out of the room. A giddiness arose in him as if his cranium had just been emptied, then filled with pure alcohol.

"What can we do?" he asked.

Emberlin arose from his chair, circled the paper-strewn desk. He stepped past the skeleton dangling lifeless on its iron frame, the pickled jars of hearts, kidneys, a fetus, part of a lung, standing on shelves next to medical tomes. He halted in front of Ethan's chair and looked at the young man with the softness of compassion in his eyes.

"Just see to it that you and Derek are ready for it. Talk to your father, if he wants to. Let him know you're ready to carry on. That ranch means the world to him."

"I know," said Ethan. "How—how long does he have?"

"Hell, I don't know, Ethan." Emberlin scratched the back of his head. "Months, years. Days, weeks. Without going inside, I just can't tell. I've told him to call me if the pain gets too bad."

"Then he knows."

"He knows."

"What did he say?" asked Ethan.

"He said he might not wait around. I gave him some strong medicine. He'll probably need it. I don't know how he stands the pain even now. There has to be considerable discomfort."

"Does he have a year? Two years?" Again, Ethan felt dizzy.

"If that. I want to get him into a hospital, in Houston or Dallas, but he won't go."

"No."

Ethan looked up at Dr. Emberlin. He felt numb. As if something had been sucked out of him. His brain swam with it, choked with the idea that his father was dying. He knew about the stomach pains. But his daddy had had those for years. The whole family had come to accept them as just like one of the scars that laced his body. Something that was there. Something that was not important. The enormity of it struck Ethan now. That Matt Baron was mortal, after all.

"Even if we got him to a hospital, we couldn't save him, Ethan. The cancer has spread too far for that, I suspect. It's like a poisonous vine. It replaces good cells with abnormal ones. It is horrible and deadly. I'm sorry."

"What about the pain?"

"He might not be able to stand it. The medicine will probably make him sick, or just not touch it toward the end."

"A year? A goddamned year? Maybe less, maybe more. Damn, damn."

Emberlin said nothing. The phone started ringing again. It made Ethan jump.

He pulled himself from the chair, stuck his straw hat on his head.

"I'll tell Derek. Thanks, Dr. Emberlin."

"I wish there was more that I could do."

"I know. Does my mother know?"

"Yes, she knows, but she hasn't faced it yet."

"Peggy?"

"I didn't tell her. Maybe you should. Incidentally, did you know your sister might turn out just like your mother?"

"What do you mean?"

"She's a drinker."

"I've never seen Peggy drunk," said Ethan.

"No, well, that's part of it, perhaps. Like mother, like daughter."

"I don't believe you, Doc."

"That's all right. It might not show up for a few years. Grace's didn't. She could tolerate alcohol for a long time. But now she's heading toward a crisis of her own, I imagine."

"Did you ever talk to my mother about her drinking?"

"No," said Emberlin. "She would have to bring it up. She never has."

Ethan laughed, a hollow laugh that was mirthless as a dead radio.

"Looks like the Barons have all kinds of troubles, Doc."

"You'll get through them, son. Call me if there's any change, if you need anything. If you have any questions."

"Questions? I've got a zillion of them and I don't know where to start. I just never thought . . . his stomach pains . . ."

"I know. He's had them a long while."

"As long as I can remember, maybe. Or at least since we had all that trouble with Bone."

"Well, you can't go back and change things, Ethan."

"No, I guess not."

Ethan left the room as the phone stopped ringing. Derek was leaning through the nurse's window, flirting with her. He turned as Ethan came through the waiting room.

"What's up, Eth?" he asked.

"Let's get out of here," said Ethan.

"You sick?"

"Come on, Dare, not here."

"Jesus, Ethan. 'Licia, I'll see you Saturday night at the Grange," said Derek, winking at Alicia Aguilar. She smiled coyly, blew him a kiss. Mrs. Hartman's baby boy started squalling again. Junior Collins groaned.

Outside, Ethan gulped in a lungful of air.

"How long you been seeing Alicia?" he asked Derek.

"She tell you that?"

"Is it a secret?"

"Hell, I've taken her to the Bijou, danced with her at the Grange Hall."

"She's grown up."

"Boy, I'll say," said Derek. "How come Doc Emberlin wanted to see you? You sick?"

"It's Daddy."

"Huh?"

"Doc Emberlin says he's dying."

"Daddy? Aw, come on, Eth. You wouldn't shit me, would you?"

"It's serious, Dare. Come on, let's get a piece of pie at Nomi's."

"Hell, I need a beer. Straight dope about Daddy?"

"Straight dope. Doc gives him a year or two, at most."

"Jesus," said Derek softly.

There was never any parking on First Street where Doc Emberlin's office sat wedged between the Baronsville Telephone Company and the Davis Veterinary Clinic. They walked past an empty storefront toward the Baronsville Bank, turned left on Main Street at the Grange Hall. Past the U.S. Post Office, they entered Mudd's Pool Hall, with its neon Jax sign flickering in the window. Since Prohibition had been repealed in 1933, Delmer Mudd was serving openly in a wet county. He had sold plenty of bootleg beer and whiskey during the dry years. There was a tavern around the corner, but most of the young people drank at Mudd's. Lupe's Cantina catered mostly to Mexicans during the day, but at night she served good Mexican food and a lot of the older folks ate and drank there, bringing in their bottles of whiskey. Lupe Carvaljo served beer and wine and setups.

"Thanks to you, we've got some places to drink now," said Derek as they crossed to the bar.

"You mean thanks to Jimmy Allred," said Ethan. "I learned a lot from that old boy."

"Why do you work for that louse? He's as crazy as Ferguson was."

"Not quite," said Ethan, as he pulled out a barstool. "Jimmy's not a great governor, but he's a very good one because he's a very good politician."

"You don't seem cut out for that stuff, Ethan," said Derek as he climbed on a stool. "And what makes Allred a good politican, anyway?"

There was a sign on the back mirror that had been printed in bold block letters. It read: NO COLOREDS, NO INDIANS.

"He knows his way around, where the back rooms are. He knows Texas and Texans. He knows we're never happy unless we're doing those things we ought not to do."

"Illegal things, you mean."

Ethan laughed.

"You've got it. Jimmy gave us plenty of law, but no enforcement. Look at his attitude toward liquor, Dare. For political reasons, he was always a dry. But when he first ran for governor, right after they appealed the Eighteenth Amendment in thirty-three, there was a caterwauling from the booze swillers, who wanted the state's dry law repealed also. Jimmy had himself a fat burr under his saddle.''

"What did he do?" asked Derek.

"I told him about Jim Ferguson's strategy of promising the tenant farmers something he knew damned well he couldn't make good on. Nobody tumbled to his trick, and it worked. So, Jimmy Allred picked up the same cards. He knew he didn't have the power to permit the people to vote on the repeal of the liquor law, but he promised that if he was elected, he would give them the chance to vote their wishes.''

"Quite a straddle," said Derek, thrumming his fingers on the bar. No one seemed eager to wait on them.

"You bet. Both the pros and the antis voted for him. He was almost unanimously elected. Jimmy and I sat down and I ran through it for him. I told him that this was not a decision by the Texans as to whether they wanted to be wet or dry. They already knew about that. They never wanted to be anything but wet. The only question Jimmy had to solve, I told him, was whether they wanted their liquor to have a legal or illegal flavor to it.''

"Beautiful," said Derek.

"Yeah. Jimmy grinned like a shit-eating ape when he signed that bill forbidding the establishment of saloons anywhere in the state. All he had to do then was sit back and let nature take its course.''

Only one of the two pool tables was occupied. Del and a man named Orville Treacher were shooting pool, as Dave Tyler and Giacomo Ingianni, Del's partner, looked on.

Del made a two-bank shot on the fifteen ball, knocking it into the corner pocket. Orville swore.

"Whooeeee," said Giacomo. "Fuckin' shot.''

"I think he had both feet off the floor," said Treacher, a sullen look on his face.

"Well, I'm short," said Delmer. Treacher, a tall, lanky man, towered over Mudd.

Derek whistled, pounded a fist on the bar top.

"Why, howdy, Derek," said Dave Tyler. "You goin' to the dance, Satidy?''

"I reckon," said Derek. "If we can ever get waited on here.''

He and Ethan sat at the little L of the bar. It was dark and cool inside, except for the light over the pool table and the rainbow neon of the jukebox against one wall. Stuffed game animals littered the shelves on the walls, back of the bar. There were several deer heads, squirrels, a pair of Gambel's quail, two jackrabbits *in flagrante delicto*, a dusty pronghorn antelope, an old buffalo head, a roadrunner and an armadillo. Winchester and Remington Arms posters were tacked below some of the shelves on the bare walls. A Blatz sign lit the back bar, and there was a Falstaff sign lighting the far end of the little L.

Dave Tyler poked Ingianni in the ribs. The man looked over at Derek with eyes dulled by the beer in his gut. He swallowed from a glass, set it on the bar, got off the stool.

Ingianni went back of the bar.

"Beer?" he asked.

"No, we just came in here to watch you watch pool, Giacomo."

"Smartass."

"Two Jaxes," said Ethan.

"Comin' right up, Mister Baron," said Ingianni sarcastically.

Del continued to clean the table, but he scratched on the eight ball, to Treacher's unabashed pleasure. A quarter disappeared off the edge of the table into the tall man's pocket. Del anted up another two bits and racked the balls for the next game.

The bottles of Jax were icy cold. Derek drank a swallow, before he turned back to his brother. So, they had talked politics and both had time to think of the enormity of the news from Doc Emberlin.

"What's he dying of?" Derek asked suddenly, as if the question had been back of his thoughts all the time.

"Cancer. It's all through him."

"What the hell is that?"

"A growth of some kind. It's real bad, Dare."

"I hope to die. Can't Doc do anything?"

Ethan shook his head.

"How goddamned long did Doc say?"

"A year or two. Maybe less."

"Does Daddy know?"

"Doc says he does."

"Well, goddamn."

Dave Tyler glanced over at the two brothers. He was drinking beer from a bottle of Falstaff. He looked away when Derek glared at him.

"Let's get the hell out of here," said Derek.

"Yeah, I think we better get home and talk to Daddy."

"God, I can't believe it," said Derek. "I just can't believe it."

"Neither can I," said Ethan. He laid a bill on the counter.

"There's your money, Del," he said.

"Don't go away mad," said Mudd.

"Just go away," laughed Treacher. Neither of the Barons knew him, but they took an instant dislike to the man. He didn't have a Texas, even a southern accent, and he wore a faded business suit, a loosened tie, a white shirt. His shoes weren't shined. His tawny straw hair was cut short. He had a rolled up sheaf of papers sticking out of his coat pocket. He took the roll out, peeled off a flyer, handed it to Derek.

"Come to the meeting Saturday night," said Treacher.

Derek glanced at the paper, showed it to Ethan.

"KKK," said Ethan.

"Shitheads," said Derek. He wadded up the paper, tossed it back to Treacher. "Wet this down real good, put some Vaseline on it and shove it up your ass," he said.

Treacher bristled, gripped the pool cue tightly, but he didn't go after Derek.

"Come on, Derek. You oughta join," said Del. "We're gonna run out every nigger in the county. Maybe some others too, who might be nigger-lovers."

"Anybody who dresses up in sheets has to be a couple of bricks shy of a load," said Derek belligerently. Dave Tyler came off the barstool, holding his Falstaff bottle like a club.

"Watch yore goddamned mouth," said Tyler.

"You going to do something about it?" asked Derek coolly.

"I might. I just goddamned might."

"Come on ahead, peckerhead."

Ethan grabbed his brother's arm.

"Derek, let's go. This isn't the time or place."

Derek sucked in a breath. His fists had already started to ball up.

"Yeah, you're right. A whole lot of white trash in this town."

"Who you callin' white trash?" asked Delmer, bringing up his pool cue as if to march with it.

"Forget it, Del," said Ethan. "You got your money. We got our beer."

Ethan hustled Derek outside. As they left, the doorway filled with Dave, Del and Treacher. They glared at the Barons as the two brothers crossed the street.

"You look out you don't see a burning cross at your place," yelled Mudd.

Derek turned and gave him the finger. Ethan slapped it down, his face turning ruddy from embarrassment.

"Nomi's looking through the window," whispered Ethan. "She saw you."

"Well, fuck her and that moronic son of hers," said Derek. He glanced over his shoulder. Naomi's Café was right next to Mudd's Pool Hall. Nomi was standing there, behind the glass, smiling like an enormous cherub. She waved.

Derek chuckled and waved back.

26

───■───

ON JUNE 10, 1938, Ethan joined W. Lee O'Daniel in Waco, bringing with him a bright red circus wagon. O'Daniel rode on the roof, singing his own songs to the accompaniment of a twangy country band. His three children, Pat, eighteen, Mike, seventeen, and Molly, sixteen, rode up there with him. There, to a raucous crowd, O'Daniel announced his candidacy for the governorship.

"Being a busy man," Lee said, "I didn't have time to write up a platform. So I borryed one. From Moses."

The crowd cheered. Ethan, sitting on the buckboard seat, beamed.

"Yes sir," continued O'Daniel, "it was the Ten Commandments. Ever hear tell of 'em?"

The crowd roared.

The politician smiled indulgently from on high.

"Well, sir, I'm goin' to run on them Ten Commandments and for the benefit of my numerous opponents, who probably never even heard of 'em, I'm putting special emphasis on the fifth plank of that platform."

"Which one's that?" yelled a voice in the crowd, one of Ethan's "plants."

"That fifth plank, ladies and gen'lmans, is: " 'Thou shalt not steal.' "

The crowd broke out into a round of enthusiastic, almost worshipful applause.

It was like that everywhere they went.

O'Daniel created a sensation at every gathering with his blatant theatrics. Newshounds suddenly wanted to know all about him. Ethan made the decision not to advertise in the Houston papers before primary day, June 23. But O'Daniel was expected in town to cast his own vote. One writer ventured the supposition that voters might take it into their heads to scatter the corpses of eleven of their niftiest politicians hither and yon all over the state.

Ethan left Brownsville that morning with the O'Daniel clan and they drove across the Baron ranch in triumphant procession. Reporters, including Dale Wilker from the *Baronsville Bugle,* caught up with them in Raymondsville, where the people had barricaded the highway so that Lee couldn't get past without speaking to them. Lee obliged, and he declaimed to a group of one thousand Texans, outlining his platform of the Decalogue.

"Cripes, Lee, you have them," whispered Ethan as he looked out over the crowd sweating in the sun in the hottest part of Texas.

"By the testicles," grinned O'Daniel.

Ethan looked at a young mother standing in the crowd with her baby in her arms. She had a look of rapturous fascination on her face. The baby squalled. She opened her dress and put the child's mouth to her breast without ever breaking her concentration on the speaker.

O'Daniel spoke for more than an hour. He and his cracker entourage sang a couple of songs he had written. At the end of his "sermon" he sent his kids, Pat, Mike and Molly, into the crowd, announcing that his youngsters "will now pass among you and take up a collection to help pay the expenses of this campaign for honest government in Texas."

The crowd did not drift apart. The people stayed and plunked money into the passed hats.

Ethan and Lee headed for dinner at Jack's Café and were buttonholed by Dale Wilker on their way there.

"Mind if I ride the rest of the way with you boys?" Dale asked.

"Son, you come right along," said O'Daniel. "You write it up the way you see it. You know this fine man, Ethan?"

"Sure, Lee. He's from Baronsville."

"Looks a hell of a lot like that writer feller who lives out in California, sails some boat with a funny name."

"Jack London," said Ethan.

"That's the man," agreed O'Daniel.

Dale smiled. Lee had made another lifelong friend.

Wilker stayed with them as the political procession, led by Ethan and Lee, wended its triumphant way toward Houston, and the three of them talked until three in the morning, after they checked into their hotel, nibbling on a late night take-out of greasy hamburgers, potato chips and Fritos with RC Colas.

"Why are Texans giving you such tremendous ovations everywhere you go, Lee?"

"Son, they want change, don't you know? They want a leader who can take them out of the bondage of corruption, give them back their decency. They want a pied piper to lead 'em out of the dens of iniquity and into the bright Texas sun."

"But that's almost biblical," said Dale. "It's nebulous."

"What's that?" asked Lee, in genuine puzzlement.

"Pie in the sky. Not concrete."

"Hellfire, boy, that's what they want. Just listen to 'em. I got 'em going, ain't I? Whoo-eeee!"

"There's another reason, Dale," said Ethan quietly, as he munched on a Frito, sipped an RC Cola. "Lee is the only one of the gubernatorial candidates who is taking his campaign to the people."

Lee put down his hamburger, brought up late by one of his faithful followers, munched what was in his mouth and swallowed.

"Tha's right," said Lee. "Those fat cats stay up there in Austin with their thumbs up their butts. This is all off the record, right?"

"Right," said Dale, who had a photographic memory. Ethan knew that Wilker was enjoying every minute he spent with the flamboyant, oddly boyish W. Lee O'Daniel.

"Well sir," said Lee, "I'm going to make them take out their stinky fingers and smell 'em."

Dale laughed louder than Lee or Ethan.

Later, after Dale left O'Daniel's room, the talk turned serious, as Ethan mapped out some ideas for Lee's campaign.

"I've got an idea, Lee," said Ethan.

"Let's have it, son. You got a say in this, that's for danged sure."

Ethan knew what Lee meant. Matt Baron had contributed to Lee's war chest in Ethan's name.

"I suggest we go to a place where none of the other eleven candidates would ever go."

"Where?" asked Lee.

"Goose Creek," said Ethan.

"Lead the way, son."

Goose Creek, fifty miles from Houston, was a small betwixt-and-between town, part farm and part factory.

"If you bring people there from fifty or a hundred miles away," Ethan had told Lee, "and they come just to hear you speak, they'll vote for you."

"By damn," said Lee, "they just might. Let's hie ourselves to the hinterland."

Ethan was right. They came from miles around. Some wag remarked on their arrival that there hadn't been anything like it in that part of Texas since the second hanging of Bill Longley back in 1870.

The first hanging didn't work out, as the rope broke and Bill got away. But the second, attended by thousands who had come from all over on horseback and in wagons to attend the ceremony, most certainly was worth the trip.

As one man put it, back then: "Old Bill finally danced real good for the folks."

The Goose Creek meeting wasn't to begin until 7:00 p.m., but Ethan arrived early to "check the house." He arrived there at four, three hours ahead of time. It was hotter than the hinges of hell, but the crowd was streaming into the little burg like ants to a jelly picnic. The crowd was jovial, "happier than a Poland China in a manure pile," as O'Daniel said privately to Dale Wilker.

In the middle of the narrow main street two cars bearing "O'Daniel for Governor" stickers and filled with country folks and fruit jars filled with ice water got all tangled up with each other, were pried apart.

"Look at them," said Dale. "Everybody grinning like a shit-eating dog and nobody cussing. Really amazing."

"That's what Lee is," said Ethan. "Just amazing."

A man in a faded chambray shirt parked his old flivver against the curb, stepped out, wiped a sheen of sweat off his face, pasted four O'Daniel stickers on his doors.

"You going to vote for W. Lee O'Daniel?" Ethan asked him.

"Sure I'm goin' to vote for him," the farmer replied. His wife stuck her head out the window and said: "You bet he's goin' to vote for him. Everybody is."

"Why?"

"Because he's honest, mister, and because he ain't no politician."

"How do you know that?" Ethan asked.

"Know it? Huh! Why, we all been a-knowin' it for years, because for years he's been talking' to us on the radio. Not about politics though. Until right lately he never mentioned politics. No sir, until now he's been tellin' us things we like to hear because listenin' to 'em makes it seem easier for us to be pore folks."

They came, the rich and the poor, to hear O'Daniel speak in person. Lee sang songs, cracked jokes as Ethan watched with approval, swelling with the energy of power politics.

Dale asked Ethan privately, at one of the political gatherings, if he really believed in W. Lee O'Daniel.

"I love politics," said Ethan. "I think I chose the right path. Daddy thinks so, too."

"You have any ambitions yourself?" asked Wilker.

Ethan looked at the crowd listening to Lee's Old Testament harangue and his eyes narrowed.

"Someday, Dale," he said, "I'll be up on a stage myself, talking to the people, not as a politician, but as a friend, a countryman."

"You planned a lot of this campaign, didn't you, Ethan?"

"Off the record?"

"Off the record," Dale laughed.

"Well, I advised Lee to stress that he was an honest man and not a politician."

"I notice he always makes the same speech."

"I told him to think of his oratory as just one big slogan," said Ethan. "Of course O'Daniel always makes the same speech. Have you listened real close?"

"Well, I've noticed one thing pretty strange," said Dale.

Ethan sipped an Orange Crush, tipped back his straw hat and lifted his eyebrows slightly in amusement.

"And what's that, Dale boy?"

"You know, don't you, Ethan? Not once, not one damned time in this whole campaign, has Lee mentioned a single one of his opponents. He hasn't called anybody specific any names. He hasn't said so-and-so was a crook. But, somehow, he's managed to smear the whole bunch with raw shit."

Ethan laughed, slapped his knee.

"Lee's plenty smart. He told me right off that he didn't want to mention the names of the other politicians, because he didn't want to give them any free advertising."

"Well, I'll be damned."

"Not only that," said Ethan, "but, if you noticed, he hasn't once mentioned politics, either."

"By the great beard of the prophet Isaiah, Eth old chap, you're absolutely right."

"You know why, Dale?"

"I guess he's probably trying to cut himself out of the herd."

"That's part of it, sure. But the real reason is that Lee doesn't know a damned thing about politics. He really doesn't."

"That's why he's got you in his camp," said Dale.

"But he does tell the people why he's a candidate for governor," said Ethan. "Just listen."

Lee was just reaching that moment in the speech Ethan had helped him write that always got the people to stomping their feet and jumping up and down like they were all afflicted with St. Vitus' dance disease.

"Yes, folks," Lee intoned, "I'm Lee O'Daniel. You all know me and you all know all about me. For ten years I've been working hard trying to make an honest living as a flour peddler in Texas, and now look at me! I'm running for governor; but you folks did it. It's your fault. Every two years, whenever there's been an election, some of you have written in asking me to do this. But until this year I never paid any attention to you.

"This time it was different; there were more letters, they were more urgent, and so one morning on a six-forty-five program, I just told you all about those letters, told you that what I needed was your advice, that I'd wait two weeks to hear from you, and that then, if enough of you had asked me to, I'd make the race for governor. But two weeks was too long. Right away the letters began to come in so fast that when I'd counted up to fifty-four thousand, four hundred ninety-nine I quit. That settled it. Most of you who wrote in asking me to be your candidate are poor people. If there's anything on earth that poor people have got plenty of, it's relatives, and so I said to myself: 'If fifty-four thousand, four hundred ninety-nine poor people in Texas and all their relatives want me to run for governor, I reckon I've got to do it.' And so I'm doing it."

"I'll be damned," murmured Dale Wilker for the hundredth time on the campaign trail.

* * *

Back in Houston, at the Rice Hotel, where the other eleven gubernatorial candidates had established their headquarters, word filtered back to them that a messiah was coming. The hotel took on the aspect of a mortuary.

Lee swept the state. He carried everything: cities, towns, villages, creek bottoms, cow camps and cotton patches. Ethan was elated. Lee had his work cut out for him, all right. He put new vitality into the state and when four men ran against him, in 1940, he steamrollered them into oblivion, and was inaugurated for a second term.

Dale Wilker remarked to the other reporters that O'Daniel was sure to win, but they'd better keep their eye on Ethan Baron, too.

"He's the young lion, that one. He'll surprise you all someday."

There were times when Mayor Ted Womack hated the location of his office inside the Baronsville Bank. While the bank dominated its corner at First and Main, Womack's office was in the back. He had a wonderful view of sagebrush and jackrabbits, but could never see who might be coming to the bank to see him. This morning, he kept making excuses to go out to his secretary's desk so he could look down Main Street and see who was coming.

Wilma Sisler, Womack's secretary, looked up from her typing for the seventh time.

"Is there something I can help you with, Mr. Womack?"

"Uh, no, Wilma. I—I'm just expecting someone."

Wilma, who had formerly been the court clerk at the Baron County Courthouse, looked at her open appointment book.

"I have no one scheduled, sir."

"Well, ah, she, uh, they might not stop by."

"I'll be glad to keep an eye out for you." Wilma's sweetness was sometimes annoying. But she was a good secretary. She was fast and neat and punctual.

"No trouble," he said, looking guiltily out the window.

This time he saw the Ford sedan pull up, park at the curb. Jane Houston Killian sat behind the wheel. Beside her sat young Steve Killian.

"Uh, I'll be in my office, if anyone drops by," Womack said abruptly. He closed his opaque glass door with his name lettered in black, with his title underneath: PRESIDENT.

Wilma watched as the Killians got out of the Ford, closed the doors. The two marched straight for the bank, came inside, headed for her desk.

"Hello Wilma," said Jane. "How are you?"

"Just fine, Mrs. Killian. May I help you?"

"Mr. Womack, please."

"Do you have an appointment?"

"No, young lady, nor do I need one. Tell Ted I'm here, or show me into his office."

"Yes, ma'am," said Wilma obediently. "Just one moment, please."

Wilma opened the door to Ted's office, stuck her head in.

"Mrs. Killian and her grandson are here, Mr. Womack."

Womack, who had been trying to look busy, nodded. "Send them in, Wilma."

"Yes, sir."

She closed the door, turned to Jane and Steve.

"Mr. Womack will see you now, Mrs. Killian."

"Thank you, Wilma," Jane said, her tone sugary as a Louisiana praline.

Wilma reopened the door to Womack's office. Jane Killian swept by her, Steve following in her wake, walked up to Womack's desk. She turned to see that the door was closed, waved Steve to a seat. She sat down then, crossed her legs, planted her purse firmly on her lap and leaned toward the banker. Womack pulled the drapes, blocking off the view of the desert landscape.

"What's on your mind, Mrs. Killian?" Womack looked nervously at Steve. The mayor was a big, florid man with purple-veined jowls, large, elephantine ears, a long, bulbous nose. He wore a suit and a vest, both a conservative blue, a Sears & Roebuck tie, a Van Heusen shirt, a gold tie-clasp, set high enough to clear the top vest button. His monogram, a large W, was on the clasp.

"I want you to foreclose on every one of Ernie Aguilar's outstanding notes," she said, her words as blunt as piano hammers.

Womack cleared his throat to keep from choking on the spot. He looked again at Steve Killian.

"Really," he said, "shouldn't we discuss this in private?"

"I want my grandson to hear this," she said. "He stands to inherit the Lazy K someday and I'm teaching him all I know."

"All you know?" Womack croaked.

"Every blessed thing," said Jane pleasantly. Her blazing blue eyes never left Womack's face. Her hennaed hair was dramatically coifed, glistened like copper wire in graceful folds. The white dress she wore only heightened her fiery complexion, and the short white gloves might have been made of mail the way she held her hands clutched to her purse strap, both balled up into tiny fists.

"Ah, how did you know . . . ?"

"Never mind, Ted. You've been carrying some of Ernie's credit like a bunch of long-past due-bills and I want him squeezed until he whistles "Dixie' and the Mexican national anthem."

"The Aguilars have always—"

"Oh, fiddle," said Jane. "I don't give a hoot in hell about Ernie's good faith or his past credit. He's become a pain in the proverbial ass. Now, you do what I say, or I'll put a bug in your wife's ear about you and Eunice Baker over at the title office."

Womack's face turned scarlet and pink as the inside of a jellyroll.

"Why this is . . . this is—"

"Pure blackmail, Ted. If you buck me on this, everybody in the county will know about your shenanigans with Eunice."

"That damned Jo-Beth," Womack spluttered.

Jane smiled sweetly, unclenched her fists from her purse strap. There was very little that Jo-Beth didn't know about. She operated the town switchboard. Everybody knew she listened in to their telephone conversations, but she had never admitted it. Every call had to go through her, and Jane made it a habit to talk to her at least once a day. And there were times when Jo-Beth Vermeil called Jane at night, after the switchboard was shut down, and spoke for hours.

"I'm sure you'll be able to call in those notes, Ted, won't you?"

"I—I don't know as I can do that to Ernie. He's a good customer. I could go to jail."

Jane looked at Steve.

"I'll remind you, Ted," she said evenly, "that I'm a stockholder in this bank and I'm on the board of directors. I helped found this bank, in case you've forgotten, and it would take only a few minutes of my time to call a meeting of the board and have you replaced."

"I'm well aware of your connections with this bank, Mrs. Killian, but I'm bound by federal banking laws and—"

"It will all be perfectly legal, Ted. I've already spoken with Jack Kearney and he assures me, since I have a vested interest in the Baronsville Bank, that I can order an audit of any account and request action on any overdue notes."

"Why, we could foreclose on half the ranchers in the county, if we exercised our options on overdue loans. We're in a depression and the government has given us a wide latitude in such matters. I don't think Ernie will actually default on any outstanding loan with us."

"He already has, Ted, as far as I'm concerned. Now, are we going to argue all day or are you going to do what I ask?"

Womack purpled again. He leaned back in his chair and made a church steeple with his large hands. He tried to swivel away from Jane, look out the window, but the drapes blocked his view. He picked up some papers, rattled them until they crackled like dry parchment.

"I, ah, I just don't know."

Jane stood up, looked at Steve as if Womack wasn't even there.

"Come along, Steve," she said. "I want to go over to the telephone office to pay my bill."

She stalked toward the door. Steve, subdued, hadn't said a word, but he glared at Womack. He looked proud of his grandmother, grateful to be in her presence.

"Now, let's not be hasty, Mrs. Killian," said Womack.

"Yes, let's do," she said, twisting the door handle like she was wringing the neck of a chicken. "Good day, Ted."

Womack spluttered, tried to say something, but his words got tangled up in a phlegmatic seizure that left his face incarnadine.

Outside, on the street, Jane stopped by the car, opened her purse.

"Are you really going to tell Mrs. Womack what her husband is doing with Eunice Baker?" Steve asked.

"I won't have to," she said. "Did you see Ted squirm, Steve?"

"Well, I dunno." Steve squirmed.

"He's a worm. He thinks he's a big shot, being the Mayor and the head of my bank. He's a big shot, all right. With a dot over the O."

It took Steve all the rest of the day to figure out what his grandmother meant.

27

RAYMOND NAYLOR LISTENED to the buzz of mud-daubers spackling a nest under the roof just outside the jail window. They were about finished. When he leaned out, he could see their shiny blue wings, their black bodies, swarming over the miniature adobe hovel. He didn't look out now, but huddled over the shamble of papers on his desk, trying to fit together disparate pieces, trying to project images of a murder a long time ago. Yet there were answers here, in the records, the files, and he knew he was close to putting together a composite, if only a skeleton, of something that had happened so long ago a less-determined man would have forgotten it.

He picked up a scrap of paper that he had copied out of the files. In the years since he had come to work for Sheriff Roy Blanchard, Naylor had filled out, grown over his belt like Roy. He was still unmarried, but his hair had begun to gray above his ears and he drank more when he was off duty than he should. But the pain had lingered so long, the injustice of the murder had badgered his mind so constantly, that his features had assumed a bulldog look, the eyes deep-sunk, the jowls thick and pendulous, the nose always quivering, it seemed, as if trying to pick up a faded, elusive scent. He was sweating through his gray uniform shirt now, the fan making lazy half-circles on top of the file cabinet as it swung on its housing, stirred the hot, dead air coming through the window into the small room.

He read his nearly illegible scrawl and his right eye began to twitch with a newly developed tic. He loosened his tie, licked his lips, cracked from the hot Texas wind, winced at the slight pain.

"Jesus the Christ," he whispered.

In the next room, he heard Roy get up from behind his desk, walk to Naylor's door, his bootheels loud and wooden in the silence of afternoon. Usually Roy didn't work on a Saturday, but they'd been short-handed since the last deputy had left after getting worked over during a fight at the Grange the month before. As usual, some kind of political argument started it all, and the new deputy—he had only been hired in 1940, late in November of the year before—had tried to break it up instead of letting the participants bash one another's heads in and cart the wounded survivors off to jail to sleep it off.

Naylor heard the footsteps stop just outside his door. He waited, then spoke up.

"Come on in, Sheriff."

The door opened. Roy stood there, a hangdog look on his face.

"Slow, huh?"

"Kinda."

"Whatcha doing there, Raymond?"

"Just looking over some old arrest records, Sheriff."

Roy walked into the room, looked at the scattered papers atop Naylor's desk. A sheepish expression softened Raymond's face as the sheriff fingered the pages atop the deputy's desk.

"You got anything solid? Or just leads," Blanchard asked.

"Leads, I think. Not sure if I can put it all together."

"Maybe the both of us can work it out. What are you lookin' for?"

"Hell, I don't want to drag none on your time, Roy."

"It's slow. Seems like either I'm workin' hard or hardly workin'." Naylor laughed.

"Well, I probably shouldn't be working on this case. It's personal."

"Damnit, Raymond, do you take me for a blind man? I been seein' you buryin' your nose in ever' goddamned file we got here and ransackin' the courthouse and pesterin' the clerks. You got one or two secrets left, but not a whole hell of a lot of time to keep 'em. I can pick up the phone any danged day of the week and ask Jo-Beth Vermeil who all you talked to about this and what you talked about."

"Damn Jo-Beth. Telephone's 'sposed to be private."

"It is, Ray, it is. It's just that sometimes she gets those wires crossed on the switchboard."

"Yeah," Naylor laughed. Blanchard laughed with him, pulled out a chair and scooted it close to the desk.

"I figure you're still trackin' down the old hit-and-run? You've been chewin' on this bone for the past six years. Two heads maybe better than one?"

"Maybe," said Naylor. "Don't want to take you away from anything you've got to do."

"What you got, Ray?"

"Mostly hunches." Naylor tapped a Camel from a battered pack, offered one to Blanchard. Roy shook his head. Blanchard looked out the window, saw the blue swarm of mud-daubers, waited as Naylor separated notes and official documents, put them in order. "I got a lot of little pieces and I'm just now putting them all to a chunk."

Naylor lit his cigarette, let the smoke curl up into his nostrils as he tossed the match in a tin ashtray painted blue.

"Shoot," said Blanchard.

"My sister was only eight years old when she got run over. My folks had a small truck farm about twenty miles from Baronsville."

"I know," said Blanchard.

"My mother, Patience, kept a-workin', but my pa, Ralph, he took to strong drink. He didn't have to work, really, and maybe that's what ruint him. The money sent to him was more'n most folks make of a month."

"Huh?"

"'Bout the time my sis got kilt, my pa started getting cash money in his mailbox."

"Who was sending it?"

"Whoever run over little Lucy, I reckon."

"Hmm," said Roy.

"Well, my pa, he broke down from the drink, and my ma, she got feebleminded. She's in a home over to Galveston. Pa, he's on the welfare in Corpus Christi. I used to visit him from time to time, but he's just one of the town drunks now. I don't know if he even knows his damned name. Ma, she long ago give up on life."

"That's tough, Raymond."

"Sure enough. So, I got to checkin', puttin' things together. The morning Lucy got kilt, Bone was in jail here. Guess who bailed him out?"

"Was he workin' for Ernie then? Yeah, maybe so."

"It was Ernie Aguilar, all right. You wasn't sheriff then."

"Nope. Jeff Cutter."

"Right. I saw old Jeff yesterday. His mind's clear as a bell. He was the one what arrested Bone the day before, for bustin' up the pool hall. He drove out to the Rocking A, told Ernie 'bout it, said he could pick Bone up and he'd drop the charges if Ernie paid the bill and kept that Indian away from town."

"Are you saying that Ernie killed your sis?"

"Well, old Jeff said that Bone had the DT's pretty bad. He was ravin' and such and when Ernie drove off, he was a-fightin' with Bone. The car was weavin' all over the place. Right after that, someone hit Lucy, and she died. The driver never stopped. I figure Bone was going' through the shiverin' fits and Ernie just couldn't handle it. The next week, my pa got a damned envelope with cash in it."

"Well, Raymond, you might be on the mark with this notion. I don't know. I don't see any proof here, though."

"No, but I can put Ernie and Bone right at the scene. If it was premeditated murder, which it ain't, you could say Ernie had the opportunity if not the motive. It was a damned accident, but he should have stopped, should have paid the price."

Blanchard let out a sigh, shook his head.

"Not much you can do, is there?"

"Well, I checked the motor vehicle records. Ernie drove a Model T. He's never sold it. I figure if I can take a look at that car, it might tell me something."

"Hell, Raymond, Ernie's long since fixed it up, likely, and painted it, banged any dents out."

"I don't know, Roy. It's a-eatin' at me. I got to find out. Everything else checks."

"Well, you can't just go out there and bust in on Ernie and start snoopin' around."

"I need a search warrant?"

"Yep, and I don't know as you could get it with what you've told me."

"I'm going to look at that flivver, Roy."

Blanchard stood up. He looked down at Naylor, a look of pity softening his eyes.

"And then what?"

"If I find any evidence, then I'll bring Aguilar in and book him for manslaughter, hit-and-run, failure to report an accident, whatever I can nail him with."

"It won't bring your little sister back, Raymond."

"No, but I'll be able to sleep nights knowing that fuckin' greaser's eatin' jailhouse grub and scratching cooties."

"I ain't a-goin' to help you none, Raymond. Ernie's a pretty big man hereabouts."

"He's just a damned killer as far as I'm concerned," said Naylor. "We couldn't get Bone for anything else, but he's damned sure an accessory. I'll bring his ass in, too."

"I might help you on that one," said Blanchard. "You keep me posted. And don't step too deep into it."

"Into what?"

"The shit, Raymond, the shit."

Grace heard a sound, lifted her fingers from the Baldwin keyboard. She had been playing some of Gene Austin's songs softly, thinking she was alone downstairs. She broke off in the middle of "I Can't Give You Anything but Love" and listened. She heard a glass clatter in the sink and twisted on the piano bench.

"Ora, is that you?"

There was no answer. Startled, Grace rose from the bench, and started toward the kitchen. Ora Cornejo had left the house at least an hour ago. Matt was out by the stables, breeding a mare that had come in heat. Derek was with him. Afterwards, they had to load several hundred head of cattle for shipment. In fact, they had probably already finished up and were headed toward the La Golondrina spread. Ethan was in Austin. She didn't know where Peggy was, but she thought she'd gone to town with Connie Killian.

Peggy stood at the kitchen counter, staring at the broken shot glass on the floor.

She looked up as her mother entered the room. Her face bore a strong resemblance to a fox's caught in the chicken coop with a pullet feather stuck to its lips.

"Shit," said Peggy.

"I don't like that kind of language," said Grace.

"I broke the goddamned glass."

"I can see that. What's the matter with you?"

"Why, Mother, there's not a thing wrong with me. I'm just fine."

"That's one of our good whiskey glasses."

"I know that, *Mother*."

Grace's eyebrows arched. She stuck her nose up in the air, sniffed the room. She eyed her daughter closely, and with considerable suspicion.

"What are you looking for in here?" Grace asked.

"I put something down in the cupboard yesterday," said Peggy.

"Yes, I suppose you did."

"Well, did you take it, Mother?"

"Take what?"

"Mother, you know very well what I'm talking about." Peggy spoke each word slowly, pronouncing each consonant precisely, clipping them crisply to disguise a tongue already thumb-thick with alcohol. She slurred her vowels as if her mouth was full of slithery, smoothly oiled ball bearings.

"Not unless you tell me," snapped Grace.

Peggy leaned against the counter, a look of cunning spreading across her face. Her blonde hair was cut short, bobbed, the bangs framing her oval face, emphasizing the deep, nut-brown coals of her eyes. Her figure was trim, but her hips flared becomingly under the cream slacks she wore. Her yellow blouse was tightly fitted, hugging her pert breasts, the pale pink bra underneath faintly outlined under the sheer shantung material.

"There was a bottle of Johnnie Walker Red Label here this morning. I put it there yesterday, behind Ora's box of starch." Ora, the maid, ate starch like candy.

"Well, it's not there now," said Grace.

"What did you do, Mother? Drink it up yourself?"

Grace stiffened. She fought back the tears that welled up in her eyes.

"I certainly did not. If I did, it wouldn't be any of your business."

"Well, it sure would. I paid money for that bottle. I need it."

"I didn't drink it. I poured it down the sink."

"You what?" Peggy's eyes flared with anger.

"You were drunk last night and this morning I found what was left of the Scotch. I haven't had a drink since Doctor Emberlin told me that your father was dying."

"Oh, sure. I'll bet."

"Peggy, if you don't want to make the same mistakes I did, you'll not drink like this. You're still tipsy from last night."

"It's a little late for advice, don't you think?"

"I hope not. I feel deeply ashamed over my drinking, young lady. For a long time I blamed your father, the terrible state of our finances when he spent all that money trying to destroy all the old brush, the drought, having you children, when all the time it was my own fault. The drinking didn't help, it only made things worse. I hope you don't make the same mistakes I did."

"Mother, I just don't need a lecture right now. My head feels like it's full of bubble gum and cobwebs and my nerves are screaming. If you threw away that Scotch, I'll just have to go into town and buy some more."

"That's stupid, Margaret."

"Well, maybe it is. But I've got a terrible hangover, damnit, and I'm suffering."

Grace's features hardened. She swept back an errant lock of hair and put her hands on her hips.

"Fix yourself a Bromo."

"I don't want a goddamned Bromo Seltzer," snapped Peggy.

"You do what you want, but I'll not have you drinking in my house. Your father can't take the strain just now."

"Well, neither can I. I stood years of your drinking, Mother. You were a real bitch when you were drunk."

"Don't sass me, young lady."

"You bitch!" Peggy screamed. "How dare you tell me what to do?"

Grace relaxed her arms, let them fall to her side.

"As long as you're in my home," she said imperiously, "you'll mind me. Now, I'll make you coffee, fix you a Bromo, or you can go back to bed, but you'll not have any liquor."

"Go to hell," said Peggy bitterly.

Grace did not reply, but turned on her heel and went back to her music room, where she picked out another piece of sheet music for another song written by Gene Austin. She put the music on the wooden stand and opened the pages. She began to play "My Blue Heaven," humming along to herself as her fingers touched the keys.

But her hands began to tremble and before she struck the final chord, tears were running down her cheeks.

The back door slammed and she knew Peggy was gone. A moment later, she heard her daughter's Chevrolet coupe start up, roar out of the driveway.

"Damn her," Grace breathed, but she knew that her curse was not really directed at Peggy, but at herself.

The knock at the door startled her.

"Who's there?" she called out.

"It's me, Gracie. Lou."

Grace closed her eyes. *Go away,* she wanted to say.

"Matt's not here."

She knew it was the wrong thing to say. Louise knew her brother wasn't at home. He and Derek had probably left for La Golondrina over a half an hour ago.

The back door opened and slammed shut. Grace winced at the sound. A moment later, Lou stood in the doorway, looking more like a ranch hand than a lady. Lou wore faded Levi's pants and jacket, a Western-cut man's blue cotton shirt, a sweaty red bandanna around her neck and a dirty, rumpled Stetson dangling between her shoulder blades on a single leather thong. A pair of rough yellow gloves sprouted from her back pocket. Her boots were scuffed, the soles rimed with dried fecal matter.

"Lou, what do you want?" Grace asked testily.

"I didn't come here to listen to you play the pianer," Lou said. Grace knew Lou could speak as well as anyone, but when she was at her most sarcastic, she sounded like a West Texas cowhand.

"Then, why did you come here?"

"Look, Gracie, don't pussyfoot with me. I just saw Peggy stagger out of here like a Corpus sailor, drunker'n seven hunnert dollars. She was plumb snockered."

"That's her business."

Lou strode to a chair, sat down, her legs spread wide like a man's. Grace sniffed disdainfully, pulled the lid over the piano keys as if closing a door on her visitor.

"She's my niece and I care about her," Lou said softly. "I care about you, too."

"Oh, really, Louise? I haven't seen much of you since Tom Casebolt died."

A shadow flickered across Lou's eyes, like wing shadows over sunny waters.

"I was in love with Tom," she said.

Grace's eyes widened.

"You? Tom? I—I never thought—"

"You don't think of me as a woman, do you, Gracie? You think because I work cows, I don't know what affection is, what being a woman is."

"Oh, Louise. I just thought—"

"I know what you thought, Gracie, for Christ's sake. Hell, Tom wasn't in love with me. He didn't even know I had a forty-rod crush on him. I never had the nerve to tell him. Truth is, I think Tom was as bat-blind as you are."

Grace fidgeted on the piano bench. She wondered where the conversation was going. Lou had begun talking about Peggy, but now she was delving into her own feelings about a dead man, an unrequited love.

"I—I just didn't know," said Grace. "And besides, it's none of my business."

"There's a point to it, Gracie. I've been watching Peggy, and it's been like seein' my own self when I was a girl. She wants to grow up mighty fast and you've kind of set a bad example."

"Me? Why, I can't imagine what you're talking about, Louise."

"Oh, don't shovel me with that horseshit, Gracie. You haven't drawn a sober breath in ten years. And your daughter's a-follerin' in your footsteps like a pet pup."

"I don't have to listen to this kind of talk," said Grace, drawing herself up straight on the bench.

"Yes, you do," said Lou. "You're heading for a hell in a handcart and taking Peggy right along with you. You think nobody knows you drink, but there just ain't no way to hide it. Peggy hasn't gotten that smart yet, but she's tryin', tryin' like hell."

"Louise, I think you'd better leave."

"I ain't leavin', Gracie. Not 'til you hear me out."

"I just won't listen."

"I ought to slap hell out of you, you make me so damned mad, but you're going to listen."

Grace turned away, wanting to run. Wanting to run and hide from Louise's accusations.

"I was in love, once," said Lou. "I had it real bad. He was a cowboy, worked for Daddy. Real tall, handsome. His name was Alex Tomkins. He was a hard-drinking, hardworking, shit-kicking, woman-loving god to me. I was fifteen years old. He used to take me to the square dances and we sparked in a haywagon like Romeo and Juliet. He took my cherry and gave me a whiskey habit in return. I was ready and willin' to marry Alex, but he was footloose and fancy-free."

"I really don't see—"

"Well, he didn't marry me and I drank myself silly on homemade whiskey and green beer. Alex got worse, himself. Daddy fired him and I run off with him to San Angelo. He worked for whiskey money and one night we were sittin' in this little roach-infested room in a fleabag hotel and the lantern was burning bright on the filthy, booze-soaked table. Alex couldn't get his breath and he tried to stand up and made this little sound in his throat. The next minute, blood started gushing from his nose, his ears, his mouth. He just seemed to explode blood all over and fell off the chair, dead as a doorknob."

"My God," said Grace. "How awful."

"I never been so rattled in my life. I was scared and I kept screaming for Alex to come back. The doctor told me that Alex had hemorrhaged inside. It was horrible. I went back home with it and realized I hadn't been no help at all to Alex. I never took another drink, though God knows I wanted to."

Grace was silent for several moments. Lou waited, watching her sister-in-law's face.

"I—I really don't see what this has to do with Peggy or me," said Grace.

"It's not too late, Gracie. For either of you. Matt needs you. He needs you sober. And I don't think he'd like it if his daughter grew up to be a common drunk. Like you."

Grace started to protest, but Lou stood up and strode close to her. Grace felt the woman's strong hands on her shoulders, gripping them in a vise.

"Matt helped me get over Alex and the whiskey," Lou said softly. "He listens real good and he's got a great big heart."

"I know that," Grace said, so soft her words were barely audible in the silence of the room. "I know that."

"It'll be tough," said Lou. "But you're the light in Matt's life and he hasn't got much left."

"How—how did you know?"

"I know a lot of things, Gracie. I know what you're going through, you and Peg. You've got to face up to it and put some light on it. Don't let the little things get you down. Don't go after something you can't ever have and don't go into the bottle for healing medicine. It ain't in there. It just means more sickness, more heartache."

Then, Louise crouched down and hugged Grace, drew her tightly against her.

"You mind what I say," she whispered, and then, as the tears began to flow down Grace's face, Lou was gone, her boots making solid thunks on the hardwood floor. Grace opened her mouth to speak, but no words would come. She crumpled up, buried her face in her hands and sobbed deeply.

"Thank you, Louise," she breathed and sat up straight. And the tears came again.

Ever since she had known that Matt was dying, Grace had faced her own fragility. She didn't know how she could live without him, even though she'd treated him badly the past few years. It was too late to change the past, but she was determined to do something about the future.

She wiped her cheeks with the back of her hand and pushed back the lid over the keys.

But she could not force herself to play anymore. Then, the tears stopped and she felt the stiffening of a resolve deep inside her. She realized that her secret pain was no longer secret. Lou had shed light on it and she could look at it from another's perspective. She felt a darkness inside her dissipate like ground fog under the brunt of a rising sun. She looked down at the dead silent keys, white and black, like everything else in life. And she could hear the music of them in their silence, hear the songs she had played over the years.

The music, especially Gene Austin's, made her think of the days when she and Matt were young and very much in love. Now, the songs only made her sad.

28

"SOMETIMES I THINK I dreamed it all," said Matt. "Or my pap dreamed it and I remember it."

"Huh?" Derek intoned.

Matt reached down, picked up a clump of grass, snatching it from the earth with an odd motion of his hand.

"All of this. The land, the cattle, the horses, you, your mother, your brother and sister. The grass." He lifted the clump of grass to his face, sniffed of the soil, bit into a blade of the Rhodes. "Today it seems like it just happened overnight, or that it was always here. Or not here, but somewhere."

"Daddy, are you all right?" asked Derek.

Matt laughed and broke it off short when the pain burrowed out of its lair and began to gnaw on his gut with razor teeth.

"Seems like when you get to the end of the picket rope, things get a hell of a sight sharper. Clearer, maybe. This grass looks more green than I ever remember it." He peered at the blades of grass in his hand, held them up to the light like a cluster of grapes. Little clods of dirt fell away. "Blue, too. Every color. Look at this grass, Derek. Soft and delicate and stubborn and persistent. Hell, it built us a kingdom here in the goddamnedest worst part of Texas. It keeps the soil from blowing away to Mexico or into the Gulf. It fattens the cattle, sleeks out the horses. People walk on it and never notice it. Hell, it looks like a magic carpet to me. Some kind of royal rug, huh? Just look at it, Derek. Look at that sweet green grass."

Matt swept the horizon with his eyes. His son looked at him, then at the sea of summer-thick grass. There was no end to it.

"Dreamed it all, like," murmured Matt and the grass moved, undulated, flowed like water out away from him and back to him and clear to the far sky like a living, breathing being and he could feel its pulse, its heartbeat, the tremors in its white roots, the nourishment flowing through its veins. He closed his eyes and they burned green fire and when he opened them again, he saw the land as it once was, barren and hostile and choked with brush and mesquite. It seemed he could hear his father's voice, whispers in the soft breeze that made the grasses wave and dance in voluptuous rhythms. He looked at his dying hands and saw the map of his own history, felt the dull, peaceful pain in every joint that had tugged at the land, roped cattle and horses, plunged a posthole digger into the hard ground, bled from barbed wire, burned from touching a hot branding iron, ached from milking cold teats, sung with the memory of caressing Grace's breasts, the dark nubbins of her nipples, her smooth tummy, the mysterious thicket between her legs, the back of her neck. He brought the clump of grass to his face and buried his nose in the blades and smelled the earth, the tangy scent of the grass filling his nostrils until his brain filled with its heady aroma and blotted out the pain in his gut.

"Sure is pretty," said Derek, self-consciously. "Mighty pretty."

"If I could just die out here, a-lyin' in it, that would suit me, son. Or if I could wallow in all two million acres of it, see it from the sky when I die, I would go happy."

"Daddy, don't talk about that." Derek's voice quavered.

"You take good care of it, Dare." Matt pulled the grass away from his face, handed the clump to Derek. "Your brother's got places to go in politics. I want him to have that. Become governor, if he wants to, maybe even president. My pa handed this land to me, and I'm passing it along to you."

Derek felt the grass sear his hand. It seemed hot, alive. He felt very strange, listening to his father talk like this. Talk about death and the land he would leave behind when he gave up his breath.

"You aren't going anywhere, yet," Derek said, but there was no conviction in his tone.

"No, but I want you to be ready for it." Matt paused, took a quick breath. "I almost let it get away from me."

"Huh?"

"This. The land. The Box B. I got into that goddamned *brasada* and lost sight of the grass."

"Well, Johnny and I've been talking about that, Daddy. He thinks we might be able to make up some kind of poison to kill all that brush, clear that strip."

Matt laughed harshly.

"No, Derek. That's a false trail."

"Might work. Johnny Bell's pretty smart."

Matt walked on, ahead of Derek, wading through the high grass, leaving a dull veridian path in his wake, as if the undersides of each blade had been turned to show where he had walked. Derek followed him, carrying the clump of grass as if it was something holy, something given to him to carry off and plant on a barren patch of soil.

"I thought I could beat it," Matt said. "Grace tried to stop me, Lord knows, but I was a stubborn son of a buck. We took the cats to it, tried to burn it up, bury it, smash it, and the *brasada* ate up money faster than I could grow it. No, that *brasada* is part of the Box B, part of the country. Maybe it's the wild part, a memento to remind us of who's boss here. Maybe something to remind us of what the land once was like, how we got to it and why we're here on it. You'll never get rid of that *brasada*. My pa tried and his pa tried and I tried and it's still there. And Bone's still there, the sonofabitch."

"It won't be there forever," said Derek.

"Maybe it will," said Matt. He stopped, looked at Derek so hard, Derek dropped his head, embarrassed. "Like Bone. He got away with murder. He's like that *brasada*, tough and hard to kill. I used to think about him and that brush all the time. Couldn't sleep at night. Couldn't get it out of my mind. Then I just quit on it. Gave it up. Maybe that's what made me so sick, worrying over something that beat me. Bone could hide in there forever. Even if we had dogs, they'd get beat by that brush. Just like I got beat."

"Naw, that's not it, Daddy."

"Well, it would take more than you and me to lick it," said Matt. "It's going to take a hero."

Derek looked up, wondering if his father had slipped a cog, finally. If this was part of his illness. If his mind was going.

Matt laughed.

"Your grandpa used to talk about such things, Derek. He loved stories of knights and chivalry and all that. He once told me and your

Aunt Lou that anytime a nation, a state, a bunch of people got in trouble, they had to look for a hero to save them. Oh, he loved history, Anson Baron did. He said something else, too."

"What?"

"He said that if you couldn't find a hero to save your butt, you had to be one yourself."

"Well, maybe I'll bring down Bone and clear that *brasada* by myself," said Derek.

"Maybe. More likely it'll be someone we don't even know, someone not even born yet."

"Haw!" snorted Derek. "It'll be me, if anyone."

Matt smiled.

"I wish I could be around to see it," said the rancher wistfully.

"You will, Daddy. Come on."

"Maybe we'd better get on back and breed that bay mare, Lady Rose. Think you can handle Squire? He's a pretty mean stud."

"I can handle him," said Derek.

"I know you can, son. Next week, you turn Chico and the other QuarterHorse mares into this pasture. Squire can have the eighty acres on the other side all to himself."

"Johnny and I talked about that yesterday. Do you think we ought to buy that Thoroughbred mare over at Goliad? Johnny says it's not for sale, that we'll have to buy a stud."

"You try for that roan Quarter mare," said Matt. "If you can't, look for one like her in Kentucky and if you can't find any mare good enough, then you buy the sorrel stud we looked at last week, Chestnut King, and see if you can't come up with a good brood mare. I don't care how old she is."

"O.K.," said Derek, grinning.

They both heard a car start up and looked toward the house.

"Peggy," said Derek. "Must be going into town. Boy, she had a snootful last night."

"Your mother doesn't like her drinking."

"Aw, Peggy can take care of herself."

"That's not the point. Grace is fighting a battle herself."

"Yeah, I noticed."

They heard the motor rev up and then the sound moved away until they no longer heard the angry roar of the engine.

"Come on, let's go on back and get it done."

Derek looked at his father's back and felt a closeness he had never felt before. It seemed that his daddy had let Derek look inside him for a few moments, see into his heart. Derek felt an intangible swelling inside him, as if his father had given something of himself, something deep and secret that he had given no one else.

Derek listened to the sound of their boots plowing susurrantly through the tall grasses, the faint crunch of their soles on the earth. He noticed, suddenly, that his father did not favor his bad leg so much anymore. Maybe, Derek thought, the pain inside him was so great, he ignored the hurt in his leg. Still, it surprised him that he had not noticed this before. Lady Rose whinnied as they approached the corral, began to toss her mane, stamp her forefeet. An answering whicker from Chico, inside the stable, rippled on the air like a series of triple-tongued cornet notes.

This was the closest Derek had ever felt to his father. For a long time, he had wanted to call him "Dad" instead of "Daddy," but he had never been able to summon up the courage. Even now, he was still hesitant. He thought it might break the mood if he was suddenly to change the form of address. But he felt the urgent need to talk to his father, to continue their conversation.

"Daddy," he said, "remember that day Bone killed Tom Casebolt?"

Matt stopped, turned around.

"Yes, son. I remember. It's not something you get over easy."

"I was mad," said Derek. "Mad as hell. I wanted to go after Bone and kill him dead. Kill those other two Indians too."

"I wanted to do the same thing."

Derek snatched a blade of grass, stuck the stem in his mouth.

"Well, that wasn't all."

"All what?"

"I wanted to quit school and run the ranch for you. I wanted to take Tom's place as foreman. I didn't, but if I had it to do all over again, I would."

"Maybe I wouldn't have let you, son," Matt said softly.

"Uh-huh. I really hated to let what Bone did go by the board. I hated to go back to school with Tom dead and all. I almost just up and quit right then."

"Do you think you could have run the ranch like Tom?"

"Damned right. I think Tom would have wanted me to."

"Seems to me you threatened to quit school that day."

"Yeah, I don't remember if I did or not. I was real mad."

"You and Johnny Bell getting along all right?"

"Oh, sure, but I think I can run the ranches better than he can."

"Pretty big for your britches, ain't you?"

Matt grinned when he said it.

"Well, I just wanted you to know."

"As long as I'm alive and Johnny works here, he'll run it. You get your law degree and then we can talk about this some more. Finish up school. I'll hang around until that's done."

"Well, sure, Daddy, but I've got three more years to go."

Matt said nothing. He turned on his heel and stalked toward the corral. Derek lagged behind, wondering if he'd said the wrong thing. Could his father last that long? He'd already gone way past the month that Doc Emberlin had given him, past six months, past one year and almost through another. Derek couldn't see that his father was that much different. A little leaner, a bit paler, but he didn't know how Matt got through the nights, whether the pain got so bad sometimes. . . .

He didn't want to think about that right now. What was just as remarkable was the change in his mother. She no longer drank. She had taken charge of the ranch's finances and even dealt with Johnny Bell and the other hands when Matt was not home or feeling bad. And she and Aunt Lou were closer than they'd ever been. They seemed almost like good friends, which was a surprise to just about everybody. His mother. She seemed pretty special lately. The hands called her "the Iron Filly" behind her back. Derek thought that was just dandy.

Matt spoke, breaking into Derek's thoughts.

"You go on in and bring Chico out. I'll hold the mare."

"I just wanted you to know," Derek said again.

"I know. Now, be careful of that stud. He'll knock you down and stomp you into the ground if you don't watch him."

Derek scrambled over the rail fence as his father climbed through. Lady Rose was haltered, hitched to the far corner of the corral. Matt dipped a bucket into the water trough and filled it. He led the mare into the center of the corral, away from the dangerous poles.

Chico made noise coming out of the stables. Derek had him snubbed down with the halter, but when the stallion caught sight of the mare, he fought all the way. He dragged Derek the last twenty feet, then mounted the mare, snorting, his penis waving frantically, spraying both men with precoital fluid.

Derek stepped back as the elegant red sorrel stud mounted the burgundy mare. He serviced her savagely, muscles glistening with sweat, rippling under his burnished hide, and Derek's trousers tautened with his own arousal. It was embarrassing and he did not look at his father. It always happened to him when he saw a stud mount a mare. When Chico had spent himself, he dismounted and sprayed father and son with milky seed as his swollen organ flapped like a loose firehose.

"Get him back inside," ordered Matt curtly as he led the mare away from the stallion. Chico reared up when Derek pulled on the halter rope, pawing the air with his hooves. Derek circled, brought the horse around, where he couldn't see the mare.

Matt grabbed the bucket of water, splashed the mare's vagina so that it tightened up, held the seed inside. She was sleek with sweat, still aroused. He walked her around until she calmed down, then opened the gate to take her to another set of stables where she could grain and rest.

Derek met his father on the way to the back stable.

"Think she'll foal?" he asked his father.

"It appeared to take."

"I'll get right on that other business, Daddy. We'll have the best QuarterHorse line in Texas."

"Put some Thoroughbred into the bloodlines, that's what we'll do," said Matt.

"I can handle it," said Derek jubilantly.

They put the mare up. Derek gave her grain, oats and corn, some wheat. The two men walked out of the stable, stood in the open as if reluctant to go back to the house.

Matt's face contorted and his body jerked with a sudden pain.

"Better get on back, I guess."

"Did you bring your pills with you?"

"Damned pills. Hate to take 'em. They knock the stuffing out of me."

Derek saw the color drain from his father's face. Something clutched at his own heart. He felt sick.

"I can run right off and get those pills."

"No, let it be."

"Daddy, Doc Emberlin could have been wrong. I mean, you might get better, huh?"

"No, he was right."

"But you don't look too bad. I mean, most of the time."

"You can't see it. But I can feel it. Eating me up."

"But, you're not—"

"Going to die? I reckon."

"What do you think is going to happen?"

"You mean when I die, or after?"

"After, I guess."

"Well, your grandpa and I talked about that when he came to the end of his days. He didn't believe in heaven or hell and neither do I. He said it didn't make much difference if a man died. He said if there was something afterwards, that was just fine. If there wasn't then it didn't make any difference. Once you shut down, you shut down."

"I've been thinking about that, about dying, a lot lately. It scares me."

Matt straightened up, shook off the pain.

He put an arm on Derek's shoulder. Derek didn't know if it was affection or a need to hold onto him.

"Son, there's nothing to be scared of. Death is just the tail end of life. Like Grandpa Anson said, if there's heaven, why that's all to the good. If there's just blackness and nothing, then you won't ever know what you lost."

"What about hell?"

Matt chuckled.

"Now, Grandpa believed in an Almighty, a Creator. He just didn't think He was stupid enough to call the square dance and condemn a bunch of worthless humans to eternal fire. So, he left without a care in the world."

Matt knew that wasn't the whole truth. His daddy had been falsely accused of murder. Only a pardon from the governor had saved him from prison. But the experience had broken him. He'd had troubles, all right. He just knew how to end them quick.

"Hmmm," said Derek, thoughtfully.

"And so will I, son. Don't you worry. We'll talk about things again before I go."

Matt squeezed Derek and started walking toward the house. Derek caught up with him and matched him stride for stride.

He had never felt more proud of his father than at that moment. Nor had he ever felt so close to this man whom he realized he hardly knew at all.

And now, it seemed too late to ever know his father well.

29

—◼—

BEN WASN'T SURPRISED to see that the bar was open in Jack Kearney's Baronsville office. It was always open, not only for Ben, but for any of Jack's clients. And for Jack himself. Killian stepped all the way inside the room, Jack's new secretary, petite little Barbara Amos, right behind him.

"Just go on in and set, Mr. Killian," Barbara said sweetly, pointing to the open door of the conference room that adjoined the front office. "Mr. Kearney will be right with you, surely."

"Thanks, Bobbie. Where is he?"

"Why, sir, he had to meet Mr. Baron real early this morning at his home. He said he would surely be back before nine. You just make yourself right to home. If you want any coffee or soda pop, it's right there yonder by the bar."

Ben smiled at Barbara. She stood no more than a smidgeon above five feet and her dark brown hair was bobbed and curled beneath her ears, a pair of Betty Boop strands streaming down just in front of her ears, her breasts tight and pointy against her poplin blouse, white as snow, and cut so low he could see the freckles on her chest. She wore a chocolate pleated skirt, silk stockings and high-heeled patent-leather shoes. Kearney liked his secretaries small, energetic and sweet. Bobbie Amos was all three, and then some. She could take Gregg shorthand faster than Jack could talk and she did most of the lawyer's research and typed up documents at better than 100 words a minute.

There was a large conference table at one end of the room. It was surrounded by eight high-backed leather chairs. Ben noticed that there was a file folder at the head of the table where Jack would sit. There were note pads and freshly sharpened pencils at three other places. There was a water glass at each place and a pitcher on a wooden tray in the center, within reach of each chair.

"Who else is coming, Bobbie?"

"Why, Mr. Baron and Mr. Aguilar, I believe."

Ben bristled.

"Why in hell didn't Jack tell me that?"

"You know Mr. Kearney," Barbara smiled.

"Not damned well enough," said Ben, and he stalked to the bar and grabbed a large shot glass, poured it full of Rebel Yell. Barbara closed the door quietly, left in discreet silence.

Ben sipped the whiskey, savored its smooth bite in his mouth.

A moment later, the door opened, and Ernesto Aguilar entered the room. Barbara wisely didn't enter, but closed the door with a touch worthy of a diamond cutter, making not a sound.

"Ben," said Ernie. Aguilar was dressed as Ben was, freshly laundered chambray workshirt, pressed Levi's, polished boots. Aguilar wore a blue bandanna around his neck and his shirt was buttoned clear to the collar. Ben's shirt was open, revealing a portion of his massive chest, a thicket of dark hair. Both men wore Stetson hats.

"Ernie."

"I did not know you would be here," said Aguilar.

"Me neither."

"What did Jack tell you?"

"He said that there were some land matters to discuss. What did he tell you?"

"Same thing, just about."

"Ben sipped from the shotglass. Ernie, you and I are going to talk about that goddamned dam you built before Jack gets here."

"Ben, I tell you the truth. I did not know about it until there was that trouble between my son, my foreman and your boys. I have told my men not to close the gate."

"Well, it's still there. I don't trust that foreman of yours, Perez."

"He is a good man, I think. I will keep the dam open. It is a lot of work to tear it down. But I do not think that is why we are here." He wondered if Ben had had anything to do with the Baronsville Bank's calling in his paper. He had made the payments, but the experience had left him shaken and suspicious. He was still trying to make things right, just in case the other ranchers meant to gang up on him.

"No," said Ben, and finished off his drink. He slammed the butt end of the glass down on the hardwood bar, walked to the window. There was a back yard, with flowers growing, a wooden fence that had lost its paint and finish over the years. Jack Kearney sometimes sat on the back porch and drank while his secretary fended off clients Kearney didn't want to see. The office had been one of the first structures to go up in Baronsville. It had been built by Anson Baron, but he'd sold it to the Baronsville Bank before he died, as he did most of the town.

"No, we're not going to talk about that goddamned dam," said Ben. "But as long it's there, there will be trouble between us. And if my creek dries up, you're going to lose some fence again and I'll blow that dam so high pieces will drop on your house."

"I don't want any trouble from you this day, Ben," Ernie said. He had had enough trouble with Ted Womack. That goddamned bank. It felt, sometimes, as if he'd had the ground pulled out from under him.

Ben sighed deeply and the room filled up with a silence between the two men.

Ben had tried to get a court order to force Aguilar to tear down his dam, but Jack had said it would take years and might never be resolved. Disputes over water were as old as the land itself. Men had been killed over water rights ever since the first Spanish land grant had been issued. But the dam still rankled Ben and always would, even though it was as Ernie had said, the water in Bandera Creek had been flowing onto Killian land ever since that day when Steve and Luke had fought with Hector and Paco.

The silence in the room did not last long. The door burst open and Jack Kearney hurtled through the door like prizefighter at the opening bell. Behind him, Derek Baron had to duck to keep from crumpling his hat. He stood a foot higher than Aguilar, more than half a foot taller than Kearney, and Ben had to look up at him from a span of at least three inches.

Jack went right to the conference table.

"Bobbie," he yelled, as he sat down, "make me one."

Barbara mixed Jack a drink of bourbon and water at the bar while the attorney went through the file folder.

"Sit down, gentlemen. This won't take a whole hell of a lot of explaining." Kearney's thick clump of black wavy hair dangled a lone curl over his forehead. He looked at the assembly with deep-set, intense brown eyes, set his jaw square, licked full, sensuous lips. Although he had a rich baritone voice, Jack was just as intimidating when silent, Ben thought. Ben told people who didn't know Jack that he was a corker in the courtroom and a pretty fair brawler at any number of roadhouses and honky-tonks. Kearney was married to a Mexican beauty named Pilar and didn't care who knew it. He was the only attorney in Baronsville, and it was not unusual for him to handle cases with conflicting interests. He got by with it because he was dead honest and people trusted him. In Baronsville, Jack Kearney often acted as a judge in minor disputes, saving the courts considerable time and money. There was no regular judge, in fact, and the town was serviced by a circuit judge who drove in at regular intervals from Galveston. Often, Jack would advise these judges of the proper sentencing and disposition of cases and usually the presiding judge would follow Jack's recommendations.

"Ben, you sit here on my left. Ernie, you and Derek sit on my right."

Barbara brought the drink and a coaster, set them before her boss.

"Bobbie, bring your pad."

Ben and the others sat down, as Jack drank two inches off the top of his bourbon and branch. Barbara returned a few moments later and sat at the far end of the table.

Killian looked at Derek. "Where's Matt?"

"He's not feeling well, sir. I'm here on his behalf."

Ben frowned. Barbara opened a steno pad and poised a yellow pencil over the lined paper.

Kearney extracted three packets of papers from his thick file folder and passed one to each man at the table.

"Take a look at these," he said. "On top is the plat map of the property in dispute. Next is an aerial map of said property. And next in succession are copies of various recorded deeds regarding said section of land. Then you will see the results of a title search I conducted, which goes clear on back to the Spanish land grants."

For the next several minutes, the men at the table read through the documents as Jack made notes on his pad.

When they had all finished reading, they looked at Jack, who grinned at them.

"A sorry mess of shit, ain't it?" he said affably. "El Rincón. No-man's-land. Goddamned mesquite and brush and rattlesnakes. Who in hell would want such a piece of property?"

"From these papers," said Ben, "it looks like we all own it."

"That's why I'm here," said Jack. "Now, that particular corner of land was never filed on properly in the first place. That is, going back to the original property descriptions, the boundaries cited were based on landmarks that have since been eradicated. Creeks have changed course or dried up, stumps have rotted away, stones have been moved. This fucking corner is a surveyor's nightmare."

"We've always thought it was Baron property," said Derek. "One of these deeds is made out to my grandfather. I've seen it before, at home."

"You're right, Derek," said Jack. "And Ben claims it, and so does Ernie here. Now, this little old chunk of land wouldn't be worth a tinker's damn to a one of you if it didn't have oil under it. And, from what I've dug up, there's oil a-plenty underneath, maybe going through that whole stretch of the *brasada.*"

"But nobody can drill there until this is settled," said Aguilar. He flashed a dark look at Ben.

"That's right," said Jack. "For the past six years I've been shuttling papers back and forth from all three of you ranchers until I'm about wore down to a nubbin. So, let's see if we can't unravel this can of worms and lay everything out straight."

"That land is mine," Ernie said stubbornly.

"Part of it's been in my family since Ernie's grandpa sold it to my pa," said Ben.

Derek said nothing. Instead, he looked through the Spanish land grants with their Spencerian calligraphy and shook his head. Once all that land had legally belonged to Ernie Aguilar's grandfather. Martin Baron, Derek's great-grandfather, had started buying it up when the Aguilars had money problems. Anson Baron bought still more, until the Box B was bigger than any of the other ranches once part of the original Spanish land grant ceded to the Aguilar family.

Jack drank half of his drink, seemed to brighten with the refreshment. He brought out a pack of Chesterfields and lit one, left the pack on the table.

Barbara, quiet as a goldfish, waited through the pause with her pencil cocked and ready.

Jack loosened his tie, rolled the cigarette to the side of his mouth, left it dangling, the smoke plumes scratching at his right eye until it developed a tic.

"All right," said Kearney, "let's get down to brass tacks. I've already talked to Matt and young Derek, who's here to see that I toe the mark on this. If you'll look at that plat map on top and the one underneath it. The three ranches come together in a point. Now, look at the aerial map and you'll see that swatch of the *brasada* cutting down through the Box B, the Baron ranches, just like a damned arrow. Now, that's all of a piece and it winds up at El Rincón, smack dab in the middle of Rocking A and Lazy K holdings."

"Hell, we know that, Jack," said Ben.

Ernie nodded.

"That wedge there is what we've got to cut up and sort out," said Kearney. "Agreed?"

Derek and Ben nodded. Ernie sat stiff and straight-backed in his chair.

"Okey-dokey, back to the original land grants. They're not clear on the boundaries. However, Anson Baron filed first on a goodly chunk of El Rincón. But so did Ernie's daddy, and yours, Ben. But, they didn't settle on exact boundaries, especially in that goddamned corner. The deeds overlap. Since then, the Barons and the Aguilars have filed claims to that corner which have put a cloud on all your titles."

"Get to the point, Jack," said Ben.

"There isn't just one point, Ben, so hold your horses."

Jack lifted his glass, rinsed out his mouth and swallowed. His cigarette continued to burn untended. He cocked his head to avoid getting smoke in his eye. The smoke tracked his eye down anyway.

"There is one principal who isn't at this table," said Kearney. He looked at Aguilar. "And maybe he doesn't belong here. But I tried to serve the sonofabitch, even went out to El Rincón myself. His house was burnt to the ground and I didn't see any sign that anyone had lived on the disputed property for at least a year. That right, Ernie?"

"Uh, somebody burned down that shack," said Aguilar.

"More than once, it looks like."

Ernie nodded. "I think it was burned twice."

"Who are we talking about here?" asked Ben, rubbing the stub of his finger with the pencil eraser.

"Jack Bone," said Kearney. "Ernie here deeded over a piece of property to him. But the problem is, Ernie doesn't own it."

"You are wrong, Jack," said Aguilar. "I do own it. I have the papers."

"Bone's been rustling cattle from me, I'm pretty sure," said Killian.

"From me, too," said Ernie. "He and his bunch are living in the *brasada* somewheres. Those two who were in prison came back. I hate it as much as you do, Ben."

"Damnit, Ernie, you're the one who gave him land, lumber to build that shack."

"That's beside the point now," said Kearney, interrupting.

Ben and Ernie eyed each other like combatants in a ring, waiting for the next bell.

Jack finished the rest of his drink, killed the smoking cigarette in his empty glass. He pulled another set of papers from his file. He passed them to Ernie, Ben and Derek.

"Look at those documents," said Kearney, "and at your maps. I've keyed everything in. The *brasada* is all of a piece and where it now ends, right at the tip of the corner, belongs to Matt Baron and his heirs. To the south and west is Aguilar's. To the north is yours, Ben. Neat, like a sliced pie. That's the way the old land deeds prove out and that's the way we're going to file the sonofabitch and clear up all your titles."

Ernie's face purpled as he looked at all of the papers. Ben scowled. Derek seemed unperturbed. He looked at Barbara and winked. She blushed. Kearney looked around the table and lit another cigarette. He nodded to Barbara and she arose, fixed him another drink. When she brought it, she took the empty glass away, held it at a distance as she set it back of the bar.

"I don't like this," said Ernie.

"Looks to me like Matt's getting the biggest slice of the pie," said Ben.

"I won't go into the legal terms, Ben. Ernie, you already know my thoughts on your claims. But that land was Baron land, bought legal from your grandfather, worked, cut, farmed, possessed, every which way, and the law says it rightly belongs to Baron. There's no way we can get rid of that corner. It's in all the land grants from the beginning of recorded deeds in Texas. Aguilar has his corner, Killian has his and cutting right through the middle is Baron land, pure and simple. Now, I want each of you to sign the documents Bobbie's going to give you and I'm going over to the courthouse and record the new deeds and clear titles. All of this other stuff—" Kearney held up a batch of papers representing the other claims. "—is just so much shit and you can use it to start a fire with or paper your outhouse walls."

"I can fight this," said Ernie, but there was no conviction in his voice.

"You'll lose, sure as shit's brown," said Jack softly.

"What about my oil wells?" asked Ben.

"You'll have to jerk 'em or work out a deal with Matt or Derek Baron. You, too, Ernie. Case closed. Bobbie, bring those papers and pass 'em out."

"Yes, Mr. Kearney."

Barbara got up, passed close to Derek. Derek lifted a hand.

"You pinch her on the ass, Derek, and she'll bite your whole hand off," said Jack amiably. He held up a hand and twisted it grotesquely. Derek laughed and withdrew his hand.

"Goddamn you," said Ernie as Barbara left the room.

"Now, no need to curse me, Ernie. You know damned well you're in the wrong. Otherwise you wouldn't have filed on this property every which way to breakfast. If you don't sign, I'll just rewrite the deeds and we'll force you off of what you're getting in this deed. We'll split your part of the corner between Matt and Ben."

Ernie cursed in Spanish under his breath.

"My, my," said Jack. "I always thought there was something suspicious about my parentage. I don't even hear it told in Spanish."

Ernie's face turned the color of sand.

Jack got up, took his drink and cigarette with him.

"So long, boys. We'll need to get those papers over to the courthouse before four o'clock. Susie Loomis won't work overtime, sweet as she is."

Ben and Ernie looked at Derek after Jack left the room. Derek smiled at both men.

"You give your daddy my best," said Ben tightly.

Ernie snorted and glowered at Derek.

"I'll sure do that, Mr. Killian. He'll be right glad you said to wish him well."

Ernie said nothing. Instead, he gripped his pencil so tightly it broke in half.

When Barbara returned with the papers, Derek was the only one in the room still smiling.

30

Twin spools of dust rose in the air as the speeding 1940 Ford coupe careened down the long lane. Peggy Baron straightened her back in the rocking chair on the front porch of the ranch house, squinted into the boiling sun. As she watched, the car sped off the road and into the wide, grassy pasture, speared a path toward a herd of shorthorns and Herefords. The herd scattered as the Ford roared through it. The Ford circled then, and began chasing the strays, moving them back to their former position. Back and forth the car wove, the driver expertly twisting the wheel, reversing his angles.

"Ethan, for Christ's sake, you better get out here," screeched Peggy. She raked a slender hand through her peroxided hair, cut short for summer. She was still trim and lean of figure, with small pert breasts that barely rumpled the summer sheath that clung to her body. She wore a blue ribbon tied in her marcelled hair, accenting the pale aquamarine dress. She wore expensive blue sandals with quarter heels. She had grown tall, a shade under five feet nine, and her dark hazel eyes glinted with gold and amber and veridian. Her thin lips quivered slightly as she waited for her brother to respond.

The screen door twanged open and creaked shut before hitting the jamb with a resounding slap.

"What the hell, Peggy . . ." Ethan looked at his kid sister. He was only a couple of inches taller than she, with dark brown hair, the same hazel eyes, a puckish, petulant mouth pouting under a straight, slightly hooked nose. He was now more corpulent than she, but not fat, not even pudgy. He was just rounder and his features reflected a seriousness that belied his thirty years.

"Looky there," said Peggy, pointing to the pasture.

"Crazy bastard. Who in hell is that?"

"I'll give you one goddamned guess."

"Derek?"

"The prodigal son returns," she said.

As they watched, the Ford streaked back to the road. The engine whined as the driver slammed the gas pedal to the floorboard. A fresh cloud of dust arose in the air. The cattle regarded the intruder with baleful eyes until the car no longer seemed a threat.

Derek Baron roared up to the fence, spun the steering wheel hard to the left and hit the brakes. The coupe slid into a skid, stopped just short of the gate. Dust shrouded it for a moment as if it were some magical object conjured up from a smoke cloud. Derek shut off the ignition, stepped out and leaned over the top of the car.

"Howdy," he said, a wide grin cracking his face.

"You bastard," scolded Peggy.

Derek grinned wider. Ethan frowned.

"Ain't you gonna say howdy to your kid brother, Ethan?" asked Derek. The youngest of the Barons, he was also the tallest, the most strikingly handsome of the three Baron offspring. His hair was darker than Ethan's, his eyes brown as coffee beans. His hair was thicker, slightly tousled from driving with the windows open. He wore white trousers, white Florsheims, a cream sport shirt bought from Neiman-Marcus in Dallas. He slammed the coupe's door shut, walked around the car, opened the gate.

He didn't bother to close it as he strode to the porch. He had to duck under the vine-covered trellis.

"How's Daddy?" Derek asked as he mounted the porch steps.

"He's dying," said Ethan. "We expected you two days ago."

"I got delayed," said Derek. He leaned over, pecked Peggy on the cheek. She giggled, softened her stern look of disapproval.

"What was the slut's name?" she asked.

"Why, I don't remember," grinned Derek. "One of those Love girls or maybe one of the Robbinses."

"Christ," said Peggy. "We're all here scared to death Daddy's goin' to die, and you're in Dallas playin' hide-the-weenie."

"Fort Worth," said Derek with a wink. "Life goes on."

"I hope you wore some protection," said Peggy, a lascivious leer flickering on her lips.

"I don't wear galoshes; never carry an umbrella."

Derek slammed Ethan on the back.

"Well, I'm here, big brother," said Derek, heartily. "How are things in Austin? Does the old man want to see me? Where's Mother?"

"She's with him," said Ethan tersely. "I don't know if Daddy wants to see you or not. Mother does. She's been a wreck waiting for you. Doc Emberlin and Aunt Lou're in there with Mother and Daddy."

"Mother a wreck? Come on, Ethan. She's got more balls than you do."

"Don't talk that way about Mother," snapped Ethan.

Peggy peered down the road, ignoring her brothers.

"Somebody else's coming," she said.

"That's just Blanchard," said Derek. "He's been tryin' to catch me for the past thirty miles."

It was indeed Sheriff Blanchard. He pulled to a stop behind the Ford coupe. The radiator on his 1936 Dodge immediately began to boil over. He got out, opened the hood. His belly sagged over his belt, and his hair was thinning, turning gray. His cheekbones were spidered with red lines, his nose pocked and warty from too much Tennessee whiskey.

"That you, Derek?" he called.

"Roy, you ought to get a couple more cylinders in that old Dodge," said Derek.

"You was speedin', son."

"Can't hardly holt that coupe down, Roy," said Derek, slipping into his down-home vernacular. He had spent time at Virginia Military Institute, was now at the University of Texas with one more year to go before he got his law degree.

"Ought to give you a ticket," grumbled the sheriff. "You didn't have troubles, I might."

"Aw, go on, Roy. You got better things to do. Come on in and have a snort. Let your car cool down. Water's at the pump."

"I know where the goddamned water is." Roy ambled up to the porch, fanned his rawboned, sweat-slick face with his hat. His cheeks were so laced with red and blue veins they looked like a county road map.

"Ethan, Peggy. I'm real sorry your daddy's under the weather. How's Gracie doin'?"

"She's O.K.," said Ethan.

When the small talk was finished, Sheriff Blanchard looked at Derek.

"I'm going to let you go this time, Derek, considerin' the circumstances. But you watch your drivin', hear?"

"Sure, Roy," said Derek. "I'll just have to lighten up my foot." He didn't wave goodbye as the sheriff left, but walked to the edge of the porch, away from Ethan and Peggy.

Derek looked around. He had not been home in a year. The yard was still the same, open in front of the large house, pecan trees, live oaks, a few huge box elders, leafing shade in generous doses, some sycamores dotting the perimeters. There, over the wisteria-covered trellis at the side, was the old cistern. Below, Derek knew, in the shadows and the grasses, there would be cool mint growing, giving off a fragrance he dearly loved. The old windmill whirled slowly in the breeze and the pump creaked reassuringly. There was the ancient carriage that belonged to his grandparents, kept up through the years for sentimental reasons. Still, it should have been in the big barn where his father housed the rest of the worn-out equipment, the sulkies, the Springfield wagons, the buckboards. Gleaming white in the sun, the private stables looked the same, the corrals as neatly groomed as the yard, and the guest house looking like an adobe fort or a mission. The other outbuildings were so far away he had to squint to see them. He could smell the oily, salty scent of the Gulf on the heavy air of early summer and his mind saw the wind-blasted trees along the coast, the wild stretches of lonely beaches, the carouseling gulls, heard the chug of the shrimp trawlers, the lobster boats, moving out of Corpus and Port Aransas.

"Well, Daddy's dying, isn't he?" Derek said.

"Doc Emberlin thinks he's mighty close," said Ethan.

"He's pissed off at you, Derek," said Peggy.

"Who the hell isn't?"

"Mother, too," said Ethan, "as if it mattered to you. You spend money like a drunken sailor."

"Ain't that what it's for?" drawled Derek. "Come on, let's go in and see the old man."

"He just wants to see *you*," said Peggy. Ethan turned away, biting off words that pumped into his mouth, swallowing them raw.

"This isn't the time to fight." said Ethan when Derek turned back to face his sister and brother. "Just go on in there, Dare. Might not be much longer."

Derek said nothing, entered the house.

Grace met him in the livingroom. She embraced him. He knew she had been crying. The corners of her mouth were taut; her face looked as if it had been scrubbed with sandpaper. The rosiness on her cheeks was false, like a cosmetologist's rouge on a corpse. Her lips were colorless, the Maybelline around her eyes faded to ash.

"I'm glad you came, son," she said.

"How's Daddy?"

"He's dying, Derek. God, I . . ." She squeezed him tightly, then released him.

"Don't cry, Mother."

"Go on. Your daddy's waiting for you."

Derek cleared his throat. He was starting to choke up too.

Doctor Emberlin was standing next to Matt's bed, putting his stethoscope in his black cowhide bag. Raw leather showed at the corners where it opened and closed. Aunt Lou sat in a chair in a dark corner of the room.

"Hello, Derek. Your father should go to the hospital, where he can get better care. He said he was just waiting for you. Maybe you can talk some sense into him."

"I'm not going," said Matt, trying to sit up in the bed. "Come on over here, Derek."

Derek walked over, looked at his father. He winced involuntarily. Matt's face had deteriorated to a skeletal thinness. His hands were almost fleshless, the fingers bony. His ribs pushed against the waxen skin. Below the waist, under the sheets, Derek could see his father's hip bones outlined faintly in white. He resembled those newsreel pictures of starving East Indians, all ribs and leg bones, skinny arms, the integument stretched so taut a touch could break it apart like a broom touching a cobweb.

The air in the room was heavy, dank, thick with the smells of medicine and sickness. Derek recoiled inwardly. He could tell that his mother had been sleeping in another room. None of her things were here, only his father's comb and brush on the highboy, a bottle of Old Taylor whiskey. The nightstand was littered with bottles and glass pill containers. The room was dark except for the lamp by the bedside. The rolltop desk that had been Grandpa Anson's stood against the wall, silent, its cubbyholes and compartments locked away under the flexible shutter. A stack of towels sat on a chair. He didn't see any of his father's clothes. An air of death clung to everything like a shroud.

Lou got up.

"I'll leave you two alone," she said. "Matt, you holler if you need anything."

"Thanks, Lou. I'll be—"

"Yeah, I know," said Lou, then left the room.

Derek waited until she had closed the door, then stepped in closer to the bed.

"Hello, Dad."

"Hello, son. I'm glad you came. Hank, you about through?"

"Not quite. Do you want something for the pain?"

"I'll tough it out," said Matt, his voice a harsh rasp. He fluttered a shaking hand toward Derek. Derek clasped it gently, afraid the bones would break if he squeezed too hard.

Emberlin started to close his bag, thought better of it. He came over to the bed, stood beside Derek.

"You really should take something, Matt," said the doctor, his tone compassionate. "It's bound to get worse. I don't know how you stand it now."

"How long do I have, Hank?"

"I don't have the answer to that, Matt. You tell Derek and me."

"Days? Weeks? Months?"

"I'm not God. You've already lasted longer than most men your age could with what you've got. A lesser man would have gone down months ago. You must be experiencing considerable discomfort."

"Some."

"It's all through you, Matt. Stomach, liver, kidneys. Lungs'll be next, maybe. The brain. You need to be in a hospital."

"Another prison," muttered Matt.

Emberlin went back to his bag, pulled out a hypodermic needle, sterile in its glass tube with a rubber stopper, fished out a small bottle of morphine.

"What do they do, Hank?" asked Baron. "Strap you down at the end? Shove a stick between your teeth? Give you a bullet to bite?"

Emberlin turned away, leaned over the nightstand.

"I'll give you something for the pain," said Emberlin.

"In a while," said Matt. "I want to talk to my boy Derek, first. Alone. That stuff puts me under, makes my mouth dry."

Grace entered the room quietly, stood beside Emberlin. The doctor turned, looked at her, a questioning look in his eyes. Grace nodded. The doctor set the vial with the hypodermic needle down next to the small bottle of morphine.

"Whatever you say, Matt," said Emberlin.

"Come with me, Hank," said Grace. "I've got some tea fixed." She stepped in close, leaned over and kissed Matt on the cheek. "We'll be back," she whispered tightly.

Emberlin and Grace walked from the room like mourners in a mortuary. The room was quiet after Grace closed the door.

"You feel like talking, Dad? You look pretty puny."

Matt tried to take a deep breath, but sagged back on the pillow with the effort.

"Your mother's pretty upset at the way you squander money," he rasped.

"Are you, Dad?"

"You'll earn it back and then some. Having a lawyer in the family will be something. My daddy always had good ones. He could barely read and write, but his documents were always clean and clear and legal. Sowing a few wild oats, are you?"

"Aw, some, I guess."

"Son, there's a glass over there on the highboy. Bring me that and the bottle of bourbon standing next to it. You bring 'em over here."

"I don't think—"

"Bring 'em over." There was still timbre in the old man's voice, but the boom of authority was gone. Derek saw that his father had suddenly grown old, with no warning. He walked over to the highboy, brought the bottle of Old Taylor over to the bedside table. Matt struggled to sit up, winced in pain.

"Dad, go easy, will you?"

"I'm leavin' you the land, son. You keep it. Fight for it, die for it. Don't ever sell it off."

"Dad . . ."

Matt pulled himself up higher on the pair of pillows. His eyes were glazed with pain, and as the sheet slid off his torso, Derek saw even more of his father's body. It looked withered and old, like thin parchment.

"See that needle there, Derek? That little bottle Hank set there?"

Derek looked again at the nightstand, saw the hypodermic needle, the array of vials, lotions, the water pitcher, the glass, a stack of fresh napkins. His foot touched something under the bed as he moved closer. A bedpan.

"If I let Hank put that needle in me, I go back to a kind of goddamned jail. The morphine drug takes me places I don't want to go. I can feel the pain, but it's way off in the distance, and it feels warm like one of your grandma's comforters, like a good shot of straight bourbon on an empty stomach. I know I've got pain, but I don't give a hoot and my mind drifts out of my body and goes off somewhere like a fat old lizard basking on a rock in the hot sun. It feels good, but it feels mighty odd, too, and I know it's false or temporary, or just no damned good for me."

"If it helps the pain—" Derek started.

"It puts the pain in another place," said Matt. "I know it's there and I can even see it and touch it and it's like playing with a rattlesnake. You're fascinated and you watch it and know you're bigger than it is, and you're not afraid—until it bites you. And when I'm in the dreams, I know that snake's going to bite me and that it won't hurt none, but I keep looking at those glittering eyes and thinking how beautiful the snake is and everything goes by so slow, you don't worry about getting bit. Except that you get to thinking that you're slow, too, and something's going to catch up to you and get you."

Matt paused, weakened by his talk, and fought for breath. Derek held his father's hand more tightly, feeling the sweat of his own hand oil his father's dry skin.

"Death maybe," sighed Matt.

"Dad, I don't know what to say. What do you want me to do? Are you not going to let Doc give you that shot?"

Matt sighed and lay back on the pillows. His fragile, cadaverous face glistened with a patina of sweat and his eyes darkened in the hollows of his sunken sockets as if he had gone to a private hell for a fleeting moment and had come back changed forever.

"Dare, listen to me," rasped Matt. "Doc doesn't know when I'm going, but it won't be long now. I can feel everything shutting down. It's hard to breathe and hard to think. I feel like my insides were dipped in boiling oil. Christ."

"Dad, let me call Doc back in here."

"No, just—just listen, son. This won't take long. I want you to run the Box B. Ethan's going to be governor some day. Did I ever tell you that? I want him to stay in politics. Anyway, he doesn't have the same feel for stock and the land as you do. You run the ranches. You and

Johnny Bell. Your mother and Aunt Lou will back you up. Take care
of Peggy. She's as wild as they come, but she'll settle down."

"Peggy?"

"A lot like your Aunt Lou used to be. She talks tough, but she's
a softie."

"O.K., Dad," said Derek, feeling that his father was starting to
ramble. The fear was still there, deeper now, blacker. "Let me get
Doc."

"No, not yet."

Matt coughed and his eyes opened wide suddenly. Derek felt the
fear claw up his father's spine and rattle across his brain like a
scuttling crab.

"Go get Johnny Bell. Tell him to come quick."

Derek hesitated. He didn't want to leave his father. But he saw the
fearful look in his father's eyes, felt the tug of filial responsibility.

"You mean Doc?"

"I mean Johnny Bell. Quick."

"Where is he?"

"I told him to wait out back, case I needed him. Fetch him right
now, son."

"I don't know, Dad—"

"Do it, son. I don't have a bunch of time . . ."

"All right."

Derek, confused, left the room. He returned a few moments later,
with Johnny Bell. The foreman entered the room cautiously, his hat
in his hand. His boots made little sound on the carpet. Bell was a
short, chunky man, dark hair, a cherubic face that belied his inner
toughness. All the flesh that looked like fat was hard muscle. His legs
were bowed so that he appeared shorter than he actually was.

"Mr. Baron," said Johnny.

"Leave us to ourselves, Derek," said Matt. "You go talk to your
mother for a while."

"Johnny, you come and get me when you and my dad are finished,
hear?" Derek said.

"Yep," said Johnny.

Derek closed the door.

Johnny looked down at his boss. He knew what was happening.
The silence between them deepened before Matt spoke.

"Pour me four fingers of that Old Taylor, will you, Johnny?"

Johnny poured whiskey into the empty glass.

"Goddamnit, Mr. Baron, I don't like this none."

"Johnny, when are you going to stop calling me 'Mr. Baron?' Call me Matt."

"Yes, sir, Mr. Baron. I mean, no, sir."

Matt reached under his pillow and dug out a swollen Bull Durham sack. He reached over, with great effort, and started pouring the crystalline contents of the tobacco sack into his glass.

"Johnny, Derek's going to take my place."

"Ain't he pretty young, Mr. Baron?"

"He can handle it. You help him."

"Sure, Mr. Baron."

Matt shook the Bull Durham sack, stirred the concoction with a bony index finger.

"What're you puttin' in there?" asked Bell.

"Johnny, you stand real close, grab my hand once I get this down."

"Jesus, Mr. Baron."

Matt drank the concoction, choked after a swallow, gripped Johnny's hand tightly. He drank some more, gagged, finished it off. He closed his eyes. He squeezed the blood out of Bell's hand with his tightening grip.

"You watch after Derek, hear?"

Bell saw Matt's eyes fill with tears.

Matt shuddered.

His eyes rolled back in their sockets. He hung on as tremors rippled through his shriveled body.

Matt struggled for breath. His eyes opened very wide once, then closed. His body spasmed into rigidity, then went slack. His grip on Bell's hand loosened. Johnny leaned over, listened to Matt's breathing. He released Matt's hand, stood there for a long moment, his heart pounding.

Then he picked up the empty glass, smelled it. His nose wrinkled and he put the glass down. He ran his finger inside the glass, touched his finger to his tongue. The taste was bitter. He knew what Matt had poured into the bourbon. He had tasted the stuff before, many times.

"Well, I'll be goddamned," he said, his voice full of wonder. "You old wolf, you."

31

JOHNNY PUT DOWN the glass and leaned over Matt again. "Mr. Baron? Matt?"

Matt's eyes opened for a moment. They filled with tears. He shuddered. Then his eyes rolled back in their sockets. He reached out, grabbed Bell's hands. He gripped them tightly as tremors rippled through his frail body. He made a gagging sound in his throat. His face purpled and his eyes began to open and shut rapidly.

"Mr. Baron, don't do this. God."

Matt's fingers relaxed. His eyes rolled backwards in their sockets, remained fixed. His mouth parted and froze in a wide, hideous rictus as his back arched and his hands twisted backward grotesquely. The hairs rose on the back of Bell's neck.

Johnny stepped back from the bed, shaking. He ran from the room, out into the hall.

"Doc," he yelled. "Better come in here. Derek, you come, too." He did not call Lou.

Derek and Emberlin entered the room.

"He's gone," said Johnny. "I think."

"What happened?" asked Derek.

Emberlin picked up the Bull Durham sack, looked inside, smelled it. He wet the tip of his finger, poked inside the sack. Then, he tasted the residue on the end of his finger. His eyes narrowed.

"Johnny, did you give this strychnine to Matt?"

"No, Doc, he took it hisself. I just poured the whiskey into that glass there." Bell put his hand on Derek's shoulder. "He didn't want it to go on, kid. Reckon he wanted to go out his own way. You need me, you come see me. I'll be working those cows out at the home pasture, cullin' some of the puny ones to put on that new Rhodes grass."

Johnny's face lost all its color. He looked as if he was about to throw up.

"I—I got to go," he said. He left the room before Derek could stop him.

"I'm afraid Johnny was right, Derek," said Emberlin as he bent over Matt's body. He took a small mirror from his satchel, held it to Matt's mouth. He put two fingers on the carotid artery under Matt's ear.

"He died?" Derek asked. "So quick?"

"Better lock that door for a while," said the doctor. "Lou will throw a fit if she finds out what happened."

Emberlin pronounced Matt Baron dead as Derek locked the bedroom door.

"Strychnine?" asked Derek, picking up the whiskey glass. His jaw hardened. Dark shadows hardened his eyes.

"That's what it looks like. Mixed in with the whiskey. I guess the pain got too rough for him, after all. I never thought Matt would go that way."

"Make out that death certificate, Doc," said Derek. "I don't want to see the word suicide anywhere on it."

"Did you give it to him?"

"No, but I know where he got it," said Derek.

"I've got to—"

"Just sit down at that desk over there, Doc, and sign that certificate."

"I'll just put down 'natural causes.'"

"That'll be fine, Doc. I don't want my Aunt Lou to know a damned thing about this. My mother, either."

Emberlin looked at Derek. He didn't see the wild brat he remembered from past visits to the Box B. He saw, instead, a hard, determined young man with steel in his spine. A man with power. The doctor knew that he was hired by Matt Baron and that he had to pass muster with the other ranchers. A word from Derek could send him packing, his practice collapsed like a Sonoran *jacal* in a windstorm.

He shrugged, sat at the rolltop desk and filled out the death certificate with a Parker pen, blew the ink dry. He retrieved his hypodermic and the morphine from the nightstand.

"Derek," said Emberlin, handing over the document he had just signed, "you have all the earmarks of becoming one purebred, unadulterated, walleyed sonofabitch."

"Thanks, Doc," said Derek, taking the death certificate from Emberlin's hand. "I intend to kick some ass around here."

"I think Matt would rest easy knowing someone would do just that. He's been worried about who would run the ranch when he was gone."

"Is there anything you can do about that grin on Dad's face?"

"I wouldn't advise it."

"Tell everyone I'll be out in a minute, Doc. I want a moment alone with my dad."

"Sure, Derek."

Derek closed his father's eyes, tried to slacken the jaw muscles so that Matt's teeth didn't show. But the rictus was set and there wasn't much he could do. He covered his father's withered body with the sheet, placed his twisted arms by his sides. He took away the whiskey glass, set the Old Taylor back on the bureau. He put the glass way in the back of the bottom drawer of the highboy, resolving to retrieve it later.

A tear streamed down Derek's face. But he fought off the urge to cry, knowing that if he broke down now, he would never get through what he had to do. He took a deep breath, swabbed away the lone teardrop with a dry handkerchief.

He did not say goodbye to his father, but left the room to face his mother, Ethan and Peggy, his Aunt Lou.

The Baron family seemed paralyzed with grief as they stood around Emberlin. Derek seemed to be the only one with a grip on himself. Peggy was numb; Ethan walked around the livingroom like a zombie. He kept picking up things that belonged to his father as if trying to bring him back through some kind of fetishistic ceremony. Grace was obviously shattered, but bore up well, living up to her reputation on the Baron Ranch as "the Iron Filly."

There was an odd look on Lou's face, but Derek managed to avoid her accusing stare.

Derek hugged his mother, kissed Peggy on the cheek. Peggy

looked at her brother, an emptiness in her eyes, as if her mind had flown.

"Ethan," said Derek, "you take care of things until I get back. There's something I have to do."

Emberlin, overhearing, looked at Derek with a puzzled look on his face.

"Where are you going?" asked Grace. "We want to see your father. Is it all right, Hank?"

"Yes," said Emberlin.

"Mother, I'll be right back," said Derek, without further explanation.

Aunt Lou's eyes narrowed, but she said nothing. Still, her lips clamped down tight as if to keep from saying something right then. Maybe, thought Derek, she knew more than he thought she did about his father's death.

Derek left the house through the back door, walked out across the patio and out the gate, on to the tack room. It was unlocked and he went inside. He switched on the light, smelled the heady musk of leather, liniment, saddle soap and oil. He searched the shelves until he found the boxes of strychnine. He took the opened box down, cringed when he saw how much was gone. He remembered, then, when he, his father and Ethan used the poison on coyotes. He knew there were only two people who could have given the poison to his father. And only one of them still smoked Bull Durham, rolled his cigarettes instead of buying ready-mades.

Derek put the box back on the shelf. It was eerily quiet and he wondered if anyone was watching him. He felt as if he was an intruder. The strychnine made him nervous. So innocent, those boxes, so deadly. Outside, he saw no one. He started walking to the barn and looking toward the stables.

"L.D.," he called.

"L. D. Johnson was his father's groom and stableman. He had been around the Box B ever since Derek could remember. He was a sour, taciturn man, and Derek had never liked him much. But he did his job and kept the horses groomed. Once, Derek and Peggy had been prowling around Johnson's house, snooping in his dresser drawers. They had found, under a stack of underwear, a series of little cartoon booklets. The cartoons featured Maggie and Jiggs, Tarzan and Jane, Blondie and Dagwood, Popeye and Olive Oyl, in a series of vignettes showing them engaged in sexual intercourse. The booklets fascinated the children, who had not yet reached puberty, and some of the positions were so outrageous they talked about them for months afterwards. When they went back a second time to look, L.D. had hidden the "fuck books," as they were called, and they couldn't find them.

There was no answer, but Derek heard sounds in the big stable. He entered through the open doors.

"You in here, L.D.?"

"Back here."

L.D. was in his late fifties, with wavy, tightly packed hair that was once red, was faded now to a graying rust. L.D. was currying Big Boy, a Tennessee Walker and Matt Baron's favorite saddle horse since Esquire had gotten too old to ride.

"Did you take some strychnine up to Daddy?"

"He ast me for it. Don't know what he wants it for."

"L.D., draw your pay and get off the Box B. I don't ever want to see your face again."

"You can't fire me, kid. Only your old daddy can do that."

"He just did, L.D. Start packin'."

"I won't. Not until I hear it from the old man's lips hisself. Hell, I been workin' here since way before his daddy died."

"You won't ever hear anything from Daddy's lips, L.D. He's deader'n a doornail. Now, pack up. Get out. I'll have your pay when you stop by the house."

A half hour later, L.D. left with a check in his hands, signed by Grace Baron. She hadn't questioned Derek's decision to fire Johnson.

"I'll be back in a while," said Derek.

"You do what you have to," she said.

Derek smiled at her reassuringly. Some things just couldn't wait.

Derek changed into ranch clothes, saddled his horse, Brigand, and rode to the herd grazing on the south pasture, where Johnny Bell had told him he would be.

"I'm real sorry, kid," said Johnny.

Billy Bob Letterman and Hank Janss were working the herd of shorthorns, culling some out, running them into a pole corral.

"Well, it was bound to happen," said Derek.

"He lasted longer'n anyone would've thought," said Bell.

"Johnny, I let L.D. go."

"He the one what gave your daddy the wolf poison?"

"Yes."

"He was probably just follerin' orders."

"Some orders you don't follow."

Johnny slid sideways in the saddle, pulled a chunk of Days Work out of his pocket, bit off a chew.

"You got a point," said Johnny. He spat.

"There's going to be some changes around here."

"Yeah, I 'spec' so."

"When you can, I want some of your best men, those you don't need for a while."

"What you got in mind, kid?"

"I'm going to clear ground for some landing strips, Johnny. And don't call me 'kid.' "

"You want me to call you mister?"

"Either Derek or Baron will do."

"What the hell's a landing strip?"

"For my airplane. I'm going to buy an airplane. I want you to hire some carpenters, too. Build me a main hangar over yonder where the road circles back of the barn."

"Ain't you got more schoolin' to do? Your daddy was set on you bein' a lawyer."

"I can hire lawyers. I'm going to run the Baron ranch."

"From an airplane?"

"Eventually. How long's it been since you've been to La Golondrina, La Rosalia or Las Arenas del Diablo?"

The Baron holdings were scattered over southwest Texas, hard to get to by road.

"Well, you got a point there, too."

"I want one strip at each of the ranches, close to the headquarters. You get a 'dozer and find an engineer."

"Anything else?"

"I'll let you know," said Derek. He nodded to Janss and Letterman.

"All right," said Bell.

After Derek rode away, Janss rode over to Johnny.

"What the hell was that all about?"

"Derek Baron's goin' to be the big chief around here, Hank."

"Well, fuck me a-runnin'. Hell, he don't know shit."

"He knows enough."

"So, what's botherin' you, Johnny?"

"It 'pears to me that Mr. Derek Baron is going to be one purebred, grade-A, homogenized, government-inspected, gaul-fisted,
bluebellied, first-class prick."

"I always thought you liked the kid."

"Yeah, but that's the danged trouble. He ain't no kid no more."

Matt Baron's body lay in state at the big house on the main ranch, La
Golondrina. Solemn clumps of friends from the various ranches
gathered in the parlor to view Matt's remains. Others came to pay
their respects from around the region, from afar, even from Washington. Neighboring ranchers came by, too. Ernie Aguilar was there with
his family, Ben Killian and his family and their hands came to pay
their respects. Keith Sherwood came down from Houston. Luke Killian was there, with his partner in advertising, Jim Goff. Jim played
and sang "Nearer My God to Thee" and "Shall We Gather at the
River." Martin and Tamar Longerbeam were there with their son
Curtis. Mayor Ted Womack, Naomi and Burt Tyler were there, but
their son David did not attend the services. Jack Kearney came, with
his secretary, Barbara Amos. Also present was Faith Emberlin, the
recently widowed doctor's beautiful, unmarried daughter. Alicia
Aguilar had become a lovely young lady, was very becoming in black.
Steve Killian seemed morbidly fascinated by the casket, the em-
balmed body of Matt Baron. His sister, April, had begun to fill out,
looked fresh and pretty standing next to her mother. Connie Killian
kept sending shy glances toward Ethan Baron. Ben offered his condo-
lences to the Baron family, looked extra hard at Derek, eye to eye.
Lou wore a dress, looked prettier than many had remembered her
ever looking. She even wore a smart hat with a black veil that gave her
face a seductive look, and real silk stockings. Jane Houston Killian
wore a gray suit that was expertly tailored, long gray gloves, patent
leather high-heeled shoes.

No fewer than three Presbyterian ministers conducted services at
the ranch on the afternoon of May 20, 1940. Cars lined the road to
the Baron home, Lincolns, Cadillacs, Hupmobiles, Packards, even a
Cord and a Graham among them. They glistened in the sun like a
giant chain of beads. Ethan delivered the eulogy. Jim Harding, Roy
Blanchard, Ben Killian, Martin Longerbeam, Merle Chandler, and
Bob Filbert were the pallbearers.

More than five thousand people stood at the graveside in the
Barons' private cemetery later that afternoon. Grace had seen to it

that there were refreshment stands near the shade trees, stocked with RC Cola, Dr. Pepper, Orange Crush and Coca-Cola.

Derek had no idea of how many people his father had known until that moment. When the Masonic ceremony was over, the cowboys from the farthest reaches of the Baron lands rode by the open grave in a final salute. Among them was Lucas Killian, the last in the procession.

Luke stood his horse by the grave and took off his battered hat, bowed his head for a moment and then rode off through the gravestones, alone. A bugler from the VFW played taps. The dying notes lingered on the afternoon air, haunting, plaintive. Derek's arms bubbled with goosebumps.

After the burial, Derek waited in his father's den for Johnny Bell. He looked at the various objects in the room, looked back down the tunnel of time at the history of the Baron family. There was the old Santa Fe saddle owned by his great grandpa; the Kentucky rifle, made in Lancaster County, Pennsylvania; the Sharps, a Henry, a succession of Winchesters, a Browning, other sporting arms rowed up in glass cabinets, the Colt Peacemaker, the flintlock pistols, his father's Colt .45 Model 1911 that he carried in the war; a shield bearing samples of Glidden's invention; barbed wire that had fenced Baron land; swatches of cowhides with the various brands burned into them, tintypes of family members long since gone to peace; a human skull with a bullet hole in the forehead; Indian artifacts; soil samples. There was even a McClellan saddle, a relic of a Baron who had ridden with Custer's 7th Cavalry under Reno, a Springfield 45-70 leaning against it, a cartridge belt dangling from the saddle ring. In a closet hung Civil War uniforms, worn by Barons who had fought on both sides during the conflict. Oddly, the room did not look cluttered. Everything in it seemed to belong there. The room was a museum, Derek thought. Each item had a history. Each object had a story to tell.

Derek had often listened to his father talk about his ancestors, his pa, and his pa's pa, and their women, their children. There were uncles and cousins who had spread out over the land and conquered it, made their mark on it. It was in this room that Matt Baron had made all of his important decisions. It was to this room that Johnny Bell came that solemn afternoon.

"I'm glad you came," said Derek.

"Kid, you only have to ask."

"I told you, Johnny, I'm not a kid anymore."

"No, I reckon you're not." Johnny remembered Derek tagging along after him when he made meat, rode the land, turned out the stock at roundup, branded, doctored beeves, fished the Nueces. Derek had been his shadow since he had come to the ranch after Tom Casebolt had been killed and he had taught him things he might have taught his own son if he'd had one.

"I'm going to need help, Johnny."

"So you're still aimin' to step into the big man's boots?"

"Someone's got to."

"Ethan will buck you. He wants the land as much as you do, and he's the oldest. He'll fight you, sure enough."

"Not if you back me up."

"Watch him. Eth's mighty quiet, like a river, but he's got whirlpools underneath."

"I know. I just wanted to know if I could count on you."

"Derek," said Johnny, "Matt told me you'd be asking me a favor one day."

"And?"

"I told him I'd see was you man enough to earn it."

"I am."

"That's what I wanted to hear. Roll your smoke."

They talked over some of the problems that lay ahead. Derek laid out the plat map of El Rincón, an aerial photograph of the *brasada.*

"I want to clear the brush out of El Rincón. I want Jack Bone out of there."

"That corner broke your daddy's heart," said Bell.

"I know. That's why I want all the varmints out of there."

"You got any ideas?"

"A few. Just keep it in mind. Daddy's policy goes back in effect as of today."

"What policy is that, Derek?"

Derek smiled. He was no longer "the kid."

"Shoot Bone and any of those Indians on sight."

"Holy shit," said Johnny.

After the foreman left, Derek sat in his father's chair, toying with a dagger that had belonged to one of his great uncles.

It was a Mexican dagger with a brass eagle's head on the butt, engraving on the blade. The legend read: *No me saques sin razón, ni me guardes sin honor.* "Do not draw me without reason, nor keep me without honor." The knife was very sharp, the blade a Toledo.

Once, Derek had seen his father cut a Mexican silver peso in half with the blade, pounding the back of it with a hammer. It hadn't even dulled the steel edge.

His daddy had loved that knife. It seemed that Derek could feel his father's energy, the pulsing of his veins, the pounding of his heart, in that beautiful blade.

He gripped the dagger's handle and brought it over his head. Angrily, he drove the blade downward, full force, and rammed it into the plat map, square on the section labeled "El Rincón." The thunk brought him out of the rage and he realized for the first time that he missed his father, would always miss him.

It was then that Derek began to cry.

32

THE BLACK UPRIGHT phone on the duty desk in the sheriff's office jangled six times before Raymond Naylor could pick it up. He and Sheriff Blanchard were locking up three men they'd picked up at Mudd's Pool Hall that afternoon. A fight had broken out between some farm boys and the local Klansmen, who were holding a meeting at the bar. Roy was still wrestling with Orville Treacher, who was still trying to get at Dale Wilker, the reporter from the *Baronsville Bugle,* who had seen the fight start and called the sheriff.

"You nigger-lovin' sonofabitch," Treacher said to Wilker. "Let me at him, Sheriff."

Roy swung a sap at Treacher's backside. Treacher staggered into the cell as the leather-bound chunk of pig iron thudded into his right kidney.

Blanchard was puffing from the exertion, his face swollen and red as a radish, every corpuscle engorged with blood. He slammed the cell door shut, twisted the key in the lock. The other two men in custody were Delmer Mudd and Giacomo Ingianni.

"Bastard," said Treacher.

"You want to wear them oversized nightshirts and burn crosses, that's one thing," huffed Roy, "but you go to beatin' up on citizens, that's another. Del, your fucking bar is closed until the judge says different."

Mudd and Ingianni glared at the sheriff.

"What about our goddamned rights?" asked Del.

"You ain't got none," said Roy. He pocketed the blackjack, walked over to the bench by the wall and sat down. Wilker, an amiable and curious young man, originally from El Paso, sat down next to Blanchard, wrote furiously in a small spiral notebook.

"Sheriff's office," said Naylor, who was still trying to catch a full breath.

The phone was silent.

"Hello," said Ray.

"You the one looking for who run over your sister?"

"Who in hell is this?"

"Bone."

Raymond slid around the end of the desk, sat in the chair. He opened a drawer, brought out a piece of paper. He pulled a pencil from his pocket, wet the lead tip on his tongue.

"Jack Bone?"

"You know who I am," said Bone.

"What about my sister?"

"I know who killed her."

Naylor finally took a deep breath, steadied himself. "You going to tell me?"

"I was there."

"Who was it?"

There was a long pause before Bone answered. "Ernie Aguilar."

"Jesus," said Naylor. "Can you prove it?"

"You can, was you to get to lookin'."

"Where? How?"

"He's still got that old flivver, stored out in the barn. You look at it real good and you'll see where your little sister left a dent."

"Why are you telling me this now?"

"Ernie's done fucked with me long enough. You go out there, Naylor, and you'll find out. He run right over that little girl and kept right on drivin', told me to keep my mouth shut. I was with him."

"When was this?" asked Naylor.

"It was in July, the fifth, back in nineteen and thirty."

Naylor wrote the date down on a piece of paper, his hand shaking. Ten years gone by. Ten years of pain. Ten years of sorrow, of frustration, of justice denied. He felt lightheaded.

"What time of day was this?"

"Mornin'. Ernie bailed me out of your damned jail and we was goin' back to his ranch."

Ray fought to keep his composure, but his hand shook so badly he had to drop the pen and lay it flat on the desk. He didn't look at Blanchard, but he knew the sheriff's eyes were fixed on him.

"Does he know you're calling me?" asked Naylor.

Bone laughed.

"That's all I'm gonna tell you. I want Ernie to pay for what he done to me."

"Hey, wait—" said Naylor, but the phone line went dead. He tapped the cradle several times, but the buzzing persisted. He hung up the receiver.

"Who in hell was that?" asked Blanchard.

Naylor looked up at him finally, then at Wilker, who was also staring in his direction.

"Tell you in a minute. Dale, you 'bout finished here?"

"Sure," said Wilker. "Give me a call, Roy, when you decide what to do with these boys."

"I will," said Blanchard.

Dale closed his notebook, rammed his pencil back into his pocket.

"Be seeing you," he said, as he left the office, walked down the hall to the front, where the switchboard was. People in town always remarked how much he resembled Jack London, with his curly hair and disarming cherubic smile. They had seen pictures of London on the newsreels and had thought he looked enough like Wilker to be his brother.

After the reporter left, Naylor got up from behind the desk.

"The damned judge wouldn't give me a search warrant before, Roy, but now I don't need one."

"What's up?"

"That was Bone. He said Aguilar was the one who ran over Lucy."

"Sure?"

"Bone was with him. The date checks out."

"Want me to go with you? I can call Freddie Beane in off of patrol." Fred Beane, from Brownwood originally, was the new deputy. He was out in the patrol car.

"No, I'll just go out there, see if Bone's story is true. If I find anything suspicious, I'll give you a call from there."

"Better tell Jack Kearney first. He might be able to get you a warrant from Judge Chowney over to Galveston."

"All right," said Naylor, trying to quell the excitement in his voice. He seemed breathless once again, but he was just anxious to drive out to the Rocking A and look in that barn of Aguilar's.

"You take it easy, Raymond."

Naylor squared his Stetson, cupped his Smith & Wesson .38 service pistol, patted the holster.

"Be seein' you, Roy."

"And wipe that shit-eating grin off your face before you go out the door," Blanchard said.

"I really like the taste of it," cracked Naylor as he strode toward the hall.

The three men in the cell, in unison, extended their middle fingers and rammed them skyward in a farewell salute to Deputy Naylor.

Elena Aguilar met Raymond Naylor at the door. She listened to him politely as he explained that he wanted to search the old barn. She looked beyond him at the official sheriff's car, her eyes darting in their sockets like shadow creatures in a woodland pond.

"I do not think you better do this," she said.

"Mrs. Aguilar, I don't need your permission. I'd like to talk to your husband first, see if he wants to cooperate."

"I will get him," she said quickly and closed the front door. Naylor's right hand rested on his pistol butt. He heard sounds inside the house.

A few moments later, he heard footsteps. The door opened and Ernie Aguilar stood there, a napkin in his hand.

"What is it that you want, Sheriff?" he asked.

"I want to take a look at that old flivver you have out in the barn, Mr. Aguilar."

"What?"

"I think you heard me, sir."

Ernie's teeth were still working on a small morsel of tortilla. He made sounds with his mouth, but didn't say anything for a moment or two.

"Why is it that you want to look at an old car?"

"I think you know why," said Naylor, bridling his impatience.

"I do not know why."

Behind Ernie, Elena stood in shadow, but Raymond could see her face, frozen with worry.

"I believe that vehicle was involved in an accident ten years ago."

Ernie laughed nervously, low in his throat.

"There was no accident. I have not driven the car in many years. It is old and has not been out of the barn." Perhaps he should have cut up the car for scrap a long time ago. Buried the pieces of it deep underground. But he had kept it, hidden away, like some part of his conscience, something he could not look at, but knew was there, under dust, like something in the back room of a museum.

"Mr. Aguilar, I'm not going to stand here and argy with you. I come to see that vehicle and you can just wait here or come with me and show it to me."

Elena touched her husband's arm gently, prodding him. Ernie slapped her hand away.

"Go with him," she whispered, just barely loud enough for Naylor to hear.

"Just a minute," said Aguilar. He closed the door, turned on Elena. She stepped back, suddenly afraid.

"I'm sorry, Ernesto," she said. "I just don't know why you won't let the sheriff see that old car."

"You be quiet," he said in a harsh whisper.

"What is wrong? Why does he come here?"

"Let me think. *Maldito.*"

Elena said nothing. Ernie thought for a moment, pushed her away.

"Go on," he said. "I will take the sheriff to the barn."

Elena opened her mouth to speak, but closed it quickly. Ernie opened the door. She waited for a moment, then turned away, retreated back to the dining room, where Hector and Alicia still sat at the table, wondering why their mother was so agitated.

"What is wrong?" asked Alicia.

"Nothing. Finish your supper."

Hector looked at his mother. He saw the warning in her eyes. He arose from the table.

"I am finished," he said, dragging his napkin from beside the plate.

He wiped his mouth with the napkin, set it down on the table.

"Where are you going?" Elena asked, her speech tight with concern.

"Outside."

"Do not interfere with your father's business."

Hector snorted and walked toward the kitchen. He had grown on the outside, but Elena wondered if he wasn't still the same frightened boy inside. He was often distant and somber of mien and she worried about him. He had not been the same since he had left Bone's camp and come home, all bloodied and torn up so badly in mind and body that she had to care for him that night as if he was still a little boy. She felt as if he had something buried deep inside him that could explode at any moment.

"Mama," said Alicia, "what is going on?"

"I don't know," said Elena honestly. "Just be quiet and finish the eating."

"Yes, Mama," said Alicia.

Elena smiled wanly at her daughter. Alicia had grown into a beauty, with her dark olive skin, like Ernesto's, the dark eyes and hair. All of the boys were calling her and taking her to dances. Elena was proud of Alicia. She worked hard, saved her money. Elena was sure Alicia was still a good girl.

Elena leaned over and patted her daughter's arm reassuringly.

"Maybe it is nothing," she said, without realizing that she was speaking in a whisper.

Ernie opened the door again, stepped outside.

"I will take you out there, Sheriff Naylor."

"Do you have electric lights in the barn?"

"Yes," Ernie said tightly, pulling the door shut behind him.

The two men walked around to the side of the house, headed toward the old barn. The sun was just above the western horizon, daubing a few far clouds in faint pastels of pink and soft indigo. They passed the chicken house. The General cackled a throaty cry, flapped his gold and brown wings. Then, he chased one of his hens into the shelter, as if asserting his authority in the presence of humans.

Ernie dug in his pocket for the keys. The padlock on the big doors was rusted. He inserted the key, twisted it back and forth inside the lock. Finally, the lock snapped open. He hung the open hook on one side of the hasp. He stepped inside the barn, reached for a lever that turned on the lights. The lever made contact and two lights came on.

The barn smelled musty. It was full of spare tractor parts, harrows, disks, an old hay baler, rolls of barbed wire, cases of dynamite, rusted tools. The lumber that formed the walls had shrunk over the years. Large cracks let in light and the weather. Over in the far corner, an old Model T Ford sat on empty tires, shrouded with a tarp. Mice, or rats, had ripped chunks of the canvas out for their nests, and it looked tattered and motheaten.

"Would you take that tarp off for me, Mr. Aguilar?" asked Naylor.

"I don't know what you want to see this old Model T for," said Ernie, his voice under control.

"I just want to take a look at it, that's all."

Ernie tugged at the tarp, threw part of it over the top. He walked around to the other side, pulled it completely away. He met Naylor, who stood in front of the car looking at the cobwebbed headlamps.

The light was bad in that corner of the barn, but Naylor leaned over, touching the car's finish with his fingers. The fender on the left side was undamaged. On the right side, he saw that the fender was crumpled, bent back toward the tire.

"How'd you get this?" he asked.

Aguilar shrugged.

"Hit something?"

"Maybe. I don't know."

Ray stepped away from the car. He knelt down and looked at the headlamp, the front bumper. There appeared to be a dark stain on the bumper, but there was so much rust he couldn't be sure.

"I'm going to have to impound this vehicle," he said as he stood up.

"What do you mean?"

"I'm going to call for a tow truck and have it taken into town. Someone will go over it and see if there's any indication that this vehicle was involved in a hit-and-run accident."

"I do not understand, Sheriff."

"I'm talking about murder, Mr. Aguilar. The murder of my little sister, Lucy Naylor. I think you did it. I think this is the car you drove."

"That is not so. Who told you this?"

"Who do you think? Who was with you, the day my sister was killed?"

"I do not know what you are talking about. I am sorry about your sister, but I did not even know her."

"No, and that's the pity, Mr. Aguilar."

"Are you accusing me?"

"Not yet. But I wouldn't go too far from this ranch for a while."

"I do not like this."

"Neither do I."

"I would like to know who sent you out here and accused me."

"Someone who was with you that day."

"What day was that?"

"July fifth, nineteen hundred and thirty."

Ray couldn't be certain in the dim light, but he was pretty sure that Aguilar's face had darkened. Aguilar said something under his breath. It was in Spanish, but Naylor couldn't hear the words clearly.

"Do you want to tell me what happened? Your side of it?"

"I did not do what you say," said Ernie. "Besides, that was a long time ago."

"I have a good long memory, Mr. Aguilar."

"It was Bone, wasn't it?"

"What did you say?"

"Nothing. Are you finished?"

"Yes. I want to use your phone. You come with me."

"Why?"

"I don't want you tampering with this vehicle. It's evidence. I'm going to call into town and wait for the tow truck."

Ernie bristled, opened his mouth to say something, but seemed to think better of it.

"Come to the house, then, Sheriff."

As Naylor closed the barn doors, attached the lock to keep the doors shut, Hector Aguilar stood just at the end of the barn, out of sight, where he had been peering through one of the cracks at the two men. He had heard every word they had spoken inside the barn.

Neither Ernie nor Ray saw the young man.

As they walked back to the house in silence, Naylor was a few paces behind Aguilar.

"Yes, it was Bone," he said softly.

Ernie stopped in mid-stride, turned around. "He is no good. He is a liar and a thief, a rustler."

"I know he is, Mr. Aguilar. He's probably a murderer, too." Naylor paused. "Maybe you and him ain't so much different."

Ernie shuddered, as if something had pierced his heart, a thin needle that drew no blood but left a tiny hole that would widen in time, widen and fester until it raged with a lethal fever.

33

—■—

ORA CORNEJO, HER skirt hiked to the knees with chubby fingers bleached by years of scrubbing clothes and washing dishes, broke for the house in a waddling run.

"Se vienen, se vienen!" she exclaimed. "Here they come!"

Grace, immaculately attired in form-fitting gabardine trousers, burgundy and cream Justin boots, a trim, tight Western-cut shirt embroidered with graceful lines over the pearl-button pockets, a bandanna encircling her wattled throat, tipped back her Stetson and looked down the road. She set down the watering can and shaded her eyes.

"Derek," she called. "Here comes company."

Her voice carried to the small office where Derek and Johnny Bell were grading grass samples brought in early that morning by Billy Bob Letterman from the ranches, La Plata, La Paloma, Santa Magdalena and La Golondrina.

Derek stepped outside the ranch office, waved to her.

Ora slowed as she neared the flower beds where Grace had been watering the azaleas, mums and new Russian roses.

"Bring the lemonade," said Grace. "Set it on the patio table over there."

Derek had hired men to build a flagstone patio just in back of the family home at La Loma de Sombra, Shadow Hill. He said they needed an open-air place, but Grace knew he had built the beautiful patio for her, designed it himself, with bordering flower beds, a trellis where honeysuckle twined and hummingbirds suckled at the blossoms in the spring.

Derek, joined by Johnny Bell, walked away from the office, the two of them wiping their dirty hands on their Levi's.

Grace looked at her watch. It was three o'clock in the afternoon and she was as excited as Derek. These were Derek's closest friends, the Longerbeam boy—she always had trouble remembering his first name—Hector Aguilar and Steve Killian. All of the boys had been born less than a year apart. They had spent their early years of schooling together. Later, Derek had to be sent away, but the bonds he had formed in childhood still held.

Derek stopped, said something to Johnny Bell, who nodded and headed for the barn and corrals, where the imported stock was quartered.

"Bring one of 'em up to the patio," Derek yelled as Johnny walked away. "Bruno."

"Shit," said Johnny, his voice carrying on the quiet air of afternoon.

Grace smiled and walked a course that would intersect Derek's.

"Your daddy would have never done a thing like this," she said. "He was very competitive."

"So am I, Mother," said Derek, as the two met. He put his arm around his mother's small waist, gave her a gentle squeeze. "But I knew they were going to hear about it anyway. We might make a little extra money if we decide to breed the new stock."

"You're smart, son," she said, "or else you're dumb as a knothole."

Derek laughed and ducked under the vine-laced trellis, the scent of honeysuckle a cloying scent in his nostrils. Hummingbirds hummed like electricity in the wires.

"How is the Rhodes grass doing?" Grace asked.

"Africa would envy us," he said. "I might even bring in some gazelles and lions."

"Oh, you," said his mother.

Steve Killian's car was the first to arrive. Curtis Longerbeam, Martin and Tamar's eldest son, drove up right afterwards. The third car stopped and parked behind Steve's new 1941 DeSoto. Hector Aguilar got out, carrying a Kodak box camera by an imitation leather strap.

"Come on over here," Derek called, waving the group on toward the patio. He released his mother. She met Ora on the steps, took the tray of tumblers and napkins from her. Ora went back inside the house.

"What you got to show us, Derek?" Steve asked as he came up. "Some kind of cattle breed nobody can pronounce?"

Derek laughed. "Hell, a Texan can pronounce anything," said Derek.

"At least a dozen different ways," said Steve, his bootheels ringing on the flagstones.

"Curtis," said Derek. "Glad you could come."

"I want to see what you brought over all the way from Switzerland," said Longerbeam. "Some kind of milk cow?"

"That's what everybody used to think," admitted Derek. "Might surprise you. Johnny's bringing one of 'em up for us to look at while we guzzle some of Ora's sour lemonade."

Ora brought another tray with a large pitcher of milky-yellow lemonade sloshing the ice against the glass with a faint tinkling bell sound.

Derek waved the two young men to the table. Hector, the last to arrive, seemed shy. As if embarrassed, Steve Killian turned away when Hector walked up. Derek saw Steve's reaction, responded by going to meet Hector, his hand outstretched.

"Hi, Heck. Glad you could come." Derek squeezed Hector's hand firmly.

"Hello, Derek. Long time."

A look passed between the two men. "How you gettin' along, Heck?"

"I don't complain much."

"Good. Have some lemonade and make yourself at home."

Hector looked around at the shade trees, the new patio. "Nice," he said.

"Thank you, Hector," said Grace, smiling at him. She and Ora began to pour the glasses full.

"Where's Peg, Mrs. Baron?" asked Steve.

"She and Lou went to Houston with Ethan. I believe she's going to see your brother Luke while she's there."

"Luke's doing pretty good," said Steve. "His advertising business is thriving."

"That's what we heard," said Grace.

"I wish Luke was here," said Derek. "He might have some ideas if we go into this new breed."

"Everybody at Nomi's is talking about it," said Curtis. He was tall, like his father, thin. Everyone thought he was going to be a professional baseball player. He had an arm like a whip. He'd played semi-pro for a year but came home to help his father, Martin, on his ranch when beef prices improved. He was engaged to Jo-Beth Vermeil, the telephone operator. They were supposed to get married in July.

"Well, here comes Johnny with Bruno."

Everyone looked at the huge bull lumbering their way, Johnny leading him on a thick rope attached to a modified hackamore with a thick come-along at the throat.

"You should call that one Brutus," said Steve Killian. "What's he weigh?"

"That bull will go twenty-five hundred," said Derek.

Curtis whistled.

"Derek, you're not going to let Johnny bring him on the patio, are you?" asked Grace, a lilt of apprehension in her voice. Ora handed full glasses of lemonade to Steve, Hector and Curtis. Grace took a glass for herself, gave one to Derek.

"Naw, Johnny's going to hold Bruno out there. Come on, let's go see him. Ora, bring Johnny some of that lemonade, will you?"

"*Por seguro,*" muttered the maid.

Johnny halted, walked the bull around in a slow circle. Ora approached the bull cautiously, handed the foreman the glass of lemonade. He thanked her in Spanish. Ora scurried to the relative safety of the patio.

"Well, what do you think?" asked Derek.

"Mighty fine-looking bull," said Steve. "What breed is he?"

"Braunvieh."

"Say what?" from Curtis.

"Born and bred in the Swiss Alps," said Derek. He walked over to the bull, rubbed its poll. "A very docile animal, so they say."

"Where did you see this breed?" asked Hector. He stepped up, touched the hide, rubbed through the hair along the top of the spine.

"Saw one over to the auction in Odessa," said Derek. "Talked to the owner. He had bought three bulls and one cow, said he was going to cross them with his shorthorns. I got in touch with a breeder over there, had him ship me three bulls, two cows."

"Looks pretty docile," said Steve.

"They are tame as pet pigs," said Johnny, grinning. He knelt down in front of the bull and nuzzled its nose with his. Even Grace laughed.

Derek stepped back, let the others inspect Bruno. The Braunvieh's head was in good proportion to his body size. The poll was wide, the forehead broad, slightly dished. The nostrils were large and open, the jawline strong. The bull had large, clear eyes, dark as coffee. The hair around the eyes was light sand.

"Ears are set funny," said Steve.

"They're big, too," said Curtis.

"Their ears are lower than the English breeds'," said Derek. "Look inside. The hair is fawn-colored, real long."

The tongue and nose were black. The horns were not too thick at the base, were straight and outthrust.

"Kind of funny-colored," said Hector.

"They come in all flavors," said Derek. "Mostly brown, like a mouse. But we've a gray-toned cow and a real dark brown one."

The three young men stepped back to admire the animal.

"I don't know, Derek," said Steve. "If they're Swiss, they'll probably die quick in high summer."

"Hell, they grow these beeves all over the world. You can breed 'em with shorthorns, Herefords, even black Angus. I think they might make a pretty good beef cattle."

"They's two kinds," said Johnny. "We got the Beef Brown Swiss here. They're registered separately from the Dairy Brown Swiss. The man in Odessa said they breed them in Canada and Mexico and that they'll work in any pasture Texas has got."

"That's right," said Derek. "I'm going to improve my stock and thought you boys might like a look-see. We can drink our lemonade on the patio there while Johnny takes Bruno back to the pen, then go down there and you can look over the cows and the other bulls."

"Fair enough," said Steve.

"You already breed the best stock around," said Hector.

"Thanks," said Derek, genuinely pleased. He led the group back to the table on the patio.

"How's Ethan doing?" asked Steve, on the way back.

"Just fine," said Derek.

"Last I heard, you two were bucking for top dog on your daddy's ranch."

"That's all in the past," said Grace tightly.

The Barons had, since 1886, been upgrading the ranch's tough Longhorn range stock by crossing it with two British beef breeds, the shorthorn (descended from Durham or Teeswater stock) and the Hereford. Since Matt's death, Derek had been keeping separate herds of about five thousand purebred Shorthorns and three thousand purebred Herefords as stud stock for the upbreeding of his range herds. The beef was better, but the cattle were not hardy, did not reproduce well, nor were they adept at foraging in the Texas heat. Derek learned from Johnny Bell that the Shorthorns and Herefords ran two to four degrees of fever when they stood exposed to the blazing South Texas summer sun. The insects of the coastal flats swarmed over them and they suffered from screwworm, cancer-eye and other diseases. During the roundups, the Barons branded only fifty percent of their normal cash stock.

Matt, following in his father's footsteps, had begun experimenting with other breeds, crossing the Shorthorn with the Brahmin blood from India. But he had still been a long way from improving his stock and he was faced with mounting debts. He was fighting with the tax appraisers and the government over his father's estate. By the time of the stock-market crash in 1929, Matt Baron had owed more than three million dollars on the estate he'd inherited from his father, Anson Baron.

Before Ethan graduated from the University of Texas, he had urged his father to lease land to one of the oil companies. When Matt signed with Sherco Oil, he was able to obtain a loan for more than three million dollars. Interest was at five percent; $500,000 of the principal was due in five years, and the remainder in twenty.

There were now a hundred oil-producing wells on the Baron ranches. These produced anywhere from fifty to a hundred and fifty barrels a day. Not a bonanza, but steady. Ben Killian's Box B had yet to earn an income from oil, and the Rocking A had but a dozen or so wells, although explorations continued on millions of acres of southwestern Texas lands. The Longerbeams were making more from oil than from cattle as the price of crude hovered at around fifty cents a barrel.

Ethan, with Lou's approval, tried to take control of the Box B after Matt died, but Derek showed surprising strength. With Ethan embroiled in politics, the eldest son was no match for Derek. Aunt Lou gracefully stepped aside, realizing that Derek might perhaps be the natural heir to Matt's boots. Whenever they argued about Derek's handling of ranch business, Grace stepped in and tried to mollify the situation. There was no open hostility between the brothers, but Derek ran the ranch with an iron hand and his mother backed him up. Later on, Lou did the same, for which Derek was grateful. He was fond of his aunt and knew if it came to a showdown, he'd be the underdog. Most of the hands would kill for Lou, and she could whip three quarters of them in a fistfight.

Late in the afternoon, after they had inspected the other Braunviehs, Derek asked Hector to stay behind.

"Want to talk to you about something," he said.

"All right."

They walked away from the house while Grace and Ora were cleaning up the sandwiches and lemonade.

"You ever see Bone anymore?" Derek asked.

"I've been looking for him."

"Me too."

"I know. He turned Ernie in for a hit-and-run that happened a long time ago. Ernie might go to prison. He's in pretty bad shape, worrying over it."

"We've got to get Bone out of that brush," said Derek. "He's stealing cattle right and left. Running them across the Rio Grande into Mexico."

"The sonofabitch," said Hector. "I know he is. From us, too."

"I flew over the *brasada* the other day, but couldn't spot his camp. What happened to the shack he used to live in?"

"I burned it down every time he got comfortable."

Derek laughed.

"Someday, let's go in there and camp and stay until we get the bastard."

"I go in there all the time. One of these days I'll catch him."

"I'd like to be there when you do."

"If there's a chance, I'll take you with me. He's pretty sneaky."

"One of these days we ought to make up a posse. You, me, Steve, maybe, and just hunt Bone and his bunch down like outlaws."

"Aw, they don't do that anymore," said Hector.

"Well, we might. I dream about it sometimes."

"Me, too," said Hector wistfully. "But I don't know about Steve. He hasn't said much to me since the fight."

"Yeah, I heard about it. What's he got against you, anyway?"

"Bad blood," said Hector cryptically.

Derek shrugged. It was none of his business, really. He liked Hector, hated what Bone had done to him. Steve had turned out all right. He had been a big help on the last roundup, and Ben Killian had given his son high marks when the Baron bunch had helped the Lazy K on their gather.

"Turn him over to the sheriff if we get Bone, Heck?"

"Turn him over to the devil," said Hector.

"Good," said Derek, slapping Hector lightly on the back. "You and your daddy getting along all right?"

Hector's face darkened. He scowled. He no longer referred to Ernesto as his father, and called him by his given name. But, in public anyway, he referred to Ernie as his father just to save getting into unresolvable arguments.

"He pretty much leaves me alone."

"Well, you get a line on Bone and need any help, you just call me, hear?"

"I'll do that, Derek," said Hector. Then, after a pause, when he looked sharply into Derek's eyes, he said, "Thanks."

Derek met his look with a hard glance of his own.

"I'm not forgetting that Bone killed Tom Casebolt, Heck. He's not going to get away with it—or anything else. His note's long overdue."

Hector choked up, nodded.

"Be seeing you, Derek."

"So long, Heck."

He watched Hector, lugging the camera, go to his car, get in. A moment later Hector was gone. Grace came out and stood by her son.

"He's a funny boy," she said.

"He's not a boy, Mother. I like him."

"Nobody else does."

"That's because he's different, not a flap-mouth."

"Well, he seems strange to me."

Derek smiled indulgently. "Mother, everyone seems strange to you."

34

SHERCO HAD DRILLED a lot of wells, but they were all failures. With petroleum so cheap, Derek Baron could not have begun to pay off the ranch's heavy debts. The same held true for Ernesto Aguilar, Ben Killian, Martin Longerbeam and the other ranchers, until Derek had stepped in and read chapter and verse to Keith Sherwood.

"From now on, Keith," Derek said, "I'll scout the oil my way and I'll tell your crews where to drill."

"It's my money that's paying for the exploration."

"It's my goddamned land that you're fucking with."

"I'll see what Ethan thinks. He has a say in this, too. He was the one who brought your father to my table."

"Ethan has no say whatsoever."

Ethan bristled when Sherwood told him what his brother had said. But Ethan had not been about to show an outsider the vulnerable underbelly of the Baron family.

"Derek runs the ranch," Ethan told Keith. "If you want to make Sherco Oil work, you'd better give him what he wants. And Aunt Lou will back him all the way. Mother, too."

Sherwood buckled under and Derek began to put his plan to work.

Derek met with Sherco's top geologist, Frank Anthony, and asked him pointed questions about the kind of terrain where they might find oil.

"Could we spot a likely formation from the air?" Derek asked.

"It's possible. We could cover a lot of ground, at least, if you could fly low enough."

Derek grinned. "I can fly so low you'll be able to count the red ants."

Derek and Frank flew to other oil fields, talked to wildcatters, stern-faced loners who, like the prospectors of old, had visions of deep, dark pools of oil, riches beyond any poor man's dreams.

Derek learned quickly. He forced Sherwood to draw up new contracts, made the stipulation that Sherco not do any wildcatting, but investigate already defined oil structures on the edges of the Baron properties in Texas. Derek knew about that business of wildcatters in East Texas striking oil and the state getting into a battle with the United States over it.

Frank flew over the vast Baron holdings with Derek flying his new Stinson like an Indian motorcycle with wings. They covered a lot of miles and began making test drills. When Derek was ready, he told Frank to call in Sherwood for the drilling.

In 1940, at the end of July, Ethan stood with his brother, Derek, and watched Sherco Oil bring in the first producing well on Baron land.

Sherco brought in other wells, all of them along the *brasada* but far from El Rincón, where everybody else had been drilling for years with mediocre results.

Derek, when he saw the royalty checks rolling in, caught the black-gold fever. By July of 1941, the number of pumping derricks had tripled on the Box B. The price of petroleum slowly climbed higher.

But always in the back of his mind was the thought of Bone living in the *brasada*, somewhere near the new oil field. He had seen plenty of sign, but he hadn't seen the man since the day Bone killed Tom Casebolt.

What Johnny Bell and the other hands noticed, however, was that Derek was always looking. And Lou Baron was doing the same.

Peggy Baron seemed a new woman when she returned to the ranch from Houston. She was even wearing a dress, and she'd had her hair trimmed, marcelled.

"You look like a movie star," Grace told her. "Like Greta Garbo. Aunt Lou will be surprised. And pleased."

"Oh, Mother."

Grace had followed her daughter upstairs to her bedroom. Peggy hefted her suitcase up on the pink bedspread, opened it, began taking out her clothes. Ora Cornejo, the maid, had kept her room cleaned, the bed made. The room was done in muted pink and lavender pastels, from bedspread to walls to bureau and dressing table. A large bookcase dominated one wall. It was crammed with books that Peggy had read, from *The Bobbsey Twins* to Charles Dickens, all of the *Lassie* books, Zane Grey, B. M. Bower, Owen Wister's *The Virginian*. She pulled a copy of Eric Ambler's *The Mask of Dimitrios* from her suitcase and placed it on one of the bookshelves, right next to C. S. Forester's *Captain Horatio Hornblower*. Stacks of magazines—*The Saturday Evening Post*, *Liberty* and *Life*—bulged from a wooden magazine stand next to an overstuffed chair, reupholstered in a darker lavender. Peggy carried her toiletries over to the dressing table, with its purple and light lavender trim, set out her brush, comb, lipstick and mascara in front of a small jewelry tray she had bought at Woolworth's in Dallas when she was twelve.

"Did you meet someone nice in Houston?"

"Oh, I met a lot of nice people. Jim Goff is an angel, you should hear him play and sing, sounds just like Bob Wills, and Luke has turned into quite a gentleman, not the rakehell he used to be. They have a wonderful office downtown with drawing boards, typewriters, they know an awful lot about advertising. They even do radio commercials and write a lot of copy for newspapers all over Texas. I had a wonderful time and, Mother, Luke wants me to come and work in his agency."

"Oh, Peggy, I don't know. Houston's so far away and I'm all alone here most of the time. Ethan hardly ever visits and Derek's always gone from dark to dark."

"Where is Derek, anyways? I want to chew the fat with him 'bout this. I want his blessing."

Grace winced at Peggy's crude language. Her daughter had always been something of a tomboy, but since her father's death, she had begun to speak more like the cowhands than a young lady of refinement and good breeding.

"Derek?" her mother asked. "You always went to your big brother, Ethan, when you wanted to talk about something serious."

"Oh, Mother, Eth is a bigshot in Austin now and wears white Palm Beach suits all the time. He's always on the phone or sitting with a bunch of men in baggy suits who smoke cigars. Derek is more like me."

"He didn't use to be."

"Well, Dare's grown up now."

"Something you might consider doing, young lady. I think Derek's coming over from La Golondrina this morning. He'll be here directly."

"Oh, Mother, I'm so excited about this job. Luke thinks I have real talent."

Grace's eyebrows arched like a pair of inchworms going over twin bumps.

"Talent? For what?"

"He thinks I could write advertising copy. I sent him some of the stuff I wrote in school."

"Oh, that," said her mother.

"Well, Luke thought it was good," said Peggy, stung by her mother's indifference. She walked to the closet with a folded skirt, opened the double doors.

"Well, you'd better talk it over with one of your brothers—I don't care which one—because Houston is a dirty little city with a lot of temptation."

"Oh, goody," said Peggy, hanging the skirt on a wooden hanger.

"Snot!" said her mother.

Derek taxied the little eighty-horse Stinson to the hangar, shut down the engine. The prop stuttered to a stop. He climbed out, carrying a small duffel bag. He put chocks under the wheels and hooked up the tie-downs just as Peggy, changed now into a pair of boy's Levi's and wearing a light-blue cotton pullover, a blue ribbon tied around her hair, ran toward him on the wobbly heels of new boots.

"Peggy!" Derek exclaimed, grinning. "You're back!"

She rushed toward him. He dropped his bag, grabbed his big sister on the fly, lifted her from the ground. She pecked him on the forehead.

"Muscles," she said.

"We just finished haying La Golondrina," he said, setting her back down on the ground. "I've got muscles I never even knew I had."

"Good crop?"

"The best ever. How was Houston?"

"So-so," she said coyly.

"Ha. I'll bet. Ethan called me over at La Golondrina and said he'd already heard Keith Sherwood raving about your beauty. He must have been into the hard stuff."

"Oh, Derek, did he tell you I was there? Keith's giving Luke's advertising agency a big oil account."

"Gulf? Texaco?"

"No, silly. Sherco Oil. He's putting in gas stations clear across Texas."

"Hoo-eee. Just to think that a few short years ago, nobody thought gasoline was worth shit."

"You ought to take a gander at Keith's new secretary. She's some punkins. She'd be perfect for you. She's got brains, which is more than I can say for the white trash you've been diddling over to Baronsville."

"Now, now, Peg, don't be runnin' them fillies down. I put a smile on their faces, a sparkle in their eyes and money in their pockets."

"Want to talk to you, baby brother," she said suddenly.

"Do you have an appointment? I got hogs to slop, horses to curry, cows to milk, sluts to put the boots to."

"Oh, shush," she said. "This is serious."

Derek stepped back, looked at his sister as if he had never seen her before.

"You look some different," he drawled.

She fluffed her hair, primped for him.

"Not that," she said. "I did get my hair cut, though."

"Looks like they emptied a peroxide bottle on it."

"Now, that's not very complimentary, Dare."

"You look pretty as a palomino foal what's been slicked up by its mama's tongue." Derek picked up his duffel bag, slung it over his shoulder. "Where do you want to talk, Sis?"

"Let's find us a stump or a nail keg to sit on. I don't want to go back to the house just yet."

"Sure," he said, seeing that she was serious. "Let's go over to the ranch office. It's quiet in there. I need to get steady. I ran into all kinds of air bumps on the way back. I think my stomach's still up there."

Peggy laughed, hooked her arm in Derek's. Together, they walked over to the office. Derek unlocked it and they went inside.

"Coffee?"

"No," she said.

"Something stronger?"

"Derek, don't be mean."

"Just checking," he said.

"I'm going to live in Houston," she said, sitting in her daddy's chair behind the desk. Derek sat in the one where Johnny Bell usually sat when they were going over ranch business. The desk was clean, for a change, except for a tattered *Farmer's Almanac* that lay on the edge nearest the map- and chart-stickered wall.

"Big move," he said, plunking his bag down at his feet.

"Luke and Jim Goff want me to work in their advertising agency." She told him all of it, the words coming in a rush, tumbling from her mouth with hardly a pause for breath. "I want to live my own life, on my own, make something of myself. I mean, Ethan's got his politics and you've got the ranch. All I have is a headful of dreams."

"Is that what you really want to do, Peg?"

"Derek, don't you ever look at life real close? I mean get down in the dirt and look into its beady little eyes?"

"Some, I guess. Since Daddy died, I've felt pretty goddamned mortal."

"Well, when Daddy died, I just thought the world was going to end. I was so angry, so damned mad that he killed himself. I don't know how you can stand to work with Johnny Bell after that."

"Johnny didn't give Daddy that strychnine."

"Well, who did?"

Derek told her.

"Why did Daddy take poison? I've thought of that a thousand times. I thought he'd shoot himself. I really did. I knew he was suffering. Aunt Lou and I talked about it."

"You did?" asked Derek, leaning forward in his chair.

"Well, sure. That's the way Grandpa died."

"Are you kidding me?"

"Didn't you know? Grandpa Anson up and blew his brains out when the TB got so bad he couldn't breathe without spraying everybody with blood. Aunt Lou told me so."

"Well, Jesus H. Christ," said Derek. "I never knew."

"So you see why I thought Daddy would do the same thing. Grandpa took that Yellow Boy of Daddy's and walked out to that big old live oak in the back yard and put the barrel in his mouth and pulled the trigger. That's what Aunt Lou told me."

"Good Christ. Well, that explains something, anyways."

"What?" she asked.

"Why Daddy didn't blow his brains out. I asked Johnny if he knew about the poison."

"What'd he say?"

"He said he didn't know about it, but that Daddy had talked about, you know, suicide. He told Johnny that he didn't want me or you or Mother, Ethan or Aunt Lou to see him die a horrible death. He said he didn't want to mess up the house or have anyone have to clean up after him. So Johnny knew Daddy was thinking about it for a long time."

Peggy sighed. With relief, Derek thought.

"Well, now I know," she said. "And I know Aunt Lou knows our daddy didn't just up and die, too."

"So, now you don't have to run away to Houston," said Derek.

Peggy looked across the desk at her brother. She smiled. "Oh, I'm going to Houston," she said. "I've already found an apartment, sharing with a girl who works for Luke and Jim. She's younger than me, homely as a mud fence, but sweet, you know?"

"Sure."

"I just wanted your blessing. Your good wishes, maybe."

"You've got both. What about this Jim Goff?"

"Oh, he's interesting. He's got a country band he calls the 'Cosmopolitan Cowboys.' They sound a lot like Bob Wills and his Texas Playboys. Jim plays guitar and sings just like Wills, but sounds some like Hank Williams, too."

"I didn't know you were interested in music," said Derek.

"I'm interested in everything. I want to write, to be a writer."

"What's that?" he said, pretending total ignorance.

"I want to live life and write about it."

"I can't think of anything more worthless," he teased.

"Derek, don't you be like Mother."

"Me, like Mother? Why, she'd have your hide if she knew you'd said that."

They laughed together.

"Well, you come visit us, Peg," he said, as he stood up.

"No, you come and visit me," she said.

"Either way. I wish you luck."

Peggy got up from behind the desk, ran to him and threw her arms around his neck. She kissed him quickly on the lips. "There, now," she said. "I can go with a clear conscience."

"You didn't need my approval, Peg."

"No, but I wanted it. I'm so excited, Dare. You might even hear me on the radio doing an advertisement."

"Well, why not? I hear Ethan every so often, talking on the news. He's getting to be about as popular as Carter's Little Liver Pills."

Derek locked the office and they walked toward the house, arm in arm.

He looked at the live oak in the back yard, a leafy umbrella over the new patio, and thought about his grandfather, and his own father. He thought, too, about that Yellow Boy Winchester in his father's den.

He wondered why his daddy had never told him the story behind that rifle.

35

ELENA AGUILAR WOULD always remember that cool September day in 1941. Not only that, but she would remember the exact time, 8:02 in the morning, when she answered the telephone that Wednesday on the third of the month.

Elena stood at the sink, scrubbing the breakfast dishes with a sponge. Alicia was drying.

"Turn down the radio, Alicia," Elena said.

"I'll get it," said Hector, who had come into the kitchen to fill his canteen before riding out to look for some missing cattle with Paco Velez. The radio was blaring a nasal-toned singer belting out "San Antonio Rose" on KBVR, Baronsville's new radio station.

Alicia stepped aside, the dish towel in her hands.

"I'm late, Mama," she said, hanging the dish towel on the counter. She leaned over, kissed her mother's cheek. No longer able to afford luxury the Aguilars had let their maid go the year before.

"Be careful," said Elena as she reached for a towel to dry her soap-flocked hands.

The phone rang four times before she picked up the receiver, just as Hector turned the dial on the radio. Bob Wills's voice went tinny, the words of the song no longer intelligible.

"Hello," she said into the mouthpiece of the upright phone on the small table by the door.

Hector turned the tap, held the canteen under the spigot. He looked at his mother. Elena was not saying anything, just listening.

"No," she said. She looked up at Hector. "Just a minute, I'll find out."

She covered the mouthpiece with her hand.

"Hector, do you know where your father is?"

Hector nodded.

"Well, where is he?"

"Shoeing that two-year-old gelding with Old Silvino."

"Tell him to come quick. There's trouble, I think."

Hector finished filling the metal canteen, capped it. His mother took her hand off the mouthpiece and put the receiver back to her ear. "He's in the barn. Hector's going to get him. What's the matter?"

There was a long pause.

"I see," said Elena. She saw that Hector was still standing there. She shooed him away silently, a scowl tightening the skin around her lips and eyes.

"O.K.," she said. Then, to Hector: *"Andale."*

"What's the matter?" he asked.

"Just a minute, Mr. Kearney," she said. She took the receiver away from her ear, but didn't bother to cover the mouthpiece.

"Go and get your father, Hector. It's very important. I think the sheriffs are going to arrest him."

Hector set down the canteen and stalked to the back hallway.

"No, wait a minute," said Elena. "Mr. Kearney wants to talk to you before you bring your father."

"Me?"

Elena pursed her lips tightly, shook the phone at her son as if it was a relay baton.

Hector walked back into the kitchen, took the receiver from his mother's trembling hand. He leaned down to speak into the mouthpiece. "Sir?"

Hector listened intently, nodding every few moments. His mother strained to hear Kearney's voice on the other end of the line.

"All right. Sure. I'll tell him. Yes, she's still here." Hector paused, listening to Kearney once again. The receiver crackled with the distorted metallic sounds of filtered speech, a tinny, off-key language that Elena couldn't translate. "Yes, I think so." Another pause, pauses in between his replies. "Not too well. I know it worries him. A lot. Yes. Yes. All right. Here she is."

He handed the phone to his mother, straightened up.

"He wants to tell you something, Mama. He told me to have Papa call him right away. I've got to go get him real quick."

"Hurry," she said, then put the black cone of the receiver to her ear.

Ernie stared at the skeletal foot protruding from the ground. The rains had washed away one section of the manure pile. The General and his flock had gouged furrows in the grave, exposing a portion of a man's femur.

Silvino stood there, slowly shaking his head, muttering in Spanish. "'Sus Maria,'" said the handyman.

Ernie took the horseshoe nail from his mouth, gripped the hammer in his hand.

"So, it didn't work, did it?"

"There was much rain. The chickens, they scratch for the bones."

Ernie saw the fear in Silvino's eyes.

"How long has it been showing like that?"

"I do not know."

"Did anyone else see it?"

"I do not know," said Silvino. "Do you want me to cover it up again?"

"No, it wants to come up. God wants José Perez to come up."

Silvino crossed himself. The General, working a patch on top of the heap, clucked a warning as Ernie stepped closer to the grave. Two of his hens were fighting over a grub. One of the others had a bug in her beak, was trying to turn away from another who eyed it lustfully. The General fixed a golden eye on Ernie as the rancher squatted down.

"I should have told someone," said Aguilar. "I know Bone killed this man."

"Si, Patron."

Ernie stood up, his shoulders sagging. "So, the rain washed the shit away," Ernie said to no one.

"Goddamned fucking chickens," said Silvino. "I am sorry."

The General flapped his wings, started clawing in the manure heap, still keeping his eyes on the two men.

"They'll still blame me," said Ernie.

"I can cover him up again."

"No," said Ernie. "It does not make any difference anymore. Come, let us finish shoeing the horse."

"*Si, Patron.*"

Ernie stuck the nail back in his mouth. He looked up as he saw Hector running toward him from the house.

"*Ay de mi,*" murmured Silvino.

Ernie tore the nail out of his mouth, threw it to the ground. He handed Silvino the hammer. "Finish shoeing the horse," he said softly.

Silvino took the hammer. He did not answer, but he shook his head ever so slightly as Hector drew closer. When no one was looking he crossed himself quickly, murmured a short prayer in Spanish.

The drone of Alicia's car engine drowned out the slam of the door as Hector dashed out. Elena sank down in the chair. The disk jockey's voice crackled faintly on the Philco radio sitting on the kitchen counter. Tears began to form in her eyes like tiny crystal beads. They welled up, flowed together in larger droplets, then trickled down her face, down lines already etched in her skin by the hard years.

Elena hung up the phone, missing the cradle twice before she anchored it. The butter-yellow walls of the room swam before her eyes. She got up slowly, lightheaded, and walked down the short hall to the back door. She looked through the screen, saw Hector and Ernie walking briskly toward her.

Ernie looked old at that moment, and Hector, taller than his father, straighter, lighter of skin, reminded her of Ben Killian. The tears burst from their ducts suddenly and she gave a sharp cry and turned to go back into the kitchen. She grabbed a dry dish towel and crushed it to her face. She reached down inside herself and found the steel she needed, the quiet center where she could compose her thoughts and look strong for her husband.

By the time the men entered the room, Elena was composed. She managed a flaccid smile.

"Do not worry, Ernesto," she said. "Everything will be all right. Come, Hector, let us wait for your father in the livingroom. You can use this phone. I wrote down Mr. Kearney's number."

"I know the number," said Ernie somberly.

Hector took his mother's arm, led her from the room as his father sat down to call Jack Kearney. They went into the livingroom. His mother pulled the drapes open, flooded the worn Karastan rug, the

Sears & Roebuck furniture, with light. Hector leaned against the fireplace.

"Sit down," she said. "We have to . . ."

"Have to what, Mama?"

"Your father—"

"I don't bear him no grudge," he said, but she knew he was pouting. For some reason—worry or concern or puzzlement—she didn't know which.

"He's your father—"

"Stop it," he said. "I know. He's the only one I have, the only one I'm likely to get."

"You mustn't let him know how you feel."

Hector pushed off the cold bricks of the hearth and swung toward the divan. His mother stood in the center of the room, straight as an Indian, her head held proudly high.

"You sit down, too," he said. "You look like you're guarding something, or waiting for more bad news."

"What did Mr. Kearney tell you?" she asked as she sat in her rocking chair by the window.

"He said the sheriffs had finally put together a case, might charge Papa with the murder of Lucy Naylor."

"Yes," she said. "He told me the same thing."

"He thinks Papa should be prepared for the worst. He asked me if he had been acting odd lately. I didn't tell him the whole story."

"You should not. Your papa will be fine once this is done with. He didn't kill that little girl on purpose. Bone was still drunk. He grabbed your father's arm. The car swerved and—"

"Don't, Mama," Hector said, his voice laden with a surprising tenderness. "I just think Papa's been acting strange lately. Talking to himself, praying all the time, begging God for forgiveness. It's embarrassing."

"He is very sad over what happened. He wishes to make amends. Did you know he had been sending money to the little girl's family all these years?"

"No," said Hector, and drew a revitalizing breath into his lungs, let the air out in a sigh.

They heard Ernesto coming and said no more.

"Jack wants me to turn myself in before that deputy, Naylor, picks me up," said Ernie. "He says I'm going to be arrested, charged with murder."

"How does he know?" asked Elena.

"He said Wilma Sisler has been keeping an eye on the case for him. Naylor went before Judge Chowney early this morning. He got a warrant for my arrest."

"Oh, no!" exclaimed Elena.

Hector arose from the divan. "You want me to drive you in, Papa?"

Ernesto looked stunned, bewildered. His eyes glanced around the room as if searching for just the right religious icon to focus on. He avoided the light from the window, as if it was a spotlight searing him in the glare of his own guilt.

"I—I must think," he said.

"We will leave you," said Elena, rising from her chair.

"No, I will go to my room," said Ernie. "Hector, I will speak to you for a few moments. Come."

Hector followed his father upstairs. At the top, Ernie turned and looked down at Elena, who stood in the sunlight streaming through the front window.

"We will talk when Hector and I have finished," he said.

"Then you are going to turn yourself in to the *policia?*" she asked.

"I will leave soon," he said.

Hector entered the little den off his parents' bedroom, where his father kept his records and books. It was small, dark, stacked with papers and ledgers. There was a painting of Jesus on the wall, his tormented face staring into infinity, a golden light surrounding the thorns attached like a sadistic crown to his head. Trickles of blood seeped from the thorn wounds onto his forehead. There was a two-way radio on one of the shelves, a spindle on the desk, skewering feed bills, receipts, grocery bills. A gun case contained Ernie's hunting rifles, drawers held his pistols. A Colt .45 hung from a worn leather holster and gun belt draped on a peg at the side of the cabinet. Hector saw his reflection in the glass that encased the rifles.

"Sit," said Ernie. Hector sat, but Ernie stood at the window, looking out over the grass-thick pasture beyond the shade trees.

"I'm sorry, Papa . . ."

Ernie turned from the window, looked at his son.

"No, it is I who am sorry, my son. I should never have let Bone blackmail me. I should have confessed to hitting the little girl ten, twelve years ago. It was a mistake."

Hector said nothing. He felt very uncomfortable seeing his father grovel in front of him. For all of his faults, his papa had always been strong, with *mucho machismo*. Now, he looked old and beaten, shriveled up by time and drained of life by carrying a lie so long in his heart.

"I may go away for a long time. I want you to stay away from Bone. He is a bad man. He has cost me much. Will you promise me that?"

"Papa, I hate Bone, too. But that is not a promise I can keep. If I see him, I will fight him. Maybe kill him."

"No, you must stay away from him. There is something very *malo* about him. I am afraid for you."

"I'll do my best to stay out of Bone's way," said Hector, standing up.

Ernie walked over to his son, put a hand on his shoulder. He had to look up at Hector, who was six inches taller.

"Once, when my grandfather was alive, we owned all the land in this county. He sold some to Matt Baron's great grandfather. Then, he sold more and more. My father sold off still more. It was as if we were destined not to live here at all."

"I don't believe that, Papa."

"Land is something that is taken from you if you don't fight for it. Even then, the cost may be too high. This land has been very dear for the Aguilar family. It has cost much. Way too much."

"It's worth it," said Hector.

"Is it? It is soaked with blood, the blood of my grandfather, the blood of my father. I can smell the blood. Can you smell it?"

Ernie looked out the window, his eyes glazed with mist. Hector did not answer. He felt a lump from in his throat, choking him.

"You pay in blood," Ernie said cryptically. He was silent for a long time. Hector looked up at him, cleared his throat. Ernie looked down at Hector.

"My son," he said.

"You want me to drive you into town?"

"No, that is not necessary. I will go by myself."

"Yes, Papa."

"Goodbye, son. Tell your mama to come up and I will speak to her."

Hector, choking to hold back a sob, nodded dumbly, left the room.

Ernie waited by the door for Elena. When she came into the room, he embraced her.

"I will go," he said. "I love you very much, Elena."

"I love you, too, Ernesto," she said, and the tears burned her eyes, washed down her cheeks. He held her tightly, felt her pounding heart against his.

"Have Hector bring the car out front," he said. "Do you want to ride to town with me?"

"I don't know if I could bear to see you go to jail," she said.

"Will you visit me?"

"Yes," she said. He chucked her under the chin, tilted her face toward his.

"Be brave. Now, leave me some moments to take some things with me that I will need."

"Yes, my husband."

She started to leave.

"Elena . . ."

"Yes?"

"Tell Hector someday soon, will you?"

"Tell him what?" Elena tried to look surprised.

"About Ben Killian. About his father."

"You know?" she asked.

"I have known since before he was born. I can count."

"But—"

"It is nothing, my dearest. I have always thought of him as my son and myself as your only husband."

She broke down then, and sobbing, left the room.

Halfway down the stairs, she heard someone knocking on the front door.

"See who it is," she told Hector.

Hector nodded and went to the door.

A moment later, as she reached the bottom of the stairs, an explosion from upstairs deafened her. She stiffened, went cold with fear.

She turned, raced back upstairs. Behind her, she heard voices, Hector's and another man's. Then, footsteps thumping down the hallway to the livingroom. She ran to Ernie's office, pushed on the door.

Her husband sat in his chair, slumped over his desk, a bullet in his temple. He had cleared the papers off his desk. A pool of blood formed under his head. A smoking pistol lay next to his hand. Raymond Naylor entered the room a moment later, Hector right behind him. Elena stood there, transfixed in horror, frozen with shock and grief.

"Jesus God," murmured Naylor. He stepped over to the desk, put two fingers just under Ernie's left ear. There was no pulse.

Elena stared at him, her eyes brimming with tears.

"What do you want?" she snapped angrily.

"I guess it don't matter no more, ma'am. Your husband, well, he's gone. I'll have to call Doc Emberlin to come out and sign a death certificate, report this to Sheriff Blanchard. I'm right sorry. Anybody you want me to call? Anything I can get for you?"

"No," she said, squaring her shoulders. She looked at the papers in the deputy's hand. He put them inside his shirt, looked sheepishly at his feet.

Hector came up behind his mother, gripped her shoulders. He stared at the top of Ernie's head, looked at the gun case. The pistol on the desk was the one that had been holstered a few moments before.

"Give us a minute," he told Naylor.

"I can't leave now."

"I know. My mother and I just want to say goodbye."

"I'll stand at the door."

Hector clenched his fists. It took all of his willpower to keep from striking Naylor.

Ray stepped to the doorway, watched as mother and son embraced wordlessly.

Hector said something under his breath. He could not have recalled what he said if anyone had asked him only seconds after he spoke. Elena murmured her husband's name, bade him farewell in Spanish. *"Adiós, mi corazón."*

Hector looked at the dead man who had been his father all these years, and was filled with a deep regret that he had never given Ernie the chance to show his love for the one he had never called son.

Elena crossed herself.

"Come, my son, let us go. There is nothing more we can do for your father."

"Mama . . ."

She touched a finger to his lips. They stopped at her bedroom, where she took a black shawl from the bottom drawer of her dresser.

"Let us pray," she said, her voice distant, as if she was in a trance. She began murmuring a prayer in Spanish as Hector led her downstairs. She walked to the window and drew the drapes closed. Then, she sat down in her rocking chair and drew the shawl tightly over her head, crossed it at her throat.

"I'm going to call Alicia," said Hector softly.

"She has not had time to get to work, but yes. Yes, call your sister. Just tell her to come back home right away."

Hector picked up the phone in the livingroom, heard Naylor's voice on it.

He couldn't help overhearing the deputy and the Sheriff speaking.

"Well, goddamnit, Raymond, you satisfied now?"

"Hell, I didn't know—"

"No, you sure as hell didn't. I'll be right out. I'll bring Doc."

Hector put the receiver back on the hook, stood there watching his mother rock slowly back and forth, her lips moving in soundless supplication to God, begging him to take Ernesto Aguilar's soul into heaven.

A wave of sadness engulfed Hector at that moment and his mind surged upward from the abyss of self-pity, leaped to a point beyond where he now stood, wrestling with the bewildering suddenness of grief. He thought of Bone out there in the *brasada*, gloating over this death, smiling that wolf smile of his and laughing at what he had done.

For as surely as if he had taken the Colt .45 in his own hand, Bone had killed Hector's father in cold blood.

36

THE CATTLE HAD been showing a profit for years, and now the Baron ranch could settle all of its debts. Derek had designed and built special barns for the storage of hay harvested from twenty thousand acres of Rhodes grass, imported from Africa. He had the barns built on the pastures, each with a capacity of 175 tons. Cattle could feed themselves from them. By the fall of 1941, Derek had 75,000 acres plowed and planted in Rhodes grass.

Ethan came down from Austin to look over the new cattle breeds and the hardy grass that seemed impervious to the vagaries of Texas weather. The boys took a week to drive to the various ranches. When they returned, they had a drink together in the den, once Matt's now Derek's. Grace was in Houston, visiting Peggy, who had done well with Killian & Goff Advertising. They heard her voice in radio commercials all the time, and she often sent newspaper clippings of the ads she had created.

"Here's to you, Derek," said Ethan, holding up his shotglass of Rebel Yell.

"No, Eth, here's to you. You gave me a free hand and I appreciate it."

"I think Daddy would have done the same."

"Thanks, Ethan. That means a lot."

Derek clinked his glass against his brother's. They drank the smooth whiskey. Ethan lazed his long legs atop Derek's desk, pushed his Stetson back on his head.

"Now, I think it's time I took a wife," Ethan said suddenly.

"Hell, I didn't even know you had a girlfriend," said Derek.

"I don't. But I'm going over to Dallas and look around."

"Be careful."

"Got any suggestions, Dare?"

"Make sure she wants you for your body, not your money."

"What body?"

The brothers laughed, but Ethan left the next day for Austin, for some politicking, then drove to Dallas on business, and there he met several young ladies of marriageable age, from good families. They gushed and cooed over him and Ethan felt very uncomfortable. He was not very smart about women. He had been raised in the company of men, and his sister was a tomboy, his mother a shadowy mystery. He danced with the Dallas girls, sat up late in their parlors talking and drinking coffee, but he couldn't make up his mind about any particular one. They all seemed superficial, descendants of the giddy flappers, smoking cigarettes and drinking liquor as if those acts implied a worldliness and sophistication they didn't actually possess.

One day, when he was in the Sherco offices, in Houston, talking to Keith Sherwood, Keith's secretary walked in and Ethan was smitten. She brought coffee for the two men and Ethan couldn't take his eyes off her. Keith, some years Ethan's senior noticed that his friend's eyes seemed to be frozen in their sockets as Samantha Deane glided across the room, graceful in high-heeled patent-leather pumps. When the door closed after she left the room, Ethan was still staring at it like a man bitten by the paralzying fangs of a sidewinder.

"Ethan, you're going to spill that coffee in your lap and start talking in a high-pitched voice."

"Huh?" Ethan jerked his head, rattled his cup in its saucer. It took some deft manipulation to keep the hot brew from scalding him.

Sherwood, a man who had posed for the Calvert's whiskey ad campaign as a "Man of Distinction," now had graying sideburns, dark hair, dark hazel eyes. He was a fine golfer, one of the best wing shots in Texas, raised fine hunting dogs for his own pleasure and for gifts to his friends. He had made a fortune in oil and had invested in prime real estate in downtown Houston, along the river in San Antonio and some of the land between Dallas and Fort Worth that would later make him even wealthier than he already was. He liked

Ethan, had been his mentor since the young man had brought him out to the Baron ranch to meet Matt. Keith's son, Barr Sherwood, and Ethan had been roommates.

"Who is she?" asked Ethan.

Sherwood told him.

"Deane? Not—"

"Yes, she's Senator Deane's youngest daughter."

Senator Everett Leroy Deane was prominent in Texas politics, had been a close friend of FDR's. He was one of Ethan's heroes, but Ethan had never met the man, although he'd seen him at several political functions. Deane had been a state senator, now was in the U.S. Senate, and some had mentioned that he might take over as chairman of the Democratic Party one day. Wendell Willkie hated him with a passion because Deane was powerful and blocked many of Willkie's pet reforms.

"What's she doing here?"

Sherwood laughed, sat on the edge of his desk, toying with a miniature putter. His coffee sat untouched, for he never drank hot liquids until they cooled.

"She's working for Sherco this summer, as she did last, before going back to school for her master's degree in business administration. She's twenty-two, single, and has no steady beau. I don't think she's looking for a husband, but I'll introduce you if you want."

"I want," said Ethan.

"Why don't you invite her to dinner at our place," said Sherwood, picking up a putter from his desk and aiming it out the window. "I'm sure Mercedes won't mind. We'd love to do some matchmaking."

"Aw, Keith, don't make it sound worse than it is."

"Ethan, I've seen that look before. It's the look of a bull in the rut, of a stallion when he sniffs a mare in season. But I warn you. Sam's a mighty headstrong young lady. She's got ideas and that's always dangerous in a woman. Also, she shuns politicians like the plague. That's probably why you never met her at any of her father's political gatherings."

"I don't care. I'll do anything to meet her. I'll crawl out there and fling myself onto her desk and offer myself as a human sacrifice."

Sherwood laughed, put down his dwarf putter and pushed a button.

Samantha Deane opened the door.

"Mr. Sherwood?" she asked. Ethan stared at her, slack-jawed. She was tall, about five foot nine, with raven-dark hair, sea-blue eyes, a figure like a goddess, trim ankles, pert breasts. She wore her hair shoulder-length and it fell gracefully about her face. It was naturally curly and shone like a crow's wing.

"I'd like you to meet my friend Ethan Baron," said Keith. "It seems he has something to ask you."

"Would you have dinner with me?" asked Ethan. The sentence came out almost as one word.

"Why, I'd be delighted," she said, and her voice struck chords in Ethan's brain that transported him to ethereal regions.

"Ethan, this is Samantha Deane."

Ethan stood up, still holding the saucer in both hands. The cup slid forward, off the saucer. Coffee spilled on Ethan's trousers. Instinctively, Samantha rushed forward, grabbed the cup and saucer. She clasped Ethan's hand, led him from Keith's office into her own. She took him into the ladies' washroom and soaked paper towels in cold water, began working on the slacks to take out the coffee stains. Her touch was quite intimate and Ethan became aroused.

"My," she said with a smile, "Mr. Rosebud doesn't take much teasing, does he?"

Ethan was dumbfounded. He fell in love with Samantha instantly, but was tongue-tied, befuddled. He didn't understand it; he just knew that she was soft and beautiful and her hands were magic.

There was an ice-breaking supper at the Sherwoods', intimate dinners at the chic Dallas restaurants, dancing at the better nightspots, a trip to Austin to meet the senator and talk to his friend, Governor W. Lee O'Daniel. It was heady stuff for Ethan and he returned to the ranch walking two feet off the ground. He didn't say much to Derek, but he called Samantha every week and made several trips to Austin via Houston on weekends. For the time being, he kept Samantha a secret from his family.

Then, the eminent Texas senator, Morris Sheppard, died. O'Daniel, without consulting Ethan, walked away from the governor's office to fill the post left vacant by Sheppard. Lieutenant Coke Stevenson stepped into the gubernatorial seat and the state automatically went back to the kind of government it had always had.

"Well, there's no accounting for people," said Ethan sadly, when he talked it over with Derek. "Lee had God on his side and when he left office, he took Him along with him to Washington."

"It won't be so bad," said Derek. "O'Daniel was a fluke. Coke has given us a government of Texas, for Texans, by a Texan. That's what everybody wants anyway."

And Ethan knew Derek was right.

"Well, I'm going after the job," he said. "And I'm going to win."

"When?"

"When I'm as well known as Lee O'Daniel," he replied with confidence.

"Go to it, Ethan. Make us proud."

Silvero drove the haywagon between the evenly spaced rows of shorn alfalfa. April and the other children stood along one row, pitching hay into the wagon as it passed, their hayforks swinging up and down like the shuttles on a loom. Mother Jane anchored the line of women on the opposite row, stood leaning on her hayfork as the wagon creaked ahead, drawn by two old dray horses wearing blinders, laboring scarcely at all in the traces, plodding with a slow-motion precision as they tugged the wagon forward, inch by inch. These were great docile beasts, trained not to feed or stray from their path. They lifted their hooves in graceful motion as they had for thirty-odd years, not only on pasture, but in Baronsville parades when their cargo was a nativity scene of cardboard wisemen bearing gifts of gold, Frankincense and myrrh, shepherds standing with crooked staffs beneath a silver foil star, or pumpkins and cornstalks and hay bales at harvest time. They appeared to be moving out of some old-world pastoral painting, wraiths in a German landscape suddenly animate after centuries of hanging on a dimlit tavern wall along the Rhine.

Motes of alfalfa dust danced and dangled in the still afternoon air, dull green lights swirling aimlessly like antic insects stirred up from the soil. Mother Jane stifled a sneeze, then staggered as if struck in the chest by a sixteen-pound maul. She gasped for breath and the pain spread through her upper body, shot down her left arm and nestled beneath her shoulder blades, burning, smothering, tearing at her flesh like meathooks.

She dropped her hayfork and lurched forward, her right arm lifted in silent supplication.

"Silvero," she gasped, but her voice did not carry above the creaking of the wagon, the rustle of hay thunking into its bed, the rattle and jingle of harnesses. The wagon moved slowly away and the children and women jumped and ran ahead of it, ready to pitch more mown alfalfa atop the growing mound. A boy jumped up onto the

bed and spread the hay evenly, then jumped back down again. He saw
Mother Jane, turned and spoke to Silvero.

"*Papá, mira.*"

Silvero turned around, saw Jane fall to the ground. He hauled in
on the reins, set the brake, leaped from the seat.

The children stopped laughing, stood mute as Silvero raced past
them.

"Where's he going?"

"What's wrong?"

The women fired questions after him.

Then, they all saw Mother Jane lying on the ground, doubled up
in agony. The women and children began to run toward her.

Silvero reached Jane first, knelt down beside her. Her face was
ashen, her eyes clenched in pain.

"What passes?" he asked in Spanish.

"My heart," she said.

"My God."

"It hurts, Silvero."

The women and children crowded around the stricken woman.
Silvero waved them away. He spoke to the women, told them to take
the children back to the wagon and wait. He told his wife to run to
the house and use the telephone to call Ben or Frances. He told her
to hurry.

Silvero laid Jane on her right side, stretched her legs out. He took
off his shirt, rolled it up and put it beneath her head.

He took her hand in his. Jane squeezed it tightly. Her face glistened strangely under a thin patina of cold sweat. He loosened the
top buttons of her blouse.

"Do you feel better?" he asked.

"Yes," she said. "Thank you, Silvero."

"We will get Doc Emberlin."

"Too late," she gasped. When she saw the concern on Silvero's
face, she smiled wanly.

Silvero murmured a brief prayer, a plea for the Virgin, with her
infinite mercy, to intercede with God on Mary's behalf.

He rubbed Jane's hand, her left arm. Jane relaxed, but her breathing was still shallow.

"I'll miss you, Silvero. Take care of Alice tonight, comfort her."

"You will not die," he said with mock sternness.

Jane rolled over on her back and smiled up at him. She looked beyond him to the sky, a cyanic blue, small patches of white clouds floating by. Just the way she liked it. She remembered lying in hayfields when she was a young girl and gazing up at the sky and wondering at its vast mystery, why it was so different during the day, almost empty, and so alive at night. She smelled the clover and the lespediza and alfalfa as if it was the first time she had smelled it. Her senses seemed so acute now, sharper than they ever had been. Everything was crystal and crisp and clear, the sky, the bleeding green field, Silvero's leathery face, his sweat-glistening bare chest, wiry with black hair, his shoulders smooth as a child's, his eyes deep and dark and moist, his jaw firm and his nose proud. He was beautiful in that moment and it was as if she could see inside him, see his soul shining and ancient and eternal and a feeling of goodness and peace washed through her, warm and loving, soothing as aged sour-mash whiskey.

She knew her lips were moving, but she heard no sound except the soft erratic beat of her own heart and she listened to it slow down and falter, then rally for a brief moment. A surge of pain collapsed her eyes, filled them with sudden tears. The sky swam, liquid cerulean, when she opened her eyes again and then the pain went away and she floated somewhere beyond it, up and away from it, until she no longer heard the beating of her heart and she wondered at it as her brain filled with darkness and the sky blackened over and Silvero's face faded into it and she thought it strange that there were no stars, only blackness and nothingness, and then she was part of that night and did not see Silvero lean over her and put his ear to her mouth or feel him shake her, or hear him begin to weep shamelessly as he held her limp hand up to his face and drenched it with tears, rubbed it back and forth across his eyes as if to soothe himself, as if to hold onto her long enough for God to have mercy and save her soul from that final journey.

Ethan kept Samantha Deane a secret from Derek for more than two months.

They loaded the dogs—Lady Kay and Prancer, English pointers—in the back of the Ford pickup one morning early in November, 1941. Prancer was a liver and white denutted male, Lady Kay a freckle-faced bitch. They were deadbroke pointers, could work the brush on their own, find birds and retrieve without much talk or whistling from the Baron brothers.

Derek had been saving a pasture and brush border for just such a morning. The sky was battened down with rolls of gray clouds, no sun, and the air was cool. He could taste the salt on the chill Gulf breeze.

"I've been mixing raw eggs and bacon drippings in their chow," said Derek. "Lady Kay came in heat in October. She's going to run fine."

"They look fine," said Ethan.

"I put them in a roading harness last August to get them in shape. I roaded them horseback."

They turned the dogs loose, loaded shells into their double-barreled Browning 12-gauge shotguns. The dogs ranged, eyes bright, noses lifted to the wind. The brothers followed after them, walking carefully and quietly, their safeties on.

Prancer, ahead of the other dog, froze. Lady Kay slunk up to honor his point, stood shoulder to shoulder.

"They're moving," whispered Derek. The two men padded up as Prancer sidled a bit, then held. Derek walked into the covey of Gambels. The dogs stayed anchored and the birds scattered like wind-blown leaves. Ethan picked out a single, swung on it. He cracked off a shot, saw the sky empty, feathers fly. Derek's Browning boomed twice and two birds tumbled from the air, leaving tiny feathers hanging in the sky like dust.

Lady Kay and Prancer picked up the quail, held them in their tender mouths like eggs. Derek took the birds, gutted them, stuffed them in the pouch attached to the back of his hunting jacket. Ethan scratched behind the dogs' ears.

"Sit," said Derek and the two dogs lolled on the grass, tongues dangling. He gave them water, pouring it from his canteen. They lapped the water in midair and their eyes brightened. They lay there, noses poked high, turning their heads to sniff the vagrant zephyrs that wafted through the grasses.

"I've found her," said Ethan.

"I didn't know you'd lost her."

"A girl. I'm going to marry her."

"Have you asked her, Ethan?"

"I thought I'd invite her out for Christmas, give her a ring."

"Told Mother and Aunt Lou yet?"

"No, not yet, Dare. I will."

"Don't move too fast," said Derek.

"Hell, I can't move fast enough to suit me."

"I can't wait to meet her," said Derek.

When they returned home that evening, Grace met them at the door, after they had put the dogs away and cleaned twenty quail, put them in the locker in the office storeroom.

"Hector Aguilar called this afternoon, Derek. Said it was urgent. Then, Steve Killian called, wanted to know if you had talked to Hector. Then, Hector called back a few minutes ago. What do you think could be the matter?" she asked.

"I haven't the slightest idea," said Derek.

But he had a damned good hunch.

37

————■————

ETHAN HELPED DEREK pack for the trip to the Rocking A.
"This could be dangerous," he told his kid brother. "It's also
against the law."

"I'm just going hunting," said Derek. "Don't tell Aunt Lou where
I've gone."

"Rustlers? Christ, this isn't the Old West."

"Bone thinks it is."

He remembered talking to Hector on the telephone earlier that
evening.

"Still want to form that posse, Derek?" Hector had asked.

"You found Bone?"

"I've got a pretty good idea about his next move. He and his
bunch stole eighteen head of cattle and six horses. Bone broke that
Old Silvino's legs, busted his head with a pistol butt."

"Jesus. When do we leave?"

"Tomorrow morning before daylight. Steve's going with us. Just
us three. Bring enough food for a week, lots of ammunition, two good
horses, rifle and pistol. Better bring chaps and a slicker, your bedroll.
This ain't goin' to be no country ride."

"You're really serious, aren't you, Heck?"

"Dead serious."

"I'll be there," said Derek.

Derek still remembered the tingle in his blood when he hung up the phone.

He had been at Ernie's funeral, talked to Hector then, afterward. He knew the story behind Ernie's suicide, or some of it. Everything seemed to go back to Bone.

"Which rifle are you taking?" Ethan asked.

"The Yellow Boy," said Derek. He walked over to the wall, took the rifle down lovingly from the rack, held it to the light. The rifle was .44-caliber, shot smokeless powder. It had been his grandfather's rifle, his favorite, the one he had killed himself with. That was probably why Matt had never shot it. But Derek had snuck it out of the house once or twice and shot it. The rifle shot true.

"You really think you're a damned cowboy, don't you? You going to pack that Colt's hogleg?"

"You bet," said Derek, grinning.

"The West is dead. It died with Grandpa."

"Well, we're going to revive it for a little while, Ethan."

Hector blew on his fingers. His breath frosted the air under the barn lamp. Inside the barn, Steve Killian finished cinching up his horse, Rowdy, tied him to a post while he went after his second mount in the stall. Derek was outside, unloading his two horses from the stock trailer. One was already saddled. It had taken him ten hours at rattletrap speed to drive to Hector's.

"I'm ready, Heck, whenever you are."

"Soon as Steve gets his other horse out here, we can go."

Derek closed the gate on the trailer, led his horse, Brig, short for Brigand, over to the barn. He trailed the other QuarterHorse, Lance, packed with food and ammunition in canvas bags attached to a wooden pannier.

"This sure as hell is some expedition," said Steve as he strode from the barn with his two horses. Hector's horses stood hipshot in the shadows outside the building.

"Where to first?" asked Derek.

"Bone figures to leave the *brasada* about now. I'm going to cut around the bottom edge, see if we can't pick up the trail."

"Where do you figure he's headed?" asked Steve.

"Mexico," said Hector. "I've been down there a lot since Papa died and I found some people willing to talk. I know where he crossed the Rio and I know where he comes out."

"You want to take him on this side?" asked Derek.

"If I can. Hell, I don't want to wind up in a Mexican jail."

"What will you do if you find him?" asked Steve.

"What do you think?" said Hector.

"My sentiments exactly," said Derek.

"Jesus, I don't know," said Steve.

"It's not too late to back out," Hector told him.

Steve thought about it for a minute or two.

"Hell, no."

"Steve," said Hector, changing the subject. "When you get back home, tell your daddy I blew up that dam on Bandera Creek."

"You did?"

"Let's go," said Hector. He switched off the light in the barn. The General crowed as the three men rode off into the darkness. They might have stepped out of the previous century, with their battered Stetsons pulled down tight on their heads, their bedrolls tied behind the cantles of their saddles, their packhorses following them in military formation. Rifles jutted from leather boots and each man wore a pistol on his hip, their gunbelts bristling with cartridges.

Elena watched them leave from the kitchen window, the house so silent, it seemed full of ghosts.

The sky began to lighten as the three riders drifted past El Rincón, the end of the mesquite grove, the dark *brasada*. A rent appeared on the eastern horizon, pale as cream, and a coyote yipped from some distant point as if running from the dawn. A sleepy armadillo lumbered out of the way of the horses and they spooked a roadrunner when they were well past the brush, in open country dotted with cactus, clumps of sawgrass and gamma grown from seeds blown by the wind decades before.

Steve lit a cigarette. He was the only one of the three who smoked. The tip winked eerily in the predawn light. Saddle leather creaked and the sound of the horses' hooves seemed to carry on the heavy, wet air, tangy with the aroma of the sea.

"Derek," whispered Hector, "you range over yonder, to my right. Steve, you drift to the left. Keep your eyes peeled. If they've left the brush, they ought to leave a pretty good trail."

"Looks like they've been this way before," said Derek, noticing the scarred ground.

"Probably with Box B and Lazy K cattle, as well as some of ours."

"What'd Ben say when you told him where you were going?" asked Derek, before Steve rode off.

"I told him we were going 'possum hunting."

"That's about right," laughed Derek.

"More like rattlesnakes," said Hector, and there was no humor in his tone.

Bone sensed something was wrong.

"You take the point, Ned," he told the man riding next to him. "I'm going to drop back. Can't hear a damned thing with all this noise."

"Ummp," grunted Ned Feather. He was still a little drunk from the night before.

Jay Black Horse led the half dozen horses on a lead rope, rode fifty yards wide of the cattle. Eddie Blue Sky and Virgil Coldwater herded the eighteen head of prime Shorthorns across the broken prairie trail they had used so many times before.

"What's up, Bone?" asked Virgil as Bone rode past him.

"Nothin', maybe. Somethin' just don't seem right."

"You been smokin' too much Mary Jane."

Bone ignored him, rode a hundred yards down the back trail. There, he stopped his horse, listened. He wet a finger, tested the wind.

At first, there was nothing. He could not sort out the sounds. He heard the cattle and the horses, then those sounds receded as the herds got farther away.

He was about to ride back when he heard something he could not, at first, identify.

Bone waited.

Nothing.

Then, he heard it. The soft crunch of horses' hooves in the sandy soil. Far off. The sounds grew closer.

"Shit," he said.

He kicked his horse in the flanks, hauled hard on the reins to turn him around.

He rode at a gallop to catch up to the others.

"Ned," he called, "kick ass. Jay, you run them horses on up ahead a mile or two to that arroyo. Eddie, you and Virg prod them cows to a run."

"What the hell?" blurted Eddie.

"We got company. Somebody's follerin' us."

"Who?" asked Virgil.

"Probably that damned Hector and I don't know who all. Get a-movin'."

The Indians whipped the stock with the tips of their reins, got the cattle moving in a ragged line toward the arroyo some two miles distant. The cattle were fat from summer feed and lumbered along at a lope, well behind the friskier horses.

"What you gonna do, Bone?" asked Virgil.

"Hole up and see who it is. You be ready to shoot."

"Maybe it's the sheriff," said Eddie, who was already panting.

"Don't make me no nevermind. Sheriff or Aguilar, they ain't gonna stop us. Now, go on. I'll catch up to you."

Bone knew it had been too easy yesterday. There had just been that old Mexican and they broke his legs, beat him senseless when he started hollering. They got the cattle and horses and no one had stopped them.

He hoped it was Hector on his trail. He had the balls of a rabbit, that one.

Hector reined up.

"Hear that?" he asked.

Steve and Derek halted their horses.

"I don't hear anything," said Steve.

"Look there," said Derek. "Fresh tracks."

Hector and Steve saw where Derek was pointing. The ground was churned up.

"And over here," said Steve, "horse tracks, plain as day."

"We've got them," said Hector. "I heard a horse running, then some other noises."

They all listened and then Derek nodded first.

"I hear them," he said.

"Me, too," said Steve.

"Now what?" asked Derek.

"We'd better think this out," said Hector.

"Do you know this country? This trail?"

Hector turned to face Derek.

"Yeah, pretty much. There's a deep arroyo up ahead. They usually go around it, but they might head there. Beyond, there's some little hills and a lot of gullies and rocks. Then, the land starts sloping down to the river."

"Places to hide?" asked Steve.

"Just that arroyo."

"How deep?" asked Derek.

"Deep enough to hide them."

Derek felt his heart pounding in his chest. Before now, it had been a lark, almost, but now they were facing bullets and Indians who didn't give a damn about human life. He began to sweat. He pulled his pistol from the holster, gripped the butt of the Colt in his gloved hand. He checked the Yellow Boy in its boot, slipped it in and out.

"So, now what?" asked Steve.

"Well, I think I'll ride on up ahead, fast, give them the idea there's just me. You and Derek can come in wide to block both sides of that arroyo. It's about a half mile long and open at both ends."

"What do we do if we hear shooting?" Derek wanted to know.

"I won't shoot first, so you'll know it's got to be Bone and his men."

"How many men?"

"Those Indians got out of prison, so I figure there's five of them. Want to know their names?"

Derek laughed, but it wasn't funny. He was just nervous. Hell, they all might die and Bone would be laughing at them.

"Let's go, then," said Derek, "before my heart jumps clean up my throat."

"Are you scared, Derek?" asked Steve.

"No, I just always shit my pants when I go riding before break-fast."

Hector put his gelding, Concho, into a hard gallop. Derek and Steve split wide, heading toward unknown destinations, hoping they would somehow find the open ends of the arroyo.

Derek put Brig into a kind of fox trot that ate up ground but didn't wear the horse out. He might need the animal's speed later on. The packhorse didn't follow that well and he had to hold on to the rope when it threatened to jerk his arm out of the socket. Maybe, he thought, he should just let the other horse loose and ride on without it. It was trained to stand and wait when he was bridled.

Up ahead, he saw Hector get smaller and smaller. Then, he saw Hector turn his packhorse loose. A moment later, Steve did the same.

"So long," said Derek and let the bitter end of the rope fly from his hand.

Ned Feather stopped at the rim of the arroyo and backed his horse around. He sidestepped the animal as the cattle came on, running like buffalo now, with Eddie and Virgil whipping them on like Apache warriors.

Jay took the horses over the lip of the arroyo and down into the bottom. Dust rose in the air and one of the horses floundered halfway down, broke a leg trying to recover from the tumble.

The cattle bawled as they went over the edge and more dust boiled up, obscuring all but their shaggy backs.

Bone rode up, reined in hard. His horse jolted to a skidding stop.

"You stay up here, Ned, and we'll see who's following us."

"I can see the bastard now. Just one, it looks like."

"There's more than one," said Bone, his eyes scanning the bleak landscape. The sun was just pushing up over the rim of the world and in a few minutes he would have its glare square in his eyes.

"Come on, goddamn you," Bone muttered.

The rider lay down on his horse, so that Bone couldn't see who it was. The galloping horse kept coming. Bone jerked his old Winchester from its scabbard, jacked a .30-30 shell into the chamber. Ned drew his own rifle, armed it and put it to his shoulder.

"Shoot when you've got a shot," ordered Bone, the thunder of the cattle strong in his ears.

"I got a bead on him now," said Ned.

"Me, too," said Bone, and his finger curled around the trigger.

As the horse and rider drew closer, Bone and Ned got set, tracked them with their sights.

They both fired at the same time when the rider was two hundred yards away and closing. The reports sounded like only one explosion. The smoke from the barrels spewed out of the muzzles and broke up, wafted away like tattered cobwebs. The smell of burnt powder hung in the air.

For a long moment, neither Indian knew where his bullet had gone.

Hector hugged his horse's neck, stayed low. He heard the shot, and his neck hairs bristled.

Then, he heard the keening whine of a bullet as it passed overhead. Another bullet plowed up ground ahead of his horse. The horse veered at the stinging spatter of dust and nearly unseated its rider.

Fear curdled Hector's insides, galvanized his stomach into a writhing, heaving mass of electrified nerve ends. He wisely let his horse take the lead. Two more rifle shots, *pop-pop*, and he heard the bullets sizzle the air as they sought his flesh, so close they made the skin on his forearms ripple with goosebumps. He heard men shouting, and the cracks of other rifles.

As the horse angled away from Bone and Feather, Hector gained control of his mount. He raised his head slightly, took his bearings.

He saw two men standing at the edge of the arroyo, levering fresh shells into their rifles. Four hundred yards to his right, he saw Derek stop his horse and lift the Yellow Boy to his shoulder.

Hector sat up in the saddle, drew his rifle from the scabbard. He cocked it quickly and tried to take aim from his slowing horse. The barrel wobbled in a semicircle and he was so nervous about shooting at a person, he couldn't really take a bead on the two Indians who were shooting at him. He squeezed the trigger, anyway, and pulled his horse up to rechamber another shell and set up for another shot.

The two men at the arroyo were shooting at Derek when Hector looked back up.

Bone shot until his barrel was hot, his Winchester 94 empty.

He yelled at Virgil and Eddie down at the bottom of the arroyo. "Get the hell up here!"

Ned Feather, wrestling with the horses, yelled something from farther down the arroyo as he jerked his rifle to his shoulder.

Bone knelt on one knee, reloaded, shoving cartridges into the loading gate.

"Look, if they get us, try to take us back, you just watch me."

"Bone, what if they tie us up?"

"Hell, I been tied up before. You just keep your eye on me, anything goes wrong."

Bone's eyes narrowed. The rider drew closer.

"Now, we'll see who's sniffin' our trail," said Bone.

"Here he comes!" yelled Ned. Bone looked up.

"It's the Aguilar kid," Bone said. "That greaser bastard."

"Shit, I got only one bullet left," said Ned Feather.

"Well, kill the sonofabitch with it," said Bone, raising his rifle to his shoulder once again.

38

DEREK PAUSED BEFORE riding down into the arroyo, just as the sun arched onto the eastern horizon like a giant molten fireball. He saw Hector's horse galloping toward the two men standing on the lip of the trench, shooting at him. Hector was either out of the saddle already, or holding so tight to his horse, Derek couldn't see him.

Why doesn't he shoot?

Then, he saw Hector's horse veer to one side and Hector bring his rifle up.

Derek plunged down into the arroyo, his rifle cocked, the butt jammed into his hip, sideways, finger on the trigger. He saw what looked like milling cattle in the center of the depression, but in the dim light of the arroyo, he could not see any men on foot or on horseback.

Dust hung in the air like a shadowy pall. A vein of faint gold appeared along the rim of the opposite bank, but it was still dark down at the bottom. Suddenly, he heard firing at the opposite end of the trench.

Derek fired a shot in the air, levered quickly and put spurs to Brig's flanks. Horse and rider charged over rocky, treacherous ground, into an unknown place where death could come with no warning, not even a sound.

He slowed Brig when he drew close to the clump of cattle, heard the bark of Steve's Remington and wondered what he was shooting at.

With dry throat and cramped belly muscles, Derek rode to the far side of the cattle, into the dust, the danger he could not see with his eyes, could only feel tightening hard fingers on his throat.

Steve saw the Indians in the bottom of the arroyo before they saw him. He watched as two of them rode toward him, trying to break out and ride back up to the flat. He reined up, brought his Remington bolt-action .30-06 to his shoulder, took aim on the lead horse's chest. He squeezed the trigger and the firing pin struck against the steel snugged against an empty chamber. Cursing, Steve pulled hard on the bolt, heard the snick of a cartridge slipping into the chamber. He aimed again, quickly, fired. The lead horse stumbled, as a puff of dust lifted from his chest. The horse crashed sideways into the other horse, throwing both riders to the ground.

As Steve pulled back the bolt again, he saw both men scramble to their feet and scrabble up the slope to the arroyo's rim. He fired twice more, then dug cartridges from his pocket and crammed them into the magazine with trembling fingers.

Bone and Ned ran out of ammunition, threw down their rifles and turned away from Hector's charge. They leaped over the edge of the arroyo, tumbled headlong into Eddie Blue Sky and Virgil Coldwater.

"What the hell?" croaked Bone.

"They're down in the arroyo," yelled Virgil. "I haven't got a gun."

"Me neither," said Eddie.

"Christ," said Bone.

"We got to get the hell out of here," said Virgil.

But as Bone looked down into the bottom of the arroyo, he knew they were trapped.

"Come on," he said. "Maybe we can get out of this."

He got to his feet and ran jerkily down the slope, Ned, Eddie and Virgil close on his heels.

Derek saw Jay Black Horse spin his horse in a tight circle. The rifle in his hand swung toward Derek.

Derek halted Brig before Jay had made his turn and brought the Yellow Boy up, pointed the muzzle toward Jay.

"Better quit it," said Derek.

Jay's horse stopped in mid-turn as the Indian jerked the reins hard.

"You sonofabitch," said Jay.

"I mean it," said Derek. His hands were no longer shaking, the fear was gone. He tightened his finger around the trigger. It had about a four- or five-pound pull. And he had a bead on Jay's chest. "One more fucking move and I drop you like a sack of shit."

Jay thought about it for a split second. Then, he dropped his rifle as if it had turned red-hot in his hands.

Hector appeared on the rim, his rifle pointed down at the Indians hopping toadlike toward the bottom.

"We got you, Bone," Hector yelled.

Bone stopped, looked back up the slope. Anger flooded his veins. His eyes hardened to twin slits of hatred.

Hector dropped the front blade sight on Bone's chest, lined it up with the rear buckhorn. His finger teased the trigger lovingly.

It would be so easy, he thought.

"Go ahead, you sonofabitch," yelled Bone. "Shoot me. You gutless bastard."

Derek herded Jay and his horse close to where Steve held his rifle pointed at Eddie and Virgil. The two ranchers looked at other.

They looked at Hector, whose face was dark, silhouetted by the sun behind the back. He looked like a dark knight atop his horse, a menacing figure holding the power of life and death in his hands.

"Is he going to shoot him?" Steve whispered.

"God, I don't know," Derek husked.

It seemed an eternity before Hector lowered his rifle. Slowly, he eased his mount over the edge of the big ditch, headed toward the frightened Indians.

"We got 'em," he said to Derek. "Let's get 'em out in the open, put some ropes on them."

"You'll never make it back with us," growled Bone, his face darkened with a scowl.

Hector's horse sidled down to level ground. Hector kept his rifle barrel fixed on Bone.

"Derek, you and Steve, back 'em up. Get off that horse, Jay. Quick."

Jay Black Horse dismounted.

"Hands up. All of you move over there and lie down on your stomachs."

For a moment, it appeared as if none of the Indians would obey.

Bone looked as if he was about to lunge toward Hector. Hector held steady, never blinked.

Then, the Indians jerked forward, lay flat on the ground.

Hector let out a sigh.

"I'll cover them while you get some rope on these boys," he said. "Bone, one funny move and I'll blow your fucking brains to mush."

Bone said nothing.

It was over in a few moments. Steve and Derek gathered up the loose stock while Hector prodded the prisoners toward the end of the arroyo.

"Ain't we gonna ride?" asked Eddie Blue Sky.

"No, you'll walk," said Hector. "We got all day and then some. You walk behind those cows, drive them back where you stole them from."

"That's right," said Steve. "We ain't in no hurry. Boy oh boy, wait'll I tell Daddy about this."

Derek grinned. So did Hector. Later, when they were heading back toward the *brasada,* the Indians walking behind the herd of cattle, their hands tied behind their back, Derek asked Hector why he hadn't shot Bone.

"Hell, you had good reason," said Derek.

"So did you," said Hector.

"Well, we ain't back yet. He might make a run for it."

"Would you shoot him?"

"I might," said Derek. "I just might."

As the cattle approached the tip of the *brasada,* Bone stumbled, fell against Ned Feather.

"Watch me," said Bone.

"Shut up there," said Derek.

Bone regained his balance, staggered toward Jay Black Horse.

"Do what I do," muttered Bone.

"What the hell there," said Steve.

"Bone, you walk straight," said Hector.

"No talking," ordered Derek.

When Derek and Hector started to swing the cattle toward the Rocking A, Bone made his move.

"Now!" he yelled, and ran toward the herd. Virgil, Ned and Jay ran too, all of them yelling, screeching war cries as if they'd suddenly gone mad.

The horses spooked. Steve's mount reared up on its hind legs. Unprepared, Steve lost his grip and slid out of the saddle. Rowdy ran into the shoulder of Derek's animal, kicking in self-defense. Three of the cows ran into Hector as he tried to bring his rifle to bear.

Steve yelled in pain as he struck the ground. Derek cursed and began shouting. "Get 'em, get 'em!"

"Sonofabitch!" yelled Hector. "They're running for the brush!"

"No!" Derek cried. "Steve, look out!"

"Christ, I can't see a fucking thing," said Hector.

Bone, hunched behind a shaggy cow, holding on to one horn, steered the animal toward Steve Killian. Steve, still groggy from the fall, tried to get up. Some of the cows turned back at Bone's charge, ran toward Steve.

Derek couldn't see any of the Indians. They were all hiding in the herd, hunched over. His spare horse, Lance, was running straight for the open, away from the mesquite.

Bone struggled with the rope that bound his wrists, jerked one way, then the other until his bonds loosened. With a mighty wrench, he pulled his hands free, the hemp burning his wrists, scratching away flesh with the stiff fibers.

Steve put up his hands to ward off the charging cow.

Bone wrestled the cow in a bulldogging grip, twisted its head to slow it down, turn it into the downed man.

The cow tried to avoid Steve, but brought Bone close enough. The Indian kicked Steve in the chest, knocked him down. Deftly, Bone snatched Steve's knife from the scabbard on his belt.

"Goddamn," said Steve, feeling the tug at his belt.

Bone bulldogged the cow back toward the *brasada*. Hector turned his horse, started chasing cows.

"Circle 'em, circle 'em!" he shouted.

Derek kept trying to draw a bead on one of the escaping Indians. Eddie Blue Sky stumbled and a steer ran over him. He screamed in pain.

"Where in hell are they?" yelled Derek. Dust rose in the air, choked him. He saw Hector riding off toward a bunch of cows and kicked his horse's flanks. He gripped his rifle tightly with sweat-slick hands.

Steve got to his feet, started trying to catch up Rowdy. The horse sidled away from him.

"Whoa up, boy," said Steve. He felt his empty scabbard.

"Bone got my knife," he yelled. No one heard him.

Cattle scattered in all directions. The Indians stopped screeching, scrambled for the safety of the brush. Hector swung Concho to head them off. He fought through the confused pack of cattle, his horse skittery under the saddle. Derek rode up on the other side of the herd, brandishing his rifle.

"Where in hell's Bone?" Derek called.

"I don't know," replied Hector, shouting above the bellowing of the cattle. "But they're all heading for the godamned brush."

"We'll stop 'em," yelled Derek.

But the loose Indian horses scattered like prairie dogs at a sharp whistle and cut in front of Hector and Derek. Hector's horse started to chase after the Indian horses. Hector jerked hard on the reins, but Concho clamped teeth on the bit and ran off to the left. Derek turned his horse, tried to run around the logjam of cattle.

"Shit fire," he muttered as two cows ran into his horse. Brig bucked and kicked both hind legs, trying to fend off his attackers. Derek slid around in the saddle as if it had been soaped and almost fell from his mount.

"Where in hell's Steve?" Hector brought Concho under control, looked around quickly.

"There's one of 'em," said Derek and spurred Brig to a run. Virgil turned, saw the horse bearing down on him and tried to get a cow between him and Derek.

Derek rode up fast, swung his rifle. He cracked the Indian in the temple. Virgil went down like a gunnysack full of sashweights.

Virgil was still tied, so Derek left him, looked around for the others. He saw Hector trying to wrestle Concho out of the pack of cattle.

"Where's Bone?" screamed Hector.

Derek twisted in the saddle as Brig swung in a tight circle.

"I don't see him! I got one of 'em."

"Goddamn!"

Hector felt his stomach roil. Sweat broke out on his face, streamed from under his armpits. He hauled Concho away from the milling cattle, galloped back toward Steve. Out of the corner of his eye he saw Derek chase after someone, leaning forward in the saddle, standing up in his stirrups.

Steve had his horse cornered, was trying to get a leg up.

"Where did Bone go?"

"Hell, I don't know," said Steve. "Sumbitch took my knife."

"Jesus, we can't let him get away."

"Hold on," said Steve, as he jumped into the saddle.

"I can't wait," said Hector. He prodded Concho in the flanks, rode back toward the *brasada*.

"There he goes!" yelled Derek.

Hector saw Bone at the same instant. The Indian was running toward the *brasada*. Derek was out of position and could not shoot. Hector knew Bone was too far away for a clean hit. Before he could bring his rifle up, Bone disappeared into the mesquite.

"I'm going in after him!" Hector called to Derek. "Don't let the others get away."

"I'm coming too!"

Hector rode up to where the brush thickened, jumped off Concho before the horse had stopped. He hit the ground running.

"Stay back, Derek. Let me get him." Hector ran headlong into the brush without thinking.

Derek watched as Hector flashed through the tangled mesquite, like a man running through a maze, like Theseus chasing after the Minotaur.

Hector looked back, caught a glimpse of Derek.

And then the mesquite trees closed in around him and he was alone.

39

HECTOR HELD HIS rifle up close to his chest, his finger cuddling the trigger. His heart pounded in his chest. He heard Steve and Derek yelling as he crouched and slunk through the thick mesquite, trying to find a track he could follow.

He looked all around him, stepped carefully. He wanted to scream for Bone to show himself, but fear gripped him. He knew Bone was at home in the *brasada*. The Indian was like an animal, some tame animal gone feral. He had learned a lot in those months he had stayed with Bone. He had learned to listen for sounds that most people didn't notice. If men were hunting Bone, the Indian always knew when they were close. He looked at the sky and watched the crows fly over, or listened to their cries of warning. He watched when the deer jumped cover and he listened to the way they ran, the sounds they made. Bone could always tell if a man was trying to come into the *brasada*.

Bone had taught him a lot without actually knowing it. For Hector had watched Bone and listened to him and the other Indians talk in English and Spanish.

Hector crept between the trees, back bent, peering in all directions. He took careful steps, held his breath so that he could hear the slightest sound. He moved, then stopped. He waited, listening.

He felt the strain in his back, but he was strangely exhilarated.

He heard nothing. He saw nothing.

Then, behind him, the sounds of the cattle, the men yelling, all faded, muffled by the mesquite jungle. He knew he had gone farther than he had thought. His blood was racing, his senses honed to a keen edge.

Carefully, Hector stepped through brackish pools of water, smelled the fetid scent of decaying vegetation, the dank pools of stagnant water, the musky stench of a small slough choked with weeds. He saw a cottonmouth slither from a sun-drenched limb jutting from the standing water. He looked at the ground, trying to find a footprint. He looked at the mesquite leaves for a sign that someone had passed through. It seemed that he was in a bewildering maze, and panic gripped him. Bands of steel tightened across his chest. His breathing came hard as claustrophobia smothered him.

A slight movement caught the corner of his eye. Hector stopped, glanced toward the source of the shadowy motion. A small pool of water rippled with wavelets. He stepped toward it, saw the glint of sunlight on floating motes of dirt. Just beyond, a moccasin track. He breathed deeply, quelling the roil of queasiness in his stomach.

Bone's track.

The hackles rose on the back of Hector's neck. He gripped the rifle tightly, slid his finger along the trigger with a gentle tracing caress.

He listened, heard nothing.

Then, the crack of a branch far behind him. Hector whirled, his scalp prickling with the rush of adrenaline that flooded his veins.

"Who—who's there?" he husked.

There was no answer.

"Jesus," he whispered to himself. Then, as an afterthought, he took his hand off the trigger, touched his forehead, then his chest and both shoulders in the sign of the cross.

"A deer, maybe," he said softly, but he shivered with a sudden chill.

He looked at the track again, a single footprint beyond the pool. His senses prickled as he stepped toward the sign. He kept on going, looking for more tracks. The trail was easy to follow, then disappeared into a jumble of broken trees, deadwood. He circled around it, rifle at the ready, heart drumming in his ears so loud it scared him.

He picked up the trail on the other side. Bone was not running, but walking carefully, picking his way. Behind him, Hector heard another sound and froze, listening for something louder, something closer. His ears ached from the strain.

"Damn," he breathed.

He knew Bone was close. Worse, he knew Bone had probably heard him. If the Indian got to his camp, he could arm himself, Hector knew. But he was armed. Wasn't he? Hadn't he taken Killian's knife? That damned Killian.

The trail of moccasin prints led through a green thick maze of mesquite. Hector's breath burned hot in his lungs. A branch whipped him in the face and the noise made him jump.

The tracks took another direction, to his left, and he realized Bone was trying to circle him. He grew even warier now, as he came to a place where Bone had stopped, walked around in a circle, then continued on.

Hector came to another small slough, waded through it. A water moccasin swam out of it and goosebumps rose on Hector's arms. He watched the snake disappear into a labyrinth of brush and young mesquite bushes. The moccasin tracks disappeared and Hector choked on the rising panic that once again smothered him. The moist earth was crisscrossed with the tracks of small deer, rats, bobcats, and the tiny prints of raccoon, looking oddly like miniature human hands. He stepped on a dry branch and it sounded like a gunshot in his ears. His heart seemed to stop and his mouth went dry.

He dropped to one knee, hoping Bone hadn't heard him. He cursed himself silently. His right eye stung where the leaves had thrashed him.

From another direction came a loud noise. Someone was running through the brush.

Then, he heard a strange cry. A human cry.

The sound was close.

Hector stood up, moved toward the place where he had heard someone cry out. He saw Bone's moccasin prints again. This time, they showed Hector that the Indian was running.

He heard other sounds now. Grunting. Someone breathing hard. Cursing. He heard a shot, then the whine of the bullet as it ricocheted.

Then, human sounds again. Two voices.

One sounded like Derek's. But Derek wasn't supposed to be in the *brasada.*

Hector moved faster, darting under the mesquite branches, dodging limbs and leaves. The brush opened up into a clearing.

Two men rolled on the ground. One was Derek, the other Bone. Their shirts were ripped, clung to their muscular torsos in ragged tatters.

They were struggling for Derek's rifle. Their hands and arms were drenched in blood. The two rolled around, first one gaining the advantage, then the other. A strange feeling gripped Hector. It was like watching himself in mortal combat with Bone. He stared in rapt fascination at Bone's arm and back muscles. They rippled like a sleek puma's under the skin. Derek's neck muscles bulged, the veins standing out like blue twine. There was something hideously sexual about the spectacle that made the fear boil in Hector like hot wine in his belly.

Hector brought his rifle up to his shoulder.

"Bone," he said, "turn him loose, or I'll shoot."

The two men ignored him. They were bathed in an eerie green light from the surrounding mesquite leaves. Each had both hands locked on the rifle. Derek's legs were oddly stiff and immobile. It was as if he was paralyzed from the waist down.

"Kill him, Heck," wheezed Derek. "Shoot him, dammit."

"I—I can't get a clear shot."

Bone laughed low in his throat. He flipped Derek and rolled again, wrenched the rifle from Derek's hands.

Hector's heart dropped in his chest. It was then that he saw the knife dangling from Derek's hip, the deerhorn handle smeared with fresh blood, the side of Derek's leg streaked black with it.

"Oh my God," breathed Hector.

Bone reached down and jerked the knife from Derek's side. Derek winced and his eyes closed in pain like clenched baby's fists.

Derek tried to rise. Bone kicked him in the side and Derek went down. He screamed.

Bone staggered away, worked the lever on Derek's rifle. A brass cartridge ejected. With a sickening feeling, Hector heard another shell slide into the chamber.

"Christ, kill him, Heck," gasped Derek.

Hector blinked, shook his head. His eyes stung from sweat. He drew a bead on Bone. Bone raised his rifle, fired from the hip. The bullet fried the air over Hector's head, made the hairs bristle on the back of his neck as if someone had scraped a cold razor over the bare flesh.

Before Hector could fire, Bone threw the rifle at Hector and broke into a dead run. He charged as Hector ducked. The rifle struck Hector's shoulder and pain shot through him as if he'd been axed. His arm went numb. The unfired rifle dropped from his hands. He tried to brace himself. He saw Bone bring the knife up and twisted to avoid the blade.

Derek sat up, tried to rise. Pain coursed through him like a charge of electricity. He groaned as Bone struck Hector, knocking him flat.

Hector clawed for his own knife, couldn't reach it. Bone pinned him to the ground in a scissorlock at the waist, squeezing the breath out of him.

Hector doubled up a fist and pounded Bone in the face. An immense satisfaction brought him renewed strength. He wriggled free of Bone's legs and crabbed away, frantically trying to draw his own knife. He saw his rifle a few feet away, reached for it with one outstretched arm.

"You Mexican bastard," growled Bone. He grabbed Hector's foot, started to drag him back toward him. Hector felt as if he was in the grip of a powerful creature. A few more inches and he'd be in range of Bone's knife. He kicked hard, broke Bone's grip. He got his knife halfway out of the scabbard before Bone leaped on his backside, shoving him facedown in the dirt.

"Just like old times, eh kid?"

Hector felt Bone on him, pressing against his buttocks. A revulsion filled him and his eyes watered with a horrible memory. He fought back tears, struggled to move.

Derek watched Bone pin Hector to the ground. He saw that Bone was in no hurry to kill Hector. Derek struggled to get up, pain wrenching his senses. His left leg throbbed, the hip, where Bone's knife had struck bone. He felt dizzy and weak, but knew that Bone would kill him as well as Hector if he didn't do something.

Derek tried to call out to Hector, but his words came out in a throaty rasp.

Hector bucked upward and twisted at the same time. He turned over until he was facing Bone. Bone's arm rose. Hector saw the knife poised to plunge downward. He freed a hand and grabbed Bone's crotch. Bone's face contorted in anger. His hand started downward, the knife pointed at Hector's chest.

Hector found Bone's testicles, squeezed them hard. Bone
screamed as Hector brought up his other hand. Hector grabbed the
Indian's wrist as the knife speared toward him. A shock of pain shot
through Hector's shoulder as he took the force of the blow. He
twisted Bone's wrist as he took another grip on the Indian's testicles
and squeezed the pulpy nuts together like two plums. He heard a *snap*
as Bone's wrist broke.

The knife fell to the ground. Hector heaved and Bone fell away
from him, drawing his legs up to his belly like a man kicked in the
groin.

Derek swayed on his feet, tried to move forward. The two figures
on the ground wavered like images in a quivering pond.

Hector grabbed up the knife in a sweat-slick hand and rammed it
into Bone's side.

Bone screamed and his body straightened out.

Hector saw the blood spurting from Bone's side. Half crazed, he
crawled atop Bone and jabbed him in the scrotum. Bone screamed
and tried to double up once more. But Hector stabbed him in the
groin again and again. Bone writhed and twisted under the onslaught.

"No, no!" Bone screamed. "Stop, Christdamn, stop!"

Hector kept stabbing Bone, slashing away his manhood, gashing
his leg and his belly, until his arm was tired, his hand covered with
blood.

Bone quivered and gagged, choking.

Derek walked stiff-legged up to Hector, put a hand on his shoulder.

"Heck, stop. Bone's all stove up. For good."

Hector looked up, saw Derek's blanched face.

"Huh?"

"You sure as hell killed Bone. Enough."

Hector looked down at the bloody rag beneath him. He crumpled
up, then, the energy draining out of him like the light from a blown-
out lamp. Bile rose up in his throat.

"He's dead?"

"Purt' near," rasped Derek. He kicked Bone's head with the toe
of his boot. Bone let out a grunt, but his eyes did not open.

Bone's head jerked from the blow.

"That's for Tom Casebolt, you sonofabitch." Derek closed his eyes
for a moment, then looked silently up at the sky.

Hector began to shake, but he steeled himself not to cry. It all seemed like a dream to him. Bone made a gurgling sound in his throat. His eyes opened, fixed on some point in space beyond the green leaves of the mesquite, then frosted over with the glaze of death.

Then, it was quiet. Hector rose to his feet, held onto Derek.

"He get you bad?" he asked.

"Naw, he just hit my hipbone. Blood's stopped. Hurts like hell. I shot at him, but he was too quick."

"God, Dare, I killed him. I killed a man."

"Well, he was trying to kill both of us."

Derek smiled wanly, wrapped an arm around Hector's shoulder. Hector dropped the knife to the ground. It landed with a dull thud.

"I can't believe Bone's dead," said Hector.

"You got him right where he lives," said Derek. "Right smack in the goddamned *brasada.*"

"Last night, after I talked to you," Hector said to Derek, "I called Jack Kearney. I asked him what the law was if we caught the rustlers. Know what he said?"

"No," said Derek. "He tell you you could shoot them?"

"Pretty much," said Hector. "If they shot at us first, we could kill them in self-defense."

"Well, that's pretty much the way it happened."

"I'm glad Bone's dead," said Hector. "Let's just leave the bastard here. Let the rats and the buzzards eat his corpse, gnaw at his bones."

"Yeah, let's get the hell out of here." Derek laughed. He felt a surge of relief flood his veins. Finally, he thought, they had done what his father hadn't been able to accomplish—get Bone. Get him out of the brush country for good. No more would Bone and his cronies roam its mesquite jungles like animals, looting and killing like marauding Apaches.

But he knew that there was a part of Texas that would never be tamed, never be conquered. The *brasada.*

The General crouched in the corner of the barn, his golden eye fixed on the nest of scorpions he had just discovered.

The Bantam hens clucked softly, waited patiently in the cool of the old weatherbeaten building.

The General struck, spearing a scorpion at the thorax, backing up as the creature stabbed at him with its stinger. He dropped the scorpion, sheared off its curled tail with a savage bite, flicked it to one of the hens.

One by one, he dragged the scorpions from their nest and murdered them. His hens devoured each scorpion, scratching and clucking among themselves. The General saved the last, the biggest, for himself, but he had to fight for it. The scorpion came at him from every angle, only to be skewered by that sharp beak and tossed aside like a squirming worm. Finally, The General tired of the battle and administered the coup de grace, crunching the scorpion's head in his beak, holding the wriggling body until it was still.

He devoured the creature, shared the last morsel with his favorite hen.

The General then led his hens out of the barn, strutting proudly into the bright Texas sun.

Outside, he flapped his wings and declared his dominion over the earth and all of its creatures.